Stories of the DOUBLE

edited by

Albert J. Guerard
Stanford University

J. B. LIPPINCOTT COMPANY
Philadelphia | *New York*

The Lippincott College English Series
Under the general editorship of
ALBERT J. GUERARD
Stanford University

Copyright © 1967 by J. B. Lippincott Company
Library of Congress Catalog Card Number: 67-15512
Printed in the United States of America

THE DOUBLE, *by Fyodor Dostoevsky, from* THE ETERNAL
HUSBAND AND OTHER STORIES, *translated from the*
Russian by Constance Garnett. Reprinted by permission
of the Macmillan Company. First published in England.

Contents

Concepts of the Double

Few concepts and dreams have haunted the human imagination as durably as those of the *double*—from primitive man's sense of a duplicated self as immortal soul to the complex mirror games and mental chess of Mann, Nabokov, Borges. The concepts and dreams are many. Primitive and decadent societies alike have conceived occult correspondences, have discerned and even deified male and female components of the soul. They have alike been fascinated by flesh-and-blood visible twins, by concepts of warfare within the soul, by myths of duality and incest among the gods; and (in art) by an imagery of multiplied limbs and doubled genitalia as well as by a sacred imagery of identical bodied souls rising from placid saintly corpses. There may be psychological insight in the most primitive and most popular forms of double literature. And there may be a component of terror, a *frisson* of the uncanny, in even the sophisticated and often ironic, nearly always self-conscious renderings of the mid-twentieth century. What common denominator is there between the haunted figure of German romantic literature who loses his shadow or sells his shadow to the Devil (or whose shadow *is* the Devil) and the poet John Shade of Nabokov's *Pale Fire?* Perhaps at least this: that *double* literature (if it proceeds from a genuine imaginative act) is rarely trivial, though not infrequently comic. The issues are real and sometimes tragic, the psychomachia definitive or barely survived—whether the experience of seeing one's double lead to a sense of resurrection or to a descent into psychosis, whether to classic split personality or to epileptic episode or to obsessive-compulsive behavior.[1]

[1] See Claire Rosenfield's "The Shadow Within," at the end of this volume, for a fuller survey of psychological and literary meanings.

1

It is a serious game—this experiencing of doubleness—even where the terms are less clinical. What is more significant than our sudden unaccountable acts of identification and vagrant sympathy, or our normal unneurotic sense of being sharply divided in our aims and inward being, or our flickering intuition that moral suppression of deep anti-social impulse may itself be immoral, a guilty act of mutilation, a destruction of vital energies? One of the recurrent pre-occupations of double literature is with the need to keep a suppressed self alive, though society may insist on annihilation: to keep alive not merely a sexual self or a self wildly dreaming of power or a self capable of vagrant fantasy, the self of childhood freedom—not merely these, but also a truly insubordinate perhaps illusory, original and fundamental self, an "être naif et forme sienne" that (in Montaigne's words) "luicte contre l'institution."[1]

There is usually a high seriousness in double stories, a deep human accent and concern, even though the writer may have been unaware of it himself.

In Poe's *William Wilson*, there is little real complexity of conception or underground creation. The namesake double is simply the projected and watching moral conscience, distressed by the first William Wilson's vices, and intervening at crucial moments in the hope of saving him. (But not projection in the Freudian sense, less a

[1]The reasonable yet virtually unattainable dream, one of the most poignant, is that of Conrad's young captain in *The Secret Sharer*, or of Cathy when she believed she could keep both Edgar Linton and Heathcliff, and would have to give up nothing.

For what the novel also imagines, at this moment when both Edgar Linton and Heathcliff must be retained, is no less than a reconciliation of our profoundest antinomies of spirit and most opposed modes of being: on the one hand the social, ethical, conscious, rational, institutional (with all the comforts these bring) and on the other the individual, free, irrational, unconscious, atavistic (with all the life energies these signify). This is a reconciliation within the personality, but has its bearing on social behavior. That other reconciliation society commends, and indeed commands, is a taming rather than a balancing; victory, not coexistence. This is what the last pages of *Wuthering Heights* also commend in a wholly conscious, doubtless intelligent way. Education and society triumph; primitive energies are leashed, very nearly annulled. But in the novel's most vital pages the dream is truly that of a happy coexistence—less harmony than coexistence—in which nothing is lost. The pleasures of control and reason are enjoyed. But the outlaw and unconscious self is nevertheless left free, still insubordinate, undamaged and alive. [From Albert J. Guerard, "Introduction," *Wuthering Heights*, by Emily Bronte. New York: Washington Square Press.]

dynamic unconscious act than an authorial idea.) And in killing his double at the end of the story, in a desperate attempt to be freed, the original Wilson discovers he has murdered himself. In a mirror it is his own features he sees "all pale and dabbled in blood." Yet even this controlled explicit parable of a detachable watching moral conscience—not super-ego but conscience—has its fine moments. Wilson's resentment of the double's affectionateness (with its homosexual, narcissistic overtones) has a Dostoevskyan unexpectedness and truth. And Poe conveys well that sense of the *uncanny* referred to by Freud. The deeply strange apparition of a *double* has its weird familiarity, since it had indeed been projected from the self. Or, as Poe puts it, "I cannot better describe the sensation which oppressed me than by saying that I could with difficulty shake off the belief of my having been acquainted with the being who stood before me, at some epoch very long ago—some point of the past even infinitely remote."

The word *double* is embarrassingly vague, as used in literary criticism. It need not imply autoscopic hallucination or even close physical resemblance. Freud, citing Stekels, observes that two dramatized human beings may constitute a single personality. The fear that stirs in Macbeth develops not in him but in Lady Macbeth; in this sense they are doubles.[1] Characters who seem occultly connected in the author's imagination (and such connection may take many forms) may also be referred to as doubles. A minor character may reenact a major character's traumatic experience, if only because the author could not leave the trauma alone. A strong feeling of sympathetic identification may lead to a sense of doubleness, an immobilizing recognition of the self one might have been. To the degree that Brierly sees himself in Lord Jim—or Lord Jim sees himself in Gentleman Brown—Jim and Brown function as doubles and elicit unexpected allegiances. In *The Devils* there are at least four senses in which the concept of the double involves Stavrogin. He has been called a double-character because his personality is so darkly and deeply divided: criminal and fallen angel, fitful eccentric and brooding theorist on Russia, a lost leader and cynic, behaving compulsively, vowed to his own destruction. Even the Stavrogin of

---

[1] Sigmund Freud, "Some Character-Types Met with in Psychoanalytic Work" (1915), *Collected Papers*, Vol. IV.

the suppressed Confession is deeply divided. We may further say that Pyotr Verkhovensky is a double for Stavrogin, or that the two are doubles for each other, since an obscure but profound relationship exists between them. Is Pyotr Mephistopheles for Stavrogin's Satan or vice-versa? At times they seem part of a single Byronic personality. But also, in a most interesting sense, the convict Fedka is a double for Stavrogin. It is he who appears at the right moment to tempt Stavrogin, and to act out the crime against Mary Lebyatkin that Stavrogin has half-consciously wished. Fedka seems an inhabitant (to use the language of Hawthorne) of Stavrogin's interior world. It should be noted, finally, that Stavrogin, in the suppressed chapter, refers to an hallucinatory Devil.

The experience of encountering a double is indeed uncanny: a response not merely to strangeness but to familiarity. For the double had once been within ourselves. The employer of Bartleby (in Melville's story) remarks that he never feels "so private" as when the scrivener is nearby, behind his screen: ". . . there was something about Bartleby that not only strangely disarmed me, but in a wonderful manner touched and disconcerted me." Golyadkin, immediately before his first encounter with his double, feels an unaccountable uneasiness. He was troubled for some unknown reason, as the stranger walked toward him. "The fact is that now this stranger somehow seemed to him familiar." If others as well as Dr. Jekyll experience Mr. Hyde as uncanny, this is perhaps because he is, more nearly than any other double, an embodiment of the savage aggressive *id* who slumbers in us all. He causes an "odd, subjective disturbance"; gives a "haunting sense of unexpressed deformity." Or, as the butler put it, "there was something queer about that gentleman—something that gave a man a turn—I don't know rightly how to say it, sir, beyond this: that you felt it in your marrow kind of cold and thin." Spencer Brydon in James' "The Jolly Corner" knows it is his own alter-ego he is stalking. Yet he too, when a figure is at last summoned up, experiences both strangeness and familiarity. James alters the double convention slightly and with characteristic irony. It is Brydon himself, not the double, who has "followed strange paths and worshipped strange gods" and led a "frivolous scandalous life." But the self he might have been, the suppressed self who would have remained in America to become a millionaire, would have had "power." And the hideous "bared identity" of that self not realized? ". . . the stranger, whoever he might be, evil, odious, blatant, vulgar, had advanced as for aggression. . . ."

The Double was Dostoevsky's second published work, written at the age of twenty-five. Yet it already displays the remarkable psychological intuition that would make Dostoevsky seem, though coming so long before Freud, the greatest of Freudian novelists. It is a pure example of the double story since, as in William Wilson, the newcomer not only resembles the subject but has the same name. There is much reason to regard Golyadkin Jr. as an autoscopic hallucination, yet reason too to suppose that a new clerk really did come to work in Golyadkin Sr.'s office. The ambiguity has often been mentioned as a weakness of the story. But surely The Double can be enjoyed both as a story of neurotic hallucination and as a terrible comic drama of real personal relationships, just as The Turn of the Screw may be enjoyed both as a true ghost story and as a story of neurotic hallucination. In any event, the double's presence is only too real for Golyadkin Sr., who is unmistakably neurotic at the start. The nature of his sickness may be debated. Otto Rank regarded the story as a classic portrayal of a paranoid state; more recently, Lawrence Kohlberg has argued that Dostoevsky's consciously "split" doubles present "classical symptoms of the obsessive-compulsive character. . . ." "The Double is not," Kohlberg writes, "the portrayal of a genuine psychiatric phenomenon of paranoia, as Dostoevsky himself may have believed. Although the feelings of persecution and the disowning of part of the self portrayed in The Double have psychiatric parallels in paranoid states, the experience of a hallucinatory duplicate of the self is not explained by, or consistent with, a paranoid psychosis."[1,2]

[1] Lawrence Kohlberg, "Psychological Analysis and Literary Form: A Study of the Double in Dostoevsky," Daedalus, Spring 1963, p. 351.

[2] Autoscopic hallucination—though claimed by a number of writers including Maupassant, Alfred De Musset and d'Annunzio—is perhaps commoner in literature than in life. Literature, as Freud remarked, is a "much more fertile province" for the uncanny than real life. The paradoxical result is that "a great deal that is not uncanny in fiction would be so if it happened in real life; and in the second place there are many more means of creating uncanny effects in fiction than there are in real life." [Sigmund Freud, "The Uncanny" (1919), Collected Papers, Vol V.]

The phenomena exist, however, though the formal literature is largely disappointing. A recent clinical study observes that the double usually appears suddenly and

Whatever the nature of Golyadkin's ailment, Dostoevsky prepares brilliantly for that dark, cold encounter on the Izmailovsky Bridge: a moment of total self-repudiation, and of actual splitting of the self. Earlier we have seen Golyadkin consult a doctor, and speak incoherently of vague persecutions. Insecure, compulsive, ashamed of his mediocre place in life, he steps into another role, that of the rich and successful man, and goes on his shopping spree, promising deposits on goods he will never return for. At the terrifying sight of his employer, Andrey Filippovich, he considers pretending that he is not himself, "but somebody else strikingly like me." To be other than himself is an overpowering psychic need. He insists on a saving duality; his private self is not his public one, and there is a "self" his friends do not know. He invites himself to a party for Klara Olsufyevna, whom he seems to love in his "underground" way. Asked to leave, he lurks in a corridor, decides to go home and at the same instant rushes back into the party, *en passant* deciding to shoot himself that night. And he is humiliated again. At this terrible moment he wants simply to efface himself; to have nothing at all to do with, be no part of the incoherent oaf who, moments later, is

---

without warning; that the spectre is seen clearly yet generally without color; that its texture is frequently misty or transparent (see especially James' *"The Jolly Corner"*); that the observer commonly feels sadness, weariness, and cold; that the experience usually lasts a few seconds at a time, though the continuous presence of a double can occur; that the majority of phantoms appear at dusk; that there seems to be "more than a mere chance affinity between autoscopy and epilepsy and migraine, but its character is at present unknown." Lukianowicz, the author of this summary, offers a "personal hypothesis (that) recognizes symptomatic autoscopy, with a known organic causation, and idiopathic autoscopy, interpreted in terms of a compensatory or a wish-fulfilling mechanism" [N. Lukianowicz, "Autoscopic Phenomena," *A.M.A. Archives on Neurology and Psychiatry*, Vol. 80 (August, 1958), 199–220.]

Lukianowicz's Case F, a young epileptic, in some ways resembles that of Golyadkin. The patient would suffer a "short-lived epileptic fugue," usually going on an aimless bus ride. The patient's own verbatim account might well apply to Golyadkin's first encounter with the double, though it was the double not the patient who did the stepping aside:

I feel dazed and 'empty' in myself. My body is like an empty shell. Then, all at once, I see and feel how my 'shadow', or 'my other me', steps out of me, of my earthly body. He makes two or three steps, then stops, and turns his head to me. I feel how my soul and my life leave my body and enter him. Soon *he* is the real me, and what is left of the 'old' me is only my 'outer body', just like an empty shell after the chick has hatched. Then he nods at me and begins to walk, and my empty body follows him like a shadow.

ejected. And now in the snowy night, longing to "hide somewhere from himself . . . to run away from himself," in exhaustion and despair, he is ready to confront or be confronted by his double. Involuntarily, he jumps aside a couple of paces—it is the very moment of splitting—and has a sense, though no one is to be seen, that someone "was standing near him, beside him" who had said something of intimate import. But only moments later the "someone," looking exactly like himself, seems to have taken on an only too solid flesh and menacing existence.

Golyadkin, Jr.—whether autoscopic hallucination or an actual stranger onto whom Golyadkin Sr. projects desperate wishes and impulsions—is more interesting than most doubles, primarily because his role changes according to the sufferer's changing needs. As in the case recorded by Lukianowicz, Golyadkin follows his double home. Is the stranger a proof of his enemies' malice, or a proof of feared madness? In any event the double at first behaves in the intolerable, humiliated, rejected, persecuted role from which Golyadkin Sr. had stepped aside. He asks for an indulgent hearing, for help, for protection. Golyadkin Sr. can bask in his power and generosity. But this humble disowned self (he too is subject to the intrigues of enemies, a man of unimpeachable behavior yet suffering from guilt) soon alarmingly turns into a highly successful self, one who begins to live Golyadkin Sr.'s old reveries of power, who has access to the boss, who begins to replace him at the office. And soon after that the double takes on a still more sinister role. He becomes an accusing conscience, or even a disowned cruel *super-ego,* and teasingly suggests acts of undefined hastiness, even homosexual advances. Golyadkin Sr. would now give (one thinks of John Jay Chapman's guilty self-mutilation) a finger of his right hand to be rid of the double. But it is Golyadkin Jr., even more strikingly, who must wipe his fingers after shaking Golyadkin Sr.'s hand. And this double —more and more dominant, more and more in control of his darkening consciousness and life—will be with him to the end. He is the worst persecutor of all.

How real is this persecutor who, whether spectre or flesh or both, was in some sense summoned from within? Was it Golyadkin Jr. who gorged himself on the other ten meat patties for which Golyadkin Sr. is compelled to pay? Did Golyadkin Sr. write to himself and also write Klara Olsufyevna's romantic letter pleading for help? The questions are perhaps irrelevant in a narrative of neurosis shading into psychosis. The measure of Dostoevsky's success (though logicians, beginning with himself, have objected to the story) is that the continuing ambiguity does not merely entrance us as a mystery. It also permits a mature reader to enjoy the two levels of the story— to enjoy the story of troubling human relationship without losing sight of the fact that we are dealing with a sick man, and to enjoy a story of neurotic behavior without ceasing to see not one physical being but two. The dramatic treatment of ambiguity (and of con- fusion and suffering surrounded by dimly seen but sane witnesses) is as impressive as anything prior to those spiritual adventures, which are yet so terribly substantial, of Franz Kafka—spiritual and visual both, as are the most meaningful dreams.

We traffic with doubles at our peril. A recurrent menace is of domination by the double or shadow; domination, it may be, by a personality we have attempted to disown. In Hans Christian Ander- sen's "The Shadow" a dissociation takes place rather casually. A "learned man" sends his shadow to explore the interior of a house across the street. At first he is without a shadow; then a new one is grown. But the lost shadow returns years later—a separate person, a rich man in fact, friendly enough yet also a harbinger of death. The identity of the scholar is more and more absorbed by that of the usurping shadow until their roles are fully exchanged. The story ends with the execution of the scholar, and with the shadow's mar- riage to a princess. In Guy de Maupassant's famous story "The Horla," the persecutor is an invisible being, though the narrator knows that this being sits, for instance, in his own chair. A crisis occurs not when the narrator sees a fleshly double but *when he fails to see himself in a mirror*. The intruder has absorbed his reflection. (We know that Maupassant himself reported coming home to find repeatedly a visible double sitting in his own chair.)

Criticism finds it hard to "place" Robert Louis Stevenson. Is he a "serious writer" or a "mere entertainer"? It is not entertainment as such that sometimes precludes "seriousness," but a manipulation of suspense too artful, an ominousness of tone too studied. Yet the *Strange Case of Dr. Jekyll and Mr. Hyde* should not be dismissed lightly. Even as psychopathology, this story of 1886 is persuasive enough, once we have allowed the necessary *donnée* of an extreme psychosomatic transformation. The story offers a convincing case of "split personality," though its larger moral intention is to convey "the thorough and primitive duality of man." (The first responses to the personality-changing drug, as it happens, seem extraordinarily similar to those attributed to LSD: the initial nausea followed by a sense of being "younger, lighter, happier in body" and the "current of disordered sensual images running like a mill race in my fancy.")

One interest of Stevenson's narrative is that it makes so explicit a meaning latent in other double stories, and in many instances of imaginative sympathy with the outlaw. This is that poignant and authentic longing to keep both selves alive, the social and civilized, the primitive and inchoate. Dr. Jekyll may at first seem a good late Victorian, concealing an "impatient gaiety of disposition" behind a "more than commonly grave countenance." But he remarks that he was, though, "so profound a double dealer . . . in no sense a hypocrite; both sides of me were in dead earnest." His longing is the longing of Cathy, to keep alive both the civilized within herself and the wild, Edgar Linton and Heathcliff. Dr. Jekyll tells himself that if each of his two impulsions "could but be housed in separate identities, life would be relieved of all that was unbearable; the unjust might go his way, delivered from the aspirations and remorse of his more upright twin; and the just could walk steadfastly and securely on his upward path. . . ." He is not repelled by the ugly image of Mr. Hyde in the mirror, but instead experiences (precisely like the liberated Michel of Gide's *The Immoralist*) a "leap of welcome." For the new countenance seems "natural and human" and bears a livelier image of the spirit than the face he had always known. Mr. Hyde is indeed a figure of evil: an unregenerate savage "brimming with images of terror, a soul boiling with causeless hatreds, and a body that seemed not strong enough to contain the raging energies of life." But when Dr. Jekyll elects the life of the "elderly and discontented doctor" (not definitively, as it happens) he does so with a certain sadness. For he knows he is sacrificing not only secret pleasures but liberty and "comparative youth," energy and vital instinct.

The belated tragic life drive and violent escape from repression is often suicidal, more often in literature (one hopes) than in life. Mann's *Death in Venice* is also, of course, a story of doubles. The bold-looking foreigner near the Funeral Hall in Munich, the outlaw gondolier, the hysterical guitar player with his carbolic smell—these are all "ghastly harbingers of death," to use Otto Rank's term for one of the double's great roles. But also they are images of the vital, lawless, instinctual life that Gustav von Aschenbach has too rigidly and too long repressed. Thus the journey to Venice is still another journey into the instinctive, the primordial, the youthful, the regressive. But it is also a journey into ultimate inertia and surrender of the will, and to death on the beach, in the presence of a beckoning sea. In Gide's *The Immoralist* various young boys are not merely objects of homosexual attraction but envied exemplars of a youthful, more instinctual life, replete with lawless but vital energies. In that sense they too function as doubles.

"Sincerity," in the odd sense Gide gives it, means a willingness to permit all potentialities of being to come alive. The double may function as an image of opportunity missed, of the road not taken. Henry James' Spencer Brydon gives this situation, not surprisingly, its most explicit definition: ". . . it's only a question of what fantastic, yet perfectly possible, development of my own nature I mayn't have missed. It comes over me that I had then a strange *alter ego* deep down somewhere within me, as the full-blown flower is in the small tight bud, and that I just took the course, I just transferred him to the climate, that blighted him once for all." But the missed opportunity or suppressed self need not be hideous and vulgar (as Brydon's turned out) or savagely regressive. Melville's Bartleby is the quietest of all doubles; passive, yet an existential hero.

At first glance, *Bartleby the Scrivener* may not seem a double story at all. The deplorable jocular flavor of the opening pages suggests that we are dealing with a minor Dickensian eccentric, stubborn in his individualist whim. And the last paragraphs—by seeming to supply a biographical clue to Bartleby's withdrawal and hopelessness—suggest, in turn, a psychological portrait. Bartleby's catatonic immobility does indeed seem pathological. But it soon becomes clear that he transcends any such limited role. He takes his place rather in Melville's total vision of spiritual isolation and personal loneliness. His story is thus a companion piece to *The Encantadas*. "Ah Bartleby! Ah humanity!" But the terms are philosophical too, and Bartleby's inaction is an act of refusal. He declines to accept the rules of a routinized and degraded game; like Camus' stranger he refuses to be "reasonable." But there is even more to his refusal than this, and once (but once only) he becomes more explicit. He has decided to give up writing; to give up, that is, his profession as scrivener. When the narrator questions him, Bartleby is staring at the blank wall ten feet from the window:

> "Why, how now? what next?" exclaimed I, "do no more writing?"
> "No more."
> "And what is the reason?"
> "Do you not see the reason for yourself," he indifferently replied.

It would be plausible to foresee in this question Melville's own abandonment of writing. His public was a blank wall. But I prefer to see the "indifference" of Camus' Meursault in *The Stranger*. Staring at the blank wall, Bartleby has recognized not a mere professional futility, but a cosmic hopelessness and absurdity. He is, in modern jargon, "opting out." He has preferred to give up a life whose terms he cannot accept. He is not the first philosopher to have ended his life in withdrawal, apparent stupor, silence.

Yet Bartleby also functions, for the narrator, as a true double, as another self and inhabitant of the mind. The "prime thing" about Bartleby is that he is *always there,* and will not quit the premises. The narrator—a safe, prudent, methodical man—installs his new employee in his own office rather than with the other scriveners. But also he sets up a folding screen which will "entirely isolate" Bartleby from his sight. (One is reminded of the narrator's care in pinning the curtains between himself and Leggatt in *The Secret Sharer.*) Bartleby is exasperating, as exasperating as the Albee of Saul Bellow's *The Victim,* yet the narrator remains strangely indulgent. He would like to dismiss Bartleby and cannot. And when at last a separation occurs, he slips something in Bartleby's hand, just as the young captain will give Leggatt both money and his hat. "But it dropped upon the floor and then—strange to say—I tore myself from him whom I had so longed to be rid of." What, precisely, has been the bond between the two? Surely the answer is that one can never, in these matters, be precise. Bartleby perhaps exists as an image of quiet insubordinate refusal to accept the safe and prudent and methodical. In psychological (and doubtless unconscious) terms he may also represent that passive feminine component with which one must come to terms: a quiet unaggressive self which may arouse hostility or anxiety in us, but of which we can hardly be rid. If this is so, then Bartleby plays a very different role from any of the other doubles we have considered.

"A mysterious communication was established already between us two—in the face of that silent, darkened tropical sea." The confrontation of the young narrator of "The Secret Sharer" and the fugitive Leggatt reflects, more than the other stories in this volume do, a normal prolonged act of introspection and unneurotic crisis of identity. The story is of a first command, and of a young man's need to test his own courage, will, and competence. But the issues are larger than these, of course—and it is significant that Conrad based his narrative both on his own trouble-ridden first command of the *Otago* in 1888 and on the story of a famous crime at sea that occurred in 1880. (The mate of the *Cutty Sark* had killed a rebellious member of his crew; his captain allowed him to escape to a nearby ship shortly afterward. But the captain committed suicide a few days later, presumably in response to his own illegal act of sympathy.) Both in real life and in Conrad's fiction, then, the radical issue is posed of identification with the outlaw. Is our sympathy for the fugitive or rebel ultimately a sympathy for one's self? Are crime and guilt always public matters to be assessed by judge and jury? Or has the man who committed an unintended or marginal crime— "the secret sharer, as though he were my second self"—the right to determine his own punishment? It is clear that Conrad (though his formal officer's ethic might have it otherwise) admired the courage of the man determined to go on living: "a proud swimmer striking out for a new destiny." It is surely too simple to ask, as a number of critics have, whether Leggatt is hero or villain, whether the narrator was "right" or "wrong." As always in Conrad's stories of boundary situation and marginal crime, the interplay of sympathy and judgment is intricate and changing. In any event the two men themselves scarcely hesitate, once their commitments have been made—

Leggatt in his decision to evade formal justice, the narrator-captain in his decision to shelter him.

The tone of *The Secret Sharer* is that of quiet, meditative self-inquiry: almost an interior monologue, or one spoken as in a whisper. The narrator scarcely expresses any surprise at all, after his first startled view of what appeared to be a headless corpse. He accepts the facts of resemblance and kinship, and repeatedly refers to Leggatt as his "double" or "second self." There is no question of literal doubling, of course, nor of autoscopic or other hallucination. But the concept of the double is obviously and consciously present. Critics have offered divers interpretations of the story, based on some of its crucial details—the rope-ladder negligently left hanging, the irregularity of the captain standing watch himself, the sleeping suit worn by Leggatt, the arrangements and even the shape of the captain's quarters, the captain's gift of money and hat, ultimately that hat floating on the night sea as a mark, at least, of saving separation.[1] I myself have spoken of the narrator's "night journey" into self and of his need to travel through Leggatt as Marlow must travel through Kurtz in *Heart of Darkness*, descending to recognize one's own potentialities for violence and reversion and one's own primitive energies.[2] At the very least we may say that "The Secret Sharer" deals with a profound experience of self-evaluation: an experience that proves temporarily crippling. Yet the meaning is unmistakably affirmed that this immobilizing experience has been necessary. At the end of the story the two men are ready to face their quite separate lives. The narrator-captain now knows his ship, and also knows himself. He will "turn out faithful," we assume, "to that ideal conception of one's own personality every man sets up for himself secretly."

Characteristically, Conrad has turned a great story of maritime adventure into a deep probing of both moral and psychological issues. And where the scope of the meaning was so large, yet the length of the story so brief, the convention of the double seems to

---

[1] See *Conrad's Secret Sharer and the Critics*, ed. Bruce Harkness. Belmont, California: Wadsworth Publishing Co.

[2] See Albert J. Guerard, *Conrad the Novelist*, Cambridge: Harvard University Press, 1958, pp. 18–29. This discussion appears also in *Conrad's Secret Sharer and The Critics*, pp. 59–74.

have served him particularly well. It permitted, without violation of an unhurried and quiet prose, a rather extraordinary economy.

Aristotle as well as Maupassant saw his double, and Plautus as well as Nabokov dramatized twins. The double convention extends to the most remote antiquity and to the most savage areas and extends also to the present day, as Claire Rosenfield's excellent article reminds us. For the bankruptcy of social realism in the novel has coincided with an ever more sophisticated (and sometimes ever more terrified) awareness of the possibilities of identity loss. The game of exchanged identities and multiple doubles has been played with Teutonic gravity or elephantine playfulness by Thomas Mann, with vertiginous subtlety by Borges, with a marvelous and demonic allusiveness by Vladimir Nabokov, in book after book. It is no paradox of literary history, but a consequence of the times, that Nabokov (who wrote his first double stories in the early 1930's, and who for so long seemed merely decadent and minor) is now regarded as one of our greatest writers. Helpless before the unrecordable chaos of social change, or recoiling before the prospects of cataclysm, feeling perhaps that there is after all nothing more important to record than the individual psyche and divided soul—at least a few of the best contemporary writers have turned within. And they have done so not always irresponsibly nor yet too solemnly, but with a new unpedantic psychological insight and also with a saving gaiety.

ALBERT J. GUERARD

The Secret Sharer

JOSEPH CONRAD

1

On my right hand there were lines of fishing stakes resembling a mysterious system of half-submerged bamboo fences, incomprehensible in its division of the domain of tropical fishes, and crazy of aspect as if abandoned forever by some nomad tribe of fishermen now gone to the other end of the ocean; for there was no sign of human habitation as far as the eye could reach. To the left a group of barren islets, suggesting ruins of stone walls, towers, and block-houses, had its foundations set in a blue sea that itself looked solid, so still and stable did it lie below my feet; even the track of light from the westering sun shone smoothly, without that animated glitter which tells of an imperceptible ripple. And when I turned my head to take a parting glance at the tug which had just left us anchored outside the bar, I saw the straight line of the flat shore joined to the stable sea, edge to edge, with a perfect and unmarked closeness, in one leveled floor half brown, half blue under the enormous dome of the sky. Corresponding in their insignificance to the islets of the sea, two small clumps of trees, one on each side of the only fault in the impeccable joint, marked the mouth of the river Meinam we had just left on the first preparatory stage of our homeward journey; and, far back on the inland level, a larger and loftier mass, the grove

Reprinted by permission of J. M. Dent and Sons, Ltd., and the Trustees of the Joseph Conrad Estate.

surrounding the great Paknam pagoda, was the only thing on which the eye could rest from the vain task of exploring the monotonous sweep of the horizon. Here and there gleams as of a few scattered pieces of silver marked the windings of the great river, and on the nearest of them, just within the bar, the tug steaming right into the land became lost to my sight, hull and funnel and masts, as though the impassive earth had swallowed her up without an effort, without a tremor. My eye followed the light cloud of her smoke, now here, now there, above the plain, according to the devious curves of the stream, but always fainter and farther away, till I lost it at last behind the miter-shaped hill of the great pagoda. And then I was left alone with my ship, anchored at the head of the Gulf of Siam.

She floated at the starting point of a long journey, very still in an immense stillness, the shadows of her spars flung far to the eastward by the setting sun. At that moment I was alone on her decks. There was not a sound in her—and around us nothing moved, nothing lived, not a canoe on the water, not a bird in the air, not a cloud in the sky. In this breathless pause at the threshold of a long passage we seemed to be measuring our fitness for a long and arduous enterprise, the appointed task of both our existences to be carried out, far from all human eyes, with only sky and sea for spectators and for judges.

There must have been some glare in the air to interfere with one's sight, because it was only just before the sun left us that my roaming eyes made out beyond the highest ridges of the principal islet of the group something which did away with the solemnity of perfect solitude. The tide of darkness flowed on swiftly; and with tropical suddenness a swarm of stars came out above the shadowy earth, while I lingered yet, my hand resting lightly on my ship's rail as if on the shoulder of a trusted friend. But, with all that multitude of celestial bodies staring down at one, the comfort of quiet communion with her was gone for good. And there were also disturbing sounds by this time—voices, footsteps forward; the steward flitted along the main-deck, a busily ministering spirit; a hand-bell tinkled urgently under the poop deck. . . .

I found my two officers waiting for me near the supper table, in the lighted cuddy. We sat down at once, and as I helped the chief mate, I said:

"Are you aware that there is a ship anchored inside the islands? I saw her mastheads above the ridge as the sun went down."

He raised sharply his simple face, overcharged by a terrible growth of whisker, and emitted his usual ejaculations: "Bless my soul, sir! You don't say so!"

My second mate was a round-cheeked, silent young man, grave beyond his years, I thought; but as our eyes happened to meet I detected a slight quiver on his lips. I looked down at once. It was not my part to encourage sneering on board my ship. It must be said, too, that I knew very little of my officers. In consequence of certain events of no particular significance, except to myself, I had been appointed to the command only a fortnight before. Neither did I know much of the hands forward. All these people had been together for eighteen months or so, and my position was that of the only stranger on board. I mention this because it has some bearing on what is to follow. But what I felt most was my being a stranger to the ship; and if all the truth must be told, I was somewhat of a stranger to myself. The youngest man on board (barring the second mate), and untried as yet by a position of the fullest responsibility, I was willing to take the adequacy of the others for granted. They had simply to be equal to their tasks; but I wondered how far I should turn out faithful to the ideal conception of one's own personality every man sets up for himself secretly.

Meantime the chief mate, with an almost visible effect of collaboration on the part of his round eyes and frightful whiskers, was trying to evolve a theory of the anchored ship. His dominant trait was to take all things into earnest consideration. He was of a painstaking turn of mind. As he used to say, he "liked to account to himself" for practically everything that came in his way, down to a miserable scorpion he had found in his cabin a week before. The why and the wherefore of that scorpion—how it got on board and came to select his room rather than the pantry (which was a dark place and more what a scorpion would be partial to), and how on earth it managed to drown itself in the inkwell of his writing desk —had exercised him infinitely. The ship within the islands was much more easily accounted for; and just as we were about to rise from table he made his pronouncement. She was, he doubted not, a ship from home lately arrived. Probably she drew too much water to cross the bar except at the top of spring tides. Therefore she went into that natural harbor to wait for a few days in preference to remaining in an open roadstead.

"That's so," confirmed the second mate, suddenly, in his slightly hoarse voice. "She draws over twenty feet. She's the Liverpool ship *Sephora* with a cargo of coal. Hundred and twenty-three days from Cardiff."

We looked at him in surprise.

"The tugboat skipper told me when he came on board for your letters, sir," explained the young man. "He expects to take her up the river the day after tomorrow."

After thus overwhelming us with the extent of his information he slipped out of the cabin. The mate observed regretfully that he "could not account for that young fellow's whims." What prevented him telling us all about it at once, he wanted to know.

I detained him as he was making a move. For the last two days the crew had had plenty of hard work, and the night before they had very little sleep. I felt painfully that I—a stranger—was doing something unusual when I directed him to let all hands turn in without setting an anchor watch. I proposed to keep on deck myself till one o'clock or thereabouts. I would get the second mate to relieve me at that hour.

"He will turn out the cook and the steward at four," I concluded, "and then give you a call. Of course at the slightest sign of any sort of wind we'll have the hands up and make a start at once."

He concealed his astonishment. "Very well, sir." Outside the cuddy he put his head in the second mate's door to inform him of my unheard-of caprice to take a five hours' anchor watch on myself. I heard the other raise his voice incredulously—"What? The Captain himself?" Then a few more murmurs, a door closed, then another. A few moments later I went on deck.

My strangeness, which had made me sleepless, had prompted that unconventional arrangement, as if I had expected in those solitary hours of the night to get on terms with the ship of which I knew nothing, manned by men of whom I knew very little more. Fast alongside a wharf, littered like any ship in port with a tangle of unrelated things, invaded by unrelated shore people, I had hardly seen her yet properly. Now, as she lay cleared for sea, the stretch of her main deck seemed to me very fine under the stars. Very fine, very roomy for her size, and very inviting. I descended the poop and paced the waist, my mind picturing to myself the coming passage through the Malay Archipelago, down the Indian Ocean, and up the Atlantic. All its phases were familiar enough to me, every characteristic, all the alternatives which were likely to face me on the high seas—everything! . . . except the novel responsibility of command. But I took heart from the reasonable thought that the ship was like other ships, the men like other men, and that the sea was not likely to keep any special surprises expressly for my discomfiture.

Arrived at that comforting conclusion, I bethought myself of a cigar and went below to get it. All was still down there. Everybody at the after end of the ship was sleeping profoundly. I came out again on the quarter-deck, agreeably at ease in my sleeping suit on that warm breathless night, barefooted, a glowing cigar in my teeth, and, going forward, I was met by the profound silence of the fore end of the ship. Only as I passed the door of the forecastle I heard a deep, quiet, trustful sigh of some sleeper inside. And suddenly I rejoiced in the great security of the sea as compared with the unrest of the land, in my choice of that untempted life presenting no disquieting problems, invested with an elementary moral beauty by the absolute straightforwardness of its appeal and by the singleness of its purpose.

The riding-light in the forerigging burned with a clear, untroubled, as if symbolic, flame, confident and bright in the mysterious shades of the night. Passing on my way aft along the other side of the ship, I observed that the rope side-ladder, put over, no doubt, for the master of the tug when he came to fetch away our letters, had not been hauled in as it should have been. I became annoyed at this, for exactitude in some small matters is the very soul of discipline. Then I reflected that I had myself peremptorily dismissed my officers from duty, and by my own act had prevented the anchor watch being formally set and things properly attended to. I asked myself whether it was wise ever to interfere with the established routine of duties even from the kindest of motives. My action might have made me appear eccentric. Goodness only knew how that

absurdly whiskered mate would "account" for my conduct, and what
the whole ship thought of that informality of their new captain. I
was vexed with myself.

Not from compunction certainly, but, as it were mechanically,
I proceeded to get the ladder in myself. Now a side-ladder of that
sort is a light affair and comes in easily, yet my vigorous tug, which
should have brought it flying on board, merely recoiled upon my
body in a totally unexpected jerk. What the devil! . . . I was so
astounded by the immovableness of that ladder that I remained
stock-still, trying to account for it to myself like that imbecile mate
of mine. In the end, of course, I put my head over the rail.

The side of the ship made an opaque belt of shadow on the
darkling glassy shimmer of the sea. But I saw at once something
elongated and pale floating very close to the ladder. Before I could
form a guess a faint flash of phosphorescent light, which seemed to
issue suddenly from the naked body of a man, flickered in the sleeping water with the elusive, silent play of summer lightning in a
night sky. With a gasp I saw revealed to my stare a pair of feet, the
long legs, a broad livid back immersed right up to the neck in a
greenish cadaverous glow. One hand, awash, clutched the bottom
rung of the ladder. He was complete but for the head. A headless
corpse! The cigar dropped out of my gaping mouth with a tiny plop
and a short hiss quite audible in the absolute stillness of all things
under heaven. At that I suppose he raised up his face, a dimly pale
oval in the shadow of the ship's side. But even then I could only
barely make out down there the shape of his black-haired head.
However, it was enough for the horrid, frost-bound sensation which
had gripped me about the chest to pass off. The moment of vain
exclamations was past, too. I only climbed on the spare spar and
leaned over the rail as far as I could, to bring my eyes nearer to
that mystery floating alongside.

As he hung by the ladder, like a resting swimmer, the sea lightning played about his limbs at every stir; and he appeared in it
ghastly, silvery, fishlike. He remained as mute as a fish, too. He
made no motion to get out of the water, either. It was inconceivable
that he should not attempt to come on board, and strangely troubling
to suspect that perhaps he did not want to. And my first words were
prompted by just that troubled incertitude.

"What's the matter?" I asked in my ordinary tone, speaking down to the face upturned exactly under mine.

"Cramp," it answered, no louder. Then slightly anxious, "I say, no need to call anyone."

"I was not going to," I said.

"Are you alone on deck?"

"Yes."

I had somehow the impression that he was on the point of letting go the ladder to swim away beyond my ken—mysterious as he came. But, for the moment, this being appearing as if he had risen from the bottom of the sea (it was certainly the nearest land to the ship) wanted only to know the time. I told him. And he, down there, tentatively:

"I suppose your captain's turned in?"

"I am sure he isn't," I said.

He seemed to struggle with himself, for I heard something like the low, bitter murmur of doubt. "What's the good?" His next words came out with a hesitating effort.

"Look here, my man. Could you call him out quietly?"

I thought the time had come to declare myself.

"*I* am the captain."

I heard a "By Jove!" whispered at the level of the water. The phosphorescence flashed in the swirl of the water all about his limbs, his other hand seized the ladder.

"My name's Leggatt."

The voice was calm and resolute. A good voice. The self-possession of that man had somehow induced a corresponding state in myself. It was very quietly that I remarked:

"You must be a good swimmer."

"Yes. I've been in the water practically since nine o'clock. The question for me now is whether I am to let go this ladder and go on swimming till I sink from exhaustion, or—to come on board here."

I felt this was no mere formula of desperate speech, but a real alternative in the view of a strong soul. I should have gathered from this that he was young; indeed, it is only the young who are ever confronted by such clear issues. But at the time it was pure intuition on my part. A mysterious communication was established already between us two—in the face of that silent, darkened tropical sea. I was young, too; young enough to make no comment. The man in the water began suddenly to climb up the ladder, and I hastened away from the rail to fetch some clothes.

Before entering the cabin I stood still, listening in the lobby at the foot of the stairs. A faint snore came through the closed door of the chief mate's room. The second mate's door was on the hook, but the darkness in there was absolutely soundless. He, too, was young and could sleep like a stone. Remained the steward, but he was not likely to wake up before he was called. I got a sleeping suit out of my room and, coming back on deck, saw the naked man from the sea sitting on the main hatch, glimmering white in the darkness, his elbows on his knees and his head in his hands. In a moment he had concealed his damp body in a sleeping suit of the same gray-stripe pattern as the one I was wearing and followed me like my double on the poop. Together we moved right aft, bare-footed, silent.

"What is it?" I asked in a deadened voice, taking the lighted lamp out of the binnacle, and raising it to his face.

"An ugly business."

He had rather regular features; a good mouth; light eyes under somewhat heavy, dark eyebrows; a smooth, square forehead; no growth on his cheeks; a small, brown mustache, and a well-shaped, round chin. His expression was concentrated, meditative, under the inspecting light of the lamp I held up to his face; such as a man thinking hard in solitude might wear. My sleeping suit was just right for his size. A well-knit young fellow of twenty-five at most. He caught his lower lip with the edge of white, even teeth.

"Yes," I said, replacing the lamp in the binnacle. The warm, heavy tropical night closed upon his head again.

"There's a ship over there," he murmured.

"Yes, I know. The *Sephora*. Did you know of us?"

"Hadn't the slightest idea. I am the mate of her——" He paused and corrected himself. "I should say I *was*."

"Aha! Something wrong?"

"Yes. Very wrong indeed. I've killed a man."

"What do you mean? Just now?"

"No, on the passage. Weeks ago. Thirty-nine south. When I say a man——"

"Fit of temper," I suggested confidently.

The shadowy, dark head, like mine, seemed to nod imperceptibly above the ghostly gray of my sleeping suit. It was, in the night, as though I had been faced by my own reflection in the depths of a somber and immense mirror.

"A pretty thing to have to own up to for a Conway boy," murmured my double distinctly.

"You're a Conway boy?"

"I am," he said, as if startled. Then, slowly . . . "Perhaps you too——"

It was so; but being a couple of years older I had left before he joined. After a quick interchange of dates a silence fell; and I thought suddenly of my absurd mate with his terrific whiskers and the "Bless my soul—you don't say so" type of intellect. My double gave me an inkling of his thoughts by saying: "My father's a parson in Norfolk. Do you see me before a judge and jury on that charge? For myself I can't see the necessity. There are fellows that an angel from heaven—— And I am not that. He was one of those creatures that are just simmering all the time with a silly sort of wickedness. Miserable devils that have no business to live at all. He wouldn't do his duty and wouldn't let anybody else do theirs. But what's the good of talking! You know well enough the sort of ill-conditioned snarling cur——"

He appealed to me as if our experiences had been as identical as our clothes. And I knew well enough the pestiferous danger of such a character where there are no means of legal repression. And I knew well enough also that my double there was no homicidal ruffian. I did not think of asking him for details, and he told me the story roughly in brusque, disconnected sentences. I needed no more. I saw it all going on as though I were myself inside that other sleeping suit.

"It happened while we were setting a reefed foresail, at dusk. Reefed foresail! You understand the sort of weather. The only sail we had left to keep the ship running; so you may guess what it had been like for days. Anxious sort of job, that. He gave me some of his cursed insolence at the sheet. I tell you I was overdone with this terrific weather that seemed to have no end to it. Terrific, I tell you—and a deep ship. I believe the fellow himself was half crazed with funk. It was no time for gentlemanly reproof, so I turned round and felled him like an ox. He up and at me. We closed just as an awful sea made for the ship. All hands saw it coming and took to the rigging, but I had him by the throat, and went on shaking him like a rat, the men above us yelling, 'Look out! look out!' Then a crash as if the sky had fallen on my head. They say that for over ten minutes hardly anything was to be seen of the ship—just the three masts and a bit of the forecastle head and of the poop all awash driving along in a smother of foam. It was a miracle that they found us, jammed together behind the forebitts. It's clear that I meant business, because I was holding him by the throat still when they picked us up. He was black in the face. It was too much for them. It seems they rushed us aft together, gripped as we were, screaming 'Murder!' like a lot of lunatics, and broke into the cuddy. And the ship running for her life, touch and go all the time, any minute her last in a sea fit to turn your hair gray only a-looking at it. I understand that the skipper, too, started raving like the rest of them. The man had been deprived of sleep for more than a week, and to have this sprung on him at the height of a furious gale nearly drove him out of his mind. I wonder they didn't fling me overboard after getting the carcass of their precious shipmate out of my fingers. They had rather a job to separate us, I've been told. A sufficiently fierce story to make an old judge and a respectable jury sit up a bit. The first thing I heard when I came to myself was the maddening howling of that endless gale, and on that the voice of the old man. He was hanging on to my bunk, staring into my face out of his sou'wester.

" 'Mr. Leggatt, you have killed a man. You can act no longer as chief mate of this ship.' "

His care to subdue his voice made it sound monotonous. He rested a hand on the end of the skylight to steady himself with, and all that time did not stir a limb, so far as I could see. "Nice little tale for a quiet tea party," he concluded in the same tone.

One of my hands, too, rested on the end of the skylight; neither did I stir a limb, so far as I knew. We stood less than a foot from each other. It occurred to me that if old "Bless my soul—you don't say so" were to put his head up the companion and catch sight of us, he would think he was seeing double, or imagine himself come upon a scene of weird witchcraft; the strange captain having a quiet confabulation by the wheel with his own gray ghost. I became very much concerned to prevent anything of the sort. I heard the other's soothing undertone.

"My father's a parson in Norfolk," it said. Evidently he had forgotten he had told me this important fact before. Truly a nice little tale.

"You had better slip down into my stateroom now," I said, moving off stealthily. My double followed my movements; our bare feet made no sound; I let him in, closed the door with care, and, after giving a call to the second mate, returned on deck for my relief.

"Not much sign of any wind yet," I remarked when he approached.

"No, sir. Not much," he assented sleepily in his hoarse voice, with just enough deference, no more, and barely suppressing a yawn.

"Well, that's all you have to look out for. You have got your orders."

"Yes, sir."

I paced a turn or two on the poop and saw him take up his position face forward with his elbow in the ratlines of the mizzen rigging before I went below. The mate's faint snoring was still going on peacefully. The cuddy lamp was burning over the table on which stood a vase with flowers, a polite attention from the ship's provision merchant—the last flowers we should see for the next three months at the very least. Two bunches of bananas hung from the beam symmetrically, one on each side of the rudder casing. Everything was as before in the ship—except that two of her captain's sleeping suits were simultaneously in use, one motionless in the cuddy, the other keeping very still in the captain's stateroom.

It must be explained here that my cabin had the form of the capital letter L, the door being within the angle and opening into the short part of the letter. A couch was to the left, the bed place to the right; my writing desk and the chronometers' table faced the door. But anyone opening it, unless he stepped right inside, had no view of what I call the long (or vertical) part of the letter. It contained some lockers surmounted by a bookcase; and a few clothes, a thick jacket or two, caps, oilskin coat, and such like, hung on hooks. There was at the bottom of that part a door opening into my bathroom, which could be entered also directly from the saloon. But that way was never used.

The mysterious arrival had discovered the advantage of this particular shape. Entering my room, lighted strongly by a big bulkhead lamp swung on gimbals above my writing desk, I did not see him anywhere till he stepped out quietly from behind the coats hung in the recessed part.

"I heard somebody moving about, and went in there at once," he whispered.

I, too, spoke under my breath.

"Nobody is likely to come in here without knocking and getting permission."

He nodded. His face was thin and the sunburn faded, as though he had been ill. And no wonder. He had been, I heard presently, kept under arrest in his cabin for nearly seven weeks. But there was nothing sickly in his eyes or in his expression. He was not a bit like me, really; yet, as we stood leaning over my bed place, whispering side by side, with our dark heads together and our backs to the door, anybody bold enough to open it stealthily would have been treated to the uncanny sight of a double captain busy talking in whispers with his other self.

"But all this doesn't tell me how you came to hang on to our side-ladder," I inquired, in the hardly audible murmurs we used, after he had told me something more of the proceedings on board the *Sephora* once the bad weather was over.

"When we sighted Java Head I had had time to think all those matters out several times over. I had six weeks of doing nothing else, and with only an hour or so every evening for a tramp on the quarter-deck."

He whispered, his arms folded on the side of my bed place, staring through the open port. And I could imagine perfectly the manner of this thinking out—a stubborn if not a steadfast operation; something of which I should have been perfectly incapable.

"I reckoned it would be dark before we closed with the land," he continued, so low that I had to strain my hearing, near as we were to each other, shoulder touching shoulder almost. "So I asked to speak to the old man. He always seemed very sick when he came to see me—as if he could not look me in the face. You know, that foresail saved the ship. She was too deep to have run long under bare poles. And it was I that managed to set it for him. Anyway, he came. When I had him in my cabin—he stood by the door looking at me as if I had the halter round my neck already—I asked him right away to leave my cabin door unlocked at night while the ship was going through Sunda Straits. There would be the Java coast within two or three miles, off Angier Point. I wanted nothing more. I've had a prize for swimming my second year in the Conway."

"I can believe it," I breathed out.

"God only knows why they locked me in every night. To see some of their faces you'd have thought they were afraid I'd go about at night strangling people. Am I a murdering brute? Do I look it? By Jove! If I had been he wouldn't have trusted himself like that into my room. You'll say I might have chucked him aside and bolted out, there and then—it was dark already. Well, no. And for the same reason I wouldn't think of trying to smash the door. There would have been a rush to stop me at the noise, and I did not mean to get into a confounded scrimmage. Somebody else might have got killed —for I would not have broken out only to get chucked back, and I did not want any more of that work. He refused, looking more sick than ever. He was afraid of the men, and also of that old second mate of his who had been sailing with him for years—a gray-headed old humbug; and his steward, too, had been with him devil knows how long—seventeen years or more—a dogmatic sort of loafer who hated me like poison, just because I was the chief mate. No chief mate ever made more than one voyage in the *Sephora*, you know. Those two old chaps ran the ship. Devil only knows what the skipper wasn't afraid of (all his nerve went to pieces altogether in that hellish spell of bad weather we had)—of what the law would do to him—of his wife, perhaps. Oh, yes! she's on board. Though I don't think she would have meddled. She would have been only too glad to have me out of the ship in any way. The 'brand of Cain' business, don't you see. That's all right. I was ready enough to go off wandering on the face of the earth—and that was price enough to pay for an Abel of that sort. Anyhow, he wouldn't listen to me. 'This thing must take its course. I represent the law here.' He was shaking like a leaf. 'So you won't?' 'No!' 'Then I hope you will be able to sleep on that,' I said, and turned my back on him. 'I wonder that *you* can,' cries he, and locks the door.

"Well, after that, I couldn't. Not very well. That was three weeks ago. We have had a slow passage through the Java Sea; drifted about Carimata for ten days. When we anchored here they thought, I suppose, it was all right. The nearest land (and that's five miles) is the ship's destination; the consul would soon set about catching me; and there would have been no object in bolting to these islets there. I don't suppose there's a drop of water on them. I don't know how it was, but tonight that steward, after bringing me my supper, went out to let me eat it, and left the door unlocked. And I ate it—all there was, too. After I had finished I strolled out on the quarter-deck. I don't know that I meant to do anything. A breath of fresh air was all I wanted, I believe. Then a sudden temptation came over me. I kicked off my slippers and was in the water before I had made up my mind fairly. Somebody heard the splash and they raised an awful hullabaloo. 'He's gone! Lower the boats! He's committed suicide! No, he's swimming.' Certainly I was swimming. It's not so easy for a swimmer like me to commit suicide by drowning. I landed on the nearest islet before the boat left the ship's side. I heard them pulling about in the dark, hailing, and so on, but after a bit they gave up. Everything quieted down and the anchorage became as still as death. I sat down on a stone and began to think. I felt certain they would start searching for me at daylight. There was no place to hide on those stony things—and if there had been, what would have been the good? But now I was clear of that ship, I was not going back. So after a while I took off all my clothes, tied them up in a bundle with a stone inside, and dropped them in the deep water on the outer side of the islet. That was suicide enough for me. Let them think what they liked, but I didn't mean to drown myself. I meant to swim till I sank—but that's not the same thing. I struck out for another of these little islands, and it was from that one that I first saw your riding-light. Something to swim for. I went on easily, and on the way I came upon a flat rock a foot or two above water. In the daytime, I dare say, you might make it out with a glass from your poop. I scrambled up on it and rested myself for a bit. Then I made another start. That last spell must have been over a mile."

His whisper was getting fainter and fainter, and all the time he stared straight out through the porthole, in which there was not even a star to be seen. I had not interrupted him. There was something that made comment impossible in his narrative, or perhaps in himself; a sort of feeling, a quality, which I can't find a name for. And when he ceased, all I found was a futile whisper: "So you swam for our light?"

"Yes—straight for it. It was something to swim for. I couldn't see any stars low down because the coast was in the way, and I couldn't see the land, either. The water was like glass. One might have been swimming in a confounded thousand feet deep cistern with no place for scrambling out anywhere; but what I didn't like was the notion of swimming round and round like a crazed bullock before I gave out; and as I didn't mean to go back . . . No. Do you see me being hauled back, stark naked, off one of these little islands by the scruff of the neck and fighting like a wild beast? Somebody would have got killed for certain, and I did not want any of that. So I went on. Then your ladder——"

"Why didn't you hail the ship?" I asked, a little louder.

He touched my shoulder lightly. Lazy footsteps came right over our heads and stopped. The second mate had crossed from the other side of the poop and might have been hanging over the rail, for all we knew.

"He couldn't hear us talking—could he?" My double breathed into my very ear, anxiously.

His anxiety was in answer, a sufficient answer, to the question I had put to him. An answer containing all the difficulty of that situation. I closed the porthole quietly, to make sure. A louder word might have been overheard.

"Who's that?" he whispered then.

"My second mate. But I don't know much more of the fellow than you do."

And I told him a little about myself. I had been appointed to take charge while I least expected anything of the sort, not quite a fortnight ago. I didn't know either the ship or the people. Hadn't had the time in port to look about me or size anybody up. And as to the crew, all they knew was that I was appointed to take the ship home. For the rest, I was almost as much of a stranger on board as himself, I said. And at the moment I felt it most acutely. I felt that it would take very little to make me a suspect person in the eyes of the ship's company.

He had turned about meantime; and we, the two strangers in the ship, faced each other in identical attitudes.

"Your ladder——" he murmured, after a silence. "Who'd have thought of finding a ladder hanging over at night in a ship anchored out here! I felt just then a very unpleasant faintness. After the life I've been leading for nine weeks, anybody would have got out of condition. I wasn't capable of swimming round as far as your rudder chains. And, lo and behold! there was a ladder to get hold of. After I gripped it I said to myself, 'What's the good?' When I saw a man's head looking over I thought I would swim away presently and leave him shouting—in whatever language it was. I didn't mind being looked at. I—I liked it. And then you speaking to me so quietly—as if you had expected me—made me hold on a little longer. It had been a confounded lonely time—I don't mean while swimming. I was glad to talk a little to somebody that didn't belong to the *Sephora*. As to asking for the captain, that was a mere impulse. It could have been no use, with all the ship knowing about me and the other people pretty certain to be round here in the morning. I don't know—I wanted to be seen, to talk with somebody, before I went on. I don't know what I would have said. . . . 'Fine night, isn't it?' or something of the sort."

"Do you think they will be round here presently?" I asked with some incredulity.

"Quite likely," he said faintly.

He looked extremely haggard all of a sudden. His head rolled on his shoulders.

"H'm. We shall see then. Meantime get into that bed," I whispered. "Want help? There."

It was a rather high bed place with a set of drawers underneath. This amazing swimmer really needed the lift I gave him by seizing his leg. He tumbled in, rolled over on his back, and flung one arm across his eyes. And then, with his face nearly hidden, he must have looked exactly as I used to look in that bed. I gazed upon my other self for a while before drawing across carefully the two green serge curtains which ran on a brass rod. I thought for a moment of pinning them together for greater safety, but I sat down on the couch, and once there I felt unwilling to rise and hunt for a pin. I would do it in a moment. I was extremely tired, in a peculiarly intimate way, by the strain of stealthiness, by the effort of whispering and the general secrecy of this excitement. It was three o'clock by now and I had been on my feet since nine, but I was not sleepy; I could not have gone to sleep. I sat there, fagged out, looking at the curtains, trying to clear my mind of the confused sensation of being in two places at once, and greatly bothered by an exasperating knocking in my head. It was a relief to discover suddenly that it was not in my head at all, but on the outside of the door. Before I could collect myself, the words "Come in" were out of my mouth, and the steward entered with a tray, bringing in my morning coffee. I had slept, after all, and I was so frightened that I shouted, "This way! I am here, steward," as though he had been miles away. He put down the tray on the table next the couch and only then said, very quietly, "I can see you are here, sir." I felt him give me a keen look, but I dared not meet his eyes just then. He must have wondered why I had drawn the curtains of my bed before going to sleep on the couch. He went out, hooking the door open as usual.

I heard the crew washing decks above me. I knew I would have been told at once if there had been any wind. Calm, I thought, and I was doubly vexed. Indeed, I felt dual more than ever. The steward reappeared suddenly in the doorway. I jumped up from the couch so quickly that he gave a start.

"What do you want here?"

"Close your port, sir—they are washing decks."

"It is closed," I said, reddening.

"Very well, sir." But he did not move from the doorway and returned my stare in an extraordinary, equivocal manner for a time. Then his eyes wavered, all his expression changed, and in a voice unusually gentle, almost coaxingly:

"May I come in to take the empty cup away, sir?"

"Of course!" I turned my back on him while he popped in and out. Then I unhooked and closed the door and even pushed the bolt. This sort of thing could not go on very long. The cabin was as hot as an oven, too. I took a peep at my double, and discovered that he had not moved, his arm was still over his eyes; but his chest heaved;

his hair was wet; his chin glistened with perspiration. I reached over him and opened the port.

"I must show myself on deck," I reflected.

Of course, theoretically, I could do what I liked, with no one to say nay to me within the whole circle of the horizon; but to lock my cabin door and take the key away I did not dare. Directly I put my head out of the companion I saw the group of my two officers, the second mate barefooted, the chief mate in long India-rubber boots, near the break of the poop, and the steward halfway down the poop ladder talking to them eagerly. He happened to catch sight of me and dived, the second ran down on the main deck shouting some order or other, and the chief mate came to meet me, touching his cap.

There was a sort of curiosity in his eye that I did not like. I don't know whether the steward had told them that I was "queer" only, or downright drunk, but I know the man meant to have a good look at me. I watched him coming with a smile which, as he got into point-blank range, took effect and froze his very whiskers. I did not give him time to open his lips.

"Square the yards by lifts and braces before the hands go to breakfast."

It was the first particular order I had given on board that ship; and I stayed on deck to see it executed, too. I had felt the need of asserting myself without loss of time. That sneering young cub got taken down a peg or two on that occasion, and I also seized the opportunity of having a good look at the face of every foremast man as they filed past me to go to the after braces. At breakfast time, eating nothing myself, I presided with such frigid dignity that the two mates were only too glad to escape from the cabin as soon as decency permitted; and all the time the dual working of my mind distracted me almost to the point of insanity. I was constantly watching myself, my secret self, as dependent on my actions as my own personality, sleeping in that bed, behind that door which faced me as I sat at the head of the table. It was very much like being mad, only it was worse because one was aware of it.

I had to shake him for a solid minute, but when at last he opened his eyes it was in the full possession of his senses, with an inquiring look.

"All's well so far," I whispered. "Now you must vanish into the bathroom."

He did so, as noiseless as a ghost, and then I rang for the steward, and facing him boldly, directed him to tidy up my stateroom while I was having my bath—"and be quick about it." As my tone admitted of no excuses, he said, "Yes, sir," and ran off to fetch his dustpan and brushes. I took a bath and did most of my dressing, splashing, and whistling softly for the steward's edification, while the secret sharer of my life stood drawn bolt upright in that little space, his face looking very sunken in daylight, his eyelids lowered under the stern, dark line of his eyebrows drawn together by a slight frown.

When I left him there to go back to my room the steward was finishing dusting. I sent for the mate and engaged him in some insignificant conversation. It was, as it were, trifling with the terrific character of his whiskers; but my object was to give him an opportunity for a good look at my cabin. And then I could at last shut, with a clear conscience, the door of my stateroom and get my double back into the recessed part. There was nothing else for it. He had to sit still on a small folding stool, half smothered by the heavy coats hanging there. We listened to the steward going into the bathroom out of the saloon, filling the water bottles there, scrubbing the bath, setting things to rights, whisk, bang, clatter—out again into the saloon—turn the key—click. Such was my scheme for keeping my second self invisible. Nothing better could be contrived under the circumstances. And there we sat; I at my writing desk ready to appear busy with some papers, he behind me out of sight of the door. It would not have been prudent to talk in daytime; and I could not have stood the excitement of that queer sense of whispering to myself. Now and then, glancing over my shoulder, I saw him far back there, sitting rigidly on the low stool, his bare feet close together, his arms folded, his head hanging on his breast—and perfectly still. Anybody would have taken him for me.

I was fascinated by it myself. Every moment I had to glance over my shoulder. I was looking at him when a voice outside the door said:

"Beg pardon, sir."

"Well!" . . . I kept my eyes on him, and so when the voice outside the door announced, "There's a ship's boat coming our way, sir," I saw him give a start—the first movement he made for hours. But he did not raise his bowed head.

"All right. Get the ladder over."

I hesitated. Should I whisper something to him? But what? His immobility seemed to have been never disturbed. What could I tell him he did not know already? . . . Finally I went on deck.

2

The skipper of the *Sephora* had a thin red whisker all round his face, and the sort of complexion that goes with hair of that color; also the particular, rather smeary shade of blue in the eyes. He was not exactly a showy figure; his shoulders were high, his stature but middling—one leg slightly more bandy than the other. He shook hands, looking vaguely around. A spiritless tenacity was his main characteristic, I judged. I behaved with a politeness which seemed to disconcert him. Perhaps he was shy. He mumbled to me as if he were ashamed of what he was saying; gave his name (it was something like Archbold—but at this distance of years I hardly am sure), his ship's name, and a few other particulars of that sort, in the manner of a criminal making a reluctant and doleful confession. He had had terrible weather on the passage out—terrible—terrible—wife aboard, too.

By this time we were seated in the cabin and the steward brought in a tray with a bottle and glasses. "Thanks! No." Never took liquor. Would have some water, though. He drank two tumblerfuls. Terrible thirsty work. Ever since daylight had been exploring the islands round his ship.

"What was that for—fun?" I asked, with an appearance of polite interest.

"No!" He sighed. "Painful duty."

As he persisted in his mumbling and I wanted my double to hear every word, I hit upon the notion of informing him that I regretted to say I was hard of hearing.

"Such a young man, too!" he nodded, keeping his smeary blue, unintelligent eyes fastened upon me. "What was the cause of it— some disease?" he inquired, without the least sympathy as if he thought that, if so, I'd got no more than I deserved.

"Yes; disease," I admitted in a cheerful tone which seemed to shock him. But my point was gained, because he had to raise his voice to give me his tale. It is not worth while to record that version. It was just over two months since all this had happened, and he had thought so much about it that he seemed completely muddled as to its bearings, but still immensely impressed.

"What would you think of such a thing happening on board your own ship? I've had the *Sephora* for these fifteen years. I am a well-known shipmaster."

He was densely distressed—and perhaps I should have sympathized with him if I had been able to detach my mental vision from the unsuspected sharer of my cabin as though he were my second self. There he was on the other side of the bulkhead, four or five feet from us, no more, as we sat in the saloon. I looked politely at Captain Archbold (if that was his name), but it was the other I saw, in a gray sleeping suit, seated on a low stool, his bare feet close together, his arms folded, and every word said between us falling into the ears of his dark head bowed on his chest.

"I have been at sea now, man and boy, for seven and thirty years, and I've never heard of such a thing happening in an English ship. And that it should be my ship. Wife on board, too."

I was hardly listening to him.

"Don't you think," I said, "that the heavy sea which, you told me, came aboard just then might have killed the man? I have seen the sheer weight of a sea kill a man very neatly, by simply breaking his neck."

"Good God!" he uttered, impressively, fixing his smeary blue eyes on me. "The sea! No man killed by the sea ever looked like that." He seemed positively scandalized at my suggestion. And as I gazed at him, certainly not prepared for anything original on his part, he advanced his head close to mine and thrust his tongue out at me so suddenly that I couldn't help starting back.

After scoring over my calmness in this graphic way he nodded wisely. If I had seen the sight, he assured me, I would never forget it as long as I lived. The weather was too bad to give the corpse a proper sea burial. So next day at dawn they took it up on the poop, covering its face with a bit of bunting; he read a short prayer, and then, just as it was, in its oilskins and long boots, they launched it amongst those mountainous seas that seemed ready every moment to swallow up the ship herself and the terrified lives on board of her.

"That reefed foresail saved you," I threw in.

"Under God—it did," he exclaimed fervently. "It was by a special mercy, I firmly believe, that it stood some of those hurricane squalls."

"It was the setting of that sail which——" I began.

"God's own hand in it," he interrupted me. "Nothing less could have done it. I don't mind telling you that I hardly dared give the order. It seemed impossible that we could touch anything without losing it, and then our last hope would have been gone."

The terror of that gale was on him yet. I let him go on for a bit, then said casually—as if returning to a minor subject.

"You were very anxious to give up your mate to the shore people, I believe?"

He was. To the law. His obscure tenacity on that point had in it something incomprehensible and a little awful; something, as it were, mystical, quite apart from his anxiety that he should not be suspected of "countenancing any doings of that sort." Seven and thirty virtuous years at sea, of which over twenty of immaculate command, and the last fifteen in the *Sephora*, seemed to have laid him under some pitiless obligation.

"And you know," he went on, groping shame-facedly amongst his feelings, "I did not engage that young fellow. His people had some interest with my owners. I was in a way forced to take him on. He looked very smart, very gentlemanly, and all that. But do you know—I never liked him, somehow. I am a plain man. You see, he wasn't exactly the sort for the chief mate of a ship like the *Sephora*."

I had become so connected in thoughts and impressions with the secret sharer of my cabin that I felt as if I, personally, were being given to understand that I, too, was not the sort that would have done for the chief mate of a ship like the *Sephora*. I had no doubt of it in my mind.

"Not at all the style of man. You understand," he insisted super-
fluously, looking hard at me.

I smiled urbanely. He seemed at a loss for a while.

"I suppose I must report a suicide."

"Beg pardon?"

"Sui-cide! That's what I'll have to write to my owners directly
I get in."

"Unless you manage to recover him before tomorrow," I assented dispassionately. . . . "I mean, alive."

He mumbled something which I really did not catch, and I
turned my ear to him in a puzzled manner. He fairly bawled:

"The land—I say, the mainland is at least seven miles off my
anchorage."

"About that."

My lack of excitement, of curiosity, of surprise, of any sort of
pronounced interest, began to arouse his distrust. But except for the
felicitous pretense of deafness I had not tried to pretend anything.
I had felt utterly incapable of playing the part of ignorance properly,
and therefore was afraid to try. It is also certain that he had brought
some ready-made suspicions with him, and that he viewed my politeness as a strange and unnatural phenomenon. And yet how else
could I have received him? Not heartily! That was impossible for
psychological reasons, which I need not state here. My only object
was to keep off his inquiries. Surlily? Yes, but surliness might have
provoked a point-blank question. From its novelty to him and from
its nature, punctilious courtesy was the manner best calculated to
restrain the man. But there was the danger of his breaking through
my defense bluntly. I could not, I think, have met him by a direct
lie, also for psychological (not moral) reasons. If he had only known
how afraid I was of his putting my feeling of identity with the other
to the test! But, strangely enough—(I thought of it only afterwards)
—I believe that he was not a little disconcerted by the reverse side of
that weird situation, by something in me that reminded him of the
man he was seeking—suggested a mysterious similitude to the young
fellow he had distrusted and disliked from the first.

However that might have been, the silence was not very prolonged. He took another oblique step.

"I reckon I had no more than a two mile pull to your ship. Not a bit more."

"And quite enough too, in this awful heat," I said.

Another pause full of mistrust followed. Necessity, they say, is mother of invention, but fear, too, is not barren of ingenious suggestions. And I was afraid he would ask me point-blank for news of my other self.

"Nice little saloon, isn't it?" I remarked, as if noticing for the first time the way his eyes roamed from one closed door to the other. "And very well fitted out, too. Here, for instance," I continued, reaching over the back of my seat negligently and flinging the door open, "is my bathroom."

He made an eager movement, but hardly gave it a glance. I got up, shut the door of the bathroom, and invited him to have a look around, as if I were very proud of my accommodation. He had to rise and be shown round, but he went through the business without any raptures whatever.

"And now we'll have a look at my stateroom," I declared, in a voice as loud as I dared to make it, crossing the cabin to the starboard side with purposely heavy steps.

He followed me in and gazed around. My intelligent double had vanished. I played my part.

"Very convenient—isn't it?"

"Very nice. Very comf . . ." He didn't finish and went out brusquely as if to escape from some unrighteous wiles of mine. But it was not to be. I had been too frightened not to feel vengeful: I felt I had him on the run, and I meant to keep him on the run. My polite insistence must have had something menacing in it, because he gave in suddenly. And I did not let him off a single item; mate's room, pantry, storerooms, the very sail locker which was also under the poop—he had to look into them all. When at last I showed him out on the quarter-deck he drew a long spiritless sigh, and mumbled dismally that he must really be going back to his ship now. I desired my mate, who had joined us, to see to the captain's boat.

The man of whiskers gave a blast on the whistle which he used to wear hanging round his neck, and yelled, *"Sephora's* away!" My double down there in my cabin must have heard, and certainly could not feel more relieved than I. Four fellows came running out from somewhere forward and went over the side, while my own men, appearing on deck too, lined the rail. I escorted my visitor to the gangway ceremoniously, and nearly overdid it. He was a tenacious beast. On the very ladder he lingered, and in that unique, guiltily conscientious manner of sticking to the point:

"I say . . . you . . . you don't think that ——"

I covered his voice loudly:

"Certainly not. . . . I am delighted. Good-by."

I had an idea of what he meant to say, and just saved myself by the privilege of defective hearing. He was too shaken generally to insist, but my mate, close witness of that parting, looked mystified and his face took on a thoughtful cast. As I did not want to appear as if I wished to avoid all communication with my officers, he had the opportunity to address me.

"Seems a very nice man. His boat's crew told our chaps a very extraordinary story, if what I am told by the steward is true. I suppose you had it from the captain, sir?"

"Yes. I had a story from the captain."

"A very horrible affair—isn't it, sir?"

"It is."

"Beats all these tales we hear about murders in Yankee ships."

"I don't think it beats them. I don't think it resembles them in the least."

"Bless my soul—you don't say so! But of course I've no acquaintance whatever with American ships, not I, so I couldn't go against your knowledge. It's horrible enough for me. . . . But the queerest part is that those fellows seemed to have some idea the man was hidden aboard here. They had really. Did you ever hear of such a thing?"

"Preposterous—isn't it?"

We were walking to and fro athwart the quarter-deck. No one of the crew forward could be seen (the day was Sunday), and the mate pursued:

"There was some little dispute about it. Our chaps took offense. 'As if we would harbor a thing like that,' they said. 'Wouldn't you like to look for him in our coalhole?' Quite a tiff. But they made it up in the end. I suppose he did drown himself. Don't you, sir?"

"I don't suppose anything."

"You have no doubt in the matter, sir?"

"None whatever."

I left him suddenly. I felt I was producing a bad impression, but with my double down there it was most trying to be on deck. And it was almost as trying to be below. Altogether a nerve-trying situation. But on the whole I felt less torn in two when I was with him. There was no one in the whole ship whom I dared take into my confidence. Since the hands had got to know his story, it would have been impossible to pass him off for anyone else, and an accidental discovery was to be dreaded now more than ever. . . .

The steward being engaged in laying the table for dinner, we could talk only with our eyes when I first went down. Later in the afternoon we had a cautious try at whispering. The Sunday quietness of the ship was against us; the stillness of air and water around her was against us; the elements, the men were against us—everything was against us in our secret partnership; time itself—for this could not go on forever. The very trust in Providence was, I suppose, denied to his guilt. Shall I confess that this thought cast me down very much? And as to the chapter of accidents which counts for so much in the book of success, I could only hope that it was closed. For what favorable accident could be expected?

"Did you hear everything?" were my first words as soon as we took up our position side by side, leaning over my bed place.

He had. And the proof of it was his earnest whisper, "The man told you he hardly dared to give the order."

I understood the reference to be to that saving foresail.

"Yes. He was afraid of it being lost in the setting."

"I assure you he never gave the order. He may think he did, but he never gave it. He stood there with me on the break of the poop after the main topsail blew away, and whimpered about our last hope—positively whimpered about it and nothing else—and the night coming on! To hear one's skipper go on like that in such weather was enough to drive any fellow out of his mind. It worked me up into a sort of desperation. I just took it into my own hands and went away from him, boiling, and—— But what's the use telling you? *You* know! . . . Do you think that if I had not been pretty fierce with them I should have got the men to do anything? Not It! The bo's'n perhaps? Perhaps! It wasn't a heavy sea—it was a sea gone mad! I suppose the end of the world will be something like that; and a man may have the heart to see it coming once and be done with it—but to have to face it day after day—— I don't blame anybody. I was precious little better than the rest. Only—I was an officer of that old coal wagon, anyhow——"

"I quite understand," I conveyed that sincere assurance into his ear. He was out of breath with whispering; I could hear him pant slightly. It was all very simple. The same strung-up force which had given twenty-four men a chance, at least, for their lives, had, in a sort of recoil, crushed an unworthy mutinous existence.

But I had no leisure to weigh the merits of the matter—footsteps in the saloon, a heavy knock. "There's enough wind to get under way with, sir." Here was the call of a new claim upon my thoughts and even upon my feelings.

"Turn the hands up," I cried through the door. "I'll be on deck directly."

I was going out to make the acquaintance of my ship. Before I left the cabin our eyes met—the eyes of the only two strangers on board. I pointed to the recessed part where the little campstool awaited him and laid my finger on my lips. He made a gesture—somewhat vague—a little mysterious, accompanied by a faint smile, as if of regret.

This is not the place to enlarge upon the sensations of a man who feels for the first time a ship move under his feet to his own independent word. In my case they were not unalloyed. I was not wholly alone with my command; for there was that stranger in my cabin. Or rather, I was not completely and wholly with her. Part of me was absent. That mental feeling of being in two places at once affected me physically as if the mood of secrecy had penetrated my very soul. Before an hour had elapsed since the ship had begun to move, having occasion to ask the mate (he stood by my side) to take a compass bearing of the pagoda, I caught myself reaching up to his ear in whispers. I say I caught myself, but enough had escaped to startle the man. I can't describe it otherwise than by saying that he shied. A grave, preoccupied manner, as though he were in possession of some perplexing intelligence, did not leave him henceforth. A little later I moved away from the rail to look at the compass with such a stealthy gait that the helmsman noticed it—and I could not help noticing the unusual roundness of his eyes. These are trifling instances, though it's to no commander's advantage to be suspected of ludicrous eccentricities. But I was also more seriously affected. There are to a seaman certain words, gestures, that should in given conditions come as naturally, as instinctively as the winking of a menaced eye. A certain order should spring on to his lips without thinking; a certain sign should get itself made, so to speak, without reflection. But all unconscious alertness had abandoned me. I had to make an effort of will to recall myself back (from the cabin) to the conditions of the moment. I felt that I was appearing an irresolute commander to those people who were watching me more or less critically.

And, besides, there were the scares. On the second day out, for instance, coming off the deck in the afternoon (I had straw slippers on my barefeet) I stopped at the open pantry door and spoke to the steward. He was doing something there with his back to me. At the sound of my voice he nearly jumped out of his skin, as the saying is, and incidentally broke a cup.

"What on earth's the matter with you?" I asked, astonished.

He was extremely confused. "Beg your pardon, sir. I made sure you were in your cabin."

"You see I wasn't."

"No, sir. I could have sworn I had heard you moving in there not a moment ago. It's most extraordinary . . . very sorry, sir."

I passed on with an inward shudder. I was so identified with my secret double that I did not even mention the fact in those scanty, fearful whispers we exchanged. I suppose he had made some slight noise of some kind or other. It would have been miraculous if he hadn't at one time or another. And yet, haggard as he appeared, he looked always perfectly self-controlled, more than calm—almost invulnerable. On my suggestion he remained almost entirely in the bathroom, which, upon the whole, was the safest place. There could be really no shadow of an excuse for anyone ever wanting to go in there, once the steward had done with it. It was a very tiny place. Sometimes he reclined on the floor, his legs bent, his head sustained on one elbow. At others I would find him on the campstool, sitting in his gray sleeping suit and with his cropped dark hair like a patient, unmoved convict. At night I would smuggle him into my bed place, and we would whisper together, with the regular footfalls of the officer of the watch passing and repassing over our heads. It was an infinitely miserable time. It was lucky that some tins of fine preserves were stowed in a locker in my stateroom; hard bread I could always get hold of; and so he lived on stewed chicken, *pâté de foie gras*, asparagus, cooked oysters, sardines—on all sorts of abominable sham delicacies out of tins. My early morning coffee he always drank; and it was all I dared do for him in that respect.

Every day there was the horrible maneuvering to go through so that my room and the bathroom should be done in the usual way. I came to hate the sight of the steward, to abhor the voice of that harmless man. I felt that it was he who would bring on the disaster of discovery. It hung like a sword over our heads.

The fourth day out, I think (we were then working down the east side of the Gulf of Siam, tack for tack, in light winds and smooth water)—the fourth day, I say, of this miserable juggling with the unavoidable, as we sat at our evening meal, that man, whose slightest movement I dreaded, after putting down the dishes ran up on deck busily. This could not be dangerous. Presently he came down again; and then it appeared that he had remembered a coat of mine which I had thrown over a rail to dry after having been wetted in a shower which had passed over the ship in the afternoon. Sitting stolidly at the head of the table I became terrified at the sight of the garment on his arm. Of course he made for my door. There was no time to lose.

"Steward!" I thundered. My nerves were so shaken that I could not govern my voice and conceal my agitation. This was the sort of thing that made my terrifically whiskered mate tap his forehead with his forefinger. I had detected him using that gesture while talking on deck with a confidential air to the carpenter. It was too far to hear a word, but I had no doubt that this pantomime could only refer to the strange new captain.

"Yes, sir," the pale-faced steward turned resignedly to me. It was this maddening course of being shouted at, checked without rhyme or reason, arbitrarily chased out of my cabin, suddenly called into it, sent flying out of his pantry on incomprehensible errands, that accounted for the growing wretchedness of his expression.

"Where are you going with that coat?"

"To your room, sir."

"Is there another shower coming?"

"I'm sure I don't know, sir. Shall I go up again and see, sir?"

"No! never mind."

My object was attained, as of course my other self in there would have heard everything that passed. During this interlude my two officers never raised their eyes off their respective plates; but the lip of that confounded cub, the second mate, quivered visibly.

I expected the steward to hook my coat on and come out at once. He was very slow about it; but I dominated my nervousness sufficiently not to shout after him. Suddenly I became aware (it could be heard plainly enough) that the fellow for some reason or other was opening the door of the bathroom. It was the end. The place was literally not big enough to swing a cat in. My voice died in my throat and I went stony all over. I expected to hear a yell of surprise and terror, and made a movement, but had not the strength to get on my legs. Everything remained still. Had my second self taken the poor wretch by the throat? I don't know what I could have done next moment if I had not seen the steward come out of my room, close the door, and then stand quietly by the sideboard.

"Saved," I thought. "But, no! Lost! Gone! He was gone!"

I laid my knife and fork down and leaned back in my chair. My head swam. After a while, when sufficiently recovered to speak in a steady voice, I instructed my mate to put the ship round at eight o'clock himself.

"I won't come on deck," I went on. "I think I'll turn in, and unless the wind shifts I don't want to be disturbed before midnight. I feel a bit seedy."

"You did look middling bad a little while ago," the chief mate remarked without showing any great concern.

They both went out, and I stared at the steward clearing the table. There was nothing to be read on that wretched man's face. But why did he avoid my eyes, I asked myself. Then I thought I should like to hear the sound of his voice.

"Steward!"

"Sir!" Startled as usual.

"Where did you hang up that coat?"

"In the bathroom, sir." The usual anxious tone. "It's not quite dry yet, sir."

For some time longer I sat in the cuddy. Had my double vanished as he had come? But of his coming there was an explanation, whereas his disappearance would be inexplicable. . . . I went slowly into my dark room, shut the door, lighted the lamp, and for a time dared not turn round. When at last I did I saw him standing bolt upright in the narrow recessed part. It would not be true to say I had a shock, but an irresistible doubt of his bodily existence flitted through my mind. Can it be, I asked myself, that he is not visible to other eyes than mine? It was like being haunted. Motionless, with a grave face, he raised his hands slightly at me in a gesture which meant clearly, "Heavens! what a narrow escape!" Narrow indeed. I think I had come creeping quietly as near insanity as any man who has not actually gone over the border. That gesture restrained me, so to speak.

The mate with the terrific whiskers was now putting the ship on the other tack. In the moment of profound silence which follows upon the hands going to their stations I heard on the poop his raised voice: "Hard alee!" and the distant shout of the order repeated on the main deck. The sails, in that light breeze, made but a faint fluttering noise. It ceased. The ship was coming round slowly: I held my breath in the renewed stillness of expectation; one wouldn't have thought that there was a single living soul on her decks. A sudden brisk shout, "Mainsail haul!" broke the spell, and in the noisy cries and rush overhead of the men running away with the main brace we two, down in my cabin, came together in our usual position by the bed place.

He did not wait for my question. "I heard him fumbling here and just managed to squat myself down in the bath," he whispered to me. "The fellow only opened the door and put his arm in to hang the coat up. All the same ——"

"I never thought of that," I whispered back, even more appalled than before at the closeness of the shave, and marveling at that something unyielding in his character which was carrying him through so finely. There was no agitation in his whisper. Whoever was being driven distracted, it was not he. He was sane. And the proof of his sanity was continued when he took up the whispering again.

"It would never do for me to come to life again."

It was something that a ghost might have said. But what he was alluding to was his old captain's reluctant admission of the theory of suicide. It would obviously serve his turn—if it had understood at all the view which seemed to govern the unalterable purpose of his action.

"You must maroon me as soon as ever you can get amongst these islands off the Cambodge shore," he went on.

"Maroon you! We are not living in a boy's adventure tale," I protested. His scornful whispering took me up.

"We aren't indeed! There's nothing of a boy's tale in this. But there's nothing else for it. I want no more. You don't suppose I am afraid of what can be done to me? Prison or gallows or whatever they may please. But you don't see me coming back to explain such things to an old fellow in a wig and twelve respectable tradesmen, do you? What can they know whether I am guilty or not—or of *what* I am guilty, either? That's my affair. What does the Bible say? 'Driven off the face of the earth.' Very well, I am off the face of the earth now. As I came at night so I shall go."

"Impossible!" I murmured. "You can't."

"Can't? . . . Not naked like a soul on the Day of Judgment. I shall freeze on to this sleeping suit. The Last Day is not yet—and . . . you have understood thoroughly. Didn't you?"

I felt suddenly ashamed of myself. I may say truly that I understood—and my hesitation in letting that man swim away from my ship's side had been a mere sham sentiment, a sort of cowardice.

"It can't be done now till next night," I breathed out. "The ship is on the off-shore tack and the wind may fail us."

"As long as I know that you understand," he whispered. "But of course you do. It's a great satisfaction to have got somebody to understand. You seem to have been there on purpose." And in the same whisper, as if we two whenever we talked had to say things to each other which were not fit for the world to hear, he added, "It's very wonderful."

We remained side by side talking in our secret way—but sometimes silent or just exchanging a whispered word or two at long intervals. And as usual he stared through the port. A breath of wind came now and again into our faces. The ship might have been moored in dock, so gently and on an even keel she slipped through the water, that did not murmur even at our passage, shadowy and silent like a phantom sea.

At midnight I went on deck, and to my mate's great surprise put the ship round on the other tack. His terrible whiskers flitted round me in silent criticism. I certainly should not have done it if it had been only a question of getting out of that sleepy gulf as quickly as possible. I believe he told the second mate, who relieved him, that it was a great want of judgment. The other only yawned. That intolerable cub shuffled about so sleepily and lolled against the rails in such a slack, improper fashion that I came down on him sharply.

"Aren't you properly awake yet?"

"Yes, sir! I am awake."

"Well, then, be good enough to hold yourself as if you were. And keep a lookout. If there's any current we'll be closing with some islands before daylight."

The east side of the gulf is fringed with islands, some solitary, others in groups. On the blue background of the high coast they seem to float on silvery patches of calm water, arid and gray, or dark green and rounded like clumps of evergreen bushes, with the larger ones, a mile or two long, showing the outlines of ridges, ribs of gray rock under the dank mantle of matted leafage. Unknown to trade, to travel, almost to geography, the manner of life they harbor is an unsolved secret. There must be villages—settlements of fishermen at least—on the largest of them, and some communication with the world is probably kept up by native craft. But all that forenoon, as we headed for them, fanned along by the faintest of breezes, I saw no sign of man or canoe in the field of the telescope I kept on pointing at the scattered group.

At noon I gave no orders for a change of course, and the mate's whiskers became much concerned and seemed to be offering themselves unduly to my notice. At last I said:

"I am going to stand right in. Quite in—as far as I can take her."

The stare of extreme surprise imparted an air of ferocity also to his eyes, and he looked truly terrific for a moment.

"We're not doing well in the middle of the gulf," I continued casually. "I am going to look for the land breezes tonight."

"Bless my soul! Do you mean, sir, in the dark amongst the lot of all them islands and reefs and shoals?"

"Well—if there are any regular land breezes at all on this coast one must get close inshore to find them, mustn't one?"

"Bless my soul!" he exclaimed again under his breath. All that afternoon he wore a dreamy, contemplative appearance which in him was a mark of perplexity. After dinner I went into my state-room as if I meant to take some rest. There we two bent our dark heads over a half-unrolled chart lying on my bed.

"There," I said. "It's got to be Koh-ring. I've been looking at it ever since sunrise. It has got two hills and a low point. It must be inhabited. And on the coast opposite there is what looks like the mouth of a biggish river—with some towns, no doubt, not far up. It's the best chance for you that I can see."

"Anything. Koh-ring let it be."

He looked thoughtfully at the chart as if surveying chances and distances from a lofty height—and following with his eyes his own figure wandering on the blank land of Cochin-China, and then passing off that piece of paper clean out of sight into uncharted regions. And it was as if the ship had two captains to plan her course for her. I had been so worried and restless running up and down that I had not had the patience to dress that day. I had re-mained in my sleeping suit, with straw slippers and a soft floppy hat. The closeness of the heat in the gulf had been most oppressive, and the crew were used to seeing me wandering in that airy attire.

"She will clear the south point as she heads now," I whispered into his ear. "Goodness only knows when, though, but certainly after dark. I'll edge her in to half a mile, as far as I may be able to judge in the dark——"

"Be careful," he murmured warningly—and I realized suddenly that all my future, the only future for which I was fit, would perhaps go irretrievably to pieces in any mishap to my first command.

I could not stop a moment longer in the room. I motioned him to get out of sight and made my way on the poop. That unplayful cub had the watch. I walked up and down for a while thinking things out, then beckoned him over.

"Send a couple of hands to open the two quarter-deck ports," I said mildly.

He actually had the impudence, or else so forgot himself in his wonder at such an incomprehensible order, as to repeat:

"Open the quarter-deck ports! What for, sir?"

"The only reason you need concern yourself about is because I tell you to do so. Have them open wide and fastened properly."

He reddened and went off, but I believe made some jeering remark to the carpenter as to the sensible practice of ventilating a ship's quarter-deck. I know he popped into the mate's cabin to impart the fact to him because the whiskers came on deck, as it were by chance, and stole glances at me from below—for signs of lunacy or drunkenness, I suppose.

A little before supper, feeling more restless than ever, I rejoined, for a moment, my second self. And to find him sitting so quietly was surprising, like something against nature, inhuman.

I developed my plan in a hurried whisper.

"I shall stand in as close as I dare and then put her round. I will presently find means to smuggle you out of here into the sail locker, which communicates with the lobby. But there is an opening, a sort of square for hauling the sails out, which gives straight on the quarter-deck and which is never closed in fine weather, so as to give air to the sails. When the ship's way is deadened in stays and all hands are aft at the main braces you will have a clear road to slip out and get overboard through the open quarter-deck port. I've had them both fastened up. Use a rope's end to lower yourself into the water so as to avoid a splash—you know. It could be heard and cause some beastly complication."

He kept silent for a while, then whispered, "I understand."

"I won't be there to see you go," I began with an effort. "The rest . . . I only hope I have understood, too."

"You have. From first to last"—and for the first time there seemed to be a faltering, something strained in his whisper. He caught hold of my arm, but the ringing of the supper bell made me start. He didn't though; he only released his grip.

After supper I didn't come below again till well past eight o'clock. The faint, steady breeze was loaded with dew; and the wet, darkened sails held all there was of propelling power in it. The night, clear and starry, sparkled darkly, and the opaque, lightless patches shifting slowly against the low stars were the drifting islets. On the port bow there was a big one more distant and shadowily imposing by the great space of sky it eclipsed.

On opening the door I had a back view of my very own self looking at a chart. He had come out of the recess and was standing near the table.

"Quite dark enough," I whispered.

He stepped back and leaned against my bed with a level, quiet glance. I sat on the couch. We had nothing to say to each other. Over our heads the officer of the watch moved here and there. Then I heard him move quickly. I knew what that meant. He was making for the companion; and presently his voice was outside my door.

"We are drawing in pretty fast, sir. Land looks rather close."

"Very well," I answered. "I am coming on deck directly."

I waited till he was gone out of the cuddy, then rose. My double moved too. The time had come to exchange our last whispers, for neither of us was ever to hear each other's natural voice.

"Look here!" I opened a drawer and took out three sovereigns. "Take this anyhow. I've got six and I'd give you the lot, only I must keep a little money to buy some fruit and vegetables for the crew from native boats as we go through Sunda Straits."

He shook his head.

"Take it," I urged him, whispering desperately. "No one can tell what——"

He smiled and slapped meaningly the only pocket of the sleeping jacket. It was not safe, certainly. But I produced a large old silk handkerchief of mine, and tying the three pieces of gold in a corner, pressed it on him. He was touched, I supposed, because he took it at last and tied it quickly round his waist under the jacket, on his bare skin.

Our eyes met; several seconds elapsed, till, our glances still mingled, I extended my hand and turned the lamp out. Then I passed through the cuddy, leaving the door of my room wide open. . . . "Steward!"

He was still lingering in the pantry in the greatness of his zeal, giving a rub-up to a plated cruet stand the last thing before going to bed. Being careful not to wake up the mate, whose room was opposite, I spoke in an undertone.

He looked round anxiously. "Sir!"

"Can you get me a little hot water from the galley?"

"I am afraid, sir, the galley fire's been out for some time now."

"Go and see."

He flew up the stairs.

"Now," I whispered loudly into the saloon—too loudly, perhaps, but I was afraid I couldn't make a sound. He was by my side in an instant—the double captain slipped past the stairs—through a tiny dark passage . . . a sliding door. We were in the sail locker, scrambling on our knees over the sails. A sudden thought struck me. I saw myself wandering barefooted, bareheaded, the sun beating on my dark poll. I snatched off my floppy hat and tried hurriedly in the dark to ram it on my other self. He dodged and fended off silently. I wonder what he thought had come to me before he understood and suddenly desisted. Our hands met gropingly, lingered united in a steady, motionless clasp for a second. . . . No word was breathed by either of us when they separated.

I was standing quietly by the pantry door when the steward returned.

"Sorry, sir. Kettle barely warm. Shall I light the spirit lamp?"

"Never mind."

I came out on deck slowly. It was now a matter of conscience to shave the land as close as possible—for now he must go overboard whenever the ship was put in stays. Must! There could be no going back for him. After a moment I walked over to leeward and my heart flew into my mouth at the nearness of the land on the bow. Under any other circumstances I would not have held on a minute longer. The second mate had followed me anxiously.

I looked on till I felt I could command my voice.

"She will weather," I said then in a quiet tone.

"Are you going to try that, sir?" he stammered out incredulously.

I took no notice of him and raised my tone just enough to be heard by the helmsman.

"Keep her good full."

"Good full, sir."

The wind fanned my cheek, the sails slept, the world was silent. The strain of watching the dark loom of the land grow bigger and denser was too much for me. I had shut my eyes—because the ship must go closer. She must! The stillness was intolerable. Were we standing still?

When I opened my eyes the second view started my heart with a thump. The black southern hill of Koh-ring seemed to hang right over the ship like a towering fragment of the ever-lasting night. On that enormous mass of blackness there was not a gleam to be seen, not a sound to be heard. It was gliding irresistibly towards us and yet seemed already within reach of the hand. I saw the vague figures of the watch grouped in the waist, gazing in awed silence.

"Are you going on, sir?" inquired an unsteady voice at my elbow. I ignored it. I had to go on.

"Keep her full. Don't check her way. That won't do now," I said warningly.

"I can't see the sails very well," the helmsman answered me, in strange, quavering tones.

Was she close enough? Already she was, I won't say in the shadow of the land, but in the very blackness of it, already swallowed up as it were, gone too close to be recalled, gone from me altogether.

"Give the mate a call," I said to the young man who stood at my elbow as still as death. "And turn all hands up."

My tone had a borrowed loudness reverberated from the height of the land. Several voices cried out together: "We are all on deck, sir."

Then stillness again, with the great shadow gliding closer, towering higher, without a light, without a sound. Such a hush had fallen on the ship that she might have been a bark of the dead floating in slowly under the very gate of Erebus.

"My God! Where are we?"

It was the mate moaning at my elbow. He was thunderstruck, and as it were deprived of the moral support of his whiskers. He clapped his hands and absolutely cried out, "Lost!"

"Be quiet," I said sternly.

He lowered his tone, but I saw the shadowy gesture of his despair. "What are we doing here?"

"Looking for the land wind."

He made as if to tear his hair, and addressed me recklessly.

"She will never get out. You have done it, sir. I knew it'd end in something like this. She will never weather, and you are too close now to stay. She'll drift ashore before she's round. O my God!"

I caught his arm as he was raising it to batter his poor devoted head, and shook it violently.

"She's ashore already," he wailed, trying to tear himself away.

"Is she? . . . Keep good full there!"

"Good full, sir," cried the helmsman in a frightened, thin, child-like voice.

I hadn't let go the mate's arm and went on shaking it. "Ready about, do you hear? You go forward"—shake—"and stop there"—shake—"and hold your noise"—shake—"and see these head-sheets properly overhauled"—shake, shake—shake.

And all the time I dared not look towards the land lest my heart should fail me. I released my grip at last and he ran forward as if fleeing for dear life.

I wondered what my double there in the sail locker thought of this commotion. He was able to hear everything—and perhaps he was able to understand why, on my conscience, it had to be thus close—no less. My first order "Hard alee!" re-echoed ominously under the towering shadow of Koh-ring as if I had shouted in a mountain gorge. And then I watched the land intently. In that smooth water and light wind it was impossible to feel the ship coming-to. No! I could not feel her. And my second self was making now ready to ship out and lower himself overboard. Perhaps he was gone already . . . ?

The great black mass brooding over our very mastheads began to pivot away from the ship's side silently. And now I forgot the secret stranger ready to depart, and remembered only that I was a total stranger to the ship. I did not know her. Would she do it? How was she to be handled?

I swung the mainyard and waited helplessly. She was perhaps stopped, and her very fate hung in the balance, with the black mass of Koh-ring like the gate of the everlasting night towering over her taffrail. What would she do now? Had she way on her yet? I stepped to the side swiftly, and on the shadowy water I could see nothing except a faint phosphorescent flash revealing the glassy smoothness of the sleeping surface. It was impossible to tell—and I had not learned yet the feel of my ship. Was she moving? What I needed was something easily seen, a piece of paper, which I could throw overboard and watch. I had nothing on me. To run down for it I didn't dare. There was no time. All at once my strained, yearning stare distinguished a white object floating within a yard of the ship's side. White on the black water. A phosphorescent flash passed under it. What was that thing? . . . I recognized my own floppy hat. It must have fallen off his head . . . and he didn't bother. Now I had what I wanted—the saving mark for my eyes. But I hardly thought of my other self, now gone from the ship, to be hidden forever from all friendly faces, to be a fugitive and a vagabond on the earth, with no brand of the curse on his sane forehead to stay a slaying hand . . . too proud to explain.

And I watched the hat—the expression of my sudden pity for his mere flesh. It had been meant to save his homeless head from the dangers of the sun. And now—behold—it was saving the ship, by serving me for a mark to help out the ignorance of my strangeness. Ha! It was drifting forward, warning me just in time that the ship had gathered sternway.

"Shift the helm," I said in a low voice to the seaman standing still like a statue.

The man's eyes glistened wildly in the binnacle light as he jumped round to the other side and spun round the wheel.

I walked to the break of the poop. On the overshadowed deck all hands stood by the forebraces waiting for my order. The stars ahead seemed to be gliding from right to left. And all was so still in the world that I heard the quiet remark, "She's round," passed in a tone of intense relief between two seamen.

"Let go and haul."

The foreyards ran round with a great noise, amidst cheery cries. And now the frightful whiskers made themselves heard giving various orders. Already the ship was drawing ahead. And I was alone with her. Nothing! no one in the world should stand now between us, throwing a shadow on the way of silent knowledge and mute affection, the perfect communion of a seaman with his first command.

Walking to the taffrail, I was in time to make out, on the very edge of a darkness thrown by a towering black mass like the very gateway of Erebus—yes, I was in time to catch an evanescent glimpse of my white hat left behind to mark the spot where the secret sharer of my cabin and of my thoughts, as though he were my second self, had lowered himself into the water to take his punishment: a free man, a proud swimmer striking out for a new destiny.

The Double

(A Petersburg Poem)

FYODOR DOSTOEVSKY

CHAPTER 1

It was a little before eight o'clock in the morning when Yakov Petrovitch Golyadkin, a titular councillor, woke up from a long sleep. He yawned, stretched, and at last opened his eyes completely. For two minutes, however, he lay in his bed without moving, as though he were not yet quite certain whether he were awake or still asleep, whether all that was going on around him were real and actual, or the continuation of his confused dreams. Very soon, however, Mr. Golyadkin's senses began more clearly and more distinctly to receive their habitual and everyday impressions. The dirty green, smoke-begrimed, dusty walls of his little room, with the mahogany chest of drawers and chairs, the table painted red, the sofa covered with American leather of a reddish colour with little green flowers on it, and the clothes taken off in haste overnight and flung in a crumpled heap on the sofa, looked at him familiarly. At last the damp autumn day, muggy and dirty, peeped into the room through the dingy window pane with such a hostile, sour grimace that Mr. Golyadkin could not possibly doubt that he was not in the

The Double, by Fyodor Dostoevsky, from *The Eternal Husband and Other Stories,* translated from the Russian by Constance Garnett. Reprinted by permission of The Macmillan Company. First published in England.

land of Nod, but in the city of Petersburg, in his own flat on the fourth storey of a huge block of buildings in Shestilavotchny Street. When he had made this important discovery, Mr. Golyadkin nervously closed his eyes, as though regretting his dream and wanting to go back to it for a moment. But a minute later he leapt out of bed at one bound, probably all at once grasping the idea about which his scattered and wandering thoughts had been revolving. From his bed he ran straight to a little round looking-glass that stood on his chest of drawers. Though the sleepy, short-sighted countenance and rather bald head reflected in the looking-glass were of such an insignificant type that at first sight they would certainly not have attracted particular attention in any one, yet the owner of the countenance was satisfied with all that he saw in the looking-glass. "What a thing it would be," said Mr. Golyadkin in an undertone, "what a thing it would be if I were not up to the mark to-day, if something were amiss, if some intrusive pimple had made its appearance, or anything else unpleasant had happened; so far, however, there's nothing wrong, so far everything's all right."

Greatly relieved that everything was all right, Mr. Golyadkin put the looking-glass back in its place and, although he had nothing on his feet and was still in the attire in which he was accustomed to go to bed, he ran to the little window and with great interest began looking for something in the courtyard, upon which the windows of his flat looked out. Apparently what he was looking for in the yard quite satisfied him too; his face beamed with a self-satisfied smile. Then, after first peeping, however, behind the partition into his valet Petrushka's little room and making sure that Petrushka was not there, he went on tiptoe to the table, opened the drawer in it and, fumbling in the farthest corner of it, he took from under old yellow papers and all sorts of rubbish a shabby green pocket-book, opened it cautiously, and with care and relish peeped into the farthest and most hidden fold of it. Probably the roll of green, gray, blue, red and particoloured notes looked at Golyadkin, too, with approval: with a radiant face he laid the open pocket-book before him and rubbed his hands vigorously in token of the greatest satisfaction. Finally, he took it out—his comforting roll of notes—and, for the hundredth time since the previous day, counted them over, carefully smoothing out every note between his forefinger and his thumb.

"Seven hundred and fifty roubles in notes," he concluded at last, in a half-whisper. "Seven hundred and fifty roubles, a noteworthy sum! It's an agreeable sum," he went on, in a voice weak and trembling with gratification as he pinched the roll with his fingers and smiled significantly; "it's a very agreeable sum! A sum agreeable to any one! I should like to see the man to whom that would be a trivial sum! There's no knowing what a man might not do with a sum like that. . . . What's the meaning of it, though?" thought Mr. Golyadkin; "where's Petrushka?" And still in the same attire he peeped behind the partition again. Again there was no sign of Petrushka; and the samovar standing on the floor was beside itself, fuming and raging in solitude, threatening every minute to boil over, hissing and lisping in its mysterious language, to Mr. Golyadkin something like, "Take me, good people, I'm boiling and perfectly ready."

"Damn the fellow," thought Mr. Golyadkin. "That lazy brute might really drive a man out of all patience; where's he dawdling now?"

In just indignation he went out into the hall, which consisted of a little corridor at the end of which was a door into the entry, and saw his servant surrounded by a good-sized group of lackeys of all sorts, a mixed rabble from outside as well as from the flats of the house. Petrushka was telling something, the others were listening. Apparently the subject of the conversation, or the conversation itself, did not please Mr. Golyadkin. He promptly called Petrushka and returned to his room, displeased and even upset. "That beast would sell a man for a halfpenny, and his master before any one," he thought to himself: "and he has sold me, he certainly has. I bet he has sold me for a farthing. Well?"

"They've brought the livery, sir."

"Put it on, and come here."

When he had put on his livery, Petrushka, with a stupid smile on his face, went in to his master. His costume was incredibly strange. He had on a much-worn green livery, with frayed gold braid on it, apparently made for a man a yard taller than Petrushka. In his hand he had a hat trimmed with the same gold braid and with a feather in it, and at his hip hung a footman's sword in a leather sheath. Finally, to complete the picture, Petrushka, who always liked to be in *négligé*, was barefooted. Mr. Golyadkin looked at Petrushka from all sides and was apparently satisfied. The livery had evidently been hired for some solemn occassion. It might be observed, too, that during his master's inspection Petrushka watched him with strange expectancy and with marked curiosity followed every movement he made, which extremely embarrassed Mr. Golyadkin.

"Well, and how about the carriage?"

"The carriage is here too."

"For the whole day?"

"For the whole day. Twenty-five roubles."

"And have the boots been sent?"

"Yes."

"Dolt! can't even say, 'Yes, sir.' Bring them here."

Expressing his satisfaction that the boots fitted, Mr. Golyadkin asked for his tea, and for water to wash and shave. He shaved with great care and washed as scrupulously, hurriedly sipped his tea and proceeded to the principal final process of attiring himself: he put on an almost new pair of trousers; then a shirt-front with brass studs, and a very bright and agreeably flowered waistcoat; about his neck he tied a gay, particoloured cravat, and finally drew on his coat, which was also newish and carefully brushed. As he dressed, he more than once looked lovingly at his boots, lifted up first one leg and then the other, admired their shape, kept muttering something to himself, and from time to time made expressive grimaces. Mr. Golyadkin was, however, extremely absent-minded that morning, for he scarcely noticed the little smiles and grimaces made at his expense by Petrushka, who was helping him dress. At last, having arranged everything properly and having finished dressing, Mr. Golyadkin put his pocket-book in his pocket, took a final admiring look at Petrushka, who had put on his boots and was therefore also quite ready, and, noticing that everything was done and that there was nothing left to wait for, he ran hurriedly and fussily out on to the stairs, with a slight throbbing at his heart. The light-blue hired carriage with a crest on it rolled noisily up to the steps. Petrushka, winking to the driver and some of the gaping crowd, helped his master into the carriage; and, hardly able to suppress an idiotic laugh, shouted in an unnatural voice: "Off!" jumped up on the footboard, and the whole turnout, clattering and rumbling noisily, rolled into the Nevsky Prospect. As soon as the light-blue carriage dashed out of the gate, Mr. Golyadkin rubbed his hands convulsively and went off into a slow, noiseless chuckle, like a jubilant man who has succeeded in bringing off a splendid performance and is as pleased as Punch with the performance himself. Immediately after his access of gaiety, however, laughter was replaced by a strange and anxious expression on the face of Mr. Golyadkin. Though the weather was damp and muggy, he let down both windows of the carriage and began carefully scrutinizing the passers-by to left and to right, at once assuming a decorous and sedate air when he thought any one was looking at him. At the turning from Liteyny Street into the Nevsky Prospect he was startled by a most unpleasant sensation and, frowning like some poor wretch whose corn has been accidentally trodden on, he huddled with almost panic-stricken haste into the darkest corner of his carriage.

He had seen two of his colleagues, two young clerks serving in the same government department. The young clerks were also, it seemed to Mr. Golyadkin, extremely amazed at meeting their colleague in such a way; one of them, in fact, pointed him out to the other. Mr. Golyadkin even fancied that the other had actually called his name, which, of course, was very unseemly in the street. Our hero concealed himself and did not respond. "The silly youngsters!" he began reflecting to himself. "Why, what is there strange in it? A man in a carriage, a man needs to be in a carriage, and so he hires a carriage. They're simply noodles! I know them—simply silly youngsters, who still need thrashing! They want to be paid a salary for playing pitch-farthing and dawdling about, that's all they're fit for. I'd let them all know, if only . . ."

Mr. Golyadkin broke off suddenly, petrified. A smart pair of Kazan horses, very familiar to Mr. Golyadkin, in a fashionable droshky, drove rapidly by on the right side of his carriage. The gentleman sitting in the droshky, happening to catch a glimpse of Mr. Golyadkin, who was rather incautiously poking his head out of the carriage window, also appeared to be extremely astonished at the unexpected meeting and, bending out as far as he could, looked with the greatest curiosity and interest into the corner of the carriage in which our hero made haste to conceal himself. The gentleman in the droshky was Andrey Filippovitch, the head of the office in which Mr. Golyadkin served in the capacity of assistant to the chief clerk. Mr. Golyadkin, seeing that Andrey Filippovitch recognized him, that he was looking at him open-eyed and that it was impossible to hide, blushed up to his ears.

"Bow or not? Call back or not? Recognize him or not?" our hero wondered in indescribable anguish. "Or pretend that I am not myself, but somebody else strikingly like me, and look as though nothing were the matter. Simply not I, not I—and that's all," said Mr. Golyadkin, taking off his hat to Andrey Filippovitch and keeping his eyes fixed upon him. "I'm . . . I'm all right," he whispered with an effort; "I'm . . . quite all right. It's not I, it's not I—and that is the fact of the matter."

Soon, however, the droshky passed the carriage, and the magnetism of his chief's eyes was at an end. Yet he went on blushing, smiling and muttering something to himself. . . .

"I was a fool not to call back," he thought at last. "I ought to have taken a bolder line and behaved with gentlemanly openness. I ought to have said, 'This is how it is, Andrey Filippovitch, I'm asked to the dinner too,' and that's all it is!"

Then, suddenly recalling how taken aback he had been, our hero flushed as hot as fire, frowned, and cast a terrible defiant glance at the front corner of the carriage, a glance calculated to reduce all his foes to ashes. At last, he was suddenly inspired to pull the cord attached to the driver's elbow, and stopped the carriage, telling him to drive back to Liteyny Street. The fact was, it was urgently necessary for Mr. Golyadkin, probably for the sake of his own peace of mind, to say something very interesting to his doctor, Krestyan Ivanovitch. And, though he had made Krestyan Ivanovitch's acquaintance quite recently, having, indeed, only paid him a single visit, and that one the previous week, to consult him about some symptom. But a doctor, as they say, is like a priest, and it would be stupid for him to keep out of sight, and, indeed, it was his duty to know his patients. "Will it be all right, though," our hero went on, getting out of the carriage at the door of a five-storey house in Liteyny Street, at which he had told the driver to stop the carriage: "Will it be all right? Will it be proper? Will it be appropriate? After all, though," he went on, thinking as he mounted the stairs out of breath and trying to suppress the beating of his heart, which had the habit of beating on all other people's staircases, "after all, it's on my own business and there's nothing reprehensible in it. . . . It would be stupid to keep out of sight. Why, of course, I shall behave as though I were quite all right, and have simply looked in as I passed. . . . He will see that it's all just as it should be."

Reasoning like this, Mr. Golyadkin mounted to the second storey and stopped before flat number five, on which there was a handsome brass door-plate with the inscription—

KRESTYAN IVANOVITCH RUTENSPITZ
Doctor of Medicine and Surgery

Stopping at the door, our hero made haste to assume an air of propriety, ease, and even of a certain affability, and prepared to pull the bell. As he was about to do so he promptly and rather appropriately reflected that it might be better to come tomorrow, and that it was not very pressing for the moment. But as he suddenly heard footsteps on the stairs, he immediately changed his mind again and at once rang Krestyan Ivanovitch's bell—with an air, moreover, of great determination.

CHAPTER 2

The doctor of medicine and surgery, Krestyan Ivanovitch Rutenspitz, a very hale, though elderly man, with thick eyebrows and whiskers that were beginning to turn grey, eyes with an expressive gleam in them that looked capable of routing every disease, and, lastly, with orders of some distinction on his breast, was sitting in his consulting-room that morning in his comfortable arm-chair. He was drinking coffee, which his wife had brought him with her own hand, smoking a cigar and from time to time writing prescriptions for his patients. After prescribing a draught for an old man who was suffering from haemorrhoids and seeing the aged patient out by the side door, Krestyan Ivanovitch sat down to await the next visitor.

Mr. Golyadkin walked in.

Apparently Krestyan Ivanovitch did not in the least expect nor desire to see Mr. Golyadkin, for he was suddenly taken aback for a moment, and his countenance unconsciously assumed a strange and, one may almost say, a displeased expression. As Mr. Golyadkin almost always turned up inappropriately and was thrown into confusion whenever he approached any one about his own little affairs, on this occasion, too, he was desperately embarrassed. Having neglected to get ready his first sentence, which was invariably a stumbling-block for him on such occasions, he muttered something—apparently an apology—and, not knowing what to do next, took a chair and sat down, but, realizing that he had sat down without being asked to do so, he was immediately conscious of his lapse, and made haste to efface his offence against etiquette and good breeding by promptly getting up again from the seat he had taken uninvited. Then, on second thoughts, dimly perceiving that he had committed two stupid blunders at once, he immediately decided to commit a third—that is, tried to right himself, muttered something, smiled, blushed, was overcome with embarrassment, sank into expressive silence, and finally sat down for good and did not get up again. Only, to protect himself from all contingencies, he looked at the doctor with that defiant glare which had an extraordinary power of figuratively crushing Mr. Golyadkin's enemies and reducing them to ashes. This glance, moreover, expressed to the full Mr. Golyadkin's independence—that is, to speak plainly, the fact that Mr. Golyadkin was "all right," that he was "quite himself, like everybody else," and that there was "nothing wrong in his upper storey." Krestyan Ivanovitch coughed, cleared his throat, apparently in token of approval and assent to all this, and bent an inquisitorial interrogative gaze upon his visitor.

"I have come to trouble you a second time, Krestyan Ivanovitch," began Mr. Golyadkin, with a smile, "and now I venture to ask your indulgence a second time. . . ." He was obviously at a loss for words.

"H'm . . . Yes!" pronounced Krestyan Ivanovitch, puffing out a spiral of smoke and putting down his cigar on the table, "but you must follow the treatment prescribed you; I explained to you that what would be beneficial to your health is a change of habits. . . . Entertainment, for instance, and, well, friends—you should visit your acquaintances, and not be hostile to the bottle; and likewise keep cheerful company."

Mr. Golyadkin, still smiling, hastened to observe that he thought he was like every one else, that he lived by himself, that he had entertainments like every one else . . . that, of course, he might go to the theatre, for he had the means like every one else, that he spent the day at the office and the evenings at home, that he was quite all right; he even observed, in passing, that he was, so far as he could see, as good as any one, that he lived at home, and, finally, that he had Petrushka. At this point Mr. Golyadkin hesitated.

"H'm! no, that is not the order of proceeding I want; and that is not at all what I would ask you. I am interested to know, in general, are you a great lover of cheerful company? Do you take advantages of festive occasions; and, well, do you lead a melancholy or a cheerful manner of life?"

"Krestyan Ivanovitch, I . . ."

"H'm! . . . I tell you," interrupted the doctor, "that you must have a radical change of life, must, in a certain sense, break in your character." (Krestyan Ivanovitch laid special stress on the words "break in," and paused for a moment with a very significant air.) "Must not shrink from gaiety, must visit entertainments and clubs, and in any case, be not hostile to the bottle. Sitting at home is not right for you . . . sitting at home is impossible for you."

"I like quiet, Krestyan Ivanovitch," said Mr. Golyadkin, with a significant look at the doctor and evidently seeking words to express his ideas more successfully: "In my flat there's only me and Petrushka. . . . I mean my man, Krestyan Ivanovitch. I mean to say, Krestyan Ivanovitch, that I go my way, my own way, Krestyan Ivanovitch. I keep myself to myself, and so far as I can see am not dependent on any one. I go out for walks, too, Krestyan Ivanovitch."

"What? Yes! well, nowadays there's nothing agreeable in walking: the climate's extremely bad."

"Quite so, Krestyan Ivanovitch. Though I'm a peaceable man, Krestyan Ivanovitch, as I've had the honour of explaining to you already, yet my way lies apart, Krestyan Ivanovitch. The ways of life are manifold. . . . I mean . . . I mean to say, Krestyan Ivano-vitch. . . . Excuse me, Krestyan Ivanovitch, I've no great gift for eloquent speaking."

"H'm . . . you say . . ."

"I say, you must excuse me, Krestyan Ivanovitch, that as far as

I can see I am no great hand at eloquence in speaking," Mr. Golyadkin articulated, stammering and hesitating, in a half-aggrieved
voice. "In that respect, Krestyan Ivanovitch, I'm not quite like
other people," he added, with a peculiar smile, "I can't talk much,
and have never learnt to embellish my speech with literary graces.
On the other hand, I act, Krestyan Ivanovitch; on the other hand, I
act, Krestyan Ivanovitch."

"H'm . . . How's that . . . you act?" responded Krestyan Ivanovitch.

Then silence followed for half a minute. The doctor looked somewhat strangely and mistrustfully at his visitor. Mr. Golyadkin, for
his part, too, stole a rather mistrustful glance at the doctor.

"Krestyan Ivanovitch," he began, going on again in the same
tone as before, somewhat irritated and puzzled by the doctor's extreme obstinacy: "I like tranquillity and not the noisy gaiety of the
world. Among them, I mean, in the noisy world, Krestyan Ivanovitch, one must be able to polish the floor with one's boots . . ."
(here Mr. Golyadkin made a slight scrape on the floor with his toe);
"they expect it, and they expect puns too . . . one must know how
to make a perfumed compliment . . . that's what they expect there.
And I've not learnt to do it, Krestyan Ivanovitch, I've never learnt
all those tricks, I've never had the time. I'm a simple person, and
not ingenious, and I've no external polish. On that side I surrender,
Krestyan Ivanovitch, I lay down my arms, speaking in that sense."

All this Mr. Golyadkin pronounced with an air which made it
perfectly clear that our hero was far from regretting that he was
laying down his arms in that sense and that he had not learnt these
tricks; quite the contrary, indeed. As Krestyan Ivanovitch listened
to him, he looked down with a very unpleasant grimace on his
face, seeming to have a presentiment of something. Mr. Golyadkin's
tirade was followed by a rather long and significant silence.

"You have, I think, departed a little from the subject," Krestyan Ivanovitch said at last, in a low voice: "I confess I cannot
altogether understand you."

"I'm not a great hand at eloquent speaking, Krestyan Ivanovitch; I've had the honour to inform you, Krestyan Ivanovitch, already," said Mr. Golyadkin, speaking this time in a sharp and resolute tone.

"H'm! . . ."

"Krestyan Ivanovitch!" began Mr. Golyadkin again in a low but more significant voice, in a somewhat solemn style and emphasizing every point: "Krestyan Ivanovitch, when I came in here I began with apologies. I repeat the same thing again, and again ask for your indulgence. There's no need for me to conceal it, Krestyan Ivanovitch. I'm an unimportant man, as you know; but, fortunately for me, I do not regret being an unimportant man. Quite the contrary, indeed, Krestyan Ivanovitch, and, to be perfectly frank, I'm proud that I'm not a great man but an unimportant man. I'm not one to intrigue and I'm proud of that too, I don't act on the sly, but openly, without cunning, and although I could do harm too, and a great deal of harm, indeed, and know to whom and how to do it, Krestyan Ivanovitch, yet I won't sully myself, and in that sense I wash my hands. In that sense, I say, I wash them, Krestyan Ivanovitch!" Mr. Golyadkin paused expressively for a moment; he spoke with mild fervour.

"I set to work, Krestyan Ivanovitch," our hero continued, "directly, openly, by no devious ways, for I disdain them, and leave them to others. I do not try to degrade those who are perhaps purer than you and I . . . that is, I mean, I and they, Krestyan Ivanovitch —I didn't mean you. I don't like insinuations; I've no taste for contemptible duplicity; I'm disgusted by slander and calumny. I only put on a mask at a masquerade, and don't wear one before people every day. I only ask you, Krestyan Ivanovitch, how you would revenge yourself upon your enemy, your most malignant enemy— the one you would consider such?" Mr. Golyadkin concluded with a challenging glance at Krestyan Ivanovitch.

Though Mr. Golyadkin pronounced this with the utmost distinctness and clearness, weighing his words with a self-confident air and reckoning on their probable effect, yet meanwhile he looked at Krestyan Ivanovitch with anxiety, with great anxiety, with extreme anxiety. Now he was all eyes, and timidly waited for the doctor's answer with irritable and agonized impatience. But to the perplexity and complete amazement of our hero, Krestyan Ivanovitch only muttered something to himself; then he moved his arm-chair up to the table, and rather drily though politely announced something to the effect that his time was precious, and that he did not quite understand; that he was ready, however, to attend to him as far as he was able, but he would not go into anything further that did not concern him. At this point he took the pen, drew a piece of paper towards him, cut out of it the usual long strip, and announced that he would immediately prescribe what was necessary.

"No, it's not necessary, Krestyan Ivanovitch! No, that's not necessary at all!" said Mr. Golyadkin, getting up from his seat, and clutching Krestyan Ivanovitch's right hand. "That isn't what's wanted, Krestyan Ivanovitch."

And, while he said this, a queer change came over him. His grey eyes gleamed strangely, his lips began to quiver, all the muscles, all the features of his face began moving and working. He was trembling all over. After stopping the doctor's hand, Mr. Golyadkin followed his first movement by standing motionless, as though he had no confidence in himself and were waiting for some inspiration for further action.

Then followed a rather strange scene.

Somewhat perplexed, Krestyan Ivanovitch seemed for a moment rooted to his chair and gazed open-eyed in bewilderment at Mr. Golyadkin, who looked at him in exactly the same way. At last Krestyan Ivanovitch stood up, gently holding the lining of Mr. Golyadkin's coat. For some seconds they both stood like that, motionless, with their eyes fixed on each other. Then, however, in an extraordinarily strange way came Mr. Golyadkin's second movement. His lips trembled, his chin began twitching, and our hero quite unexpectedly burst into tears. Sobbing, shaking his head and striking himself on the chest with his right hand, while with his left clutching the lining of the doctor's coat, he tried to say something and to make some explanation, but could not utter a word.

At last Krestyan Ivanovitch recovered from his amazement.

"Come, calm yourself!" he brought out at last, trying to make Mr. Golyadkin sit down in an arm-chair.

"I have enemies, Krestyan Ivanovitch, I have enemies; I have malignant enemies who have sworn to ruin me. . . ." Mr. Golyadkin answered in a frightened whisper.

"Come, come, why enemies? You mustn't talk about enemies! You really mustn't. Sit down, sit down," Krestyan Ivanovitch went on, getting Mr. Golyadkin once for all into the arm-chair.

Mr. Golyadkin sat down at last, still keeping his eyes fixed on the doctor. With an extremely displeased air, Krestyan Ivanovitch strode from one end of the room to another. A long silence followed.

"I'm grateful to you, Krestyan Ivanovitch, I'm very grateful, and I'm very sensible of all you've done for me now. To my dying day I shall never forget your kindness, Krestyan Ivanovitch," said Mr. Golyadkin, getting up from his seat with an offended air.

"Come, give over! I tell you, give over!" Krestyan Ivanovitch responded rather sternly to Mr. Golyadkin's outburst, making him sit down again.

"Well, what's the matter? Tell me what is unpleasant," Krestyan Ivanovitch went on, "and what enemies are you talking about? What is wrong?"

"No, Krestyan Ivanovitch, we'd better leave that now," answered Mr. Golyadkin, casting down his eyes; "let us put all that aside for the time. . . . Till another time, Krestyan Ivanovitch, till a more convenient moment, when everything will be discovered and the mask falls off certain faces, and something comes to light. But, meanwhile, now, of course, after what has passed between us . . . you will agree yourself, Krestyan Ivanovitch . . . Allow me to wish you good-morning, Krestyan Ivanovitch," said Mr. Golyadkin, getting up gravely and resolutely and taking his hat.

"Oh, well . . . as you like . . . h'm . . ." (A moment of silence followed.) "For my part, you know . . . whatever I can do . . . and I sincerely wish you well."

"I understand you, Krestyan Ivanovitch, I understand: I understand you perfectly now. . . . In any case excuse me for having troubled you, Krestyan Ivanovitch."

"H'm, no, I didn't mean that. However, as you please; go on taking the medicines as before. . . ."

"I will go on with the medicines as you say, Krestyan Ivanovitch. I will go on with them, and I will get them at the same chemist's. . . . To be a chemist nowadays, Krestyan Ivanovitch, is an important business. . . ."

"How so? In what sense do you mean?"

"In a very ordinary sense, Krestyan Ivanovitch. I mean to say that nowadays that's the way of the world. . . ."

"H'm . . ."

"And that every silly youngster, not only a chemist's boy, turns up his nose at respectable people."

"H'm. How do you understand that?"

"I'm speaking of a certain person, Krestyan Ivanovitch . . . of a common acquaintance of ours, Krestyan Ivanovitch, of Vladimir Semyonovitch. . . ."

"Ah!"

"Yes, Krestyan Ivanovitch: and I know certain people, Krestyan Ivanovitch, who don't quite keep to the general rule of telling the truth, sometimes."

"Ah! How so?"

"Why, yes, it is so: but that's neither here nor there: they sometimes manage to serve you up a fine egg in gravy."

"What? Serve up what?"

"An egg in gravy, Krestyan Ivanovitch. It's a Russian saying. They know how to congratulate some one at the right moment, for instance; there are people like that."

"Congratulate?"

"Yes, congratulate, Krestyan Ivanovitch, as some one I know very well did the other day!"

"Some one you know very well . . . Ah! how was that?" said Krestyan Ivanovitch, looking attentively at Mr. Golyadkin.

"Yes, some one I know very well indeed congratulated some one else I know very well—and, what's more, a comrade, a friend of his heart, on his promotion, on his receiving the rank of assessor. This was how it happened to come up: 'I am exceedingly glad of the opportunity to offer you, Vladimir Semyonovitch, my congratulations, my *sincere* congratulations, on your receiving the rank of assessor. And I'm the more pleased, as all the world knows that there are old women nowadays who tell fortunes.'"

At this point Mr. Golyadkin gave a sly nod, and screwing up his eyes, looked at Krestyan Ivanovitch.

"H'm. So he said that. . . ."

"He did, Krestyan Ivanovitch, he said it and glanced at once at Andrey Filippovitch, the uncle of our Prince Charming, Vladimir Semyonovitch. But what is it to me, Krestyan Ivanovitch, that he has been made an assessor? What is it to me? And he wants to get married and the milk is scarcely dry on his lips, if I may be allowed the expression. And I said as much. Vladimir Semyonovitch, said I! I've said everything now; allow me to withdraw."

"H'm . . ."

"Yes, Krestyan Ivanovitch, allow me now, I say, to withdraw. But, to kill two birds with one stone, as I twitted our young gentleman with the old women, I turned to Klara Olsufyevna (it all happened the day before yesterday at Olsufy Ivanovitch's), and she had only just sung a song full of feeling, 'You've sung songs full of feeling, madame,' said I, 'but they've not been listened to with a pure heart.' And by that I hinted plainly, Krestyan Ivanovitch, hinted plainly, that they were not running after her now, but looking higher. . . ."

"Ah! And what did he say?"

"He swallowed the pill, Krestyan Ivanovitch, as the saying is."

"H'm . . ."

"Yes, Krestyan Ivanovitch. To the old man himself, too, I said, 'Olsufy Ivanovitch,' said I, 'I know how much I'm indebted to you, I appreciate to the full all the kindness you've showered upon me from my childhood up. But open your eyes, Olsufy Ivanovitch,' I said 'Look about you. I myself do things openly and aboveboard, Olsufy Ivanovitch.'"

"Oh, really!"

"Yes, Krestyan Ivanovitch. Really. . . ."

"What did he say?"

"Yes, what, indeed, Krestyan Ivanovitch? He mumbled one thing and another, and 'I know you,' and that 'his Excellency was a benevolent man'—he rambled on. . . . But, there, you know! he's begun to be a bit shaky, as they say, with old age."

"Ah! so that's how it is now. . . ."

"Yes, Krestyan Ivanovitch. And that's how we all are! Poor old man! He looks towards the grave, breathes incense, as they say, while they concoct a piece of womanish gossip and he listens to it; without him they wouldn't . . ."

"Gossip, you say?"

"Yes, Krestyan Ivanovitch, they've concocted a womanish scandal. Our bear, too, had a finger in it, and his nephew, our Prince Charming. They've joined hands with the old women and, of course, they've concocted the affair. Would you believe it? They plotted the murder of some one! . . ."

"The murder of some one?"

"Yes, Krestyan Ivanovitch, the moral murder of some one. They spread about . . . I'm speaking of a man I know very well."

Krestyan Ivanovitch nodded.

"They spread rumours about him . . . I confess I'm ashamed to repeat them, Krestyan Ivanovitch."

"H'm . . ."

"They spread a rumour that he had signed a promise to marry though he was already engaged in another quarter . . . and would you believe it, Krestyan Ivanovitch, to whom?"

"Really?"

"To a cook, to a disreputable German woman from whom he used to get his dinners; instead of paying what he owed, he offered her his hand."

"Is that what they say?"

"Would you believe it, Krestyan Ivanovitch? A low German, a nasty shameless German, Karolina Ivanovna, if you know . . ."

"I confess, for my part . . ."

"I understand you, Krestyan Ivanovitch, I understand, and for my part I feel it. . . ."

"Tell me, please, where are you living now?"

"Where am I living now, Krestyan Ivanovitch?"

"Yes . . . I want . . . I believe, you used to live . . ."

"Yes, Krestyan Ivanovitch, I did, I used to. To be sure I lived!" answered Mr. Golyadkin, accompanying his words with a little laugh, and somewhat disconcerting Krestyan Ivanovitch by his answer.

"No, you misunderstood me; I meant to say . . ."

"I, too, meant to say, Krestyan Ivanovitch, I meant it too," Mr. Golyadkin continued, laughing. "But I've kept you far too long, Krestyan Ivanovitch. I hope you will allow me now, to wish you good-morning."

"H'm . . ."

"Yes, Krestyan Ivanovitch, I understand you; I fully understand you now," said our hero, with a slight flourish before Krestyan Ivanovitch. "And so permit me to wish you good-morning. . . ."

At this point our hero made a scrape with the toe of his boot and walked out of the room, leaving Krestyan Ivanovitch in the utmost amazement. As he went down the doctor's stairs he smiled and rubbed his hands gleefully. On the steps, breathing the fresh air and feeling himself at liberty, he was certainly prepared to admit that he was the happiest of mortals, and thereupon to go straight to his office—when suddenly his carriage rumbled up to the door: he glanced at it and remembered everything. Petrushka was already opening the carriage door. Mr. Golyadkin was completely overwhelmed by a strong and unpleasant sensation. He blushed, as it were, for a moment. Something seemed to stab him. He was just about to raise his foot to the carriage step when he suddenly turned round and looked towards Krestyan Ivanovitch's window. Yes, it was so! Krestyan Ivanovitch was standing at the window, was stroking his whiskers with his right hand and staring with some curiosity at the hero of our story.

"That doctor is silly," thought Mr. Golyadkin, huddling out of sight in the carriage; "extremely silly. He may treat his patients all right, but still . . . he's as stupid as a post."

Mr. Golyadkin sat down, Petrushka shouted "Off!" and the carriage rolled towards Nevsky Prospect again.

CHAPTER 3

All that morning was spent by Mr. Golyadkin in a strange bustle of activity. On reaching the Nevsky Prospect our hero told the driver to stop at the bazaar. Skipping out of his carriage, he ran to the Arcade, accompanied by Petrushka, and went straight to a shop where gold and silver articles were for sale. One could see from his very air that he was overwhelmed with business and had a terrible amount to do. Arranging to purchase a complete dinner-and-tea service for fifteen hundred roubles and including in the bargain for that sum a cigar-case of ingenious form and a silver shaving-set, and finally, asking the price of some other articles, useful and agreeable in their own way, he ended by promising to come without fail next day, or to send for his purchases the same day. He took the number of the shop, listening attentively to the shopkeeper, who

was very pressing for a small deposit, said that he should have it all
in good time. After which he took leave of the amazed shopkeeper
and, followed by a regular flock of shopmen, walked along the Arcade, continually looking round at Petrushka and diligently seeking
out fresh shops. On the way he dropped into a money-changer's
and changed all his big notes into small ones, and though he lost
on the exchange, his pocket-book was considerably fatter, which
evidently afforded him extreme satisfaction. Finally, he stopped at a
shop for ladies' dress-materials. Here, too, after deciding to purchase
goods for a considerable sum, Mr. Golyadkin promised to come
again, took the number of the shop and, on being asked for a deposit, assured the shopkeeper that he "should have a deposit too,
all in good time." Then he visited several other shops, making purchases in each of them, asked the price of various things, sometimes
arguing a long time with the shopkeeper, going out of the shop
and returning two or three times—in fact, he displayed exceptional
activity. From the Arcade our hero went to a well-known furniture
shop, where he ordered furniture for six rooms; he admired a fashionable and very ingenious toilet table for ladies' use in the latest
style, and, assuring the shopkeeper that he would certainly send for
all these things, walked out of the shop, as usual promising a deposit.
Then he went off somewhere else and ordered something more. In
short, there seemed to be no end to the business he had to get
through. At last, Mr. Golyadkin seemed to grow heartily sick of it
all, and he began, goodness knows why, to be tormented by the
stings of conscience. Nothing would have induced him now, for
instance, to meet Andrey Filippovitch, or even Krestyan Ivanovitch.

At last, the town clock struck three. When Mr. Golyadkin finally
took his seat in the carriage, of all the purchases he had made that
morning he had, it appeared, in reality only got a pair of gloves
and a bottle of scent that cost a rouble and a half. As it was still
rather early, he ordered his coachman to stop near a well-known
restaurant in Nevsky Prospect which he only knew by reputation,
got out of the carriage, and hurried in to have a light lunch, to rest
and to wait for the hour fixed for the dinner.

Lunching as a man lunches who has the prospect before him of
going out to a sumptuous dinner, that is, taking a snack of something
in order to still the pangs, as they say, and drinking one small glass

of vodka, Mr. Golyadkin established himself in an arm-chair and, modestly looking about him, peacefully settled down to an emaciated nationalist paper. After reading a couple of lines he stood up and looked in the looking-glass, set himself to rights and smoothed himself down; then he went to the window and looked to see whether his carriage was there . . . then he sat down again in his place and took up the paper. It was noticeable that our hero was in great excitement. Glancing at his watch and seeing that it was only a quarter past three and that he had consequently a good time to wait and, at the same time, opining that to sit like that was unsuitable, Mr. Golyadkin ordered chocolate, though he felt no particular inclination for it at the moment. Drinking the chocolate and noticing that the time had moved on a little, he went up to pay his bill.

He turned round and saw facing him two of his colleagues, the same two he had met that morning in Liteyny Street—young men, very much his juniors both in age and in rank. Our hero's relations with them were neither one thing nor the other, neither particularly friendly nor openly hostile. Good manners were, of course, observed on both sides: there was no closer intimacy, nor could there be. The meeting at this moment was extremely distasteful to Mr. Golyadkin. He frowned a little, and was disconcerted for an instant.

"Yakov Petrovitch, Yakov Petrovitch!" chirped the two register clerks. "You here? What brings you? . . ."

"Ah, it is you, gentlemen," Mr. Golyadkin interrupted hurriedly, somewhat embarrassed and scandalized by the amazement of the clerks and by the abruptness of their address, but feeling obliged, however, to appear jaunty and free and easy. "You've deserted, gentlemen, he-he-he. . . ." Then, to keep up his dignity and to condescend to the juveniles, with whom he never overstepped certain limits, he attempted to slap one of the youths on the shoulder; but this effort at good fellowship did not succeed and, instead of being a well-bred little jest, produced quite a different effect.

"Well, and our bear, is he still at the office?"

"Who's that, Yakov Petrovitch?"

"Why, the bear. Do you mean to say you don't know whose name that is? . . ." Mr. Golyadkin laughed and turned to the cashier to take his change.

"I mean Andrey Filippovitch, gentlemen," he went on, finishing with the cashier, and turning to the clerks this time with a very serious face. The two register clerks winked at one another.

"He's still at the office and asking for you, Yakov Petrovitch," answered one of them.

"At the office, eh! In that case, let him stay, gentlemen. And asking for me, eh?"

"He was asking for you, Yakov Petrovitch; but what's up with you, scented, pomaded, and such a swell? . . ."

"Nothing, gentlemen, nothing! that's enough," answered Mr. Golyadkin, looking away with a constrained smile. Seeing that Mr. Golyadkin was smiling, the clerks laughed aloud. Mr. Golyadkin was a little offended.

"I'll tell you as friends, gentlemen," our hero said, after a brief silence, as though making up his mind (which, indeed, was the case) to reveal something to them. "You all know me, gentlemen, but hitherto you've known me only on one side. No one is to blame for that and I'm conscious that the fault has been partly my own."

Mr. Golyadkin pursed up his lips and looked significantly at the clerks. The clerks winked at one another again.

"Hitherto, gentlemen, you have not known me. To explain myself here and now would not be quite appropriate. I will only touch on it lightly in passing. There are people, gentlemen, who dislike roundabout ways and only mask themselves at masquerades. There are people who do not see man's highest avocation in polishing the floor with their boots. There are people, gentlemen, who refuse to say that they are happy and enjoying a full life, when, for instance, their trousers set properly. There are people, finally, who dislike dashing and whirling about for no object, fawning, and licking the dust, and above all, gentlemen, poking their nose where they are not wanted. . . . I've told you almost everything, gentlemen; now allow me to withdraw. . . ."

Mr. Golyadkin paused. As the register clerks had now got all that they wanted, both of them with great incivility burst into shouts of laughter. Mr. Golyadkin flared up.

"Laugh away, gentlemen, laugh away for the time being! If you live long enough you will see," he said, with a feeling of offended dignity, taking his hat and retreating to the door.

"But I will say more, gentlemen," he added, turning for the last time to the register clerks. "I will say more—you are both here with me face to face. This, gentlemen, is my rule: if I fail I don't lose heart, if I succeed I persevere, and in any case I am never underhand. I'm not one to intrigue—and I'm proud of it. I've never prided myself on diplomacy. They say, too, gentlemen, that the bird flies itself to the hunter. It's true and I'm ready to admit it; but who's the hunter, and who's the bird in this case? That is still the question, gentlemen!"

Mr. Golyadkin subsided into eloquent silence, and, with a most significant air, that is, pursing up his lips and raising his eyebrows as high as possible, he bowed to the clerks and walked out, leaving them in the utmost amazement.

"What are your orders now?" Petrushka asked, rather gruffly; he was probably weary of hanging about in the cold. "What are your orders?" he asked Mr. Golyadkin, meeting the terrible, withering glance with which our hero had protected himself twice already that morning, and to which he had recourse now for the third time as he came down the steps.

"To the Ismailovsky Bridge."

"To the Ismailovsky Bridge! Off!"

"Their dinner will not begin till after four, or perhaps five o'clock," thought Mr. Golyadkin; "isn't it early now? However, I can go a little early; besides, it's only a family dinner. And so I can go *sans façons*, as they say among well-bred people. Why shouldn't I go *sans façons*? The bear told us, too, that it would all be *sans façons*, and so I will be the same. . . ." Such were Mr. Golyadkin's reflections and meanwhile his excitement grew more and more acute. It could be seen that he was preparing himself for some great enterprise, to say nothing more; he muttered to himself, gesticulated with his right hand, continually looked out of his carriage window, so that, looking at Mr. Golyadkin, no one would have said that he was on his way to a good dinner, and only a simple dinner, in his family circle—*sans façons*, as they say among well-bred people. Finally, just at Ismailovsky Bridge, Mr. Golyadkin pointed out a house; and the carriage rolled up noisily and stopped at the first entrance on the right. Noticing a feminine figure at the second-storey window, Mr. Golyadkin kissed his hand to her. He had, however, not the slightest idea what he was doing, for he felt more dead than alive at the moment. He got out of the carriage pale, distracted; he mounted the steps, took off his hat, mechanically straightened himself, and though he felt a slight trembling in his knees, he went upstairs.

"Olsufy Ivanovitch?" he inquired of the man who opened the door.

"At home, sir; at least he's not at home, his honour's not at home."

"What? What do you mean, my good man? I—I've come to dinner, brother. Why, you know me?"

"To be sure I know you! I've orders not to admit you."

"You . . . you, brother . . . you must be making a mistake. It's I, my boy, I'm invited; I've come to dinner," Mr. Golyadkin announced, taking off his coat and displaying unmistakable intentions of going into the room.

"Allow me, sir, you can't, sir. I've orders not to admit you. I've orders to refuse you. That's how it is."

Mr. Golyadkin turned pale. At that very moment the door of the inner room opened and Gerasimitch, Olsufy Ivanovitch's old butler, came out.

"You see the gentleman wants to go in, Emelyan Gerasimitch, and I . . ."

"And you're a fool, Alexeitch. Go inside and send the rascal Semyonitch here. It's impossible," he said politely but firmly, addressing Mr. Golyadkin. "It's quite impossible. His honour begs you to excuse him: he can't see you."

"He said he couldn't see me?" Mr. Golyadkin asked uncertainly. "Excuse me, Gerasimitch, why is it impossible?"

"It's quite impossible. I've informed your honour; they said 'Ask him to excuse us.' They can't see you."

"Why not? How's that? Why?"

"Allow me, allow me! . . ."

"How is it, though? It's out of the question! Announce me. . . . How is it? I've come to dinner. . . ."

"Excuse me, excuse me. . . ."

"Ah, well, that's a different matter, they asked to be excused: but, allow me, Gerasimitch; how is it, Gerasimitch?"

"Excuse me, excuse me!" replied Gerasimitch, very firmly putting away Mr. Golyadkin's hand and making way for two gentlemen who walked into the entry that very instant. The gentlemen in question were Andrey Filippovitch and his nephew, Vladimir Semyonovitch. Both of them looked with amazement at Mr. Golyadkin. Andrey Filippovitch seemed about to say something, but Mr. Golyadkin had by now made up his mind; he was by now walking out of Olsufy Ivanovitch's entry, blushing and smiling, with eyes cast down and a countenance of helpless bewilderment. "I will come afterwards, Gerasimitch; I will explain myself: I hope that all this will without delay be explained in due season. . . ."

"Yakov Petrovitch, Yakov Petrovitch . . . ." He heard the voice of Andrey Filippovitch following him.

Mr. Golyadkin was by that time on the first landing. He turned quickly to Andrey Filippovitch.

"What do you desire, Andrey Filippovitch?" he said in a rather resolute voice.

"What's wrong with you, Yakov Petrovitch? In what way?"

"No matter, Andrey Filippovitch. I'm on my own account here. This is my private life, Andrey Filippovitch."

"What's that?"

"I say, Andrey Filippovitch, that this is my private life, and as for my being here, as far as I can see, there's nothing reprehensible to be found in it as regards my official relations."

"What! As regards your official . . . . What's the matter with you, my good sir?"

"Nothing, Andrey Filippovitch, absolutely nothing; an impudent slut of a girl, and nothing more. . . ."

"What! What?" Andrey Filippovitch was stupefied with amazement. Mr. Golyadkin, who had up till then looked as though he would fly into Andrey Filippovitch's face, seeing that the head of his office was laughing a little, almost unconsciously took a step forward. Andrey Filippovitch jumped back. Mr. Golyadkin went up one step and then another. Andrey Filippovitch looked about him uneasily. Mr. Golyadkin mounted the stairs rapidly. Still more rapidly Andrey Filippovitch darted into the flat and slammed the door after him. Mr. Golyadkin was left alone. Everything grew dark before his eyes. He was utterly nonplussed, and stood now in a sort of senseless hesitation, as though recalling something extremely senseless, too, that had happened quite recently. "Ech, ech!" he muttered, smiling with constraint. Meanwhile, there came the sounds of steps and voices on the stairs, probably of other guests invited by Olsufy Ivanovitch. Mr. Golyadkin recovered himself to some extent; put up his raccoon collar, concealing himself behind it as far as possible, and began going downstairs with rapid little steps, tripping and stumbling in his haste. He felt overcome by a sort of weakness and numbness. His confusion was such that, when he came out on the steps, he did not even wait for his carriage but walked across the muddy court to it. When he reached his carriage and was about to get into it, Mr. Golyadkin inwardly uttered a desire to sink into the earth, or to hide in a mousehole together with his carriage. It seemed to him that everything in Olsufy Ivanovitch's house was looking at him now out of every window. He knew that he would certainly die on the spot if he were to go back.

"What are you laughing at, blockhead?" he said in a rapid mutter to Petrushka, who was preparing to help him into the carriage.

"What should I laugh at? I'm not doing anything; where are we to drive now?"

"Go home, drive on. . . ."

"Home, off!" shouted Petrushka, climbing on to the footboard.

"What a crow's croak!" thought Mr. Golyadkin. Meanwhile, the carriage had driven a good distance from Ismailovsky Bridge. Suddenly our hero pulled the cord with all his might and shouted to the driver to turn back at once. The coachman turned his horses and within two minutes was driving into Olsufy Ivanovitch's yard again.

"Don't, don't, you fool, back!" shouted Mr. Golyadkin—and, as though he were expecting this order, the driver made no reply but, without stopping at the entrance, drove all round the courtyard and out into the street again.

Mr. Golyadkin did not drive home, but, after passing the Semyonovsky Bridge, told the driver to return to a side street and stop near a restaurant of rather modest appearance. Getting out of the carriage, our hero settled up with the driver and so got rid of his equipage at last. He told Petrushka to go home and await his return, while he went into the restaurant, took a private room and ordered dinner. He felt very ill and his brain was in the utmost confusion and chaos. For a long time he walked up and down the room in agitation; at last he sat down in a chair, propped his brow in his hands and began doing his very utmost to consider and settle something relating to his present position.

CHAPTER 4

That day the birthday of Klara Olsufyevna, the only daughter of the civil councillor, Berendyev, at one time Mr. Golyadkin's benefactor and patron, was being celebrated by a brilliant and sumptuous dinner-party, such as had not been seen for many a long day within the walls of the flats in the neighbourhood of Ismailovsky Bridge—a dinner more like some Balthazar's feast, with a suggestion of something Babylonian in its brilliant luxury and style, with Veuve Clicquot champagne, with oysters and fruit from Eliseyev's and Milyutin's, with all sorts of fatted calves, and all grades of the government service. This festive day was to conclude with a brilliant ball, a small birthday ball, but yet brilliant in its taste, its distinction and its style. Of course, I am willing to admit that similar balls do happen sometimes, though rarely. Such balls, more like family rejoicings than balls, can only be given in such houses as that of the civil councillor, Berendyev. I will say more: I even doubt if such balls could be given in the houses of all civil councillors. Oh, if I were a poet! such as Homer or Pushkin, I mean, of course; with any lesser talent one would not venture—I should certainly have painted all that glorious day for you, oh, my readers, with a free brush and brilliant colours! Yes, I should begin my poem with my dinner, I should lay special stress on that striking and solemn moment when the first goblet was raised to the honour of the queen of the fête. I should describe to you the guests plunged in a reverent silence and expectation, as eloquent as the rhetoric of Demosthenes; I should describe for you, then, how Andrey Filippovitch, having as the eldest of the guests some right to take precedence, adorned with his grey hairs and the orders that well befit grey hairs, got up from his seat and raised above his head the congratulatory glass of sparkling wine—brought from a distant kingdom to celebrate such occasions and more like heavenly nectar than plain wine. I would portray for you the guests and the happy parents raising their glasses, too, after Andrey Filippovitch, and fastening upon him eyes full of expectation. I would describe for you how the same Andrey Filippovitch, so often mentioned, after dropping a tear in the glass, delivered his congratulations and good wishes, proposed the toast and drank the health . . . but I confess, I freely confess, that I could not do justice to the solemn moment when the queen of the fête, Klara Olsufyevna, blushing like a rose in spring, with the glow of bliss and of modesty, was so overcome by her feelings that she sank into the arms of her tender mamma; how that tender mamma shed tears, and how the father, Olsufy Ivanovitch, a hale old man and a privy councillor, who had lost the use of his legs in his long years of service and been rewarded by destiny for his devotion with investments, a house, some small estates, and a beautiful daughter, sobbed like a little child and announced through his tears that his Excellency was a benevolent man.

I could not, I positively could not, describe the enthusiasm that followed that moment in every heart, an enthusiasm clearly evinced in the conduct of a youthful register clerk (though at that moment he was more like a civil councillor than a register clerk), who was moved to tears, too, as he listened to Andrey Filippovitch. In his turn, too, Andrey Filippovitch was in that solemn moment quite unlike a collegiate councillor and the head of an office in the department—yes, he was something else . . . what, exactly, I do not know, but not a collegiate councillor. He was more exalted! Finally . . . . Oh, why do I not possess the secret of lofty, powerful language, of the sublime style, to describe these grand and edifying moments of human life, which seem created expressly to prove that virtue sometimes triumphs over ingratitude, free-thinking, vice and envy! I will say nothing, but in silence—which will be better than any eloquence—I will point to that fortunate youth, just entering on his twenty-sixth spring—to Vladimir Semyonovitch, Andrey Filippovitch's nephew, who in his turn now rose from his seat, who in his turn proposed a toast, and upon whom were fastened the tearful eyes of the parents, the proud eyes of Andrey Filippovitch, the modest eyes of the queen of the fête, the solemn eyes of the guests, and even the decorously envious eyes of some of the young man's youthful colleagues. I will say nothing of that, though I cannot refrain from observing that everything in that young man—who was, indeed, speaking in a complimentary sense, more like an elderly than a young man—everything, from his blooming cheeks to his assessorial rank, seemed almost to proclaim aloud the lofty pinnacle a man can attain through morality and good principles! I will not describe how Anton Antonovitch Syetotchkin, a little old man as grey as a badger, the head clerk of a department, who was a colleague of Andrey Filippovitch's and had once been also of Olsufy Ivanovitch's, and was an old friend of the family and Klara Olsufyevna's godfather, in his turn proposed a toast, crowed like a cock, and cracked many little jokes; how by this extremely proper breach of propriety, if one may use such an expression, he made the whole company laugh till they cried, and how Klara Olsufyevna, at her parents' bidding, rewarded him for his jocularity and politeness with a kiss. I will only say that the guests, who must have felt like kinsfolk and brothers after such a dinner, at last rose from the table, and the elderly and more solid guests, after a brief interval spent in friendly conversation, interspersed with some candid, though, of course, very polite and proper, observations, went decorously into the next room and, without losing valuable time, promptly divided themselves up into parties and, full of the sense of their own dignity, installed themselves at tables covered with green baize. Meanwhile, the ladies established in the drawing-room suddenly became very affable and began talking about dress materials. And the venerable host, who had lost the use of his legs in the service of loyalty and religion, and had been rewarded with all the blessings we have enumerated above, began walking about on crutches among his guests, supported by Vladimir Semyonovitch and Klara Olsufyevna, and he, too, suddenly becoming extremely affable, decided to improvise a modest little dance, regardless of expense; to that end a nimble youth (the one who was more like a civil councillor than a youth) was despatched to fetch musicians, and musicians to the number of eleven arrived, and exactly at half-past eight struck up the inviting strains of a French quadrille, followed by various other dances. . . . It is needless to say that my pen is too weak, dull, and spiritless to describe the dance that owed its inspiration to the genial hospitality of the grey-headed host. And how, I ask, can the modest chronicler of Mr. Golyadkin's adventures, extremely interesting as they are in their own way, how can I depict the choice and rare mingling of beauty, brilliance, style, gaiety, polite solidity and solid politeness, sportiveness, joy, all the mirth and playfulness of these wives and daughters of petty officials, more like fairies than ladies—in a complimentary sense—with their lily shoulders and their rosy faces, their ethereal figures, their playfully agile homeopathic—to use the exalted language appropriate—little feet? How can I describe to you, finally, the gallant officials, their partners—gay and solid youths, steady, gleeful, decorously vague, smoking a pipe in the intervals between the dancing in a little green room apart, or not smoking a pipe in the intervals between the dances, every one of them with a highly respectable surname and rank in the service—all steeped in a sense of the elegant and a sense of their own dignity; almost all speaking French to their partners, or if Russian, using only the most well-bred expressions, compliments and profound observations, and only in the smoking-room permitting themselves some genial lapses from this high tone, some phrases of cordial and friendly brevity, such, for instance, as: " 'Pon my soul, Petka, you rake, you did kick off that polka in style," or "I say, Vasya, you dog, you did give your partner a time of it." For all this, as I've already had the honour of explaining, oh, my readers! my pen fails me, and therefore I am dumb. Let us rather return to Mr. Golyadkin, the true and only hero of my very truthful tale.

The fact is that he found himself now in a very strange position, to say the least of it. He was here also, gentlemen—that is, not at the dance, but almost at the dance; he was "all right, though; he could take care of himself," yet at this moment he was a little astray; he was standing at that moment, strange to say—on the landing of the back stairs to Olsufy Ivanovitch's flat. But it was "all right" his standing there; he was "quite well." He was standing in a corner, huddled in a place which was not very warm, though it was dark, partly hidden by a huge cupboard and an old screen, in the midst of rubbish, litter, and odds and ends of all sorts, concealing himself for the time being and watching the course of proceedings as a disinterested spectator. He was only looking on now, gentlemen; he, too, gentlemen, might go in, of course . . . why should he not go in? He had only to take one step and he would go in, and would go in very adroitly. Just now, though he had been standing nearly three hours between the cupboard and the screen in the midst of the rubbish, litter, and odds and ends of all sorts, he was only quoting, in his own justification, a memorable phrase of the French minister, Villesle: "All things come in time to him who has the strength to wait." Mr. Golyadkin had read this sentence in some book on quite a different subject, but now very aptly recalled it. The phrase, to begin with, was exceedingly appropriate to his present position, and, indeed, why should it not occur to the mind of a man who had been waiting for almost three hours in the cold and the dark in expectation of a happy ending to his adventures? After quoting very appropriately the phrase of the French minister, Villesle, Mr. Golyadkin immediately thought of the Turkish vizier, Martsimiris, as well as of the beautiful Margravine Luise, whose story he had read also in some book. Then it occurred to his mind that the Jesuits made it their rule that any means were justified if only the end were attained. Fortifying himself somewhat with this historical fact, Mr. Golyadkin said to himself, What were the Jesuits? The Jesuits were every one of them very great fools; that he was better than any of them; that if only the refreshment-room would be empty for one minute (the door of the refreshment-room opened straight into the passage to the back stairs, where Mr. Golyadkin was in hiding now), he would, in spite of all the Jesuits in the world, go straight in, first from the refreshment-room into the tea-room, then into the room where they were now playing cards, and then straight into the hall where they were now dancing the polka, and he would go in, he would certainly go in, in spite of anything he would go in—he would slip through—and that would be all, no one would notice him; and once there he would know what to do.

Well, so this is the position in which we find the hero of our perfectly true story, though, indeed, it is difficult to explain what was passing in him at that moment. The fact is that he had made his way to the back stairs, and to the passage, on the ground that, as he said, "Why shouldn't he? And everyone did go that way"; but he had not ventured to penetrate further, evidently he did not dare to do so . . . "not because there was anything he did not dare, but just because he did not care to, because he preferred to be in hiding"; so here he was, waiting now for a chance to slip in, and he

had been waiting for it two hours and a half. "Why not wait? Villesle himself had waited. But what had Villesle to do with it?"
thought Mr. Golyadkin: "How does Villesle come in? But how am I
to . . . to go and walk in? . . . Ech, you dummy!" said Mr. Golyadkin,
pinching his benumbed cheek with his benumbed fingers; "you silly
fool, you silly old Golyadkin—silly fool of a surname! . . ."

But these compliments paid to himself were only by the way
and without any apparent aim. Now he was on the point of pushing
forward and slipping in; the refreshment-room was empty and no
one was in sight. Mr. Golyadkin saw all this through the little window; in two steps he was at the door and had already opened it.
"Should he go in or not? Come, should he or not? I'll go in . . . why
not? to the bold all ways lie open!" Reassuring himself in this way,
our hero suddenly and quite unexpectedly retreated behind the
screen. "No," he thought. "Ah, now, somebody's coming in? Yes,
they've come in; why did I dawdle when there were no people
about? Even so, shall I go and slip in? . . . No, how slip in when a
man has such a temperament! Fie, what a low tendency! I'm as
scared as a hen! Being scared is our special line, that's the fact of
the matter! To be abject on every occasion is our line: no need to
ask us about that. Just stand here like a post and that's all! At home
I should be having a cup of tea now. . . . It would be pleasant, too,
to have a cup of tea. If I come in later Petrushka'll grumble, maybe.
Shall I go home? Damnation take all this! I'll go and that'll be the
end of it!" Reflecting on his position in this way, Mr. Golyadkin
dashed forward as though some one had touched a spring in him;
in two steps he found himself in the refreshment-room, flung off his
overcoat, took off his hat, hurriedly thrust these things into a corner,
straightened himself and smoothed himself down; then . . . then he
moved on to the tea-room, and from the tea-room darted into the
next room, slipped almost unnoticed between the card-players, who
were at the tip-top of excitement, then . . . Mr. Golyadkin forgot
everything that was going on about him, and went straight as an
arrow into the drawing-room.

As luck would have it they were not dancing. The ladies were
promenading up and down the room in picturesque groups. The
gentlemen were standing about in twos and threes or flitting about
the room engaging partners. Mr. Golyadkin noticed nothing of this.

He saw only Klara Olsufyevna, near her Andrey Filippovitch, then Vladimir Semyonovitch, two or three officers, and, finally, two or three other young men who were also very interesting and, as any one could see at once, were either very promising or had actually done something. . . . He saw some one else, too. Or, rather, he saw nobody and looked at nobody . . . but, moved by the same spring which had sent him dashing into the midst of a ball to which he had not been invited, he moved forward, and then forwarder and forwarder. On the way he jostled against a councillor and trod on his foot, and incidentally stepped on a very venerable old lady's dress and tore it a little, pushed against a servant with a tray and then ran against somebody else, and, not noticing all this, or rather noticing it but at the same time looking at no one, pressing farther and farther forward, he suddenly found himself facing Klara Olsuf-yevna. There is no doubt whatever that he would, with the utmost delight, without winking an eyelid, have sunk through the earth at that moment; but what has once been done cannot be recalled . . . can never be recalled. What was he to do? "If I fail I don't lose heart, if I succeed I persevere."

Mr. Golyadkin was, of course, not "one to intrigue," and "not accomplished in the art of polishing the floor with his boots." . . . And so, indeed, it proved. Besides, the Jesuits had some hand in it too . . . though Mr. Golyadkin had no thoughts to spare for them now! All the moving, noisy, talking, laughing groups were suddenly hushed as though at a signal and, little by little, crowded round Mr. Golyadkin. He, however, seemed to hear nothing, to see nothing, he could not look . . . he could not possibly look at anything; he kept his eyes on the floor and so stood, giving himself his word of honour, in passing, to shoot himself one way or another that night. Making this vow, Mr. Golyadkin inwardly said to himself, "Here goes!" and to his own great astonishment began unexpectedly to speak.

He began with congratulations and polite wishes. The congratu-lations went off well, but over the good wishes our hero stammered. He felt that if he stammered all would be lost at once. And so it turned out—he stammered and floundered . . . floundering, he blushed crimson; blushing, he was overcome with confusion. In his confusion he raised his eyes; raising his eyes he looked about him; looking about him—he almost swooned. . . . Every one stood still, every one was silent, every one was waiting; a little way off there was whispering; a little nearer there was laughter. Mr. Golyadkin fastened a humble, imploring look on Andrey Filippovitch. Andrey Filippovitch responded with such a look that if our hero had not been utterly crushed already he certainly would have been crushed a second time—that is, if that were possible. The silence lasted long.

"This is rather concerned with my domestic circumstances and my private life, Andrey Filippovitch," our hero, half-dead, articulated in a scarcely audible voice; "it is not an official incident, Andrey Filippovitch. . . ."

"For shame, sir, for shame!" Andrey Filippovitch pronounced in a half-whisper, with an indescribable air of indignation; he pronounced these words and, giving Klara Olsufyevna his arm, he turned away from Mr. Golyadkin.

"I've nothing to be ashamed of, Andrey Filippovitch," answered Mr. Golyadkin, also in a whisper, turning his miserable eyes about him, trying helplessly to discover in the amazed crowd something on which he could gain a footing and retrieve his social position.

"Why, it's all right, it's nothing, gentlemen! Why, what's the matter? Why, it might happen to any one," whispered Mr. Golyadkin, moving a little away and trying to escape from the crowd surrounding him.

They made way for him. Our hero passed through two rows of inquisitive and wondering spectators. Fate drew him on. He felt that himself, that fate was leading him on. He would have given a great deal, of course, for a chance to be back in the passage by the back stairs, without having committed a breach of propriety; but as that was utterly impossible, he began trying to creep away into a corner and to stand there—modestly, decorously apart, without interfering with any one, without attracting especial attention, but at the same time to win the favourable notice of his host and the company. At the same time Mr. Golyadkin felt as though the ground were giving way under him, as though he were staggering, falling. At last he made his way to a corner and stood in it, like an unconcerned, rather indifferent spectator, leaning his arms on the backs of two chairs, taking complete possession of them in that way, and trying, as far as he could, to glance confidently at Olsufy Ivanovitch's guests, grouped about him. Standing nearest him was an officer, a tall and handsome fellow, beside whom Golyadkin felt himself an insect.

"These two chairs, Lieutenant, are intended, one for Klara Olsufyevna, and the other for Princess Tchevtchehanov; I'm taking care of them for them," said Mr. Golyadkin breathlessly, turning his imploring eyes on the officer. The lieutenant said nothing, but turned away with a murderous smile. Checked in this direction, our hero was about to try his luck in another quarter, and directly addressed an important councillor with a cross of great distinction on his breast. But the councillor looked him up and down with such a frigid stare that Mr. Golyadkin felt distinctly as though a whole bucketful of cold water had been thrown over him. He subsided into silence. He made up his mind that it was better to keep quiet, not to open his lips, and to show that he was "all right," that he was "like every one else," and that his position, as far as he could see, was quite a proper one. With this object he riveted his gaze on the lining of his coat, then raised his eyes and fixed them upon a very respectable-looking gentleman. "That gentleman has a wig on," thought Mr. Golyadkin; "and if he takes off that wig he will be bald, his head will be as bare as the palm of my hand." Having made this important discovery, Mr. Golyadkin thought of the Arab emirs, whose heads are left bare and shaven if they take off the green turbans they wear as a sign of their descent from the prophet Mahomet. Then, probably from some special connection of ideas with the Turks, he thought of Turkish slippers and at once, apropos of that, recalled the fact that Andrey Filippovitch was wearing boots, and that his boots were more like slippers than boots. It was evident that Mr. Golyadkin had become to some extent reconciled to his position. "What if that chandelier," flashed through Mr. Golyadkin's mind, "were to come down from the ceiling and fall upon the company? I should rush at once to save Klara Olsufyevna. 'Save her!' I should cry. 'Don't be alarmed, madame, it's of no consequence, I will rescue you, I.' Then . . . ." At that moment Mr. Golyadkin looked about in search of Klara Olsufyevna, and saw Gerasimitch, Olsufy Ivanovitch's old butler. Gerasimitch, with a most anxious and solemnly official air, was making straight for him. Mr. Golyadkin started and frowned from an unaccountable but most dis-

agreeable sensation; he looked about him mechanically; it occurred
to his mind if only he could somehow creep off somewhere, unob-
served, on the sly—simply disappear, that is, behave as though he
had done nothing at all, as though the matter did not concern him
in the least! . . . But before our hero could make up his mind to do
anything, Gerasimitch was standing before him.

"Do you see, Gerasimitch," said our hero, with a little smile,
addressing Gerasimitch; "you go and tell them—do you see the
candle there in the chandelier, Gerasimitch?—it will be falling down
directly: so, you know, you must tell them to see to it; it really will
fall down, Gerasimitch. . . ."

"The candle? No, the candle's standing straight; but somebody
is asking for you, sir."

"Who is asking for me, Gerasimitch?"

"I really can't say, sir, who it is. A man with a message. 'Is
Yakov Petrovitch Golyadkin here?' says he. 'Then call him out,'
says he, 'on very urgent and important business . . .' you see."

"No, Gerasimitch, you are making a mistake; in that you are
making a mistake, Gerasimitch."

"I doubt it, sir."

"No, Gerasimitch, it isn't doubtful; there's nothing doubtful
about it, Gerasimitch. Nobody's asking for me, but I'm quite at
home here—that is, in my right place, Gerasimitch."

Mr. Golyadkin took breath and looked about him. Yes! every
one in the room, all had their eyes fixed upon him, and were listening in a sort of solemn expectation. The men had crowded a little
nearer and were all attention. A little farther away the ladies were
whispering together. The master of the house made his appearance
at no great distance from Mr. Golyadkin, and though it was impossible to detect from his expression that he, too, was taking a close
and direct interest in Mr. Golyadkin's position, for everything was
being done with delicacy, yet, nevertheless, it all made our hero
feel that the decisive moment had come for him. Mr. Golyadkin
saw clearly that the time had come for a bold stroke, the chance of
putting his enemies to shame. Mr. Golyadkin was in great agitation.
He was aware of a sort of inspiration and, in a quivering and impressive voice, he began again, addressing the waiting butler—

"No, my dear fellow, no one's calling for me. You are mistaken.
I will say more: you were mistaken this morning, too, when you

assured me . . . dared to assure me, I say," (he raised his voice) "that
Olsufy Ivanovitch, who has been my benefactor as long as I can
remember and has, in a sense, been a father to me, was shutting his
door upon me at the moment of solemn family rejoicing for his
paternal heart." (Mr. Golyadkin looked about him complacently, but
with deep feeling. A tear glittered on his eyelash.) "I repeat, my
friend," our hero concluded, "you were mistaken, you were cruelly
and unpardonably mistaken. . . ."

The moment was a solemn one. Mr. Golyadkin felt that the
effect was quite certain. He stood with modestly downcast eyes,
expecting Olsufy Ivanovitch to embrace him. Excitement and perplexity were apparent in the guests, even the inflexible and terrible
Gerasimitch faltered over the words "I doubt it . . ." when suddenly
the ruthless orchestra, apropos of nothing, struck up a polka. All was
lost, all was scattered to the winds. Mr. Golyadkin started; Gerasimitch stepped back; everything in the room began undulating like the
sea; and Vladimir Semyonovitch led the dance with Klara Olsufyevna, while the handsome lieutenant followed with Princess Tchevtchehanov. Onlookers, curious and delighted, squeezed in to watch
them dancing the polka—an interesting, fashionable new dance
which every one was crazy over. Mr. Golyadkin was, for the time,
forgotten. But suddenly all were thrown into excitement, confusion
and bustle; the music ceased . . . a strange incident had occurred.
Tired out with the dance, and almost breathless with fatigue, Klara
Olsufyevna, with glowing cheeks and heaving bosom, sank into an
arm-chair, completely exhausted. . . . All hearts turned to the fasci-
nating creature, all vied with one another in complimenting her and
thanking her for the pleasure conferred on them—all at once there
stood before her Mr. Golyadkin. He was pale, extremely perturbed;
he, too, seemed completely exhausted, he could scarcely move. He
was smiling for some reason, he stretched out his hand imploringly.
Klara Olsufyevna was so taken aback that she had not time to withdraw hers and mechanically got up at his invitation. Mr. Golyadkin
lurched forward, first once, then a second time, then lifted his leg,
then made a scrape, then gave a sort of stamp, then stumbled . . . he,
too, wanted to dance with Klara Olsufyevna. Klara Olsufyevna uttered a shriek; every one rushed to release her hand from Mr. Golyadkin's, and in a moment our hero was carried almost ten paces
away by the rush of the crowd. A circle formed round him, too.

Two old ladies, whom he had almost knocked down in his retreat, raised a great shrieking and outcry. The confusion was awful; all were asking questions, every one was shouting, every one was finding fault. The orchestra was silent. Our hero whirled round in his circle and mechanically, with a semblance of a smile, muttered something to himself, such as "Why not?" and "that the polka, so far, at least, as he could see, was a new and very interesting dance, invented for the diversion of the ladies . . . but that since things had taken this turn, he was ready to consent." But Mr. Golyadkin's consent no one apparently thought of asking. Our hero was suddenly aware that some one's hand was laid on his arm, that another hand was pressed against his back, that he was with peculiar solicitude being guided in a certain direction. At last he noticed that he was going straight to the door. Mr. Golyadkin wanted to say something, to do something. . . . But no, he no longer wanted to do anything. He only mechanically kept laughing in answer. At last he was aware that they were putting on his greatcoat, that his hat was thrust over his eyes; finally he felt that he was in the entry on the stairs in the dark and cold. At last he stumbled, he felt that he was falling down a precipice; he tried to cry out—and suddenly found himself in the courtyard. The air blew fresh on him, he stood still for a minute; at that very instant, the strains reached him of the orchestra striking up again. Mr. Golyadkin suddenly recalled it all; it seemed to him that all his flagging energies came back to him again. He had been standing as though riveted to the spot, but now he started off and rushed away headlong, anywhere, into the air, into freedom, wherever chance might take him.

CHAPTER 5

It was striking midnight from all the clock towers in Petersburg when Mr. Golyadkin, beside himself, ran out on the Fontanka Quay, close to the Ismailovsky Bridge, fleeing from his foes, from persecution, from a hailstorm of nips and pinches aimed at him, from the shrieks of excited old ladies, from the Ohs and Ahs of women and from the murderous eyes of Andrey Filippovitch. Mr. Golyadkin was killed—killed entirely, in the full sense of the word, and if he still preserved the power of running, it was simply through some sort of miracle, a miracle in which at last he refused himself to believe. It was an awful November night—wet, foggy, rainy, snowy, teeming with colds in the head, fevers, swollen faces, quinsies, inflammations of all kinds and descriptions—teeming, in fact, with all the gifts of a Petersburg November. The wind howled in the deserted streets, lifting up the black water of the canal above the rings on the bank, and irritably brushing against the lean lamp-posts which chimed in with its howling in a thin, shrill creak, keeping up the endless squeaky, jangling concert with which every inhabitant of Petersburg is so familiar. Snow and rain were falling both at once. Lashed by the wind, the streams of rain-water spurted almost horizontally, as though from a fireman's hose, pricking and stinging the face of the luckless Mr. Golyadkin like a thousand pins and needles. In the stillness of the night, broken only by the distant rumbling of carriages, the howl of the wind and the creaking of the lamp-posts, there was the dismal sound of the splash and gurgle of water, rushing from every roof, every porch, every pipe and every cornice, on to the granite of the pavement. There was not a soul, near or far, and, indeed, it seemed there could not be at such an hour and in such weather. And so only Mr. Golyadkin, alone with his despair, was fleeing in terror along the pavement of Fontanka, with his usual rapid little step, in haste to get home as soon as possible to his flat on the fourth storey in Shestilavotchny Street.

Though the snow, the rain, and all the nameless horrors of a raging snowstorm and fog, under a Petersburg November sky, were attacking Mr. Golyadkin, already shattered by misfortunes, were showing him no mercy, giving him no rest, drenching him to the bone, glueing up his eyelids, blowing right through him from all sides, baffling and perplexing him—though all this was hurled upon Mr. Golyadkin at once, as though conspiring and combining with all his enemies to make a grand day, evening, and night for him, in spite of all this Mr. Golyadkin was almost insensible to this final proof of the persecution of destiny: so violent had been the shock and the impression made upon him a few minutes before at the civil councillor Berendyev's! If any disinterested spectator could have glanced casually at Mr. Golyadkin's painful progress, he would instantly have grasped the awful horror of his pitiful plight and would certainly have said that Mr. Golyadkin looked as though he wanted to hide from himself, as though he were trying to run away from himself! Yes! It was really so. One may say more: Mr. Golyadkin did not want only to run away from himself, but to be obliterated, to cease to be, to return to dust. At the moment he took in nothing surrounding him, understood nothing of what was going on about him, and looked as though the miseries of the stormy night, of the long tramp, the rain, the snow, the wind, all the cruelty of the weather, did not exist for him. The golosh slipping off the boot on Mr. Golyadkin's right foot was left behind in the snow and slush on the pavement of Fontanka, and Mr. Golyadkin did not think of turning back to get it, did not, in fact, notice that he had lost it. He was so perplexed that, in spite of everything surrounding him, he stood several times stock-still in the middle of the pavement, completely possessed by the thought of his recent horrible humiliation; at that instant he was dying, disappearing; then he suddenly set off again like mad and ran and ran without looking back, as though he were pursued, as though he were fleeing from some still more awful calamity. . . . The position was truly awful! . . . At last Mr. Golyadkin halted in exhaustion, leaned on the railing in the attitude of a man whose nose has suddenly begun to bleed, and began looking intently at the black and troubled waters of the canal. There is no knowing what length of time he spent like this. All that is known is that at that instant Mr. Golyadkin reached such a pitch of despair, was so harassed, so tortured, so exhausted, and so weakened in what feeble faculties were left him that he forgot everything, forgot the Ismailovsky Bridge, forgot Shestilavotchny Street, forgot his present plight. . . . After all, what did it matter to him? The thing was done. The decision was affirmed and ratified; what could he do? All at once . . . all at once he started and involuntarily skipped a couple of paces aside. With unaccountable uneasiness he began gazing about him; but no one was there, nothing special had happened, and yet . . . and yet he fancied that just now, that very minute, some one was standing near him, beside him, also leaning on the railing, and—marvellous to relate!—had even said something to him, said something quickly, abruptly, not quite intelligibly, but something quite private, something concerning himself.

"Why, was it my fancy?" said Mr. Golyadkin, looking round once more. "But where am I standing? . . . Ech, ech," he thought finally, shaking his head, though he began gazing with an uneasy, miserable feeling into the damp, murky distance, straining his sight and doing his utmost to pierce with his short-sighted eyes the wet darkness that stretched all round him. There was nothing new, however, nothing special caught the eye of Mr. Golyadkin. Everything seemed to be all right, as it should be, that is, the snow was falling more violently, more thickly and in larger flakes, nothing could be seen twenty paces away, the lamp-posts creaked more shrilly than ever and the wind seemed to intone its melancholy song even more tearfully, more piteously, like an importunate beggar whining for a copper to get a crust of bread. At the same time a new sensation took possession of Mr. Golyadkin's whole being: agony upon agony, terror upon terror . . . a feverish tremor ran through his veins. The moment was insufferably unpleasant! "Well, it's no matter," he said, to encourage himself. "Well, no matter; perhaps it's no matter at all, and there's no stain on any one's honour. Perhaps it's as it should be," he went on, without understanding what he was saying. "Perhaps it will all be for the best in the end, and there will be nothing to complain of, and every one will be justified."

Talking like this and comforting himself with words, Mr. Golyadkin shook himself a little, shook off the snow which had drifted in thick layers on his hat, his collar, his overcoat, his tie, his boots and everything—but his strange feeling, his strange, obscure misery he could not get rid of, could not shake off. Somewhere in the distance there was the boom of a cannon shot. "Ach, what weather!" thought our hero. "Tchoo! Isn't there going to be a flood? It seems as though the water has risen so violently."

Mr. Golyadkin had hardly said or thought this when he saw a person coming towards him, belated, no doubt, like him, through some accident. An unimportant, casual incident, one might suppose, but for some unknown reason Mr. Golyadkin was troubled, even scared, and rather flurried. It was not that he was exactly afraid of some ill-intentioned man, but just that "perhaps . . . after all, who knows, this belated individual," flashed through Mr. Golyadkin's mind, "maybe he's that very thing, maybe he's the very principal thing in it, and isn't here for nothing, but is here with an object, crossing my path and provoking me." Possibly, however, he did not think this precisely, but only had a passing feeling of something like it—and very unpleasant. There was no time, however, for thinking and feeling. The stranger was already within two paces. Mr. Golyadkin, as he invariably did, hastened to assume a quite peculiar air, an air that expressed clearly that he, Golyadkin, kept himself to himself, that he was "all right," that the road was wide enough for all, and that he, Golyadkin, was not interfering with any one. Suddenly, he stopped short as though petrified, as though struck by lightning, and quickly turned round after the figure which had only just passed him—turned as though some one had given him a tug from behind, as though the wind had turned him like a weathercock. The passer-by vanished quickly in the snowstorm. He, too, walked quickly; he was dressed like Mr. Golyadkin and, like him, too, wrapped up from head to foot, and he, too, tripped and trotted along the pavement of Fontanka with rapid little steps that suggested that he was a little scared.

"What—what is it?" whispered Mr. Golyadkin, smiling mistrustfully, though he trembled all over. An icy shiver ran down his back. Meanwhile, the stranger had vanished completely; there was no sound of his step, while Mr. Golyadkin still stood and gazed after him. At last, however, he gradually came to himself.

"Why, what's the meaning of it?" he thought with vexation. "Why, have I really gone out of my mind, or what?" He turned and went on his way, making his footsteps more rapid and frequent, and doing his best not to think of anything at all. He even closed his eyes at last with the same object. Suddenly, through the howling of the wind and the uproar of the storm, the sound of steps very close at hand reached his ears again. He started and opened his eyes. Again a rapidly approaching figure stood out black before him, some twenty paces away. This little figure was hastening, tripping along, hurrying nervously; the distance between them grew rapidly less. Mr. Golyadkin could by now get a full view of this second belated companion. He looked full at him and cried out with amazement and horror; his legs gave way under him. It was the same individual who had passed him ten minutes before, and who now quite unexpectedly turned up facing him again. But this was not the only marvel that struck Mr. Golyadkin. He was so amazed that he stood still, cried out, tried to say something, and rushed to overtake the stranger, even shouted something to him, probably anxious to stop him as quickly as possible. The stranger did, in fact, stop ten paces from Mr. Golyadkin, so that the light from the lamp-post that stood near fell full upon his whole figure—stood still, turned to Mr. Golyadkin, and with impatient and anxious face waited to hear what he would say.

"Excuse me, possibly I'm mistaken," our hero brought out in a quavering voice.

The stranger in silence, and with an air of annoyance, turned and rapidly went on his way, as though in haste to make up for the two seconds he had wasted on Mr. Golyadkin. As for the latter, he was quivering in every nerve, his knees shook and gave way under him, and with a moan he squatted on a stone at the edge of the pavement. There really was reason, however, for his being so overwhelmed. The fact is that this stranger seemed to him now somehow familiar. That would have been nothing, though. But he recognized, almost certainly recognized this man. He had often seen him, that man, had seen him some time, and very lately too; where could it have been? Surely not yesterday? But, again, that was not the chief thing, that Mr. Golyadkin had often seen him before; there was hardly anything special about the man; the man at first sight would not have aroused any special attention. He was just a man like any one else, a gentleman like all other gentlemen, of course, and perhaps he had some good qualities and very valuable ones too—in fact, he was a man who was quite himself. Mr. Golyadkin cherished no sort of hatred or enmity, not even the slightest hostility towards this man—quite the contrary, it would seem, indeed—and yet (and this was the real point) he would not for any treasure on earth have been willing to meet that man, and especially to meet him as he had done now, for instance. We may say more: Mr. Golyadkin knew that man perfectly well: he even knew what he was called, what his name was; and yet nothing would have induced him, and again, for no treasure on earth would he have consented to name him, to consent to acknowledge that he was called so-and-so, that his father's name was this and his surname was that.

Whether Mr. Golyadkin's stupefaction lasted a short time or a long time, whether he was sitting for a long time on the stone of the pavement I cannot say; but, recovering himself a little at last, he suddenly fell to running, without looking round, as fast as his legs could carry him; his mind was preoccupied, twice he stumbled and almost fell—and through this circumstance his other boot was also bereaved of its golosh. At last Mr. Golyadkin slackened his pace a little to get breath, looked hurriedly round and saw that he had already, without being aware of it, run right across Fontanka, had crossed the Anitchkov Bridge, had passed part of the Nevsky Prospect and was now standing at the turning into Liteyny Street. Mr. Golyadkin turned into Liteyny Street. His position at that instant was like that of a man standing at the edge of a fearful precipice, while the earth is bursting open under him, is already shaking, moving, rocking for the last time, falling, drawing him into the abyss, and yet the luckless wretch has not the strength, nor the resolution, to leap back, to avert his eyes from the yawning gulf below; the abyss draws him and at last he leaps into it of himself, himself hastening the moment of his destruction.

Mr. Golyadkin knew, felt and was firmly convinced that some other evil would certainly befall him on the way, that some unpleasantness would overtake him, that he would, for instance, meet his stranger once more: but—strange to say—he positively desired this meeting, considered it inevitable, and all he asked was that it might all be quickly over, that he should be relieved from his position in one way or another, but as soon as possible. And meanwhile he ran on and on, as though moved by some external force, for he felt a weakness and numbness in his whole being: he could not think of anything, though his thoughts caught at everything like brambles. A little lost dog, soaked and shivering, attached itself to Mr. Golyadkin, and ran beside him, scurrying along with tail and ears drooping, looking at him from time to time with timid comprehension. Some remote, long-forgotten idea—some memory of something that had happened long ago—came back into his mind now, kept knocking at his brain as with a hammer, vexing him and refusing to be shaken off.

"Ech, that horrid little cur!" whispered Mr. Golyadkin, not understanding himself.

At last he saw his stranger at the turning into Italyansky Street. But this time the stranger was not coming to meet him, but was going in the same direction as he was, and he, too, was running, a few steps in front. At last they turned into Shestilavotchny Street.

Mr. Golyadkin caught his breath. The stranger stopped exactly before the house in which Mr. Golyadkin lodged. He heard a ring at the bell and almost at the same time the grating of the iron bolt. The gate opened, the stranger stooped, darted in and disappeared. Almost at the same instant Mr. Golyadkin reached the spot and like an arrow flew in at the gate. Heedless of the grumbling porter, he ran, gasping for breath, into the yard, and immediately saw his interesting companion, whom he had lost sight of for a moment.

The stranger darted towards the staircase which led to Mr. Golyadkin's flat. Mr. Golyadkin rushed after him. The stairs were dark, damp and dirty. At every turning there were heaped-up masses of refuse from the flats, so that any unaccustomed stranger who found himself on the stairs in the dark was forced to travel to and fro for half an hour in danger of breaking his legs, cursing the stairs as well as the friends who lived in such an inconvenient place. But Mr. Golyadkin's companion seemed as though familiar with it, as though at home; he ran up lightly, without difficulty, showing a perfect knowledge of his surroundings. Mr. Golyadkin had almost caught him up; in fact, once or twice the stranger's coat flicked him on the nose. His heart stood still. The stranger stopped before the door of Mr. Golyadkin's flat, knocked on it, and (which would, however, have surprised Mr. Golyadkin at any other time) Petrushka, as though he had been sitting up in expectation, opened the door at once and, with a candle in his hand, followed the stranger as the latter went in. The hero of our story dashed into his lodging beside himself; without taking off his hat or coat he crossed the little passage and stood still in the doorway of his room, as though thunderstruck. All his presentiments had come true. All that he had dreaded and surmised was coming to pass in reality. His breath failed him, his head was in a whirl. The stranger, also in his coat and hat, was sitting before him on his bed, and with a faint smile, screwing up his eyes, nodded to him in a friendly way. Mr. Golyadkin wanted to scream, but could not—to protest in some way, but his strength failed him. His hair stood on end, and he almost fell down with horror. And, indeed, there was good reason. He recognized his nocturnal visitor. The nocturnal visitor was no other than himself—Mr. Golyadkin himself, another Mr. Golyadkin, but absolutely the same as himself—in fact, what is called a double in every respect. . . .

CHAPTER 6

At eight o'clock next morning Mr. Golyadkin woke up in his bed. At once all the extraordinary incidents of the previous day and the wild, incredible night, with all its almost impossible adventures, presented themselves to his imagination and memory with terrifying vividness. Such intense, diabolical malice on the part of his enemies, and, above all, the final proof of that malice, froze Mr. Golyadkin's heart. But at the same time it was all so strange, incomprehensible, wild, it seemed so impossible that it was really hard to credit the whole business; Mr. Golyadkin was, indeed, ready to admit himself that it was all an incredible delusion, a passing aberration of the fancy, a darkening of the mind, if he had not fortunately known by bitter experience to what lengths spite will sometimes carry any one, what a pitch of ferocity an enemy may reach when he is bent on revenging his honour and prestige. Besides, Mr. Golyadkin's exhausted limbs, his heavy head, his aching back, and the malignant cold in his head bore vivid witness to the probability of his expedition of the previous night and upheld the reality of it, and to some extent of all that had happened during that expedition. And, indeed, Mr. Golyadkin had known long, long before that something was being got up among them, that there was some one else with them. But after all, thinking it over thoroughly, he made up his mind to keep quiet, to submit and not to protest for the time.

"They are simply plotting to frighten me, perhaps, and when they see that I don't mind, that I make no protest, but keep perfectly quiet and put up with it meekly, they'll give it up, they'll give it up of themselves, give it up of their own accord."

Such, then, were the thoughts in the mind of Mr. Golyadkin as,

stretching in his bed, trying to rest his exhausted limbs, he waited
for Petrushka to come into his room as usual. . . . He waited for a
full quarter of an hour. He heard the lazy scamp fiddling about
with the samovar behind the screen, and yet he could not bring himself to call him. We may say more: Mr. Golyadkin was a little afraid
of confronting Petrushka.

"Why, goodness knows," he thought, "goodness knows how that
rascal looks at it all. He keeps on saying nothing, but he has his own
ideas."

At last the door creaked and Petrushka came in with a tray in
his hands. Mr Golyadkin stole a timid glance at him, impatiently
waiting to see what would happen, waiting to see whether he would
not say something about a certain circumstance. But Petrushka said
nothing; he was, on the contrary, more silent, more glum and ill-
humoured than usual; he looked askance from under his brows at
everything; altogether it was evident that he was very much put out
about something; he did not even once glance at his master, which,
by the way, rather piqued the latter. Setting all he had brought on
the table, he turned and went out of the room without a word.

"He knows, he knows, he knows all about it, the scoundrel!"
Mr. Golyadkin grumbled to himself as he took his tea. Yet our hero
did not address a single question to his servant, though Petrushka
came into his room several times afterwards on various errands. Mr.
Golyadkin was in great trepidation of spirit. He dreaded going to
the office. He had a strong presentiment that there he would find
something that would not be "just so."

"You may be sure," he thought, "that as soon as you go you
will light upon something! Isn't it better to endure in patience?
Isn't it better to wait a bit now? Let them do what they like there;
but I'd better stay here a bit today, recover my strength, get better,
and think over the whole affair more thoroughly, then afterwards I
could seize the right moment, fall upon them like snow from the
sky, and get off scot free myself."

Reasoning like this, Mr. Golyadkin smoked pipe after pipe;
time was flying. It was already nearly half-past nine.

"Why, it's half-past nine already," thought Mr. Golyadkin; "it's
late for me to make my appearance. Besides, I'm ill, of course I'm
ill, I'm certainly ill; who denies it? What's the matter with me? If

they send to make inquiries, let the executive clerk come; and, indeed, what is the matter with me really? My back aches, I have a cough, and a cold in my head; and, in fact, it's out of the question for me to go out, utterly out of the question in such weather. I might be taken ill and, very likely, die; nowadays especially the death-rate is so high. . . ."

With such reasoning Mr. Golyadkin succeeded at last in setting his conscience at rest, and defended himself against the reprimands he expected from Andrey Filippovitch for neglect of his duty. As a rule in such cases our hero was particularly fond of justifying himself in his own eyes with all sorts of irrefutable arguments, and so completely setting his conscience at rest. And so now, having completely soothed his conscience, he took up his pipe, filled it, and had no sooner settled down comfortably to smoke, when he jumped up quickly from the sofa, flung away the pipe, briskly washed, shaved, and brushed his hair, got into his uniform and so on, snatched up some papers, and flew off to the office.

Mr. Golyadkin went into his department timidly, in quivering expectation of something unpleasant—an expectation which was none the less disagreeable for being vague and unconscious; he sat timidly down in his invariable place next the head clerk, Anton Antonovitch Syetotchkin. Without looking at anything or allowing his attention to be distracted, he plunged into the contents of the papers that lay before him. He made up his mind and vowed to himself to avoid, as far as possible, anything provocative, anything that might compromise him, such as indiscreet questions, jests, or unseemly allusions to any incidents of the previous evening; he made up his mind also to abstain from the usual interchange of civilities with his colleagues, such as inquiries after health and such like. But evidently it was impossible, out of the question, to keep to this. Anxiety and uneasiness in regard to anything near him that was annoying always worried him far more than the annoyance itself. And that was why, in spite of his inward vows to refrain from entering into anything, whatever happened, and to keep aloof from everything, Mr. Golyadkin from time to time, on the sly, very, very quietly, raised his head and stealthily looked about him to right and to left, peeped at the countenances of his colleagues, and tried to gather whether there were not something new and particular in them referring to himself and with sinister motives concealed from him. He assumed that there must be a connection between all that had happened yesterday and all that surrounded him now. At last, in his misery, he began to long for something—goodness knows what— to happen to put an end to it—even some calamity—he did not care. At this point destiny caught Mr. Golyadkin: he had hardly felt this desire when his doubts were solved in the strangest and most unexpected manner.

The door leading from the next room suddenly gave a soft and timid creak, as though to indicate that the person about to enter was a very unimportant one, and a figure, very familiar to Mr. Golyadkin, stood shyly before the very table at which our hero was seated. The latter did not raise his head—no, he only stole a glance at him, the tiniest glance; but he knew all, he understood all, to every detail. He grew hot with shame, and buried his devoted head in his papers with precisely the same object with which the ostrich, pursued by hunters, hides his head in the burning sand. The new arrival bowed to Andrey Filippovitch, and thereupon he heard a voice speaking in the regulation tone of condescending politeness with which all persons in authority address their subordinates in public offices.

"Take a seat here," said Andrey Filippovitch, motioning the newcomer to Anton Antonovitch's table. "Here, opposite Mr. Golyadkin, and we'll soon give you something to do."

Andrey Filippovitch ended by making a rapid gesture that decorously admonished the newcomer of his duty, and then he immediately became engrossed in the study of the papers that lay in a heap before him.

Mr. Golyadkin lifted his eyes at last, and that he did not fall into a swoon was simply because he had foreseen it all from the first, that he had been forewarned from the first, guessing in his soul who the stranger was. Mr. Golyadkin's first movement was to look quickly about him, to see whether there were any whispering, any office joke being cracked on the subject, whether any one's face was agape with wonder, whether, indeed, some one had not fallen under the table from terror. But to his intense astonishment there was no sign of anything of the sort. The behavior of his colleagues and companions surprised him. It seemed contrary to the dictates of

commonsense. Mr. Golyadkin was positively scared at this extraordinary reticence. The fact spoke for itself; it was a strange, horrible, uncanny thing. It was enough to rouse any one. All this, of
course, only passed rapidly through Mr. Golyadkin's mind. He felt
as though he were burning in a slow fire. And, indeed, there was
enough to make him. The figure that was sitting opposite Mr. Golyadkin now was his terror, was his shame, was his nightmare of the
evening before; in short, was Mr. Golyadkin himself, not the Mr.
Golyadkin who was sitting now in his chair with his mouth wide-
open and his pen petrified in his hand, not the one who acted as
assistant to his chief, not the one who liked to efface himself and
slink away in the crowd, not the one whose deportment plainly
said, "Don't touch me and I won't touch you," or, "Don't interfere
with me, you see I'm not touching you"; no, this was another Mr.
Golyadkin, quite different, yet, at the same time, exactly like the
first—the same height, the same figure, the same clothes, the same
baldness; in fact, nothing, absolutely nothing, was lacking to complete the likeness, so that if one were to set them side by side,
nobody, absolutely nobody, could have undertaken to distinguish
which was the real Golyadkin and which was the counterfeit,
which was the old one and which was the new one, which was the
original and which was the copy.

Our hero was—if the comparison can be made—in the position
of a man upon whom some practical joker has stealthily, by the way
of jest, turned a burning-glass.

"What does it mean? Is it a dream?" he wondered. "Is it reality
or the continuation of what happened yesterday? And besides, by
what right is this all being done? Who sanctioned such a clerk, who
authorized this? Am I asleep, am I in a waking dream?"

Mr. Golyadkin tried pinching himself, even tried to screw up
his courage to pinch some one else. . . . No, it was not a dream,
and that was all about it. Mr. Golyadkin felt that the sweat was
trickling down him in big drops; he felt that what was happening
to him was something incredible, unheard-of, and for that very
reason was, to complete his misery, utterly unseemly, for Mr. Golyadkin realized and felt how disadvantageous it was to be the first
example of such a burlesque adventure. He even began to doubt his
own existence, and though he was prepared for anything and had

been longing for his doubts to be settled in any way whatever, yet the actual reality was startling in its unexpectedness. His misery was poignant and overwhelming. At times he lost all power of thought and memory. Coming to himself after such a moment, he noticed that he was mechanically and unconsciously moving the pen over the paper. Mistrustful of himself, he began going over what he had written—and could make nothing of it. At last the other Mr. Golyadkin, who had been sitting discreetly and decorously at the table, got up and disappeared through the door into the other room. Mr. Golyadkin looked round—everything was quiet; he heard nothing but the scratching of pens, the rustle of turning over pages, and conversation in the corners farthest from Andrey Filippovitch's seat. Mr. Golyadkin looked at Anton Antonovitch, and as, in all probability, our hero's countenance fully reflected his real condition and harmonized with the whole position, and was consequently, from one point of view, very remarkable, good-natured Anton Antonovitch, laying aside his pen, inquired after his health with marked sympathy.

"I'm very well, thank God, Anton Antonovitch," said Mr. Golyadkin, stammering. "I am perfectly well, Anton Antonovitch. I am all right now, Anton Antonovitch," he added uncertainly, not yet fully trusting Anton Antonovitch, whose name he had mentioned so often.

"I fancied you were not quite well: though that's not to be wondered at; no, indeed! Nowadays especially there's such a lot of illness going about. Do you know . . ."

"Yes, Anton Antonovitch, I know there is such a lot of illness . . . I did not mean that, Anton Antonovitch," Mr. Golyadkin went on, looking intently at Anton Antonovitch. "You see, Anton Antonovitch, I don't even know how you, that is, I mean to say, how to approach this matter, Anton Antonovitch. . . ."

"How so? I really . . . do you know . . . I must confess I don't quite understand; you must . . . you must explain, you know, in what way you are in difficulties," said Anton Antonovitch, beginning to be in difficulties himself, seeing that there were actually tears in Mr. Golyadkin's eyes.

"Really, Anton Antonovitch . . . I . . . here . . . there's a clerk here, Anton Antonovitch . . ."

"Well! I don't understand now."

"I mean to say, Anton Antonovitch, there's a new clerk here."

"Yes, there is; a namesake of yours."

"What?" cried Mr. Golyadkin.

"I say a namesake of yours; his name's Golyadkin too. Isn't he a brother of yours?"

"No, Anton Antonovitch, I . . ."

"H'm! you don't say so! Why, I thought he must be a relation of yours. Do you know, there's a sort of family likeness."

Mr. Golyadkin was petrified with astonishment, and for the moment he could not speak. To treat so lightly such a horrible, unheard-of thing, a thing undeniably rare and curious in its way, a thing which would have amazed even an unconcerned spectator, to talk of a family resemblance when he could see himself as in a looking-glass!

"Do you know, Yakov Petrovitch, what I advise you to do?" Anton Antonovitch went on. "Go and consult a doctor. Do you know, you look somehow quite unwell. Your eyes look peculiar . . . you know, there's a peculiar expression in them."

"No, Anton Antonovitch, I feel, of course . . . that is, I keep wanting to ask about this clerk."

"Well?"

"That is, have not you noticed, Anton Antonovitch, something peculiar about him, something very marked?"

"That is . . . ?"

"That is, I mean, Anton Antonovitch, a striking likeness with somebody, for instance; with me, for instance? You spoke just now, you see, Anton Antonovitch, of a family likeness. You let slip the remark. . . . You know there really are sometimes twins exactly alike, like two drops of water, so that they can't be told apart. Well, it's that that I mean."

"To be sure," said Anton Antonovitch, after a moment's thought, speaking as though he were struck by the fact for the first time; "yes, indeed! You are right, there is a striking likeness, and you are quite right in what you say. You really might be mistaken for one another," he went on, opening his eyes wider and wider; "and, do you know, Yakov Petrovitch, it's positively a marvellous likeness, fantastic, in fact, as the saying is; that is, just as you . . . Have you observed, Yakov Petrovitch? I wanted to ask you to explain it; yes, I must confess I didn't take particular notice at first. It's wonderful, it's really wonderful! And, you know, you are not a native of these parts, are you, Yakov Petrovitch?"

"No."

"He is not from these parts, you know, either. Perhaps he comes from the same part of the country as you do. Where, may I make bold to inquire, did your mother live for the most part?"

"You said . . . you say, Anton Antonovitch, that he is not a native of these parts?"

"No, he is not. And, indeed, how strange it is!" continued the talkative Anton Antonovitch, for whom it was a genuine treat to gossip. "It may well arouse curiosity; and yet, you know, you might often pass him by, brush against him, without noticing anything. But you mustn't be upset about it. It's a thing that does happen. Do you know, the same thing, I must tell you, happened to my aunt on my mother's side; she saw her own double before her death . . ."

"No, I—excuse my interrupting you, Anton Antonovitch—I wanted to find out, Anton Antonovitch, how that clerk . . . that is, on what footing is he here?"

"In place of Semyon Ivanovitch, to fill the vacancy left by his death; the post was vacant, so he was appointed. Do you know, I'm told poor dear Semyon Ivanovitch left three children, all tiny tots. The widow fell at the feet of his Excellency. They do say she's hiding something; she's got a bit of money, but she's hiding it."

"No, Anton Antonovitch, I was still referring to that circumstance."

"You mean . . .? To be sure! But why are you so interested in that? I tell you not to upset yourself. All this is temporary to some extent. Why, after all, you know, you have nothing to do with it. So it has been ordained by God Almighty, it's His will, and it is sinful repining. His wisdom is apparent in it. And as far as I can make out, Yakov Petrovitch, you are not to blame in any way. There are all sorts of strange things in the world! Mother Nature is liberal with her gifts, and you are not called upon to answer for it, you won't be responsible. Here, for instance, you have heard, I expect, of those—what's their name?—oh, the Siamese twins who are joined together at the back, live and eat and sleep together. I'm told they get a lot of money."

"Allow me, Anton Antonovitch . . ."

"I understand, I understand! Yes! But what of it? It's no matter, I tell you, as far as I can see there's nothing for you to upset yourself about. After all, he's a clerk—as a clerk he seems to be a capable man. He says his name is Golyadkin, that he's not a native of this district, and that he's a titular councillor. He had a personal interview with his Excellency."

"And how did his Excellency . . . ?"

"It was all right; I am told he gave a satisfactory account of himself, gave his reasons, said, 'It's like this, your Excellency,' and that he was without means and anxious to enter the service, and would be particularly flattered to be serving under his Excellency . . . all that was proper, you know; he expressed himself neatly. He must be a sensible man. But of course he came with a recommendation; he couldn't have got in without that. . . ."

"Oh, from whom . . . that is, I mean, who is it has had a hand in this shameful business?"

"Yes, a good recommendation, I'm told; his Excellency, I'm told, laughed with Andrey Filippovitch."

"Laughed with Andrey Filippovitch?"

"Yes, he only just smiled and said that it was all right, and that he had nothing against it, so long as he did his duty. . . ."

"Well, and what more? You relieve me to some extent, Anton Antonovitch; go on, I entreat you."

"Excuse me, I must tell you again. . . . Well, then, come, it's nothing, it's a very simple matter; you mustn't upset yourself, I tell you, and there's nothing suspicious about it. . . ."

"No. I . . . that is, Anton Antonovitch, I want to ask you, didn't his Excellency say anything more . . . about me, for instance?"

"Well! To be sure! No, nothing of the sort; you can set your mind quite at rest. You know it is, of course, a rather striking circumstance, and at first . . . why, here, I, for instance, I scarcely noticed it. I really don't know why I didn't notice it till you mentioned it. But you can set your mind at rest entirely. He said nothing

particular, absolutely nothing," added good-natured Anton Antonovitch, getting up from his chair.

"So then, Anton Antonovitch, I . . ."

"Oh, you must excuse me. Here I've been gossiping about these
trivial matters, and I've business that is important and urgent. I
must inquire about it."

"Anton Antonovitch!" Andrey Filippovitch's voice sounded,
summoning him politely, "his Excellency has been asking for you."

"This minute, I'm coming this minute, Andrey Filippovitch."
And Anton Antonovitch, taking a pile of papers, flew off first to
Andrey Filippovitch and then into his Excellency's room.

"Then what is the meaning of it?" thought Mr. Golyadkin. "Is
there some sort of game going on? So the wind's in that quarter
now. . . . That's just as well; so things have taken a much pleasanter
turn," our hero said to himself, rubbing his hands, and so delighted
that he scarcely knew where he was. "So our position is an ordinary
thing. So it turns out to be all nonsense, it comes to nothing at all.
No one has done anything really, and they are not budging, the
rascals, they are sitting busy over their work; that's splendid, splendid! I like the good-natured fellow, I've always liked him, and I'm
always ready to respect him . . . though it must be said one doesn't
know what to think; this Anton Antonovitch . . . I'm afraid to trust
him; his hair's very grey, and he's so old he's getting shaky. It's an
immense and glorious thing that his Excellency said nothing, and let
it pass! It's a good thing! I approve! Only, why does Andrey Filippovitch interfere with his grins? What's he got to do with it? The
old rogue. Always on my track, always, like a black cat, on the
watch to run across a man's path, always thwarting and annoying a
man, always annoying and thwarting a man. . . ."

Mr. Golyadkin looked around him again, and again his hopes
revived. Yet he felt that he was troubled by one remote idea, an
unpleasant idea. It even occurred to him that he might try somehow
to make up to the clerks, to be the first in the field even (perhaps
when leaving the office or going up to them as though about his
work), to drop a hint in the course of conversation, saying, "This is
how it is, what a striking likeness, gentlemen, a strange circumstance,
a burlesque farce!"—that is, treat it all lightly, and in this way

sound the depth of the danger. "Devils breed in still waters," our hero concluded inwardly.

Mr. Golyadkin, however, only contemplated this; he thought better of it in time. He realized that this would be going too far. "That's your temperament," he said to himself, tapping himself lightly on the forehead; "as soon as you gain anything you are delighted! You're a simple soul! No, you and I had better be patient, Yakov Petrovitch; let us wait and be patient!"

Nevertheless, as we have mentioned already, Mr. Golyadkin was buoyed up with the most confident hopes, feeling as though he had risen from the dead.

"No matter," he thought, "it's as though a hundred tons had been lifted off my chest! Here is a circumstance, to be sure! The box has been opened by lifting the lid. Krylov is right, a clever chap, a rogue, that Krylov, and a great fable-writer! And as for him, let him work in the office, and good luck to him so long as he doesn't meddle or interfere with any one; let him work in the office—I consent and approve!"

Meanwhile the hours were passing, flying by, and before he noticed the time, it struck four. The office was closed. Andrey Filippovitch took his hat, and all followed his example in due course. Mr. Golyadkin dawdled a little on purpose, long enough to be the last to go out when all the others had gone their several ways. Going out into the street he felt as though he were in Paradise, so that he even felt inclined to go a longer way round, and to walk along the Nevsky Prospect.

"To be sure this is destiny," thought our hero, "this unexpected turn in affairs. And the weather's more cheerful, and the frost and the little sledges. And the frost suits the Russian, the Russian gets on capitally with the frost. I like the Russian. And the dear little snow, and the first few flakes in autumn; the sportsman would say, 'It would be nice to go shooting hares in the first snow.' Well, there, it doesn't matter."

This was how Mr. Golyadkin's enthusiasm found expression. Yet something was fretting in his brain, not exactly melancholy, but at times he had such a gnawing at his heart that he did not know how to find relief.

"Let us wait for the day, though, and then we shall rejoice.

And, after all, you know, what does it matter? Come, let us think it over, let us look at it. Come, let us consider it, my young friend, let us consider it. Why, a man's exactly like you in the first place, absolutely the same. Well, what is there in that? If there is such a man, why should I weep over it? What is it to me? I stand aside, I whistle to myself, and that's all! That's what I laid myself open to, and that's all about it! Let him work in the office! Well, it's strange and marvellous, they say, that the Siamese twins . . . . But why bring in the Siamese twins? They are twins, of course, but even great men, you know, sometimes seem queer creatures. In fact, we know from history that the famous Suvorov used to crow like a cock. . . . But there, he did all that with political motives; and he was a great general . . . but what are generals, after all? But I keep myself to myself, that's all, and I don't care about any one else, and, secure in my innocence, I scorn my enemies. I am not one to intrigue, and I'm proud of it. Genuine, straightforward, neat and nice, meek and mild."

All at once Mr. Golyadkin broke off, his tongue failed him and he began trembling like a leaf; he even closed his eyes for a minute. Hoping, however, that the object of his terror was only an illusion, he opened his eyes at last and stole a timid glance to the right. No, it was not an illusion! . . . His acquaintance of that morning was tripping along by his side, smiling, peeping into his face, and apparently seeking an opportunity to begin a conversation with him. The conversation was not begun, however. They both walked like this for about fifty paces. All Mr. Golyadkin's efforts were concentrated on muffling himself up, hiding himself in his coat and pulling his hat down as far as possible over his eyes. To complete his mortification, his companion's coat and hat looked as though they had been taken off Mr. Golyadkin himself.

"Sir," our hero articulated at last, trying to speak almost in a whisper, and not looking at his companion, "we are going different ways, I believe. . . . I am convinced of it, in fact," he said, after a brief pause. "I am convinced, indeed, that you quite understand me," he added, rather severely, in conclusion.

"I could have wished . . ." his companion pronounced at last, "I could have wished . . . no doubt you will be magnanimous and pardon me . . . I don't know to whom to address myself here . . . my circumstances . . . I trust you will pardon my intrusiveness. I fancied, indeed, that, moved by compassion, you showed some interest in me this morning. On my side, I felt drawn to you from the first moment. I . . ."

A this point Mr. Golyadkin inwardly wished that his companion might sink into the earth.

"If I might venture to hope that you would accord me an indulgent hearing, Yakov Petrovitch . . ."

"We—here, we—we . . . you had better come home with me," answered Mr. Golyadkin. "We will cross now to the other side of the Nevsky Prospect, it will be more convenient for us there, and then by the little back street . . . we'd better go by the back street."

"Very well, by all means let us go by the back street," our hero's meek companion responded timidly, suggesting by the tone of his reply that it was not for him to choose, and that in his position he was quite prepared to accept the back street. As for Mr. Golyadkin, he was utterly unable to grasp what was happening to him. He could not believe in himself. He could not get over his amazement.

CHAPTER 7

He recovered himself a little on the staircase as he went up to his flat.

"Oh, I'm a sheep's-head," he railed at himself inwardly. "Where am I taking him? I am thrusting my head into the noose. What will Petrushka think, seeing us together? What will the scoundrel dare to imagine now? He's suspicious. . . ."

But it was too late to regret it. Mr. Golyadkin knocked at the door; it was opened, and Petrushka began taking off the visitor's coat as well as his master's. Mr. Golyadkin looked askance, just stealing a glance at Petrushka, trying to read his countenance and divine what he was thinking. But to his intense astonishment he saw that his servant showed no trace of surprise, but seemed, on the contrary, to be expecting something of the sort. Of course he did look morose, as it was; he kept his eyes turned away and looked as though he would like to fall upon somebody.

"Hasn't somebody bewitched them all today?" thought our hero. "Some devil must have got round them. There certainly must be something peculiar in the whole lot of them today. Damn it all, what a worry it is!"

Such were Mr. Golyadkin's thoughts and reflections as he led his visitor into his room and politely asked him to sit down. The visitor appeared to be greatly embarrassed, he was very shy, and humbly watched every movement his host made, caught his glance, and seemed trying to divine his thoughts from them. There was a downtrodden, crushed, scared look about all his gestures, so that—if the comparison may be allowed—he was at that moment rather like the man who, having lost his clothes, is dressed up in somebody else's: the sleeves work up to the elbows, the waist is almost up to his neck, and he keeps every minute pulling down the short waistcoat; he wriggles sideways and turns away, tries to hide himself, or peeps into every face, and listens whether people are talking of his position, laughing at him or putting him to shame—and he is crimson with shame and overwhelmed with confusion and wounded vanity. . . . Mr. Golyadkin put down his hat in the window, and carelessly sent it flying to the floor. The visitor darted at once to pick it up, brushed off the dust, and carefully put it back, while he laid his own on the floor near a chair, on the edge of which he meekly seated himself. This little circumstance did something to open Mr. Golyadkin's eyes; he realized that the man was in great straits, and so did not put himself out for his visitor as he had done at first, very properly leaving all that to the man himself. The visitor, for his part, did nothing either; whether he was shy, a little ashamed, or from politeness was waiting for his host to begin is not certain and would be difficult to determine. At that moment Petrushka came in; he stood still in the doorway, and fixed his eyes in the direction farthest from where the visitor and his master were seated.

"Shall I bring in dinner for two?" he said carelessly, in a husky voice.

"I—I don't know . . . you . . . yes, bring dinner for two, my boy."

Petrushka went out. Mr. Golyadkin glanced at his visitor. The latter crimsoned to his ears. Mr. Golyadkin was a kind-hearted

man, and so in the kindness of his heart he at once elaborated a
theory.

"The fellow's hard up," he thought. "Yes, and in his situation
only one day. Most likely he's suffered in his time. Maybe his good
clothes are all that he has, and nothing to get him a dinner. Ah,
poor fellow, how crushed he seems! But no matter; in a way it's
better so. . . . Excuse me," began Mr. Golyadkin, "allow me to ask
what I may call you."

"I . . . I . . . I'm Yakov Petrovitch," his visitor almost whispered,
as though conscience-stricken and ashamed, as though apologizing for
being called Yakov Petrovitch too.

"Yakov Petrovitch!" repeated our hero, unable to conceal his
confusion.

"Yes, just so. . . . The same name as yours," responded the meek
visitor, venturing to smile and speak a little jocosely. But at once he
drew back, assuming a very serious air, though a little disconcerted,
noticing that his host was in no joking mood.

"You . . . allow me to ask you, to what am I indebted for the
honour . . . ?"

"Knowing your generosity and your benevolence," interposed
the visitor in a rapid but timid voice, half rising from his seat, "I
have ventured to appeal to you and to beg for your . . . acquaintance
and protection . . ." he concluded, choosing his phrases with difficulty and trying to select words not too flattering or servile, that
he might not compromise his dignity and not be so bold as to suggest
an unseemly inequality. In fact, one may say the visitor behaved
like a gentlemanly beggar with a darned waistcoat, with an honourable passport in his pocket, who has not yet learnt by practice to
hold out his hand properly for alms.

"You perplex me," answered Mr. Golyadkin, gazing round at
himself, his walls and his visitor. "In what could I . . . that is, I
mean, in what way could I be of service to you?"

"I felt drawn to you, Yakov Petrovitch, at first sight, and, graciously forgive me, I built my hopes on you—I made bold to build
my hopes on you, Yakov Petrovitch. I . . . I'm in a desperate plight
here, Yakov Petrovitch; I'm poor, I've had a great deal of trouble,
Yakov Petrovitch, and have only recently come here. Learning that

you, with your innate goodness and excellence of heart, are of the same name . . ."

Mr. Golyadkin frowned.

"Of the same name as myself and a native of the same district, I made up my mind to appeal to you, and to make known to you my difficult position."

"Very good, very good; I really don't know what to say," Mr. Golyadkin responded in an embarrassed voice. "We'll have a talk after dinner. . . ."

The visitor bowed; dinner was brought in. Petrushka laid the table, and Mr. Golyadkin and his visitor proceeded to partake of it. The dinner did not last long, for they were both in a hurry, the host because he felt ill at ease, and was, besides, ashamed that the dinner was a poor one—he was partly ashamed because he wanted to give the visitor a good meal, and partly because he wanted to show him he did not live like a beggar. The visitor, on his side too, was in terrible confusion and extremely embarrassed. When he had finished the piece of bread he had taken, he was afraid to put out his hand to take another piece, was ashamed to help himself to the best morsels, and was continually assuring his host that he was not at all hungry, that the dinner was excellent, that he was absolutely satisfied with it, and should not forget it to his dying day. When the meal was over, Mr. Golyadkin lighted his pipe, and offered a second, which was brought in, to the visitor. They sat facing each other, and the visitor began telling his adventures.

Mr. Golyadkin junior's story lasted for three or four hours. His history was, however, composed of the most trivial and wretched, if one may say so, incidents. It dealt with details of service in some lawcourt in the provinces, of prosecutors and presidents, of some department intrigues, of the depravity of some registration clerks, of an inspector, of the sudden appointment of a new chief in the department, of how the second Mr. Golyadkin had suffered, quite without any fault on his part; of his aged aunt, Pelagea Semyonovna; of how, through various intrigues on the part of his enemies, he had lost his situation, and had come to Petersburg on foot; of the harassing and wretched time he had spent here in Petersburg, how for a long time he had tried in vain to get a job, had spent all his money, had nothing left, had been living almost in the street, lived on a crust of bread and washed it down with his tears, slept on the bare floor, and finally, how some good Christian had exerted himself on his behalf, had given him an introduction, and had nobly got him into a new berth. Mr. Golyadkin's visitor shed tears as he told his story, and wiped his eyes with a blue-check handkerchief that looked like oilcloth. He ended by making a clean breast of it to Mr. Golyadkin, and confessing that he was not only for the time without means of subsistence and money for a decent lodging, but had not even the wherewithal to fit himself out properly, so that he had not, he said in conclusion, been able to get together enough for a pair of wretched boots, and that he had had to hire a uniform for the time.

Mr. Golyadkin was melted; he was genuinely touched. Even though his visitor's story was the paltriest story, every word of it was like heavenly manna to his heart. The fact was that Mr. Golyadkin was beginning to forget his last misgivings, to surrender his soul to freedom and rejoicing, and at last mentally dubbed himself a fool. It was all so natural! And what a thing to break his heart over, what a thing to be so distressed about! To be sure there was, there really was, one ticklish circumstance—but, after all, it was not a misfortune; it could be no disgrace to a man, it could not cast a slur on his honour or ruin his career, if he were innocent, since Nature herself was mixed up in it. Moreover, the visitor begged for protection, wept, railed at destiny, seemed such an artless, pitiful, insignificant person, with no craft or malice about him, and he seemed now to be ashamed himself, though perhaps on different grounds, of the strange resemblance of his countenance with that of Mr. Golyadkin's. His behaviour was absolutely unimpeachable; his one desire was to please his host, and he looked as a man looks who feels conscience-stricken and to blame in regard to some one else. If any doubtful point were touched upon, for instance, the visitor at once agreed with Mr. Golyadkin's opinion. If, by mistake, he advanced an opinion in opposition to Mr. Golyadkin's, and afterwards noticed that he had made a slip, he immediately corrected his mistake, explained himself and made it clear that he meant the same thing as his host, that he thought as he did and took the same view of everything as he did. In fact, the visitor made every possible effort to "make up to" Mr. Golyadkin, so that the latter made up his mind at last that his visitor must be a very amiable person in every way. Meanwhile, tea was brought in; it was nearly nine o'clock. Mr. Golyadkin felt in a very good humour, grew lively and skittish, let himself go a little, and finally plunged into a most animated and interested conversation with his visitor. In his festive moments Mr. Golyadkin was fond of telling interesting anecdotes. So now he told the visitor a great deal about Petersburg, about its entertainments and attractions, about the theatre, the clubs, about Brülov's picture, and about the two Englishmen who came from England to Petersburg on purpose to look at the iron railing of the Summer Garden, and returned at once when they had seen it; about the office; about Olsufy Ivanovitch and Andrey Filippovitch; about the way that Russia was progressing, was hour by hour progressing towards a state of perfection, so that

Arts and letters flourish here today;

about an anecdote he had lately read in the *Northern Bee* concerning a boa-constrictor in India of immense strength; about Baron Brambeus, and so on. In short, Mr. Golyadkin was quite happy; first, because his mind was at rest; secondly, because, so far from being afraid of his enemies, he was quite prepared now to challenge them all to mortal combat; thirdly, because he was now in the role of patron and was doing a good deed. Yet he was conscious at the bottom of his heart that he was not perfectly happy, that there was still a hidden worm gnawing at his heart, though it was only a tiny one. He was extremely worried by the thought of the previous evening at Olsufy Ivanovitch's. He would have given a great deal now for nothing to have happened of what took place then.

"It's no matter, though!" our hero decided at last, and he firmly resolved in his heart to behave well in future and never to be guilty of such pranks again. As Mr. Golyadkin was now completely worked up, and had suddenly become almost blissful, the fancy took him to have a jovial time. Rum was brought in by Petrushka, and punch was prepared. The visitor and his host drained a glass each, and then a second. The visitor appeared even more amiable than before, and gave more than one proof of his frankness and charming character; he entered keenly into Mr. Golyadkin's joy, seemed only to rejoice in his rejoicing, and to look upon him as his one and only benefactor. Taking up a pen and a sheet of paper, he asked Mr. Golyadkin not to look at what he was going to write, but afterwards showed his host what he had written. It turned out to be a verse of four lines, written with a good deal of feeling, in excellent language and handwriting, and evidently was the composition of the amiable visitor himself. The lines were as follows—

> *If thou forget me,*
> *I shall not forget thee;*
> *Though all things may be,*
> *Do not thou forget me.*

With tears in his eyes Mr. Golyadkin embraced his companion, and, completely overcome by his feelings, he began to initiate his friend into some of his own secrets and private affairs, Andrey Filippovitch and Klara Olsufyevna being prominent in his remarks.

"Well, you may be sure we shall get on together, Yakov Petrovitch," said our hero to his visitor. "You and I will take to each other like fish to the water, Yakov Petrovitch; we shall be like brothers; we'll be cunning, my dear fellow, we'll work together; we'll get up an intrigue, too, to pay them out. To pay them out we'll get up an intrigue too. And don't you trust any of them. I know you, Yakov Petrovitch, and I understand your character; you'll tell them everything straight out, you know, you're a guileless soul! You must hold aloof from them all, my boy."

His companion entirely agreed with him, thanked Mr. Golyadkin, and he, too, grew tearful at last.

"Do you know, Yasha," Mr. Golyadkin went on in a shaking voice, weak with emotion, "you must stay with me for a time, or stay with me for ever. We shall get on together. What do you say, brother, eh? And don't you worry or repine because there's such a strange circumstance about us now; it's a sin to repine, brother; it's nature! And Mother Nature is liberal with her gifts, so there, brother Yasha! It's from love for you that I speak, from brotherly love. But we'll be cunning, Yasha; we'll lay a mine, too, and we'll make them laugh out of the other side of their mouths."

They reached their third and fourth glasses of punch at last, and then Mr. Golyadkin began to be aware of two sensations: the one that he was extraordinarily happy, and the other that he could not stand upon his legs. The guest was, of course, invited to stay the night. A bed was somehow made up on two chairs. Mr. Golyadkin junior declared that under a friend's roof the bare floor would be a soft bed, that for his part he could sleep anywhere, humbly and gratefully; that he was in Paradise now, that he had been through a great deal of trouble and grief in his time; he had seen ups and downs, had all sorts of things to put up with, and—who could tell what the future would be?—maybe he would have still more to put up with. Mr. Golyadkin senior protested against this, and began to maintain that one must put one's faith in God. His guest entirely agreed, observing that there was, of course, no one like God. At this point Mr. Golyadkin senior observed that in certain respects the Turks were right in calling upon God even in their sleep. Then, though disagreeing with certain learned professors in the slanders they had promulgated against the Turkish prophet Mahomet and recognizing him as a great politician in his own line, Mr. Golyadkin passed to a very interesting description of an Algerian barber's shop which he had read in a book of miscellanies. The friends laughed heartily at the simplicity of the Turks, but paid due tribute to their fanaticism, which they ascribed to opium. . . . At last the guest began undressing, and thinking in the kindness of his heart that very likely he hadn't even a decent shirt, Mr. Golyadkin went behind the screen to avoid embarrassing a man who had suffered enough, and partly to reassure himself as far as possible about Petrushka, to sound him, to cheer him up if he could, to be kind to the fellow so that every one might be happy and that everything might be pleasant all round. It must be remarked that Petrushka still rather bothered Mr. Golyadkin.

"You go to bed now, Pyotr," Mr. Golyadkin said blandly, going into his servant's domain; "you go to bed now and wake me up at eight o'clock. Do you understand, Petrushka?"

Mr. Golyadkin spoke with exceptional softness and friendliness. But Petrushka remained mute. He was busy making his bed, and did not even turn round to face his master, which he ought to have done out of simple respect.

"Did you hear what I said, Pyotr?" Mr. Golyadkin went on. "You go to bed now and wake me tomorrow at eight o'clock; do you understand?"

"Why, I know that; what's the use of telling me?" Petrushka grumbled to himself.

"Well, that's right, Petrushka; I only mentioned it that you might be happy and at rest. Now we are all happy, so I want you, too, to be happy and satisfied. And now I wish you good-night. Sleep, Petrushka, sleep; we all have to work. . . . Don't think anything amiss, my man . . ." Mr. Golyadkin began, but stopped short. "Isn't this too much?" he thought. "Haven't I gone too far? That's how it always is; I always overdo things."

Our hero felt much dissatisfied with himself as he left Petrushka. He was, besides, rather wounded by Petrushka's grumpiness and rudeness. "One jests with the rascal, his master does him too much honour, and the rascal does not feel it," thought Mr. Golyadkin. "But there, that's the nasty way of all that sort of people!"

Somewhat shaken, he went back to his room, and, seeing that his guest had settled himself for the night, he sat down on the edge of his bed for a minute.

"Come, you must own, Yasha," he began in a whisper, wagging his head, "you're a rascal, you know; what a way you've treated me! You see, you've got my name, do you know that?" he went on, jesting in a rather familiar way with his visitor. At last, saying a friendly good-night to him, Mr. Golyadkin began preparing for the night. The visitor meanwhile began snoring. Mr. Golyadkin in his turn got into bed, laughing and whispering to himself: "You are drunk today, my dear fellow, Yakov Petrovitch, you rascal, you old Golyadkin— what a surname to have! Why, what are you so pleased about? You'll be crying tomorrow, you know, you sniveller; what am I to do with you?"

At this point a rather strange sensation pervaded Mr. Golyadkin's whole being, something like doubt or remorse.

"I've been over-excited and let myself go," he thought; "now I've a noise in my head and I'm drunk; I couldn't restrain myself, ass that I am! and I've been babbling bushels of nonsense, and, like a rascal, I was planning to be so sly. Of course, to forgive and forget injuries is the height of virtue; but it's a bad thing, nevertheless! Yes, that's so!"

At this point Mr. Golyadkin got up, took a candle and went on tiptoe to look once more at his sleeping guest. He stood over him for a long time, meditating deeply.

"An unpleasant picture! A burlesque, a regular burlesque, and that's the fact of the matter!"

At last Mr. Golyadkin settled down finally. There was a humming, a buzzing, a ringing in his head. He grew more and more drowsy . . . tried to think about something, to remember something very interesting, to decide something very important, some delicate question—but could not. Sleep descended upon his devoted head, and he slept as people generally do sleep who are not used to drinking and have consumed five glasses of punch at some festive gathering.

CHAPTER 8

Mr. Golyadkin woke up next morning at eight o'clock as usual; as soon as he was awake he recalled all the adventures of the previous evening—and frowned as he recalled them. "Ugh, I did play the fool last night!" he thought, sitting up and glancing at his visitor's bed. But what was his amazement when he saw in the room no trace, not only of his visitor, but even of the bed on which his visitor had slept!

"What does it mean?" Mr. Golyadkin almost shrieked. "What can it be? What does this new circumstance portend?"

While Mr. Golyadkin was gazing in open-mouthed bewilderment at the empty spot, the door creaked and Petrushka came in with the tea-tray.

"Where, where?" our hero said in a voice hardly audible, pointing to the place which had been occupied by his visitor the night before.

At first Petrushka made no answer and did not look at his master, but fixed his eyes upon the corner to the right till Mr. Golyad-kin felt compelled to look into that corner too. After a brief silence, however, Petrushka in a rude and husky voice answered that his master was not at home.

"You idiot; why, *I'm* your master, Petrushka!" said Mr. Golyadkin in a breaking voice, looking open-eyed at his servant.

Petrushka made no reply, but he gave Mr. Golyadkin such a look that the latter crimsoned to his ears—looked at him with an insulting reproachfulness almost equivalent to open abuse. Mr. Gol-yadkin was utterly flabbergasted, as the saying is. At last Petrushka explained that the *other one* had gone away an hour and a half ago, and would not wait. His answer, of course, sounded truthful and probable; it was evident that Petrushka was not lying; that his insulting look and the phrase the *other one* employed by him were only the result of the disgusting circumstance with which he was already familiar, but still he understood, though dimly, that some-thing was wrong, and that destiny had some other surprise, not alto-gether a pleasant one, in store for him.

"All right, we shall see," he thought to himself. "We shall see in due time; we'll get to the bottom of all this. . . . Oh, Lord, have mercy upon us!" he moaned in conclusion, in quite a different voice. "And why did I invite him, to what end did I do all that? Why, I am thrusting my head into their thievish noose myself; I am tying the noose with my own hands. Ach, you fool, you fool! You can't resist babbling like some silly boy, some chancery clerk, some wretched creature of no class at all, some rag, some rotten dish-clout; you're a gossip, an old woman! . . . Oh, all ye saints! And he wrote verses, the rogue, and expressed his love for me! How could . . . How can I show him the door in a polite way if he turns up again, the rogue? Of course, there are all sorts of ways and means. I can say this is how it is, my salary being so limited . . . Or scare him off in some way saying that, taking this and that into considera-tion, I am forced to make clear . . . that he would have to pay an equal share of the cost of board and lodging, and pay the money in advance. H'm! No, damn it all, no! That would be de-grading to me. It's not quite delicate! Couldn't I do something like this: suggest to Petrushka that he should annoy him in some way, should be disrespectful, be rude, and get rid of him in that way.

Set them at each other in some way. . . . No, damn it all, no! It's dangerous and again, if one looks at it from that point of view—it's not the right thing at all! Not the right thing at all! But there, even if he doesn't come, it will be a bad look-out, too! I babbled to him last night! . . . Ach, it's a bad look-out, a bad look-out! Ach, we're in a bad way! Oh, I'm a cursed fool, a cursed fool! You can't train yourself to behave as you ought, you can't conduct yourself reasonably. Well, what if he comes, and refuses. And God grant he may come! I should be very glad if he did come. . . ."

Such were Mr. Golyadkin's reflections as he swallowed his tea and glanced continually at the clock on the wall.

"It's a quarter to nine; it's time to go. And something will happen! What will there be there? I should like to know what exactly lies hidden in this—that is, the object, the aim, and the various intrigues. It would be a good thing to find out what all these people are plotting, and what will be their first step. . . ."

Mr. Golyadkin could endure it no longer. He threw down his unfinished pipe, dressed and set off for the office, anxious to ward off the danger if possible and to reassure himself about everything by his presence in person. There was danger: he knew himself that there was danger.

"We . . . will get to the bottom of it," said Mr. Golyadkin, taking off his coat and goloshes in the entry. "We'll go into all these matters immediately."

Making up his mind to act in this way, our hero put himself to rights, assumed a correct and official air, and was just about to pass into the adjoining room, when suddenly, in the very doorway, he jostled against his acquaintance of the day before, his friend and companion. Mr. Golyadkin junior seemed not to notice Mr. Golyadkin senior, though they met almost nose to nose. Mr. Golyadkin junior seemed to be busy, to be hastening somewhere, was breathless; he had such an official, such a business-like air that it seemed as though any one could read in his face: 'Entrusted with a special commission. . . .'

"Oh, it's you, Yakov Petrovitch!" said our hero, clutching the hand of his last night's visitor.

"Presently, presently, excuse me, tell me about it afterwards," cried Mr. Golyadkin junior, dashing on.

"But, excuse me; I believe, Yakov Petrovitch, you wanted . . ."

"What is it? Make haste and explain."

At this point his visitor of the previous night halted as though reluctantly and against his will, and put his ear almost to Mr. Golyadkin's nose.

"I must tell you, Yakov Petrovitch, that I am surprised at your behaviour . . . behaviour which seemingly I could not have expected at all."

"There's a proper form for everything. Go to his Excellency's secretary and then appeal in the proper way to the directors of the office. Have you got your petition?"

"You . . . I really don't know, Yakov Petrovitch! You simply amaze me, Yakov Petrovitch! You certainly don't recognize me or, with your characteristic gaiety, you are joking."

"Oh, it's you," said Mr. Golyadkin junior, seeming only now to recognize Mr. Golyadkin senior. "So it's you? Well, have you had a good night?"

Then, smiling a little—a formal and conventional smile, by no means the sort of smile that was befitting (for, after all, he owed a debt of gratitude to Mr. Golyadkin senior)—smiling this formal and conventional smile, Mr. Golyadkin junior added that he was very glad Mr. Golyadkin senior had had a good night; then he made a slight bow and shuffling a little with his feet, looked to the right, and to the left, then dropped his eyes to the floor, made for the side door and muttering in a hurried whisper that he had a special commission, dashed into the next room. He vanished like an apparition.

"Well, this is queer!" muttered our hero, petrified for a moment; "this is queer! This is a strange circumstance."

At this point Mr. Golyadkin felt as though he had pins and needles all over him.

"However," he went on to himself, as he made his way to his department, "however, I spoke long ago of such a circumstance: I had a presentiment long ago that he had a special commission. Why, I said yesterday that the man must certainly be employed on some special commission."

"Have you finished copying out the document you had yesterday, Yakov Petrovitch?" Anton Antonovitch Syetotchkin asked Mr. Golyadkin, when the latter was seated beside him. "Have you got it here?"

"Yes," murmured Mr. Golyadkin, looking at the head clerk with a rather helpless glance.

"That's right! I mention it because Andrey Filippovitch has asked for it twice. I'll be bound his Excellency wants it. . . ."

"Yes, it's finished. . . ."

"Well, that's all right then."

"I believe, Anton Antonovitch, I have always performed my duties properly. I'm always scrupulous over the work entrusted to me by my superiors, and I attend to it conscientiously."

"Yes. Why, what do you mean by that?"

"I mean nothing, Anton Antonovitch. I only want to explain, Anton Antonovitch, that I . . . that is, I meant to express that spite and malice sometimes spare no person whatever in their search for their daily and revolting food. . . ."

"Excuse me, I don't quite understand you. What person are you alluding to?"

"I only meant to say, Anton Antonovitch, that I'm seeking the straight path and I scorn going to work in a roundabout way. That I am not one to intrigue, and that, if I may be allowed to say so, I may very justly be proud of it. . . ."

"Yes. That's quite so, and to the best of my comprehension I thoroughly endorse your remarks; but allow me to tell you, Yakov Petrovitch, that personalities are not quite permissible in good society, that I, for instance, am ready to put up with anything behind my back—for every one's abused behind his back—but to my face, if you please, my good sir, I don't allow any one to be impudent. I've grown grey in the government service, sir, and I don't allow any one to be impudent to me in my old age. . . ."

"No, Anton Antonovitch . . . you see, Anton Antonovitch . . . you haven't quite caught my meaning. To be sure, Anton Antonovitch, I, for my part, could only think it an honour. . . ."

"Well, then, I ask your pardon, too. We've been brought up in the old school. And it's too late for us to learn your new-fangled ways. I believe we've had understanding enough for the service of our country up to now. As you are aware, sir, I have an order of merit for twenty-five years' irreproachable service. . . ."

"I feel it, Anton Antonovitch, on my side, too, I quite feel all that. But I didn't mean that, I am speaking of a mask, Anton Antonovitch. . . ."

"A mask?"

"Again you . . . I am apprehensive that you are taking this, too, in a wrong sense, that is the sense of my remarks, as you say yourself, Anton Antonovitch. I am simply enunciating a theory, that is, I am advancing the idea, Anton Antonovitch, that persons who wear a mask have become far from uncommon, and that nowadays it is hard to recognize the man beneath the mask. . . ."

"Well, do you know, it's not altogether so hard. Sometimes it's fairly easy. Sometimes one need not go far to look for it."

"No, you know, Anton Antonovitch, I say, I say of myself, that I, for instance, do not put on a mask except when there is need of it; that is, simply at carnival time or at some festive gathering, speaking in the literal sense; but that I do not wear a mask before people in daily life, speaking in another less obvious sense. That's what I meant to say, Anton Antonovitch."

"Oh, well, but we must drop all this, for now I've no time to spare," said Anton Antonovitch, getting up from his seat and collecting some papers in order to report upon them to his Excellency. "Your business, as I imagine, will be explained in due course without delay. You will see for yourself whom you should censure and whom you should blame, and thereupon I humbly beg you to spare me from further private explanations and arguments which interfere with my work. . . ."

"No, Anton Antonovitch," Mr. Golyadkin, turning a little pale, began to the retreating figure of Anton Antonovitch: "I had no thought of the kind."

"What does it mean?" our hero went on to himself, when he was left alone. "What quarter is the wind in now, and what is one to make of this new turn?"

At the very time when our bewildered and half-crushed hero was setting himself to solve this new question, there was a sound of movement and bustle in the next room, the door opened and Andrey Filippovitch, who had been on some business in his Excellency's study, appeared breathless in the doorway, and called to Mr. Golyadkin. Knowing what was wanted and anxious not to keep Andrey Filippovitch waiting, Mr. Golyadkin leapt up from his seat, and, as was fitting, immediately bustled for all he was worth getting the manuscript that was required finally neat and ready and preparing to follow the manuscript and Andrey Filippovitch into his Excellency's study. Suddenly, almost slipping under the arm of Andrey Filippovitch, who was standing right in the doorway, Mr. Golyadkin junior darted into the room in breathless haste and bustle, with a solemn and resolutely official air; he bounded straight up to Mr. Golyadkin senior, who was expecting nothing less than such a visitation.

"The papers, Yakov Petrovitch, the papers . . . His Excellency has been pleased to ask for them; have you got them ready?" Mr. Golyadkin senior's friend whispered in a hurried undertone. "Andrey Filippovitch is waiting for you. . . ."

"I know he is waiting without your telling me," said Mr. Golyadkin senior, also in a hurried whisper.

"No, Yakov Petrovitch, I did not mean that; I did not mean that at all, Yakov Petrovitch, not that at all; I sympathize with you, Yakov Petrovitch, and am moved by genuine interest."

"Which I most humbly beg you to spare me. Allow me, allow me . . ."

"You'll put it in an envelope, of course, Yakov Petrovitch, and you'll put a mark in the third page; allow me, Yakov Petrovitch. . . ."

"You allow me, if you please. . . ."

"But, I say, there's a blot here, Yakov Petrovitch; did you know there was a blot here? . . ."

At this point Andrey Filippovitch called Yakov Petrovitch a second time.

"One moment, Andrey Filippovitch, I'm only just . . . Do you understand Russian, sir?"

"It would be best to take it out with a penknife, Yakov Petrovitch. You had better rely upon me; you had better not touch it yourself, Yakov Petrovitch, rely upon me—I'll do it with a penknife. . . ."

Andrey Filippovitch called Mr. Golyadkin a third time.

"But, allow me, where's the blot? I don't think there's a blot at all."

"It's a huge blot. Here it is! Here, allow me, I saw it here . . . you just let me, Yakov Petrovitch, I'll just touch it with the penknife, I'll scratch it out with the penknife from true-hearted sympathy. There, like this; see, it's done."

At this point, and quite unexpectedly, Mr. Golyadkin junior overpowered Mr. Golyadkin senior in the momentary struggle that had arisen between them, and so, entirely against the latter's will, suddenly, without rhyme or reason, took possession of the document required by the authorities, and, instead of scratching it out with the penknife in true-hearted sympathy as he had perfidiously promised Mr. Golyadkin senior, hurriedly rolled it up, put it under his arm, in two bounds was beside Andrey Filippovitch, who noticed none of his manoeuvres, and flew with the latter into the Director's room. Mr. Golyadkin remained as though riveted to the spot, holding the penknife in his hand and apparently on the point of scratching something out with it. . . .

Our hero could not yet grasp his new position. He could not at once recover himself. He felt the blow, but thought that it was somehow all right. In terrible, indescribable misery he tore himself at last from his seat, rushed straight to the Director's room, imploring heaven on the way that it might somehow all be arranged satisfactorily and so would be all right. . . . In the furthermost room, which adjoined the Director's private room, he ran straight upon Andrey Filippovitch in company with his namesake. Both of them were coming back; Mr. Golyadkin moved aside. Andrey Filippovitch was talking with a good-humoured smile, Mr. Golyadkin senior's namesake was smiling, too, fawning upon Andrey Filippovitch and tripping about at a respectful distance from him, and was whispering something in his ear with a delighted air, to which Andrey Filippovitch assented with a gracious nod. In a flash our hero grasped the whole position. The fact was that the work had surpassed his Excellency's expectations (as he learnt afterwards), and was finished punctually by the time it was needed. His Excellency was extremely pleased with it. It was even said that his Excellency had said "Thank you" to Mr. Golyadkin junior, had thanked him warmly, had said that he would remember it on occasion and would never forget it. . . . Of course, the first thing Mr. Golyadkin did was to protest, to protest with the utmost vigour of which he was capable. Pale as death, and hardly knowing what he was doing, he rushed up to Andrey Filippovitch. But the latter, hearing that Mr. Golyadkin's business was a private matter, refused to listen, observing firmly that he had not a minute to spare even for his own affairs.

The curtness of his tone and his refusal struck Mr. Golyadkin. "I had better, perhaps, try in another quarter. . . . I had better appeal to Anton Antonovitch."

But to his disappointment Anton Antonovitch was not available either: he, too, was busy over something somewhere!

"Ah, it was not without design that he asked me to spare him explanation and discussion!" thought our hero. "This was what the old rogue had in his mind! In that case I shall simply make bold to approach his Excellency."

Still pale and feeling that his brain was in a complete ferment, greatly perplexed as to what he ought to decide to do, Mr. Golyadkin sat down on the edge of the chair. "It would have been a great deal better if it had all been just nothing," he kept incessantly thinking to himself. "Indeed, such a mysterious business was utterly improbable. In the first place, it was nonsense, and secondly it could not happen. Most likely it was imagination, or something else happened, and not what really did happen; or perhaps, I went myself . . . and somehow mistook myself for some one else . . . in short, it's an utterly impossible thing."

Mr. Golyadkin had no sooner made up his mind that it was an utterly impossible thing than Mr. Golyadkin junior flew into the room with papers in both hands as well as under his arm. Saying two or three words about business to Andrey Filippovitch as he passed, exchanging remarks with one, polite greetings with another, and familiarities with a third, Mr. Golyadkin junior, having apparently no time to waste, seemed on the point of leaving the room, but luckily for Mr. Golyadkin senior he stopped near to the door to say a few words as he passed two or three clerks who were at work there. Mr. Golyadkin senior rushed straight at him. As soon as Mr. Golyadkin junior saw Mr. Golyadkin senior's movement he began immediately, with great uneasiness, looking about him to make his escape. But our hero already held his last night's guest by the sleeve. The clerks surrounding the two titular councillors stepped back and waited with curiosity to see what would happen. The senior titular councillor realized that public opinion was not on his side, he realized that they were intriguing against him: which made it all the more necessary to hold his own now. The moment was a decisive one.

"Well!" said Mr. Golyadkin junior, looking rather impatiently at Mr. Golyadkin senior.

The latter could hardly breathe.

"I don't know," he began, "in what way to make plain to you the strangeness of your behaviour, sir."

"Well. Go on." At this point Mr. Golyadkin junior turned round and winked to the clerks standing round, as though to give them to understand that a comedy was beginning.

"The impudence and shamelessness of your manners with me, sir, in the present case, unmasks your true character . . . better than any words of mine could do. Don't rely on your trickery: it is worthless. . . ."

"Come, Yakov Petrovitch, tell me now, how did you spend the night?" answered Mr. Golyadkin junior, looking Mr. Golyadkin senior straight in the eye.

"You forget yourself, sir," said the titular councillor, completely flabbergasted, hardly able to feel the floor under his feet. "I trust that you will take a different tone. . . ."

"My darling!" exclaimed Mr. Golyadkin junior, making a rather unseemly grimace at Mr. Golyadkin senior, and suddenly, quite unexpectedly, under the pretence of caressing him, he pinched his chubby cheek with two fingers.

Our hero grew as hot as fire. . . . As soon as Mr. Golyadkin junior noticed that his opponent, quivering in every limb, speechless with rage, as red as a lobster, and exasperated beyond all endurance, might actually be driven to attack him, he promptly and in the most shameless way hastened to be beforehand with his victim. Patting him two or three times on the cheek, tickling him two or three times, playing with him for a few seconds in this way while his victim stood rigid and beside himself with fury to the no little diversion of the young men standing round, Mr. Golyadkin junior ended with a most revolting shamelessness by giving Mr. Golyadkin senior a poke in his rather prominent stomach, and with a most venomous and suggestive smile said to him: "You're mischievous, brother Yakov, you are mischievous! We'll be sly, you and I, Yakov Petrovitch, we'll be sly."

Then, and before our hero could gradually come to himself

after the last attack, Mr. Golyadkin junior (with a little smile before-hand to the spectators standing round) suddenly assumed a most businesslike, busy and official air, dropped his eyes to the floor and, drawing himself in, shrinking together, and pronouncing rapidly "on a special commission" he cut a caper with his short leg, and darted away into the next room. Our hero could not believe his eyes and was still unable to pull himself together. . . .

At last he roused himself. Recognizing in a flash that he was ruined, in a sense annihilated, that he had disgraced himself and sullied his reputation, that he had been turned into ridicule and treated with contempt in the presence of spectators, that he had been treacherously insulted by one whom he had looked on only the day before as his greatest and most trustworthy friend, that he had been put to utter confusion, Mr. Golyadkin senior rushed in pursuit of his enemy. At the moment he would not even think of the witnesses of his ignominy.

"They're all in a conspiracy together," he said to himself; "they stand by each other and set each other on to attack me." After taking a dozen steps, however, our hero perceived clearly that all pursuit would be vain and useless, and so he turned back. "You won't get away," he thought, "you will get caught one day; the wolf will have to pay for the sheep's tears."

With ferocious composure and the most resolute determination Mr. Golyadkin went up to his chair and sat down upon it. "You won't escape," he said again.

Now it was not a question of passive resistance: there was determination and pugnacity in the air, and any one who had seen how Mr. Golyadkin at that moment, flushed and scarcely able to restrain his excitement, stabbed his pen into the inkstand and with what fury he began scribbling on the paper, could be certain beforehand that the matter would not pass off like this, and could not end in a simple, womanish way. In the depth of his soul he formed a resolution, and in the depth of his heart swore to carry it out. To tell the truth he still did not quite know how to act, or rather did not know at all, but never mind, that did not matter!

"Imposture and shamelessness do not pay nowadays, sir. Imposture and shamelessness, sir, lead to no good, but lead to the halter.

Grishka Otrepyov was the only one, sir, who gained by imposture, deceiving the blind people and even that not for long."

In spite of this last circumstance, Mr. Golyadkin proposed to wait till such time as the mask should fall from certain persons and something should be made manifest. For this, it was necessary, in the first place, that office hours should be over as soon as possible, and till then our hero proposed to take no step. Then, when office hours were over, he would take one step. He knew then how he must act after taking that step, how to arrange his whole plan of action, to abase the horn of arrogance and crush the snake gnawing the dust in contemptible impotence. To allow himself to be treated like a rag used for wiping dirty boots, Mr. Golyadkin could not. He could not consent to that, especially in the present case. Had it not been for that last insult, our hero might, perhaps, have brought himself to control his anger; he might, perhaps, have been silent, have submitted and not have protested too obstinately; he would just have disputed a little, have made a slight complaint, have proved that he was in the right, then he would have given way a little, then, perhaps, he would have given way a little more, then he would have come round altogether, then, especially when the opposing party solemnly admitted that he was right, perhaps, he would have overlooked it completely, would even have been a little touched, there might even, perhaps—who could tell?—spring up a new, close, warm friendship, on an even broader basis than the friendship of last night, so that this friendship might, in the end, completely eclipse the unpleasantness of the rather unseemly resemblance of the two individuals, so that both the titular councillors might be highly delighted, and might go on living till they were a hundred, and so on. To tell the whole truth, Mr. Golyadkin began to regret a little that he had stood up for himself and his rights, and had at once come in for unpleasantness in consequence.

"Should he give in," thought Mr. Golyadkin, "say he was joking, I would forgive him. I would forgive him even more if he would acknowledge it aloud. But I won't let myself be treated like a rag. And I have not allowed even persons very different from him to treat me so, still less will I permit a depraved person to attempt it. I am not a rag. I am not a rag, sir!"

In short, our hero made up his mind. "You're in fault yourself, sir!" he thought. He made up his mind to protest, and to protest with all his might to the very last. That was the sort of man he was! He could not consent to allow himself to be insulted, still less to allow himself to be treated as a rag, and, above all, to allow a thoroughly vicious man to treat him so. No quarrelling, however, no quarrelling! Possibly, if some one wanted, if some one, for instance, actually insisted on turning Mr. Golyadkin into a rag, he might have done so, might have done so without opposition or punishment (Mr. Golyadkin was himself conscious of this at times), and he would have been a rag and not Golyadkin—yes, a nasty, filthy rag; but that rag would not have been a simple rag, it would have been a rag possessed of dignity, it would have been a rag possessed of feelings and sentiments, even though dignity was defenceless and feelings could not assert themselves, and lay hidden deep down in the filthy folds of the rag, still the feelings were there. . . .

The hours dragged on incredibly slowly; at last it struck four. Soon after, all got up and, following the head of the department, moved each on his homeward way. Mr. Golyadkin mingled with the crowd; he kept a vigilant look-out, and did not lose sight of the man he wanted. At last our hero saw that his friend ran up to the office attendants who handed the clerks their overcoats, and hung about near them waiting for his in his usual nasty way. The minute was a decisive one. Mr. Golyadkin forced his way somehow through the crowd and, anxious not to be left behind, he, too, began fussing about his overcoat. But Mr. Golyadkin's friend and companion was given his overcoat first because on this occasion, too, he had succeeded, as he always did, in making up to them, whispering something to them, cringing upon them and getting round them.

After putting on his overcoat, Mr. Golyadkin junior glanced ironically at Mr. Golyadkin senior, acting in this way openly and defiantly, looked about him with his characteristic insolence, finally he tripped to and fro among the other clerks—no doubt in order to leave a good impression on them—said a word to one, whispered something to another, respectfully accosted a third, directed a smile at a fourth, gave his hand to a fifth, and gaily darted downstairs. Mr. Golyadkin senior flew after him, and to his inexpressible delight overtook him on the last step, and seized him by the collar of his overcoat. It seemed as though Mr. Golyadkin junior was a little disconcerted, and he looked about him with a helpless air.

"What do you mean by this?" he whispered to Mr. Golyadkin at last in a weak voice.

"Sir, if you are a gentleman, I trust that you remember our friendly relations yesterday," said our hero.

"Ah, yes! Well? Did you sleep well?"

Fury rendered Mr. Golyadkin senior speechless for a moment.

"I slept well, sir . . . but allow me to tell you, sir, that you are playing a very complicated game. . . ."

"Who says so? My enemies say that," answered abruptly the man who called himself Mr. Golyadkin, and saying this, he unexpectedly freed himself from the feeble hand of the real Mr. Golyadkin. As soon as he was free he rushed away from the stairs, looked around him, saw a cab, ran up to it, got in, and in one moment vanished from Mr. Golyadkin senior's sight. The despairing titular councillor, abandoned by all, gazed about him, but there was no other cab. He tried to run but his legs gave way under him. With a look of open-mouthed astonishment on his countenance, feeling crushed and shrivelled up, he leaned helplessly against a lamp-post, and remained so for some minutes in the middle of the pavement. It seemed as though all were over for Mr. Golyadkin.

CHAPTER 9

Everything, apparently, and even nature itself, seemed up in arms against Mr. Golyadkin; but he was still on his legs and unconquered; he felt that he was unconquered. He was ready to struggle. He rubbed his hands with such feeling and such energy when he recovered from his first amazement that it could be deduced from his very air that he would not give in. Yet the danger was imminent; it was evident; Mr. Golyadkin felt it; but how to grapple with

it, with this danger?—that was the question. The thought even
flashed through Mr. Golyadkin's mind for a moment, "After all, why
not leave it so, simply give it up? Why, what is it? Why, it's nothing.
I'll keep apart as though it were not I," thought Mr. Golyadkin.
"I'll let it all pass; it's not I, and that's all about it; he's separate,
too, maybe he'll give it up, too; he'll hang about, the rascal, he'll
hang about. He'll come back and give it up again. That's how it
will be! I'll take it meekly. And, indeed, where is the danger? Come,
what danger is there? I should like any one to tell me where the
danger lies in this business. It is a trivial affair. An everyday affair. . . ."

At this point Mr. Golyadkin's tongue failed; the words died away
on his lips; he even swore at himself for this thought; he convicted
himself on the spot of abjectness, of cowardice for having this
thought; things were no forwarder, however. He felt that to make
up his mind to some course of action was absolutely necessary for
him at the moment; he even felt that he would have given a great
deal to any one who could have told him what he must decide to
do. Yes, but how could he guess what? Though, indeed, he had no
time to guess. In any case, that he might lose no time, he took a cab
and dashed home.

"Well? What are you feeling now?" he wondered; "what are you
graciously pleased to be thinking of, Yakov Petrovitch? What are you
doing? What are you doing now, you rogue, you rascal? You've
brought yourself to this plight, and now you are weeping and
whimpering!"

So Mr. Golyadkin taunted himself as he jolted along in the vehicle. To taunt himself and so to irritate his wounds was, at this time,
a great satisfaction to Mr. Golyadkin, almost a voluptuous enjoyment.

"Well," he thought, "if some magician were to turn up now, or
if it could come to pass in some official way and I were told: 'Give
a finger of your right hand, Golyadkin—and it's a bargain with you;
there shall not be the other Golyadkin, and you will be happy, only
you won't have your finger'—yes, I would sacrifice my finger, I
would certainly sacrifice it, I would sacrifice it without winking. . . .
The devil take it all!" the despairing titular councillor cried at last.
"Why, what is it all for? Well, it all had to be; yes, it absolutely had
to; yes, just this had to be, as though nothing else were possible!

And it was all right at first. Every one was pleased and happy. But there, it had to be! There's nothing to be gained by talking, though; you must act."

And so, almost resolved upon some action, Mr. Golyadkin reached home, and without a moment's delay snatched up his pipe and, sucking at it with all his might and puffing out clouds of smoke to right and to left, he began pacing up and down the room in a state of violent excitement. Meanwhile, Petrushka began laying the table. At last Mr. Golyadkin made up his mind completely, flung aside his pipe, put on his overcoat, said he would not dine at home and ran out of the flat. Petrushka, panting, overtook him on the stairs, bringing the hat he had forgotten. Mr. Golyadkin took his hat, wanted to say something incidentally to justify himself in Petrushka's eyes that the latter might not think anything particular, such as, "What a queer circumstance! here he forgot his hat—and so on," but as Petrushka walked away at once and would not even look at him, Mr. Golyadkin put on his hat without further explanation, ran downstairs, and repeating to himself that perhaps everything might be for the best, and that affairs would somehow be arranged, though he was conscious among other things of a cold chill right down to his heels, he went out into the street, took a cab and hastened to Andrey Filippovitch's.

"Would it not be better tomorrow, though?" thought Mr. Golyadkin, as he took hold of the bell-rope of Andrey Filippovitch's flat. "And, besides, what can I say in particular? There is nothing particular in it. It's such a wretched affair, yes, it really is wretched, paltry, yes, that is, almost a paltry affair . . . yes, that's what it all is, the incident. . . ." Suddenly Mr. Golyadkin pulled at the bell; the bell rang; footsteps were heard within. . . . Mr. Golyadkin cursed himself on the spot for his hastiness and audacity. His recent unpleasant experiences, which he had almost forgotten over his work, and his encounter with Andrey Filippovitch immediately came back into his mind. But by now it was too late to run away: the door opened. Luckily for Mr. Golyadkin he was informed that Andrey Filippovitch had not returned from the office and had not dined at home.

"I know where he dines: he dines near the Ismailovsky Bridge," thought our hero; and he was immensely relieved. To the footman's inquiry what message he would leave, he said: "It's all right, my good man, I'll look in later," and he even ran downstairs with a certain cheerful briskness. Going out into the street, he decided to dismiss the cab and paid the driver. When the man asked for something extra, saying he had been waiting in the street and had not spared his horse for his honour, he gave him five kopecks extra, and even willingly; and then walked on.

"It really is such a thing," thought Mr. Golyadkin, "that it cannot be left like that; though, if one looks at it that way, looks at it sensibly, why am I hurrying about here, in reality? Well, yes, though, I will go on discussing why I should take a lot of trouble; why I should rush about, exert myself, worry myself and wear myself out. To begin with, the thing's done and there's no recalling it . . . of course, there's no recalling it! Let us put it like this: a man turns up with a satisfactory reference, said to be a capable clerk, of good conduct, only he is a poor man and has suffered many reverses—all sorts of ups and downs—well, poverty is not a crime: so I must stand aside. Why, what nonsense it is! Well, he came; he is so made, the man is so made by nature itself, that he is as like another man as though they were two drops of water, as though he were a perfect copy of another man; how could they refuse to take him into the department on that account? If it is fate, if it is only fate, if it is only blind chance that is to blame—is he to be treated like a rag, is he to be refused a job in the office? . . . Why, what would become of justice after that? He is a poor man, hopeless, downcast; it makes one's heart ache: compassion bids one care for him! Yes! There's no denying, there would be a fine set of head officials, if they took the same view as a reprobate like me! What an addlepate I am! I have foolishness enough for a dozen! Yes, yes! They did right, and many thanks to them for being good to a poor, luckless fellow. . . . Why, let us imagine for a moment that we are twins, that we had been born twin brothers, and nothing else—there it is! Well, what of it? Why, nothing! All the clerks can get used to it. . . . And an outsider, coming into our office, would certainly find nothing unseemly or offensive in the circumstance. In fact, there is really something touching in it; to think that the divine Providence created two men exactly alike, and the heads of the department, seeing the divine handiwork, provided for two twins. It would, of course," Mr. Golyadkin went on, drawing a breath and dropping his voice, "it would,

of course . . . it would, of course, have been better if there had
been . . . if there had been nothing of this touching kindness, and if
there had been no twins either. . . . The devil take it all! And what
need was there for it? And what was the particular necessity that
admitted of no delay! My goodness! The devil has made a mess of
it! Besides, he has such a character, too, he's of such a playful, horrid
disposition—he's such a scoundrel, he's such a nimble fellow! He's
such a toady! Such a lickspittle! He's such a Golyadkin! I daresay
he will misconduct himself; yes, he'll disgrace my name, the black-
guard! And now I have to look after him and wait upon him! What
an infliction! But, after all, what of it? It doesn't matter. Granted,
he's a scoundrel, well, let him be a scoundrel, but to make up for it,
the other one's honest; so he will be a scoundrel and I'll be honest,
and they'll say that this Golyadkin's a rascal, don't take any notice
of him, and don't mix him up with the other; but the other one's
honest, virtuous, mild, free from malice, always to be relied upon
in the service, and worthy of promotion; that's how it is, very
good . . . but what if . . . what if they get us mixed up! . . . He is
equal to anything! Ah, Lord, have mercy upon us! . . . He will counterfeit a man, he will counterfeit him, the rascal—he will change
one man for another as though he were a rag, and not reflect that a
man is not a rag. Ach, mercy on us! Ough, what a calamity!" . . .

Reflecting and lamenting in this way, Mr. Golyadkin ran on,
regardless of where he was going. He came to his senses in Nevsky
Prospect, only owing to the chance that he ran so neatly full tilt
into a passer-by that he saw stars in his eyes. Mr. Golyadkin muttered his excuses without raising his head, and it was only after the
passer-by, muttering something far from flattering, had walked a
considerable distance away, that he raised his nose and looked about
to see where he was and how he had got there. Noticing when he
did so that he was close to the restaurant in which he had sat for a
while before the dinner-party at Olsufy Ivanovitch's, our hero was
suddenly conscious of a pinching and nipping sensation in his stomach; he remembered that he had not dined; he had no prospect of
a dinner-party anywhere. And so, without losing precious time, he
ran upstairs into the restaurant to have a snack of something as
quickly as possible, and to avoid delay by making all the haste he
could. And though everything in the restaurant was rather dear,

that little circumstance did not on this occasion make Mr. Golyadkin pause, and, indeed, he had no time to pause over such a trifle. In the brightly lighted room the customers were standing in rather a crowd round the counter, upon which lay heaps of all sorts of such edibles as are eaten by well-bred persons at lunch. The waiter scarcely had time to fill glasses, to serve, to take money and give change. Mr. Golyadkin waited for his turn and modestly stretched out his hand for a savoury patty. Retreating into a corner, turning his back on the company and eating with appetite, he went back to the attendant, put down his plate and, knowing the price, took out a ten-kopeck piece and laid the coin on the counter, catching the waiter's eye as though to say, "Look, here's the money, one pie," and so on.

"One rouble ten kopecks is your bill," the waiter filtered through his teeth.

Mr. Golyadkin was a good deal surprised.

"You are speaking to me? . . . I . . . I took one pie, I believe."

"You've had eleven," the man retorted confidently.

"You . . . so it seems to me . . . I believe, you're mistaken. . . . I really took only one pie, I think."

"I counted them; you took eleven. Since you've had them, you must pay for them; we don't give anything away for nothing."

Mr. Golyadkin was petrified. "What sorcery is this, what is happening to me?" he wondered. Meanwhile, the man waited for Mr. Golyadkin to make up his mind; people crowded round Mr. Golyadkin; he was already feeling in his pocket for a silver rouble, to pay the full amount at once, to avoid further trouble. "Well, if it was eleven, it was eleven," he thought, turning as red as a lobster. "Why, what does it matter if eleven pies have been eaten? Why, a man's hungry, so he eats eleven pies; well, let him eat, and may it do him good; and there's nothing to wonder at in that, and there's nothing to laugh at. . . ."

At that moment something seemed to stab Mr. Golyadkin. He raised his eyes and—at once he guessed the riddle. He knew what the sorcery was. All his difficulties were solved. . . .

In the doorway of the next room, almost directly behind the waiter and facing Mr. Golyadkin, in the doorway which, till that moment, our hero had taken for a looking-glass, a man was standing

—he was standing, Mr. Golyadkin was standing—not the original Mr. Golyadkin, the hero of our story, but the other Mr. Golyadkin, the new Mr. Golyadkin. The second Mr. Golyadkin was apparently in excellent spirits. He smiled to Mr. Golyadkin the first, nodded to him, winked, shuffled his feet a little, and looked as though in another minute he would vanish, would disappear into the next room, and then go out, maybe, by a back way out; and there it would be, and all pursuit would be in vain. In his hand he had the last morsel of the tenth pie, and before Mr. Golyadkin's very eyes he popped it into his mouth and smacked his lips.

"He has impersonated me, the scoundrel!" thought Mr. Golyadkin, flushing hot with shame. "He is not ashamed of the publicity of it! Do they see him? I fancy no one notices him. . . ."

Mr. Golyadkin threw down his rouble as though it burnt his fingers, and without noticing the waiter's insolently significant grin, a smile of triumph and serene power, he extricated himself from the crowd, and rushed away without looking round. "We must be thankful that at least he has not completely compromised any one!" thought Mr. Golyadkin senior. "We must be thankful to him, the brigand, and to fate, that everything was satisfactorily settled. The waiter was rude, that was all. But, after all, he was in the right. One rouble and ten kopecks were owing: so he was in the right. 'We don't give things away for nothing,' he said! Though he might have been more polite, the rascal. . . ."

All this Mr. Golyadkin said to himself as he went downstairs to the entrance, but on the last step he stopped suddenly, as though he had been shot, and suddenly flushed till the tears came into his eyes at the insult to his dignity. After standing stock-still for half a minute, he stamped his foot resolutely, at one bound leapt from the step into the street and, without looking round, rushed breathless and unconscious of fatigue back home to his flat in Shestilavotchny Street. When he got home, without changing his coat, though it was his habit to change into an old coat at home, without even stopping to take his pipe, he sat down on the sofa, drew the inkstand towards him, took up a pen, got a sheet of notepaper, and with a hand that trembled from inward excitement, began scribbling the following epistle.

DEAR SIR YAKOV PETROVITCH!

I should not take up my pen if my circumstances, and your own action, sir, had not compelled me to that step. Believe me that nothing but necessity would have induced me to enter upon such a discussion with you, and therefore, first of all, I beg you, sir, to look upon this step of mine not as a premeditated design to insult you, but as the inevitable consequence of the circumstance that is a bond between us now.

("I think that's all right, proper, courteous, though not lacking in force and firmness. . . . I don't think there is anything for him to take offence at. Besides, I'm fully within my rights," thought Mr. Golyadkin, reading over what he had written.)

Your strange and sudden appearance, sir, on a stormy night, after the coarse and unseemly behaviour of my enemies to me, for whom I feel too much contempt even to mention their names, was the starting point of all the misunderstanding existing between us at the present time. Your obstinate desire to persist in your course of action, sir, and forcibly to enter the circle of my existence and all my relations in practical life, transgresses every limit imposed by the merest politeness and every rule of civilized society. I imagine there is no need, sir, for me to refer to the seizure by you of my papers, and particularly to your taking away my good name, in order to gain the favour of my superiors—favour you have not deserved. There is no need to refer here either to your intentional and insulting refusal of the necessary explanation in regard to us. Finally, to omit nothing, I will not allude here to your last strange, one may even say, your incomprehensible behaviour to me in the coffee-house. I am far from lamenting over the needless—for me—loss of a rouble; but I cannot help expressing my indignation at the recollection of your public outrage upon me, to the detriment of my honour, and what is more, in the presence of several persons of good breeding, though not belonging to my circle of acquaintance.

("Am I not going too far?" thought Mr. Golyadkin. "Isn't it too much; won't it be too insulting—that taunt about good breeding, for instance? . . . But there, it doesn't matter! I must show him the resoluteness of my character. I might, however, to soften him, flatter him, and butter him up at the end. But there, we shall see.")

But I should not weary you with my letter, sir, if I were not firmly convinced that the nobility of your sentiments and your open, candid character would suggest to you yourself a means for retrieving all lapses and returning everything to its original position.

With full confidence, I venture to rest assured that you will not take my letter in a sense derogatory to yourself, and at the same time that you will not refuse to explain yourself expressly on this occasion by letter, sending the same by my man.

In expectation of your reply, I have the honour, dear sir, to remain,

Your humble servant,

Y. GOLYADKIN.

"Well, that is quite all right. The thing's done, it has come to letter writing. But who is to blame for that? He is to blame himself: by his own action he reduces a man to the necessity of resorting to epistolary composition. And I am within my rights. . . ."

Reading over his letter for the last time, Mr. Golyadkin folded it up, sealed it and called Petrushka. Petrushka came in looking, as usual, sleepy and cross about something.

"You will take this letter, my boy . . . do you understand?"

Petrushka did not speak.

"You will take it to the department; there you must find the secretary on duty, Vahramyev. He is the one on duty today. Do you understand that?"

"I understand."

" 'I understand'! He can't even say, 'I understand, sir!' You must ask for the secretary, Vahramyev, and tell him that your master desired you to send his regards, and humbly requests him to refer to the address book of our office and find out where the titular councillor, Golyadkin, is living?"

Petrushka remained mute, and, as Mr. Golyadkin fancied, smiled.

"Well, so you see, Pyotr, you have to ask him for the address, and find out where the new clerk, Golyadkin, lives."

"Yes."

"You must ask for the address and then take this letter there. Do you understand?"

"I understand."

"If there . . . where you have to take the letter, that gentleman to whom you have to give the letter, that Golyadkin . . . What are you laughing at, you blockhead?"

"What is there to laugh at? What is it to me! I wasn't doing anything, sir. It's not for the likes of us to laugh. . . ."

"Oh, well . . . if that gentleman should ask, 'How is your master, how is he?'; if he . . . well, if he should ask you anything—you hold your tongue, and answer, 'My master is all right, and begs you for an answer to his letter.' Do you understand?"

"Yes, sir."

"Well, then, say, 'My master is all right and quite well,' say, 'and is just getting ready to pay a call: and he asks you,' say, 'for an answer in writing.' Do you understand?"

"Yes."

"Well, go along, then."

"Why, what a bother I have with this blockhead, too! He's laughing, and there's nothing to be done. What's he laughing at? I've lived to see trouble. Here I've lived like this to see trouble. Though perhaps it may all turn out for the best. . . . That rascal will be loitering about for the next two hours now, I expect; he'll go off somewhere else. . . . There's no sending him anywhere. What a misery it is! . . . What misery has come upon me!"

Feeling his troubles to the full, our hero made up his mind to remain passive for two hours till Petrushka returned. For an hour of the time he walked about the room, smoked, then put aside his pipe and sat down to a book, then he lay down on the sofa, then took up his pipe again, then again began running about the room. He tried to think things over but was absolutely unable to think about anything. At last the agony of remaining passive reached the climax and Mr. Golyadkin made up his mind to take a step. "Petrushka will come in another hour," he thought. "I can give the key to the porter, and I myself can, so to speak . . . I can investigate the matter; I shall investigate the matter in my own way."

Without loss of time, in haste to investigate the matter, Mr. Golyadkin took his hat, went out of the room, locked up his flat, went in to the porter, gave him the key, together with ten kopecks —Mr. Golyadkin had become extraordinarily free-handed of late— and rushed off. Mr. Golyadkin went first on foot to the Ismailovsky Bridge. It took him half an hour to get there. When he reached the goal of his journey, he went straight into the yard of the house so familiar to him, and glanced up at the windows of the civil councillor Berendyev's flat. Except for three windows hung with red curtains all the rest was dark.

"Olsufy Ivanovitch has no visitors today," thought Mr. Golyadkin; "they must all be staying at home today."

After standing for some time in the yard, our hero tried to decide on some course of action. But he was apparently not destined to reach a decision. Mr. Golyadkin changed his mind, and with a wave of his hand went back into the street.

"No, there's no need for me to go today. What could I do here? . . . No, I'd better, so to speak . . . I'll investigate the matter personally."

Coming to this conclusion, Mr. Golyadkin rushed off to his office. He had a long way to go. It was horribly muddy, besides, and the wet snow lay about in thick drifts. But it seemed as though difficulty did not exist for our hero at the moment. He was drenched through, it is true, and he was a good deal spattered with mud.

"But that's no matter, so long as the object is obtained."

And Mr. Golyadkin certainly was nearing his goal. The dark mass of the huge government building stood up black before his eyes.

"Stay," he thought; "where am I going, and what am I going to do here? Suppose I do find out where he lives? Meanwhile, Petrushka will certainly have come back and brought me the answer. I am only wasting my precious time, I am simply wasting my time. Though, shouldn't I, perhaps, go in and see Vahramyev? But, no, I'll go later. . . . Ech! There was no need to have gone out at all. But, there, it's my temperament! I've a knack of always seizing a chance of rushing ahead of things, whether there is a need to or not. . . . H'm! . . . what time is it? It must be nine by now. Petrushka might come and not find me at home. It was pure folly on my part to go out. . . . Ech, it is really a nuisance!"

Sincerely acknowledging that he had been guilty of an act of folly, our hero ran back to Shestilavotchny Street. He arrived there, weary and exhausted. From the porter he learned that Petrushka had not dreamed of turning up yet.

"To be sure! I foresaw it would be so," thought our hero; "and meanwhile, it's nine o'clock. Ech, he's such a good-for-nothing chap! He's always drinking somewhere! Mercy on us! What a day has fallen to my miserable lot!"

Reflecting in this way, Mr. Golyadkin unlocked his flat, got a light, took off his outdoor things, lighted his pipe and, tired, worn out, exhausted and hungry, lay down on the sofa and waited for Petrushka. The candle burnt dimly; the light flickered on the wall. . . . Mr. Golyadkin gazed and gazed, and thought and thought, and feel asleep at last, worn out.

It was late when he woke up. The candle had almost burnt down, was smoking and on the point of going out. Mr. Golyadkin jumped up, shook himself, and remembered it all, absolutely all. Behind the screen he heard Petrushka snoring lustily. Mr. Golyadkin rushed to the window—not a light anywhere. He opened the movable pane—all was still; the city was asleep as though it were dead: so it must have been two or three o'clock; so it proved to be, indeed; the clock behind the partition made an effort and struck two. Mr. Golyadkin rushed behind the partition.

He succeeded, somehow, though only after great exertions, in rousing Petrushka, and making him sit up in his bed. At that moment the candle went out completely. About ten minutes passed before Mr. Golyadkin succeeded in finding another candle and lighting it. In the interval Petrushka had fallen asleep again.

"You scoundrel, you worthless fellow!" said Mr. Golyadkin, shaking him up again. "Will you get up, will you wake?" After half an hour of effort, Mr. Golyadkin succeeded, however, in rousing his servant thoroughly, and dragging him out from behind the partition. Only then, our hero remarked the fact that Petrushka was what is called dead-drunk and could hardly stand on his legs.

"You good-for-nothing fellow!" cried Mr. Golyadkin; "you ruf-

fian! You'll be the death of me! Good heavens! whatever has he
done with the letter? Ach, my God! where is it? . . . And why did
I write it? As though there were any need for me to have written
it! I went scribbling away out of pride, like a noodle! I've got myself into this fix out of pride! That is what dignity does for you, you
rascal, that is dignity! . . . Come, what have you done with the
letter, you ruffian? To whom did you give it?"

"I didn't give any one any letter; and I never had any letter
. . . so there!"

Mr. Golyadkin wrung his hands in despair.

"Listen, Pyotr . . . listen to me, listen to me. . . ."

"I am listening. . . ."

"Where have you been?—Answer. . . ."

"Where have I been? . . . I've been to see good people! What
is it to me!"

"Oh, Lord, have mercy on us! Where did you go, to begin
with? Did you go the the department? . . . Listen, Pyotr, perhaps
you're drunk?"

"Me drunk! If I should be struck on the spot this minute, not a
drop, not a drop—so there. . . ."

"No, no, it's no matter you're being drunk. . . . I only asked;
it's all right your being drunk; I don't mind, Petrushka, I don't
mind. . . . Perhaps it's only that you have forgotten, but you'll
remember it all. Come, try to remember—have you been to that
clerk's, to Vahramyev's; have you been to him or not?"

"I have not been, and there's no such clerk. Not if I were this
minute . . ."

"No, no, Pyotr! No, Petrushka, you know I don't mind. Why,
you see I don't mind. . . . Come, what happened? To be sure, it's
cold and damp in the street, and so a man has a drop, and it's no
matter. I am not angry. I've been drinking myself today, my boy.
. . . Come, think and try and remember, did you go to Vahramyev?"

"Well, then, now, this is how it was, it's the truth—I did go, if
this very minute . . ."

"Come, that is right, Petrushka, that is quite right that you've
been. You see I'm not angry. . . . Come, come," our hero went on,
coaxing his servant more and more, patting him on the shoulder
and smiling to him, "come, you had a little nip, you scoundrel. . . .
You had two-penn'orth of something, I suppose? You're a sly rogue!

Well, that's no matter; come, you see that I'm not angry. . . . I'm not angry, my boy, I'm not angry. . . ."

"No, I'm not a sly rogue, say what you like. . . . I only went to see some good friends. I'm not a rogue, and I never have been a rogue. . . ."

"Oh, no, no, Petrushka; listen, Petrushka, you know I'm not scolding when I called you a rogue. I said that in fun, I said it in a good sense. You see, Petrushka, it is sometimes a compliment to a man when you call him a rogue, a cunning fellow, that he's a sharp chap and would not let any one take him in. Some men like it. . . . Come, come, it doesn't matter! Come, tell me, Petrushka, without keeping anything back, openly, as to a friend . . . did you go to Vahramyev's, and did he give you the address?"

"He did give me the address, he did give me the address, too. He's a nice gentleman! 'Your master,' says he, 'is a nice man,' says he, 'very nice man,' says he, 'I send my regards,' says he, 'to your master, thank him and say that I like him,' says he—'how I do respect your master,' says he. 'Because,' says he, 'your master, Petrushka,' says he, 'is a good man, and you,' says he, 'Petrushka, are a good man too. . . .'"

"Ah, mercy on us! But the address, the address! You Judas!" The last word Mr. Golyadkin uttered almost in a whisper.

"And the address . . . he did give the address too."

"He did? Well, where does Golyadkin, the clerk Golyadkin, the titular councillor, live?"

"'Why,' says he, 'Golyadkin will be now at Shestilavotchny Street. When you get into Shestilavotchny Street, take the stairs on the right and it's the fourth floor. And there,' says he, 'you'll find Golyadkin. . . .'"

"You scoundrel!" our hero cried, out of patience at last. "You're a ruffian! Why, that's my address; why, you are talking about me. But there's another Golyadkin; I'm talking of the other one, you scoundrel!"

"Well, that's as you please! What is it to me? Have it your own way. . . ."

"And the letter, the letter? . . ."

"What letter? There wasn't any letter, and I didn't see any letter."

"But what have you done with it, you rascal?"

"I delivered the letter, I delivered it. He sent his regards. 'Thank you,' says he, 'your master's a nice man,' says he. 'Give my regards,' says he, 'to your master. . . .'"

"But who said that? Was it Golyadkin said it?"

Petrushka said nothing for a moment, and then, with a broad grin, he stared straight into his master's face. . . .

"Listen, you scoundrel!" began Mr. Golyadkin, breathless, beside himself with fury; "listen, you rascal, what have you done to me? Tell me what you've done to me! You've destroyed me, you villain, you've cut the head off my shoulders, you Judas!"

"Well, have it your own way! I don't care," said Petrushka in a resolute voice, retreating behind the screen.

"Come here, come here, you ruffian. . . ."

"I'm not coming to you now, I'm not coming at all. What do I care, I'm going to good folks. . . . Good folks live honestly, good folks live without falsity, and they never have doubles. . . ."

Mr. Golyadkin's hands and feet went icy cold, his breath failed him. . . .

"Yes," Petrushka went on, "they never have doubles. God doesn't afflict honest folk. . . ."

"You worthless fellow, you are drunk! Go to sleep now, you ruffian! And tomorrow you'll catch it," Mr. Golyadkin added in a voice hardly audible. As for Petrushka, he muttered something more; then he could be heard getting into bed, making the bed creak. After a prolonged yawn, he stretched; and at last began snoring, and slept the sleep of the just, as they say. Mr. Golyadkin was more dead than alive. Petrushka's behaviour, his very strange hints, which were yet so remote that it was useless to be angry at them, especially as they were uttered by a drunken man, and, in short, the sinister turn taken by the affair altogether, all this shook Mr. Golyadkin to the depths of his being.

"And what possessed me to go for him in the middle of the night?" said our hero, trembling all over from a sickly sensation. "What the devil made me have anything to do with a drunken man! What could I expect from a drunken man? Whatever he says is a lie. But what was he hinting at, the ruffian? Lord, have mercy on us! And why did I write all that letter? I'm my own enemy, I'm my own murderer! As if I couldn't hold my tongue? I had to go scribbling nonsense! And what now! You are going to ruin, you are like an old rag, and yet you worry about your pride; you say, 'my honour is wounded,' you must stick up for your honour! My own murderer, that is what I am!"

Thus spoke Mr. Golyadkin and he hardly dared to stir for terror. At last his eyes fastened upon an object which excited his interest to the utmost. In terror lest the object that caught his attention should prove to be an illusion, a deception of his fancy, he stretched out his hand to it with hope, with dread, with indescribable curiosity. . . . No, it was not a deception! Not a delusion! It was a letter, really a letter, undoubtedly a letter, and addressed to him. Mr. Golyadkin took the letter from the table. His heart beat terribly.

"No doubt that scoundrel brought it," he thought, "put it there, and then forgot it; no doubt that is how it happened: no doubt that is just how it happened. . . ."

The letter was from Vahramyev, a young fellow-clerk who had once been his friend. "I had a presentiment of this though," thought our hero, "and I had a presentiment of all that there will be in the letter. . . ."

The letter was as follows—

DEAR SIR YAKOV PETROVITCH!

Your servant is drunk, and there is no getting any sense out of him. For that reason, I prefer to reply by letter. I hasten to inform you that the commission you've entrusted to me—that is, to deliver a letter to a certain person you know, I agree to carry out carefully and exactly. That person, who is very well known to you and who has taken the place of a friend to me, whose name I will refrain from mentioning (because I do not wish unnecessarily to blacken the reputation of a perfectly innocent man), lodges with us at Karolina Ivanovna's, in the room in which, when you were among us, the infantry officer from Tambov used to be. That person, however, is always to be found in the company of honest and true-hearted persons, which is more than one can say for some people. I intend from this day to break off all connection with you; it's impossible for us to remain on friendly terms and to keep up the appearance of comradeship congruous with them. And, therefore, I beg you, my dear sir, immediately on the receipt of this candid letter from me, to send me the two roubles you owe me for the razor of foreign make which I sold you seven months ago, if you will kindly remember, when you were still living with us in the lodgings of Karolina Ivanovna, a lady whom I respect from the bottom of my heart. I am acting in this way because you, from the accounts I hear from sensible persons, have lost your dignity and reputation and have become a source of danger to the morals of the innocent and uncontaminated. For some persons are not straightforward, their words are full of falsity and their show of good intentions is suspicious. People can always be found capable of insulting Karolina Ivanovna, who is always irreproachable in her conduct, and an honest woman, and, what's more, a maiden lady, though no longer young—though, on the other hand, of a good foreign family—and this fact I've been asked to mention in this letter by several persons, and I speak also for myself. In any case you will learn all in due time, if you haven't learnt it yet, though you've made yourself notorious from one end of the town to the other, according to the accounts I hear from sensible people, and consequently might well have received intelligence relating to you, my dear sir, in many places. In conclusion, I beg to inform you, my dear sir, that a certain person you know, whose name I will not mention here, for certain honourable reasons, is highly respected by right-thinking people, and is, moreover, of lively and agreeable disposition, and is equally successful in the service and in the society of persons of common sense, is true in word and in friendship, and does not insult behind their back those with whom he is on friendly terms to their face.

In any case, I remain

Your obedient servant,

N. VAHRAMYEV.

P.S. You had better dismiss your man: he is a drunkard and probably gives you a great deal of trouble; you had better engage Yevstafy, who used to be in service here, and is now out of a place. Your present servant is not only a drunkard, but, what's more, he's a thief, for only last week he sold a pound of lump sugar to Karolina Ivanovna at less than cost price, which, in my opinion, he could not have done otherwise than by robbing you in a very sly way, little by little, at different times. I write this to you for your own good, although some people can do nothing but insult and deceive everybody, especially persons of honesty and good nature; what is more, they slander them behind their back and misrepresent them, simply from envy, and because they can't call themselves the same.

V.

After reading Vahramyev's letter our hero remained for a long time sitting motionless on his sofa. A new light seemed breaking through the obscure and baffling fog which had surrounded him for the last two days. Our hero seemed to reach a partial understanding. . . . He tried to get up from the sofa to take a turn about the room, to rouse himself, to collect his scattered ideas, to fix them upon a certain subject and then to set himself to rights a little, to think over his position thoroughly. But as soon as he tried to stand up he fell back again at once, weak and helpless. "Yes, of course, I had a presentiment of all that; how he writes though, and what is the real meaning of his words? Supposing I do understand the meaning; but what is it leading to? He should have said straight out: this and that is wanted, and I would have done it. Things have taken such a turn, things have come to such an unpleasant pass! Oh, if only tomorrow would make haste and come, and I could make haste and get to work! I know now what to do. I shall say this and that, I shall agree with his arguments, I won't sell my honour, but . . . maybe; but he, that person we know of, that disagreeable person, how does he come to be mixed up in it? And why has he turned up here? Oh, if tomorrow would make haste and come! They'll slander me before then, they are intriguing, they are working to spite me! The great thing is not to lose time, and now, for instance, to write a letter, and to say this and that and that I agree to this and that. And as soon as it is daylight tomorrow send it off, before he can do anything . . . and so checkmate them, get in before them, the darlings. . . . They will ruin me by their slanders, and that's the fact of the matter!"

Mr. Golyadkin drew the paper to him, took up a pen and wrote the following missive in answer to the secretary's letter—

DEAR SIR NESTOR IGNATYEVITCH!

With amazement mingled with heartfelt distress I have perused your insulting letter to me, for I see clearly that you are referring to me when you speak of certain discreditable persons and false friends. I see with genuine sorrow how rapidly the calumny has spread and how deeply it has taken root, to the detriment of my prosperity, my honour and my good name. And this is the more distressing and mortifying that even honest people of a genuinely noble way of thinking and, what is even more important, of straight-forward and open dispositions, abandon the interests of honourable men and with all the qualities of their hearts attach themselves to the pernicious corruption, which in our difficult and immoral age has unhappily increased and multiplied so greatly and so disloyally. In conclusion, I will say that the debt of two roubles of which you remind me I regard as a sacred duty to return to you in its entirety.

As for your hints concerning a certain person of the female sex, concerning the intentions, calculations and various designs of that person, I can only tell you, sir, that I have but a very dim and obscure understanding of those insinuations. Permit me, sir, to preserve my honourable way of thinking and my good name undefiled, in any case. I am ready to stoop to an explanation in person, preferring a personal interview to a written explanation as more secure, and I am, moreover, ready to enter into conciliatory proposal on mutual terms, of course. To that end, I beg you, my dear sir, to convey to that person my readiness for a personal arrangement and, what is more, to beg her to fix the time and place of the interview. It grieved me, sir, to read your hints of my having insulted you, having been treacherous to our original friendship and having spoken ill of you. I ascribe this misunderstanding to the abominable calumny, envy and ill will of those whom I may justly stigmatize as my bitterest foes. But I suppose they do not know that innocence is strong through its very innocence, that the shamelessness, the insolence and the revolting familiarity of some persons sooner or later gains the stigma of universal contempt; and that such persons come to ruin through nothing but their own worthlessness and the corruption of their own hearts. In conclusion, I beg you, sir, to convey to those per-

sons that their strange pretensions and their dishonourable and
fantastic desire to squeeze others out of the position which those
others occupy by their very existence in this world, and to take
their place, are deserving of contempt, amazement, compassion
and, what is more, the madhouse; moreover, such efforts are severely prohibited by law, which, in my opinion, is perfectly just,
for every one ought to be satisfied with his own position. Every
one has his fixed position, and if this is a joke, it is a joke in very
bad taste. I will say more: it is utterly immoral, for, I make bold
to assure you, sir, my own views which I have expounded above,
in regard to keeping *one's own place,* are purely moral.

In any case, I have the honour to remain
Your humble servant,
Y. GOLYADKIN.

CHAPTER 10

Altogether, we may say, the adventures of the previous day had
thoroughly unnerved Mr. Golyadkin. Our hero passed a very bad
night; that is, he did not get thoroughly off to sleep for five minutes:
as though some practical joker had scattered bristles in his bed. He
spent the whole night in a sort of half-sleeping state, tossing from
side to side, from right to left, moaning and groaning, dozing off for
a moment, waking up again a minute later, and all was accompanied
by a strange misery, vague memories, hideous visions—in fact, everything disagreeable that can be imagined. . . .

At one moment the figure of Andrey Filippovitch appeared
before him in a strange, mysterious half-light. It was a frigid, wrath-
ful figure, with a cold, harsh eye and with stiffly polite words of
blame on its lips . . . and as soon as Mr. Golyadkin began going up
to Andrey Filippovitch to defend himself in some way and to prove
to him that he was not at all such as his enemies represented him,
that he was like this and like that, that he even possessed innate
virtues of his own, superior to the average—at once a person only

too well known for his discreditable behaviour appeared on the
scene, and by some most revolting means instantly frustrated poor
Mr. Golyadkin's efforts, on the spot, almost before the latter's eyes,
blackened his reputation, trampled his dignity in the mud, and then
immediately took possession of his place in the service and in society.

At another time Mr. Golyadkin's head felt sore from some sort
of slight blow of late conferred and humbly accepted, received
either in the course of daily life or somehow in the performance of
his duty, against which blow it was difficult to protest. . . . And while
Mr. Golyadkin was racking his brains over the question why it was
so difficult to protest even against such a blow, this idea of a blow
gradually melted away into a different form—into the form of some
familiar, trifling or rather important piece of nastiness which he had
seen, heard or even himself committed—and frequently committed,
indeed, and not on nasty grounds, not from any nasty impulse, even,
but just because it happened—sometimes, for instance, out of delicacy, another time owing to his absolute defencelessness—in fact,
because . . . because, in fact, Mr. Golyadkin knew perfectly well
because of what! At this point Mr. Golyadkin blushed in his sleep,
and, smothering his blushes, muttered to himself that in this case he
ought to be able to show the strength of his character, he ought to be
able to show in this case the remarkable strength of his character,
and then wound up by asking himself, "What, after all, is strength
of character? Why understand it now? . . ."

But what irritated and enraged Mr. Golyadkin most of all was
that invariably, at such a moment, a person well known for his undignified burlesque behaviour turned up uninvited, and, regardless
of the fact that the matter was apparently settled, he, too, would
begin muttering, with an unseemly little smile, "What's the use of
strength of character! How could you and I, Yakov Petrovitch, have
strength of character? . . ."

Then Mr. Golyadkin would dream that he was in the company
of a number of persons distinguished for their wit and good breeding;
that he, Mr. Golyadkin, too, was conspicuous for his wit and politeness, that everybody liked him, even some of his enemies who were
present began to like him, which was very agreeable to Mr. Golyadkin; that every one gave him precedence, and that at last Mr. Golyadkin himself, with gratification, overheard the host, drawing one

of the guests aside, speak in his, Mr. Golyadkin's, praise . . . and all
of a sudden, apropos of nothing, there appeared again a person,
notorious for his treachery and brutal impulses, in the form of Mr.
Golyadkin junior, and on the spot, at once, by his very appearance
on the scene, Mr. Golyadkin junior destroyed the whole triumph and
glory of Mr. Golyadkin senior, eclipsed Mr. Golyadkin senior, trampled him in the mud, and, at last, proved clearly that Golyadkin
senior—that is, the genuine one—was not the genuine one at all but
the sham, and that he, Golyadkin junior, was the real one; that, in
fact, Mr. Golyadkin senior was not at all what he appeared to be,
but something very disgraceful, and that, consequently, he had no
right to mix in the society of honourable and well-bred people. And
all this was done so quickly that Mr. Golyadkin had not time to
open his mouth before all of them were subjugated, body and soul,
by the wicked, sham Mr. Golyadkin, and with profound contempt
rejected him, the real and innocent Mr. Golyadkin. There was not
one person left whose opinion the infamous Mr. Golyadkin would
not have changed round. There was not left one person, even the
most insignificant of the company, to whom the false and worthless
Mr. Golyadkin would not make up in his blandest manner, upon
whom he would not fawn in his own way, before whom he would
not burn sweet and agreeable incense, so that the flattered person
simply sniffed and sneezed till the tears came in token of the
intensest pleasure.

And the worst of it was that all this was done in a flash: the
swiftness of movement of the false and worthless Mr. Golyadkin was
marvellous! He scarcely had time, for instance, to make up to one
person and win his good graces—and before one could wink an eye
he was at another. He stealthily fawns on another, drops a smile of
benevolence, twirls on his short, round, though rather wooden-
looking leg, and already he's at a third, and is cringing upon a third,
he's making up to him in a friendly way; before one has time to
open one's mouth, before one has time to feel surprised, he's at a
fourth, at the same manoeuvres with him—it was horrible; sorcery
and nothing else! And every one was pleased with him, and everybody liked him, and every one was exalting him, and all were pro-
claiming in chorus that his politeness and sarcastic wit were infinitely superior to the politeness and sarcastic wit of the real Mr.

Golyadkin and putting the real and innocent Mr. Golyadkin to shame thereby and rejecting the veritable Mr. Golyadkin, and shoving and pushing out the loyal Mr. Golyadkin, and showering blows on the man so well known for his love towards his fellow-creatures! . . .

In misery, in terror and in fury, the cruelly treated Mr. Golyadkin ran out into the street and began trying to take a cab in order to drive straight to his Excellency's, or, at any rate, to Andrey Filippovitch's, but—horror! the cabman absolutely refused to take Mr. Golyadkin, saying, "We cannot drive two gentlemen exactly alike, sir; a good man tries to live honestly, your honour, and never has a double." Overcome with shame, the unimpeachable, honest Mr. Golyadkin looked round and did, in fact, assure himself with his own eyes that the cabman and Petrushka, who had joined them, were all quite right, for the depraved Mr. Golyadkin was actually on the spot, beside him, close at hand, and with his characteristic nastiness was again, at this critical moment, certainly preparing to do something very unseemly, and quite out of keeping with that gentlemanliness of character which is usually acquired by good breeding—that gentlemanliness of which the loathsome Mr. Golyadkin the second was always boasting on every opportunity. Beside himself with shame and despair, the utterly ruined though perfectly just Mr. Golyadkin dashed headlong away, wherever fate might lead him; but with every step he took, with every thud of his foot on the granite of the pavement, there leapt up as though out of the earth a Mr. Golyadkin precisely the same, perfectly alike, and of a revolting depravity of heart. And all these precisely similar Golyadkins set to running after one another as soon as they appeared, and stretched in a long chain like a file of geese, hobbling after the real Mr. Golyadkin, so there was nowhere to escape from these duplicates—so that Mr. Golyadkin, who was in every way deserving of compassion, was breathless with terror; so that at last a terrible multitude of duplicates had sprung into being; so that the whole town was obstructed at last by duplicate Golyadkins, and the police officer, seeing such a breach of decorum, was obliged to seize all these duplicates by the collar and to put them into the watchhouse, which happened to be beside him. . . . Numb and chill with horror, our hero woke up, and numb and chill with horror felt that his waking state was hardly more cheerful. . . . It was oppressive and harrowing. . . . He was overcome by such anguish that it seemed as though some one were gnawing at his heart.

At last Mr. Golyadkin could endure it no longer. "This shall not be!" he cried, resolutely sitting up in bed, and after this exclamation he felt fully awake.

It seemed as though it were rather late in the day. It was unusually light in the room. The sunshine filtered through the frozen panes and flooded the room with light, which surprised Mr. Golyadkin not a little and, so far as Mr. Golyadkin could remember, at least, there had scarcely ever been such exceptions in the course of the heavenly luminary before. Our hero had hardly time to wonder at this when he heard the clock buzzing behind the partition as though it were just on the point of striking. "Now," thought Mr. Golyadkin, and he prepared to listen with painful suspense. . . .

But to complete Mr. Golyadkin's astonishment, the clock whirred and only struck once.

"What does this mean?" cried our hero, finally leaping out of bed. And, unable to believe his ears, he rushed behind the screen just as he was. It actually was one o'clock. Mr. Golyadkin glanced at Petrushka's bed; but the room did not even smell of Petrushka: his bed had long been made and left, his boots were nowhere to be seen either—an unmistakable sign that Petrushka was not in the house. Mr. Golyadkin rushed to the door: the door was locked. "But where is he, where is Petrushka?" he went on in a whisper, conscious of intense excitement and feeling a perceptible tremor run all over him . . . Suddenly, a thought floated into his mind . . . Mr. Golyadkin rushed to the table, looked all over it, felt all round— yes, it was true, his letter of the night before to Vahramyev was not there. Petrushka was nowhere behind the screen either, the clock had just struck one, and some new points were evident to him in Vahramyev's letter, points that were obscure at first sight though now they were fully explained. Petrushka had evidently been bribed at last! "Yes, yes, that was so!"

"So this was how the chief plot was hatched!" cried Mr. Golyadkin, slapping himself on the forehead, opening his eyes wider and wider; "so in the filthy German woman's den the whole power of evil lies hidden now! So she was only making a strategic diversion in directing me to the Ismailovsky Bridge—she was putting me off the scent, confusing me (the worthless witch), and in that way laying her mines! Yes, that is so! If one only looks at the thing from that point of view, all of this is bound to be so, and the scoundrel's appearance on the scene is fully explained: it's all part and parcel of the same thing. They've kept him in reserve a long while, they had him in readiness for the evil day. This is how it has all turned out! This is what it has come to. But there, never mind. No time has been lost so far."

At this point Mr. Golyadkin recollected with horror that it was past one in the afternoon. "What if they have succeeded by now? . . ." He uttered a moan. . . . "But, no, they are lying, they've not had time—we shall see. . . ."

He dressed after a fashion, seized paper and a pen, and scribbled the following missive—

DEAR SIR YAKOV PETROVITCH!

Either you or I, but both together is out of the question! And so I must inform you that your strange, absurd, and at the same time impossible desire to appear to be my twin and to give yourself out as such serves no other purpose than to bring about your complete disgrace and discomfiture. And so I beg you, for the sake of your own advantage, to step aside and make way for really honourable men of loyal aims. In the opposite case I am ready to determine upon extreme measures. I lay down my pen and wait . . . However, I remain ready to oblige or to meet you with pistols.

Y. GOLYADKIN.

Our hero rubbed his hands energetically when he had finished the letter. Then, pulling on his greatcoat and putting on his hat, he unlocked his flat with a spare key and set off for the department. He reached the office but could not make up his mind to go in—it was by now too late. It was half-past two by Mr. Golyadkin's watch. All at once a circumstance of apparently little importance settled some doubts in Mr. Golyadkin's mind: a flushed and breathless figure suddenly made its appearance from behind the screen of the department building and with a stealthy movement like a rat he darted up the steps and into the entry. It was a copying clerk called Ostafyev, a man Mr. Golyadkin knew very well, who was rather useful and ready to do anything for a trifle. Knowing Ostafyev's weak spot and surmising that after his brief, unavoidable absence he would probably be greedier than ever for tips, our hero made up his mind not to be sparing of them, and immediately darted up the steps, and then into the entry after him, called to him and, with a mysterious air, drew him aside into a convenient corner behind a huge iron stove. And having led him there, our hero began questioning him.

"Well, my dear fellow, how are things going in there . . . you understand me?" . . .

"Yes, your honour, I wish you good health, your honour."

"All right, my good man, all right; but I'll reward you, my good fellow. Well, you see, how are things?"

"What is your honour asking?" At this point Ostafyev held his hand as though by accident before his open mouth.

"You see, my dear fellow, this is how it is . . . but don't you imagine . . . Come, is Andrey Filippovitch here? . . ."

"Yes, he is here."

"And are the clerks here?"

"Yes, sir, they are here as usual."

"And his Excellency, too?"

"And his Excellency, too." Here the man held his hand before his open mouth again and looked rather curiously and strangely at Mr. Golyadkin, so at least our hero fancied.

"And there's nothing special there, my good man?"

"No, sir, certainly not, sir."

"So there's nothing concerning me, my friend. Is there nothing going on there—that is, nothing more than . . . eh? nothing more, you understand, my friend?"

"No, sir, I've heard nothing so far, sir." Again the man put his hand before his mouth and again looked rather strangely at Mr. Golyadkin. The fact was, Mr. Golyadkin was trying to read Ostafyev's countenance, trying to discover whether there was not something hidden in it. And, in fact, he did look as though he were hiding something: Ostafyev seemed to grow colder and more churlish, and did not enter into Mr. Golyadkin's interests with the same sympathy as at the beginning of the conversation. "He is to some extent justi-

fied," thought Mr. Golyadkin. "After all, what am I to him? Perhaps
he has already been bribed by the other side, and that's why he has
just been absent. But, here, I'll try him. . . ." Mr. Golyadkin realized
that the moment for kopecks had arrived.

"Here, my dear fellow. . . ."

"I'm feelingly grateful for your honour's kindness."

"I'll give you more than that."

"Yes, your honour."

"I'll give you some more directly, and when the business is over,
I'll give you as much again. Do you understand?"

The clerk did not speak. He stood at attention and stared fixedly
at Mr. Golyadkin.

"Come, tell me now: have you heard nothing about me? . . ."

"I think, so far, I have not . . . so to say . . . nothing so far."
Ostafyev, like Mr. Golyadkin, spoke deliberately and preserved a
mysterious air, moving his eyebrows a little, looking at the ground,
trying to fall into the suitable tone, and, in fact, doing his very
utmost to earn what had been promised him, for what he had received
already he reckoned as already earned.

"And you know nothing?"

"So far, nothing, sir."

"Listen . . . you know . . . maybe you will know . . ."

"Later on, of course, maybe I shall know."

"It's a poor look-out," thought our hero. "Listen: here's something more, my dear fellow."

"I am truly grateful to your honour."

"Was Vahramyev here yesterday? . . ."

"Yes, sir."

"And . . . somebody else? . . . Was he? . . . Try and remember,
brother."

The man ransacked his memory for a moment, and could think
of nothing appropriate.

"No, sir, there wasn't anybody else."

"H'm!" a silence followed.

"Listen, brother, here's some more; tell me all, every detail."

"Yes, sir," Ostafyev had by now become as soft as silk; which
was just what Mr. Golyadkin needed.

"Explain to me now, my good man, what footing is he on?"

"All right, sir, a good one, sir," answered the man, gazing open-eyed at Mr. Golyadkin.

"How do you mean, all right?"

"Well, it's just like that, sir." Here Ostafyev twitched his eyebrows significantly. But he was utterly nonplussed and didn't know what more to say.

"It's a poor look-out," thought Mr. Golyadkin.

"And hasn't anything more happened . . . in there . . . about Vahramyev?"

"But everything is just as usual."

"Think a little."

"There is, they say . . ."

"Come, what?"

Ostafyev put his hand in front of his mouth.

"Wasn't there a letter . . . from here . . . to me?"

"Mihyeev the attendant went to Vahramyev's lodging, to their German landlady, so I'll go and ask him, if you like."

"Do me the favour, brother, for goodness' sake! . . . I only mean . . . you mustn't imagine anything, brother, I only mean . . . Yes, you question him, brother, find out whether they are not getting up something concerning me. Find out how he is acting. That is what I want; that is what you must find out, my dear fellow, and then I'll reward you, my good man. . . ."

"I will, your honour, and Ivan Semyonovitch sat in your place today, sir."

"Ivan Semyonovitch? Oh! really, you don't say so."

"Andrey Filippovitch told him to sit there."

"Re-al-ly! How did that happen? You must find out, brother; for God's sake find out, brother; find it all out—and I'll reward you, my dear fellow; that's what I want to know . . . and don't you imagine anything, brother. . . ."

"Just so, sir, just so; I'll go at once. And aren't you going in today, sir?"

"No, my friend; I only looked round, I only looked round, you know. I only came to have a look round, my friend, and I'll reward you afterwards, my friend."

"Yes, sir." The man ran rapidly and eagerly up the stairs and Mr. Golyadkin was left alone.

"It's a poor look-out!" he thought. "Ech, it's a bad business, a bad business! Ech! things are in a bad way with us now! What does it all mean? What did that drunkard's insinuations mean, for instance, and whose trickery was it? Ah! I know now whose it was. And what a thing this is. No doubt they found out and made him sit there. . . . But, after all, did they sit him there? It was Andrey Filippovitch sat him there, he sat Ivan Semyonovitch there himself; why did he make him sit there and with what object? Probably they found out . . . That is Vahramyev's work—that is, not Vahramyev, he is as stupid as an ashen post, Vahramyev is, and they are all at work on his behalf, and they egged that scoundrel on to come here for the same purpose, and the German woman brought up her grievance, the one-eyed hussy. I always suspected that this intrigue was not without an object and that in all this old-womanish gossip there must be something, and I said as much to Krestyan Ivanovitch, telling him they'd sworn to cut a man's throat—in a moral sense, of course—and they pounced upon Karolina Ivanovna. Yes, there are master hands at work in this, one can see! Yes, sir, there are master hands at work here, and not Vahramyev's. I've said already that Vahramyev is stupid, but . . . I know who it is behind it all, it's that rascal, that impostor! It's only that he relies upon, which is partly proved by his successes in the best society. And it would certainly be desirable to know on what footing he stands now. What is he now among them? Only, why have they taken Ivan Semyonovitch? What the devil do they want with Ivan Semyonovitch? Could not they have found any one else? Though it would come to the same thing whoever it had been, and the only thing I know is that I have suspected Ivan Semyonovitch for a long time past. I noticed long ago what a nasty, horrid old man he was—they say he lends money and takes interest like any Jew. To be sure, the bear's the leading spirit in the whole affair. One can detect the bear in the whole affair. It began in this way. It began at the Ismailovsky Bridge; that's how it began. . . ."

At this point Mr. Golyadkin frowned, as though he had taken a bite out of a lemon, probably remembering something very unpleasant.

"But, there, it doesn't matter," he thought. "I keep harping on my own troubles. What will Ostafyev find out? Most likely he is staying on or has been delayed somehow. It is a good thing, in a sense, that I am intriguing like this, and am laying mines on my side too. I've only to give Ostafyev ten kopecks and he's . . . so to speak, on my side. Only the point is, is he really on my side? Perhaps they've got him on their side too . . . and they are carrying on an intrigue by means of him on their side too. He looks a ruffian, the rascal, a regular ruffian; he's hiding something, the rogue. 'No, nothing,' says he, 'and I am deeply grateful to your honour,' says he. You ruffian, you!"

He heard a noise . . . Mr. Golyadkin shrank up and skipped behind the stove. Some one came downstairs and went out into the street. "Who could that be going away now?" our hero thought to himself. A minute later footsteps were audible again. . . . At this point Mr. Golyadkin could not resist poking the very tip of his nose out beyond his corner—he poked it out and instantly withdrew it again, as though some one had pricked it with a pin. This time some one he knew well was coming—that is, the scoundrel, the intriguer and the reprobate—he was approaching with his usual mean, tripping little step, prancing and shuffling with his feet as though he were going to kick some one.

"The rascal," said our hero to himself.

Mr. Golyadkin could not, however, help observing that the rascal had under his arm a huge green portfolio belonging to his Excellency.

"He's on a special commission again," thought Mr. Golyadkin, flushing crimson and shrinking into himself more than ever from vexation.

As soon as Mr. Golyadkin junior had slipped past Mr. Golyadkin senior without observing him in the least, footsteps were heard for the third time, and this time Mr. Golyadkin guessed that these were Ostafyev's. It was, in fact, the sleek figure of a copying clerk, Pisarenko by name. This surprised Mr. Golyadkin. Why had he mixed up other people in their secret? our hero wondered. What barbarians! Nothing is sacred to them! "Well, my friend?" he brought out, addressing Pisarenko: "who sent you, my friend? . . ."

"I've come about your business. There's no news so far from any one. But should there be any we'll let you know."

"And Ostafyev?"

"It was quite impossible for him to come, your honour. His

Excellency has walked through the room twice, and I've no time to stay."

"Thank you, my good man, thank you . . . only, tell me . . ."

"Upon my word, sir, I can't stay. . . . They are asking for us every minute . . . but if your honour will stay here, we'll let you know if anything happens concerning your little affair."

"No, my friend, you just tell me . . ."

"Excuse me, I've no time to stay, sir." said Pisarenko, tearing himself away from Mr. Golyadkin, who had clutched him by the lapel of his coat. "I really can't. If your honour will stay here, we'll let you know."

"In a minute, my good man, in a minute! In a minute, my good fellow! I tell you what, here's a letter; and I'll reward you, my good man."

"Yes, sir."

"Try and give it to Mr. Golyadkin, my dear fellow."

"Golyadkin?"

"Yes, my man, to Mr. Golyadkin."

"Very good, sir; as soon as I get off I'll take it, and you stay here, meanwhile; no one will see you here. . . ."

"No, my good man, don't imagine . . . I'm not standing here to avoid being seen. But I'm not going to stay here now, my friend. . . . I'll be close here in the side street. There's a coffee-house near here; so I'll wait there, and if anything happens, you let me know about anything, you understand?"

"Very good, sir. Only let me go; I understand."

"And I'll reward you," Mr. Golyadkin called after Pisarenko, when he had at last released him. . . .

"The rogue seemed to be getting rather rude," our hero reflected as he stealthily emerged from behind the stove. "There's some other dodge here. That's clear. . . . At first it was one thing and another . . . he really was in a hurry, though; perhaps there's a great deal to do in the office. And his Excellency had been through the room twice. . . . How did that happen? . . . Ough! never mind! It may mean nothing, perhaps; but now we shall see. . . ."

At this point Mr. Golyadkin was about to open the door, intending to go out into the street, when suddenly, at that very instant, his Excellency's carriage dashed up to the door. Before Mr. Golyadkin had time to recover from the shock, the door of the carriage was opened from within and a gentleman jumped out. This gentleman was no other than Mr. Golyadkin junior, who had only gone out ten minutes before. Mr. Golyadkin senior remembered that the Director's flat was only a couple of paces away.

"He has been out on a special commission," our hero thought to himself.

Meanwhile, Mr. Golyadkin junior took out of the carriage a thick green portfolio and other papers. Finally, giving some orders to the coachman, he opened the door, almost ran up against Mr. Golyadkin senior, purposely avoided noticing him, acting in this way expressly to annoy him, and mounted the office staircase at a rapid canter.

"It's a bad look-out," thought Mr. Golyadkin. "This is what it has come to now! Oh, good Lord! look at him."

For half a minute our hero remained motionless. At last he made up his mind. Without pausing to think, though he was aware of a violent palpitation of the heart and a tremor in all his limbs, he ran up the stairs after his enemy.

"Here goes; what does it matter to me? I have nothing to do with the case," he thought, taking off his hat, his greatcoat and his goloshes in the entry.

When Mr. Golyadkin walked into his office, it was already getting dusk. Neither Andrey Filippovitch nor Anton Antonovitch was in the room. Both of them were in the Director's room, handing in reports. The Director, so it was rumoured, was in haste to report to a still higher Excellency. In consequence of this, and also because twilight was coming on, and the office hours were almost over, several of the clerks, especially the younger ones, were, at the moment when our hero entered, enjoying a period of inactivity; gathered together in groups, they were talking, arguing, and laughing, and some of the most youthful—that is, belonging to the lowest grades in the service, had got up a game of pitch-farthing in a corner, by a window. Knowing what was proper, and feeling at the moment a special need to conciliate and get on with them, Mr. Golyadkin immediately approached those with whom he used to get on best, in order to wish them good-day, and so on. But his colleagues answered his greetings rather strangely. He was unpleasantly impressed by a certain coldness, even curtness, one might almost say severity, in their manner. No one shook hands with him. Some simply said, "Good-day" and walked away; others barely nodded; one simply turned away and pretended not to notice him; at last some of them—and what mortified Mr. Golyadkin most of all, some of the youngsters of the lowest grades, mere lads who, as Mr. Golyadkin justly observed about them, were capable of nothing but hanging about and playing pitch-farthing at every opportunity—little by little collected round Mr. Golyadkin, formed a group round him and almost barred his way. They all looked at him with a sort of insulting curiosity.

It was a bad sign. Mr. Golyadkin felt this, and very judiciously decided not to notice it. Suddenly, a quite unexpected event completely finished him off, as they say, and utterly crushed him.

At the moment most trying to Mr. Golyadkin senior, suddenly, as though by design, there appeared in the group of fellow clerks surrounding him the figure of Mr. Golyadkin junior, gay as ever, smiling a little smile as ever, nimble, too, as ever; in short, mischievous, skipping and tripping, chuckling and fawning, with sprightly tongue and sprightly toe, as always, precisely as he had been the day before at a very unpleasant moment for Mr. Golyadkin senior, for instance.

Grinning, tripping and turning with a smile that seemed to say "good-evening" to every one, he squeezed his way into the group of clerks, shaking hands with one, slapping another on the shoulder, putting his arm round another, explaining to a fourth how he had come to be employed by his Excellency, where he had been, what he had done, what he had brought with him; to the fifth, probably his most intimate friend, he gave a resounding kiss—in fact, everything happened as it had in Mr. Golyadkin's dream. When he had skipped about to his heart's content, polished them all off in his usual way, disposed them all in his favour, whether he needed them or not, when he had lavished his blandishments to the delectation of all the clerks, Mr. Golyadkin junior suddenly, and most likely by mistake, for he had not yet had time to notice his senior, held out his hand to Mr. Golyadkin senior also. Probably also by mistake—though he had had time to observe the dishonourable Mr. Golyadkin junior thoroughly, our hero at once eagerly seized the hand so unexpectedly held out to him and pressed it in the warmest and friendliest way, pressed it with a strange, quite unexpected, inner feeling, with a tearful emotion. Whether our hero was misled by the first movement of his worthless foe, or was taken unawares, or, without recognizing it, felt at the bottom of his heart how defenceless he was—it is difficult to say. The fact remains that Mr. Golyadkin senior, apparently knowing what he was doing, of his own free will, before witnesses, solemnly shook hands with him whom he called his mortal foe. But what was the amazement, the stupefaction and fury, what was the horror and the shame of Mr. Golyadkin senior, when his enemy and mortal foe, the dishonourable Mr. Golyadkin junior, noticing the mistake of that persecuted, innocent, perfidiously deceived man, without a trace of shame, of feeling, of compassion or of conscience, pulled his hand away with insufferable rudeness and insolence. What was worse, he shook the hand as though it had been polluted with something horrid; what is more, he spat aside with disgust, accompanying this with a most insulting gesture; worse still, he drew out his handkerchief and, in the most unseemly way, wiped all the fingers that had rested for one moment in the hand of Mr. Golyadkin senior. While he did this Mr. Golyadkin junior looked about him in his characteristic horrid way, took care that every one should see what he was doing, glanced into people's eyes and evidently tried to insinuate to every one everything that was most unpleasant in regard to Mr. Golyadkin senior. Mr. Golyadkin junior's revolting behaviour seemed to arouse general indignation among the clerks that surrounded them; even the frivolous youngsters showed their displeasure. A murmur of protest rose on all sides. Mr. Golyadkin could not but discern the general feeling; but suddenly—an appropriate witticism that bubbled from the lips of Mr. Golyadkin junior shattered, annihilated our hero's last hopes, and inclined the balance again in favour of his deadly and undeserving foe.

"He's our Russian Faublas, gentlemen; allow me to introduce the youthful Faublas," piped Mr. Golyadkin junior, with his characteristic insolence, pirouetting and threading his way among the clerks, and directing their attention to the petrified though genuine Mr. Golyadkin. "Let us kiss each other, darling," he went on with insufferable familiarity, addressing the man he had so treacherously insulted. Mr. Golyadkin junior's unworthy jest seemed to touch a responsive chord, for it contained an artful allusion to an incident with which all were apparently familiar. Our hero was painfully conscious of the hand of his enemies. But he had made up his mind by now. With glowing eyes, with pale face, with a fixed smile he tore himself somehow out of the crowd and with uneven, hurried steps made straight for his Excellency's private room. In the room next to the last he was met by Andrey Filippovitch, who had only just come out from seeing his Excellency, and although there were present in this room at the moment a good number of persons of whom Mr. Golyadkin knew nothing, yet our hero did not care to take such a fact into consideration. Boldly, resolutely, directly, almost wondering at himself and inwardly admiring his own courage, without loss of time he accosted Andrey Filippovitch, who was a good deal surprised by this unexpected attack.

"Ah! . . . What is it . . . what do you want?" asked the head of the division, not hearing Mr. Golyadkin's hesitating words.

"Andrey Filippovitch, may . . . might I, Andrey Filippovitch, may I have a conversation with his Excellency at once and in private?" our hero said resolutely and distinctly, fixing the most determined glance on Andrey Filippovitch.

"What next! Of course not." Andrey Filippovitch scanned Mr. Golyadkin from head to foot.

"I say all this, Andrey Filippovitch, because I am surprised that no one here unmasks the impostor and scoundrel."

"Wha-a-at!"

"Scoundrel, Andrey Filippovitch!"

"Of whom are you pleased to speak in those terms?"

"Of a certain person, Andrey Filippovitch; I'm alluding, Andrey Filippovitch, to a certain person; I have the right . . . I imagine, Andrey Filippovitch, that the authorities would surely encourage such action," added Mr. Golyadkin, evidently hardly knowing what he was saying. "Andrey Filippovitch . . . but no doubt you see yourself, Andrey Filippovitch, that this honourable action is a mark of my loyalty in every way—of my looking upon my superior as a father, Andrey Filippovitch; I, as much as to say, look upon my benevolent superior as a father and blindly trust my fate to him. It's as much as to say . . . you see . . ." At this point Mr. Golyadkin's voice trembled and two tears ran down his eyelashes.

As Andrey Filippovitch listened to Mr. Golyadkin he was so astonished that he could not help stepping back a couple of paces.

Then he looked about him uneasily. . . . It is difficult to say how the matter would have ended. But suddenly the door of his Excellency's room was opened, and he himself came out, accompanied by several officials. All the persons in his room followed in a string. His Excellency called Andrey Filippovitch and walked beside him, beginning to discuss some business details. When all had set off and gone out of the room, Mr. Golyadkin woke up. Growing calmer, he took refuge under the wing of Anton Antonovitch, who came last in the procession and who, Mr. Golyadkin fancied, looked stern and anxious. "I've been talking nonsense, I've been making a mess of it again, but there, never mind," he thought.

"I hope, at least, that you, Anton Antonovitch, will consent to listen to me and to enter into my position," he said quietly, in a voice that still trembled a little. "Rejected by all, I appeal to you. I am still at a loss to understand what Andrey Filippovitch's words mean, Anton Antonovitch. Explain them to me if you can. . . ."

"Everything will be explained in due time," Anton Antonovitch replied sternly and emphatically, and, as Mr. Golyadkin fancied, with an air that gave him plainly to understand that Anton Antonovitch did not wish to continue the conversation, "You will soon know all about it. You will be officially informed about everything today."

"What do you mean by officially informed, Anton Antonovitch? Why officially?" our hero asked timidly.

"It is not for you and me to discuss what our superiors decide upon, Yakov Petrovitch."

"Why our superiors, Anton Antonovitch?" said our hero, still more intimidated; "why our superiors? I don't see what reason there is to trouble our superiors in the matter, Anton Antonovitch. . . . Perhaps you mean to say something about yesterday's doing, Anton Antonovitch?"

"Oh no, nothing to do with yesterday; there's something else amiss with you."

"What is there amiss, Anton Antonovitch? I believe, Anton Antonovitch, that I have done nothing amiss."

"Why, you were meaning to be sly with some one," Anton Antonovitch cut in sharply, completely flabbergasting Mr. Golyadkin.

Mr. Golyadkin started, and turned as white as a pocket-handkerchief.

"Of course, Anton Antonovitch," he said, in a voice hardly

audible, "if one listens to the voice of calumny and hears one's enemies' tales, without heeding what the other side has to say in its defence, then, of course . . . then, of course, Anton Antonovitch, one must suffer innocently and for nothing."

"To be sure; but your unseemly conduct, in injuring the reputation of a virtuous young lady belonging to that benevolent, highly distinguished and well-known family who had befriended you . . ."

"What conduct do you mean, Anton Antonovitch?"

"What I say. Do you know anything about your praiseworthy conduct in regard to that other young lady who, though poor, is of honourable foreign extraction?"

"Allow me, Anton Antonovitch . . . if you would kindly listen to me, Anton Antonovitch . . ."

"And your treacherous behaviour and slander of another person, your charging another person with your own sins. Ah, what do you call that?"

"I did not send him away, Anton Antonovitch," said our hero, with a tremor; "and I've never instructed Petrushka, my man, to do anything of the sort. . . . He has eaten my bread, Anton Antonovitch, he has taken advantage of my hospitality," our hero added expressively and with deep emotion, so much so that his chin twitched a little and tears were ready to start again.

"That is only your talk, that he has eaten your bread," answered Anton Antonovitch, somewhat offended, and there was a perfidious note in his voice which sent a pang to Mr. Golyadkin's heart.

"Allow me most humbly to ask you again, Anton Antonovitch, is his Excellency aware of all this business?"

"Upon my word, you must let me go now, though. I've no time for you now. . . . You'll know everything you need to know today."

"Allow me, for God's sake, one minute, Anton Antonovitch."

"Tell me afterwards. . . ."

"No, Anton Antonovitch; I . . . you see, Anton Antonovitch . . . only listen . . . I am not one for free-thinking, Anton Antonovitch; I shun free-thinking; I am quite ready for my part . . . and, indeed, I've given up that idea. . . ."

"Very good, very good. I've heard that already."

"No, you have not heard it, Anton Antonovitch. It is something else, Anton Antonovitch; it's a good thing, really, a good thing and pleasant to hear. . . . As I've explained to you, Anton Antonovitch, I admit that idea, that divine Providence has created two men exactly alike, and that a benevolent government, seeing the hand of Providence, provided a berth for two twins. That is a good thing, Anton Antonovitch. You see that it is a very good thing, Anton Antonovitch, and that I am very far from free-thinking. I look upon my benevolent government as a father; I say 'yes,' by all means; you are benevolent authorities, and you, of course . . . A young man must be in the service. . . . Stand up for me, Anton Antonovitch, take my part, Anton Antonovitch. . . . I am all right . . . Anton Antonovitch, for God's sake, one little word more . . . Anton Antonovitch. . . ."

But by now Anton Antonovitch was far away from Mr. Golyadkin. . . . Our hero was so bewildered and overcome by all that had happened and all that he had heard that he did not know where he was standing, what he had heard, what he had done, what was being done to him, and what was going to be done to him.

With imploring eyes he sought for Anton Antonovitch in the crowd of clerks, that he might justify himself further in his eyes and say something to him extremely high-toned and very agreeable, and creditable to himself. . . . By degrees, however, a new light began to break upon our hero's bewildered mind, a new and awful light that revealed at once a whole perspective of hitherto unknown and utterly unsuspected circumstances. . . . At that moment somebody gave our bewildered hero a poke in the ribs. He looked around. Pisarenko was standing before him.

"A letter, your honour."

"Ah, you've been out already, then, my good man?"

"No, it was brought at ten o'clock this morning. Sergey Mihyeev, the attendant, brought it from Mr. Vahramyev's lodging."

"Very good, very good, and I'll reward you now, my dear fellow."

Saying this, Mr. Golyadkin thrust the letter in the side pocket of his uniform and buttoned up every button of it; then he looked round him, and to his surprise, found that he was by now in the hall of the department, in a group of clerks crowding at the outer door, for office hours were over. Mr. Golyadkin had not only failed till that moment to observe this circumstance, but had no notion how he suddenly came to be wearing his greatcoat and goloshes and to be holding his hat in his hand. All the clerks were standing motionless, in reverential expectation. The fact was that his Excellency was standing at the bottom of the stairs waiting for his carriage, which was for some reason late in arriving, and was carrying on a very interesting conversation with Andrey Filippovitch and two councillors. At a little distance from Andrey Filippovitch stood Anton Antonovitch and several other clerks, who were all smiles, seeing that his Excellency was graciously making a joke. The clerks who were crowded at the top of the stairs were smiling too, in expectation of his Excellency's laughing again. The only one who was not smiling was Fedosyevitch, the corpulent hall porter, who stood stiffly at attention, holding the handle of the door, waiting impatiently for the daily gratification that fell to his share— that is, the task of flinging one half of the door wide open with a swing of his arm, and then, with a low bow, reverentially making way for his Excellency to pass. But the one who seemed to be more de-lighted than any and to feel the most satisfaction of all was the worthless and ungentlemanly enemy of Mr. Golyadkin. At that instant he positively forgot all the clerks, and even gave up tripping and pirouetting in his usual odious way; he even forgot to make up to anybody. He was all eyes and ears, he even doubled himself up strangely, no doubt in the strained effort to hear, and never took his eyes off his Excellency, and only from time to time his arms, legs and head twitched with faintly perceptible tremors that be-trayed the secret emotions of his soul.

"Ah, isn't he in a state!" thought our hero. "He looks like a favourite, the rascal! I should like to know how it is that he deceives society of every class. He has neither brains nor character, neither education nor feeling; he's a lucky rogue! Mercy on us! How can a man, when you think of it, come and make friends with every one so quickly! And he'll get on, I swear the fellow will get on, the rogue will make his way—he's a lucky rascal! I should like to know, too, what he keeps whispering to every one—what plots he is hatch-ing with all these people, and what secrets they are talking about. Lord, have mercy on us! If only I could . . . get on with them a little too . . . say this and that and the other. Hadn't I better ask him . . . tell him I won't do it again; say 'I'm in fault, and a young man must serve nowadays, your Excellency'? I am not in the least abashed by my obscure position—so there! I am not going to protest in any way, either; I shall bear it all with meekness and patience, so there! Is that the way to behave? . . . Though you'll never see through him, though, the rascal; you can't reach him with anything you say; you can't hammer reason into his head. . . . We'll make an effort, though. I may happen to hit on a good moment, so I'll make an effort. . . ."

Feeling in his uneasiness, his misery and his bewilderment that he couldn't leave things like this, that the critical moment had come, that he must explain himself to some one, our hero began to move a little towards the place where his worthless and undeserving enemy stood: but at that very moment his Excellency's long-expected carriage rolled up into the entrance, Fedosyevitch flung open the door and, bending double, let his Excellency pass out. All the waiting clerks streamed out towards the door, and for a moment separated Mr. Golyadkin senior from Mr. Golyadkin junior.

"You shan't get away!" said our hero, forcing his way through the crowd while he kept his eyes fixed on the man he wanted. At last the crowd dispersed. Our hero felt he was free and flew in pursuit of his enemy.

CHAPTER 11

Mr. Golyadkin's breath failed him; he flew as though on wings after his rapidly retreating enemy. He was conscious of immense energy. Yet in spite of this terrible energy he might confidently have said that at that moment a humble gnat—had a gnat been able to exist in Petersburg at that time of the year—could very easily have knocked him down. He felt, too, that he was utterly weak again, that he was carried along by a peculiar outside force, that it was not he himself who was running, but, on the contrary, that his legs were giving way under him, and refused to obey him. This all might turn out for the best, however.

"Whether it is for the best or not for the best," thought Mr. Golyadkin, almost breathless from running so quickly, "but that the game is lost there cannot be the slightest doubt now; that I am utterly done for is certain, definite, signed and ratified."

In spite of all this our hero felt as though he had risen from the dead, as though he had withstood a battalion, as though he had won a victory when he succeeded in clutching the overcoat of his enemy, who had already raised one foot to get into the cab he had engaged.

"My dear sir! My dear sir!" he shouted to the infamous Mr. Golyadkin junior, holding him by the button. "My dear sir, I hope that you . . ."

"No, please do not hope for anything," Mr. Golyadkin's heartless enemy answered evasively, standing with one foot on the step of the cab and vainly waving the other leg in the air, in his efforts to get in, trying to preserve his equilibrium, and at the same time trying with all his might to wrench his coat away from Mr. Golyadkin senior, while the latter held on to it with all the strength that had been vouchsafed to him by nature.

"Yakov Petrovitch, only ten minutes . . ."

"Excuse me, I've no time . . ."

"You must admit, Yakov Petrovitch . . . please, Yakov Petrovitch. . . . For God's sake, Yakov Petrovitch . . . let us have it out— in a straightforward way . . . one little second, Yakov Petrovitch . . ."

"My dear fellow, I can't stay," answered Mr. Golyadkin's dishonourable enemy, with uncivil familiarity, disguised as good-natured heartiness; "another time, believe me, with my whole soul and all my heart; but now I really can't . . ."

"Scoundrel!" thought our hero. "Yakov Petrovitch," he cried miserably. "I have never been your enemy. Spiteful people have described me unjustly. . . . I am ready, on my side . . . Yakov Petrovitch, shall we go in here together, at once, Yakov Petrovitch? And with all my heart, as you have so justly expressed it just now, and in straightforward, honourable language, as you have expressed it just now—here into this coffee-house; there the facts will explain themselves: they will really, Yakov Petrovitch. Then everything will certainly explain itself. . . ."

"Into the coffee-house? Very good. I am not against it. Let us go into the coffee-house on one condition only, my dear, on one condition—that these things shall be cleared up. We will have it all out, darling," said Mr. Golyadkin junior, getting out of the cab and shamelessly slapping our hero on the shoulder. "You friend of my heart, for your sake, Yakov Petrovitch, I am ready to go by the back street (as you were pleased to observe so aptly on one occasion, Yakov Petrovitch). Why, what a rogue he is! Upon my word, he does just what he likes with one!" Mr. Golyadkin's false friend went on, fawning upon him and cajoling him with a little smile. The coffee-house which the two Mr. Golyadkins entered stood some distance away from the main street and was at the moment quite empty. A rather stout German woman made her appearance behind the counter. Mr. Golyadkin and his unworthy enemy went into the second room, where a puffy-looking boy with a closely shaven head was busy with a bundle of chips at the stove, trying to revive the smouldering fire. At Mr. Golyadkin junior's request chocolate was served.

"And a sweet little lady-tart," said Mr. Golyadkin junior, with a sly wink at Mr. Golyadkin senior.

Our hero blushed and was silent.

"Oh, yes, I forgot, I beg your pardon. I know your taste. We are sweet on charming little Germans, sir; you and I are sweet on charming and agreeable little Germans, aren't we, you upright soul? We take their lodgings, we seduce their morals, they win our hearts with their beer-soup and their milk-soup, and we give them notes of different sorts, that's what we do, you Faublas, you deceiver!" All this Mr. Golyadkin junior said, making an unworthy though villainously artful allusion to a certain personage of the female sex, while he fawned upon our hero, smiled at him with an amiable air, with a deceitful show of being delighted with him and pleased to have met him. Seeing that Mr. Golyadkin senior was by no means so stupid and deficient in breeding and the manners of good society as to believe in him, the infamous man resolved to change his tactics and to make a more open attack upon him. After uttering his disgusting speech, the false Mr. Golyadkin ended by slapping the real and substantial Mr. Golyadkin on the shoulder, with a revolting effrontery and familiarity. Not content with that, he began playing pranks utterly unfit for well-bred society; he took it into his head to repeat his old, nauseous trick—that is, regardless of the resistance and faint cries of the indignant Mr. Golyadkin senior, he pinched the latter on the cheek. At the spectacle of such depravity our hero boiled within, but was silent . . . only for the time, however.

"That is the talk of my enemies," he answered at last, in a trembling voice, prudently restraining himself. At the same time our hero looked round uneasily towards the door. The fact was that Mr. Golyadkin junior seemed in excellent spirits, and ready for all sorts of little jokes, unseemly in a public place, and, speaking generally, not permissible by the laws of good manners, especially in well-bred society.

"Oh, well, in that case, as you please," Mr. Golyadkin junior gravely responded to our hero's thought, setting down upon the table the empty cup which he had gulped down with unseemly greed. "Well, there's no need for me to stay long with you, however. . . . Well, how are you getting on now, Yakov Petrovitch?"

"There's only one thing I can tell you, Yakov Petrovitch," our hero answered, with sangfroid and dignity; "I've never been your enemy."

"H'm. . . . Oh, what about Petrushka? Petrushka is his name, I fancy? Yes, it is Petrushka! Well, how is he? Well? The same as ever?"

"He's the same as ever, too, Yakov Petrovitch," answered Mr. Golyadkin senior, somewhat amazed. "I don't know, Yakov Petrovitch . . . from my standpoint . . . from a candid, honourable standpoint, Yakov Petrovitch, you must admit, Yakov Petrovitch . . ."

"Yes, but you know yourself, Yakov Petrovitch," Mr. Golyadkin junior answered in a soft and expressive voice, so posing falsely as a sorrowful man overcome with remorse and deserving compassion. "You know yourself we live in difficult times. . . . I appeal to you, Yakov Petrovitch; you are an intelligent man and your reflections are just," Mr. Golyadkin junior said in conclusion, flattering Mr. Golyadkin senior in an abject way. "Life is not a game, you know yourself, Yakov Petrovitch," Mr. Golyadkin junior added, with vast significance, assuming the character of a clever and learned man, who is capable of passing judgments on lofty subjects.

"For my part, Yakov Petrovitch," our hero answered warmly, "for my part, scorning to be roundabout and speaking boldly and openly, using straightforward, honourable language and putting the whole matter on an honourable basis, I tell you I can openly and honourably assert, Yakov Petrovitch, that I am absolutely pure, and that, you know it yourself, Yakov Petrovitch, the error is mutual— it may all be the world's judgment, the opinion of the slavish crowd. . . . I speak openly, Yakov Petrovitch, everything is possible. I will say, too, Yakov Petrovitch, if you judge it in this way, if you look at the matter from a lofty, noble point of view, then I will boldly say, without false shame I will say, Yakov Petrovitch, it will positively be a pleasure to me to discover that I have been in error, it will positively be a pleasure to me to recognize it. You know yourself you are an intelligent man and, what is more, you are a gentleman. Without shame, without false shame, I am ready to recognize it," he wound up with dignity and nobility.

"It is the decree of destiny, Yakov Petrovitch . . . but let us drop all this," said Mr. Golyadkin junior. "Let us rather use the brief moment of our meeting for a more pleasant and profitable conversation, as is only suitable between two colleagues in the service. . . . Really, I have not succeeded in saying two words to you all this time. . . . I am not to blame for that Yakov Petrovitch. . . ."

"Nor I," answered our hero warmly, "nor I, either! My heart tells me, Yakov Petrovitch, that I'm not to blame in all this matter. Let us blame fate for all this, Yakov Petrovitch," added Mr. Golyadkin senior, in a quick, conciliatory tone of voice. His voice began little by little to soften and to quaver.

"Well! How are you in health?" said the sinner in a sweet voice.

"I have a little cough," answered our hero, even more sweetly.

"Take care of yourself. There is so much illness going about, you may easily get quinsy; for my part I confess I've begun to wrap myself up in flannel."

"One may, indeed, Yakov Petrovitch, very easily get quinsy," our hero pronounced after a brief silence; "Yakov Petrovitch, I see that I have made a mistake, I remember with softened feelings those happy moments which we were so fortunate as to spend together, under my poor, though I venture to say, hospitable roof . . ."

"In your letter, however, you wrote something very different," said Mr. Golyadkin junior reproachfully, speaking on this occasion —though only on this occasion—quite justly.

"Yakov Petrovitch, I was in error. . . . I see clearly now that I was in error in my unhappy letter too. Yakov Petrovitch, I am ashamed to look at you, Yakov Petrovitch, you wouldn't believe . . . Give me that letter that I may tear it to pieces before your eyes, Yakov Petrovitch, and if that is utterly impossible, I entreat you to read it the other way before—precisely the other way before—that is, expressly with a friendly intention, giving the opposite sense to the whole letter. I was in error. Forgive me, Yakov Petrovitch, I was quite . . . I was grievously in error, Yakov Petrovitch."

"You say so?" Mr. Golyadkin's perfidious friend inquired, rather casually and indifferently.

"I say that I was quite in error, Yakov Petrovitch, and that for my part, quite without false shame, I am . . ."

"Ah, well, that's all right! That's a nice thing your being in error," answered Mr. Golyadkin junior.

"I even had an idea, Yakov Petrovitch," our candid hero answered in a gentlemanly way, completely failing to observe the horrible perfidy of his deceitful enemy, "I even had an idea that here were two people created exactly alike. . . ."

"Ah, is that your idea?"

At this point the notoriously worthless Mr. Golyadkin took up his hat. Still failing to observe his treachery, Mr. Golyadkin senior, too, got up and with a noble, simple-hearted smile to his false friend, tried in his innocence to be friendly to him, to encourage him, and in that way to form a new friendship with him.

"Good-bye, your Excellency," Mr. Golyadkin junior called out suddenly. Our hero started, noticing in his enemy's face something positively Bacchanalian, and, solely to get rid of him, put two fingers into the unprincipled man's outstretched hand; but then . . . then his enemy's shamelessness passed all bounds. Seizing the two fingers of Mr. Golyadkin's hand and at first pressing them, the worthless fellow on the spot, before Mr. Golyadkin's eyes, had the effrontery to repeat the shameful joke of the afternoon. The limit of human patience was exhausted.

He had just hidden in his pocket the handkerchief with which he had wiped his fingers when Mr. Golyadkin senior recovered from the shock and dashed after him into the next room, into which his irreconcilable foe had in his usual hasty way hastened to decamp. As though perfectly innocent, he was standing at the counter eating pies, and with perfect composure, like a virtuous man, was making polite remarks to the German woman behind the counter.

"I can't go into it before ladies," thought our hero, and he, too, went up to the counter, so agitated that he hardly knew what he was doing.

"The tart is certainly not bad! What do you think?" Mr. Golyadkin junior began upon his unseemly sallies again, reckoning, no doubt, upon Mr. Golyadkin's infinite patience. The stout German, for her part, looked at both her visitors with pewtery, vacant-looking eyes, smiling affably and evidently not understanding Russian. Our hero flushed red as fire at the words of the unabashed Mr. Golyadkin junior, and, unable to control himself, rushed at him with the evident intention of tearing him to pieces and finishing him off completely, but Mr. Golyadkin junior, in his usual mean way, was already far off; he took flight, he was already on the steps. It need hardly be said that, after the first moment of stupefaction with which Mr. Golyadkin senior was naturally overcome, he recovered himself and went at full speed after his insulting enemy, who had already got into a cab, whose driver was obviously in collusion with him. But at that very instant the stout German, seeing both her customers make off, shrieked and rang her bell with all her might. Our hero was on the point of flight, but he turned back, and, without asking for change, flung her money for himself and for the shameless man who had left without paying, and although thus delayed, he succeeded in catching up with his enemy. Hanging on to the side of the cab with all the force bestowed on him by nature, our hero was carried for some time along the street, clambering upon the vehicle, while Mr. Golyadkin junior did his utmost to dislodge him. Meanwhile the cabman, with whip, with reins, with kicks and with shouts urged on his exhausted nag, who quite unexpectedly dropped into a gallop, biting at the bit, and kicking with his hind legs in a horrid way. At last our hero succeeded in climbing into the cab, facing his enemy and with his back to the driver, his knees touching the knees and his right hand clutching the very shabby fur collar of his depraved and exasperated foe.

The enemies were borne along for some time in silence. Our hero could scarcely breathe. It was a bad road and he was jolted at every step and in peril of breaking his neck. Moreover, his exasperated foe still refused to acknowledge himself vanquished and was trying to shove him off into the mud. To complete the unpleasantness of his position the weather was detestable. The snow was falling in heavy flakes and doing its utmost to creep under the unfastened overcoat of the genuine Mr. Golyadkin. It was foggy and nothing could be seen. It was difficult to tell through what street and in what direction they were being taken. . . . It seemed to Mr. Golyadkin that what was happening to him was somehow familiar. One instant he tried to remember whether he had had a presentiment of it the day before, in a dream, for instance. . . .

At last his wretchedness reached the utmost pitch of agony. Leaning upon his merciless opponent, he was beginning to cry out. But his cries died away upon his lips. . . . There was a moment when Mr. Golyadkin forgot everything and made up his mind that all this was of no consequence and that it was all nothing, that it was happening in some inexplicable manner, and that, therefore, to protest was effort thrown away. . . . But suddenly and almost at the same instant that our hero was drawing this conclusion, an unexpected jolt gave quite a new turn to the affair. Mr. Golyadkin fell off the cab like a sack of flour and rolled on the ground, quite correctly recognizing, at the moment of his fall, that his excitement had been very inappropriate. Jumping up at last, he saw that they had arrived somewhere; the cab was standing in the middle of some courtyard, and from the first glance our hero noticed that it was the courtyard of the house in which was Olsufy Ivanovitch's flat. At the same instant he noticed that his enemy was mounting the steps, probably on his way to Olsufy Ivanovitch's. In indescribable misery he was about to pursue his enemy, but, fortunately for himself, prudently thought better of it. Not forgetting to pay the cabman, Mr. Golyadkin ran with all his might along the street, regardless of where he was going. The snow was falling heavily as before; as before it was muggy, wet and dark. Our hero did not walk, but flew, coming into collision with every one on the way—men, women and children, and himself rebounding from everyone—men, women and children. About him and after him he heard frightened voices, squeals, screams. . . . But Mr. Golyadkin seemed unconscious and would pay no heed to anything. . . . He came to himself, however, on the Semyonovsky Bridge, and then only through succeeding in tripping against and upsetting two peasant women and the wares they were selling, and tumbling over them.

"That's no matter," thought Mr. Golyadkin, "that can easily be set right," and he felt in his pocket at once, intending to make up for the cakes, apples, nuts and various trifles he had scattered, with a rouble. Suddenly, a new light dawned upon Mr. Golyadkin; in his pocket he felt the letter given him in the morning by the clerk. Remembering that there was a tavern he knew close by, he ran to it without a moment's delay, settled himself at a little table lighted up by a tallow candle, and, taking no notice of anything, regardless of the waiter who came to ask for his orders, broke the seal and began reading the following letter, which completely astounded him—

You noble man, who are suffering for my sake, and will be dear to my heart for ever!

I am suffering, I am perishing—save me! The slanderer, the intriguer, notorious for the immorality of his tendencies, has entangled me in his snares and I am undone! I am lost! But he is abhorrent to me, while you! . . . They have separated us, they have intercepted my letters to you—and all this has been the work of the vicious man who has taken advantage of his one good quality—his likeness to you. A man can always be plain in appearance, yet fascinate by his intelligence, his strong feelings and his agreeable manners. . . . I am ruined! I am being married against my will, and the chief part in this intrigue is taken by my parent, benefactor and civil councillor, Olsufy Ivanovitch, no doubt desirous of securing me a place and relations in well-bred society. . . . But I have made up my mind and I protest by all the powers bestowed on me by nature. Be waiting for me with a carriage at nine o'clock this evening at the window of Olsufy Ivanovitch's flat. We are having another ball and a handsome lieutenant is coming. I will come out and we will fly. Moreover, there are other government offices in which one can be of service to one's country. In any case, remember, my friend, that innocence is strong in its very innocence. Farewell. Wait with the carriage at the entrance. I shall throw myself into the protection of your arms at two o'clock in the night.

Yours till death,

KLARA OLSUFYEVNA.

After reading the letter our hero remained for some minutes as though petrified. In terrible anxiety, in terrible agitation, white as a sheet, with the letter in his hand, he walked several times up and down the room; to complete the unpleasantness of his position, though our hero failed to observe it, he was at that moment the object of the exclusive attention of every one in the room. Probably the disorder of his attire, his unrestrained excitement, his walking or rather running about the room, his gesticulating with both hands, perhaps some enigmatic words unconsciously addressed to the air, probably all this prejudiced Mr. Golyadkin in the opinion of the customers, and even the waiter began to look at him suspiciously. Coming to himself, Mr. Golyadkin noticed that he was standing in the middle of the room and was in an almost unseemly, discourteous manner staring at an old man of very respectable appearance who, having dined and said grace before the ikon, had sat down again and fixed his eyes upon Mr. Golyadkin. Our hero looked vaguely about him and noticed that every one, actually every one, was looking at him with a hostile and suspicious air. All at once a retired military man in a red collar asked loudly for the *Police News*. Mr. Golyadkin started and turned crimson: he happened to look down and saw that he was in such disorderly attire as he would not have worn even at home, much less in a public place. His boots, his trousers and the whole of his left side were covered with mud; the trouser-strap was torn off his right foot, and his coat was even torn in many places. In extreme misery our hero went up to the table at which he had read the letter, and saw that the attendant was coming up to him with a strange and impudently peremptory expression of face. Utterly disconcerted and crestfallen, our hero began to look about the table at which he was now standing. On the table stood a dirty plate, left there from somebody's dinner, a soiled table-napkin and a knife, fork and spoon that had just been used. "Who has been having dinner?" thought our hero. "Can it have been I? Anything is possible! I must have had dinner without noticing it; what am I to do?"

Raising his eyes, Mr. Golyadkin again saw beside him the waiter who was about to address him.

"How much is my bill, my lad?" our hero inquired, in a trembling voice.

A loud laugh sounded round Mr. Golyadkin, the waiter himself grinned. Mr. Golyadkin realized that he had blundered again, and had done something dreadfully stupid. He was overcome by confusion, and to avoid standing there with nothing to do he put his hand in his pocket to get out his handkerchief; but to the indescribable amazement of himself and all surrounding him, he pulled out instead of his handkerchief the bottle of medicine which Krestyan Ivanovitch had prescribed for him four days earlier. "Get the medicine at the same chemist's," floated through Mr. Golyadkin's brain. . . .

Suddenly he started and almost cried out in horror. A new light dawned. . . . The dark reddish and repulsive liquid had a sinister gleam to Mr. Golyadkin's eyes. . . . The bottle dropped from his hands and was instantly smashed. Our hero cried out and stepped back a pace to avoid the spilled medicine . . . he was trembling in every limb, and drops of sweat came out on to his brow and temples. "So my life is in danger!" Meantime there was a stir, a commotion in the room; every one surrounded Mr. Golyadkin, every one talked to Mr. Golyadkin, some even caught hold of Mr. Golyadkin. But our hero was dumb and motionless, seeing nothing, hearing nothing, feeling nothing. . . . At last, as though tearing himself from the place, he rushed out of the tavern, pushing away all and each who tried to detain him; almost unconscious, he got into the first cab that passed him and drove to his flat.

In the entry of his flat he met Mihyeev, an attendant from the office, with an official envelope in his hand.

"I know, my good man, I know all about it," our exhausted hero answered, in a weak, miserable voice; "it's official. . . ."

The envelope did, in fact, contain instructions to Mr. Golyadkin, signed by Andrey Filippovitch, to give up the business in his hands to Ivan Semyonovitch. Taking the envelope and giving ten kopecks to the man, Mr. Golyadkin went into his flat and saw that Petrushka was collecting all his odds and ends, all his things into a heap, evidently intending to abandon Mr. Golyadkin and move to the flat of Karolina Ivanovna, who had enticed him to take the place of Yevstafy.

CHAPTER 12

Petrushka came in swaggering, with a strangely casual manner
and an air of vulgar triumph on his face. It was evident that he had
some idea in his head, that he felt thoroughly within his rights, and
he looked like an unconcerned spectator—that is, as though he were
anybody's servant rather than Mr. Golyadkin's.

"I say, you know, my good lad," our hero began breathlessly,
"what time is it?"

Without speaking, Petrushka went behind his partition, then
returned, and in a rather independent tone announced that it was
nearly half-past seven.

"Well, that's all right, my lad, that's all right. Come, you see,
my boy . . . allow me to tell you, my good lad, that everything, I
fancy, is at an end between us."

Petrushka said nothing.

"Well, now as everything is over between us, tell me openly,
as a friend, where you have been."

"Where I've been? To see good people, sir."

"I know, my good lad, I know. I have always been satisfied
with you, and I give you a character. . . . Well, what are you doing
with them now?"

"Why, sir! You know yourself. We all know a decent man won't
teach you any harm."

"I know, my dear fellow, I know. Nowadays good people are
rare, my lad; prize them, my friend. Well, how are they?"

"To be sure, they . . . Only I can't serve you any longer, sir, as
your honour must know."

"I know, my dear fellow, I know your zeal and devotion; I have
seen it all, my lad, I've noticed it. I respect you, my friend. I respect
a good and honest man, even though he's a lackey."

"Why, yes, to be sure! The likes of us, of course, as you know yourself, are as good as anybody. That's so. We all know, sir, that there's no getting on without a good man."

"Very well, very well, my boy, I feel it. . . . Come, here's your money and here's your character. Now we'll kiss and say good-bye, brother. . . . Come, now, my lad, I'll ask one service of you, one last service," said Mr. Golyadkin, in a solemn voice. "You see, my dear boy, all sorts of things happen. Sorrow is concealed in gilded palaces, and there's no escaping it. You know, my boy, I've always been kind to you, my boy."

Petrushka remained mute.

"I believe I've always been kind to you, my dear fellow. . . . Come, how much linen have we now, my dear boy?"

"Well, it's all there. Linen shirts six, three pairs of socks; four shirt-fronts; flannel vests; of underlinen two sets. You know all that yourself. I've got nothing of yours, sir. . . . I look after my master's belongings, sir. I am like that, sir . . . we all know . . . and I've . . . never been guilty of anything of the sort, sir, you know yourself, sir. . . ."

"I trust you, my lad, I trust you. I didn't mean that, my friend, I didn't mean that, you know, my lad; I tell you what . . ."

"To be sure, sir, we know that already. Why, when I used to be in service at General Stolbnyakov's . . . I lost the place through the family's going away to Saratov . . . they've an estate there. . . ."

"No; I didn't mean that, my lad, I didn't mean that; don't think anything of the sort, my dear fellow. . . ."

"To be sure. It's easy, as you know yourself, sir, to take away the character of folks like us. And I've always given satisfaction—ministers, generals, senators, counts—I've served them all. I've been at Prince Svintchatkin's, at Colonel Pereborkin's, at General Nedobarov's—they've gone away too, they've gone to their property. As we all know . . ."

"Yes, my lad, very good, my lad, very good. And now I'm going away, my friend. . . . A different path lies before each man, no one can tell what road he may have to take. Come, my lad, put out my clothes now, lay out my uniform too . . . and my other trousers, my sheets, quilts and pillows. . . ."

"Am I to pack them all in the bag?"

"Yes, my lad, yes; the bag, please. Who knows what may happen to us? Come, my dear boy, you can go and find a carriage. . . ."

"A carriage? . . ."

"Yes, my lad, a carriage; a roomy one, and take it by the hour. And don't you imagine anything. . . ."

"And are you meaning to go far away, sir?"

"I don't know, my lad, I don't know that either. I think you had better pack my feather-bed too. What do you think, my lad? I am relying on you, my dear fellow. . . ."

"Is your honour setting off at once?"

"Yes, my friend, yes! Circumstances have turned out so . . . so it is, my dear fellow, so it is. . . ."

"To be sure, sir; when we were in the regiment the same thing happened to the lieutenant; they eloped from a country gentleman's. . . ."

"Eloped? . . . How? My dear fellow!"

"Yes, sir, eloped, and they were married in another house. Everything was got ready beforehand. There was a hue and cry after them; the late prince took their part, and so it was all settled. . . ."

"They were married, but . . . how is it, my dear fellow? . . . How did you come to know, my boy?"

"Why, to be sure! The earth is full of rumours, sir. We know, sir, we've all . . . to be sure, there's no one without sin. Only I'll tell you now, sir, let me speak plainly and vulgarly, sir; since it has come to this, I must tell you, sir; you have an enemy—you've a rival, sir, a powerful rival, so there. . . ."

"I know, my dear fellow, I know; you know yourself, my dear fellow. . . . So, you see, I'm relying upon you. What are we to do now, my friend? How do you advise me?"

"Well, sir, if you are in that way now, if you've come, so to say, to such a pass, sir, you'll have to make some purchases, sir—say some sheets, pillows, another feather-bed, a double one, a good quilt—here at the neighbours downstairs—she's a shopkeeper, sir—she has a good fox-fur cloak, so you might look at it and buy it, you might have a look at it at once. You'll need it now, sir; it's a good cloak, sir, satin lined with fox. . . ."

"Very good, my lad, very good, I agree; I rely upon you, I rely upon you entirely; a cloak by all means, if necessary. . . . Only make haste, make haste! For God's sake make haste! I'll buy the cloak—only please make haste! It will soon be eight o'clock. Make haste for God's sake, my dear lad! Hurry up, my lad. . . ."

Petrushka ran to gather together a bundle of linens, pillows, quilt, sheets, and all sorts of odds and ends, tied them up and rushed headlong out of the room. Meanwhile, Mr. Golyadkin seized the letter once more, but he could not read it. Clutching his devoted head, he leaned against the wall in a state of stupefaction. He could not think of anything, he could do nothing either, and could not even tell what was happening to him. At last, seeing that time was passing and neither Petrushka nor the fur cloak had made an appearance, Mr. Golyadkin made up his mind to go himself. Opening the door into the entry, he heard below noise, talk, disputing, scuffling. . . . Several of the women of the neighbouring flats were shouting, talking and protesting about something—Mr. Golyadkin knew what. Petrushka's voice was heard: then there was a sound of footsteps.

"My goodness! They'll bring all the world in here," moaned Mr. Golyadkin, wringing his hands in despair and rushing back into his room. Running back into his room, he fell almost senseless on the sofa with his face in the pillow. After lying a minute in this way, he jumped up and, without waiting for Petrushka, he put on his goloshes, his hat and his greatcoat, snatched up his papers and ran headlong downstairs.

"Nothing is wanted, nothing, my dear fellow! I will manage myself—everything myself. I don't need you for the time, and meantime, things may take a better turn, perhaps," Mr. Golyadkin muttered to Petrushka, meeting him on the stairs; then he ran out into the yard, away from the house. There was a faintness at his heart, he had not yet made up his mind what was his position, what he was to do, how he was to act in the present critical position.

"Yes, how am I to act? Lord, have mercy on me! And that all this should happen!" he cried out at last in despair, tottering along the street at random; "that all this must needs happen! Why, but for this, but for just this, everything would have been put right; at one stroke, at one skillful, vigorous, firm stroke it would have been set right. I would have my finger cut off to have it set right! And I know, indeed, how it would have been settled. This is how it would have

been managed: I'd have gone on the spot . . . said how it was . . .
'with your permission, sir, I'm neither here nor there in it . . . things
aren't done like that,' I would say, 'my dear sir, things aren't done
like that, there's no accepting an impostor in our office; an impostor
. . . my dear sir, is a man . . . who is worthless and of no service
to his country. Do you understand that? Do you understand that,
my dear sir?' I should say! That's how it would be. . . . But no . . .
after all, things are not like that . . . not a bit like that . . . I am
talking nonsense, like a fool! A suicidal fool! It's not like that at
all, you suicidal fool. . . . This is how things are done, though, you
profligate man! . . . Well, what am I to do with myself now? Well,
what am I going to do with myself now? What am I fit for now?
Come, what are you fit for now, for instance, you Golyadkin, you,
you worthless fellow! Well, what now? I must get a carriage; 'hire
a carriage and bring it here,' says she, 'we shall get our feet wet
without a carriage,' says she. . . . And who could ever have thought
it! Fie, fie, my young lady! Fie, fie, a young lady of virtuous behaviour! Well, well, the girl we all thought so much of! You've
distinguished yourself, madame, there's no doubt of that! you've
distinguished yourself! . . . And it all comes from immoral education.
And now that I've looked into it and seen through it all, I see that
it is due to nothing else but immorality. Instead of looking after
her as a child . . . and the rod at times . . . they stuff her with
sweets and dainties, and the old man is always doting over her:
saying 'my dear, my love, my beauty,' saying, 'we'll marry you to
a count!' . . . And now she has come forward herself and shown
her cards, as though to say that's her little game! Instead of keeping
her at home as a child, they sent her to a boarding-school, to a
French madame, an *émigrée*, a Madame Falbalas or something, and
she learned all sorts of things at that Madame Falbalas', and this is
how it always turns out. 'Come,' says she, 'and be happy! Be in a
carriage,' she says, 'at such a time, under the windows, and sing a
sentimental serenade in the Spanish style; I await you and I know
you love me, and we will fly together and live in a hut.' But the
fact is it's impossible; since it has come to that, madame, it's impossible, it is against the law to abduct an innocent, respectable girl from her parents' roof without their sanction! And, if you
come to that, why, what for and what need is there to do it?

Come, she should marry a suitable person, the man marked out by destiny, and that would be the end of it. But I'm in the government service, I might lose my berth through it: I might be arrested for it, madame! I tell you that! If you did not know it. It's that German woman's doing. She's at the bottom of it all, the witch; she cooked the whole kettle of fish. For they've slandered a man, for they've invented a bit of womanish gossip about him, a regular performance by the advice of Andrey Filippovitch, that's what it came from. Otherwise how could Petrushka be mixed up in it? What has he to do with it? What need for that rogue to be in it? No, I cannot, madame, I cannot possibly, not on any account. . . . No, madame, this time you must really excuse me. It's all your doing, madame, it's not all the German's doing, it's not the witch's doing at all, but simply yours. For the witch is a good woman, for the witch is not to blame in any way; it's your fault, madame; it's you who are to blame, let me tell you! I shall be charged with a crime through you, madame. . . . A man might be ruined . . . a man might lose sight of himself, and not be able to restrain himself—a wedding, indeed! And how is it all going to end? And how will it all be arranged? I would give a great deal to know all that! . . ."

So our hero reflected in his despair. Coming to himself suddenly, he observed that he was standing somewhere in Liteyny Street. The weather was awful: it was a thaw; snow and rain were falling—just as at that memorable time when at the dread hour of midnight all Mr. Golyadkin's troubles had begun. "This is a nice night for a journey!" thought Mr. Golyadkin, looking at the weather; "It's death all round. . . . Good Lord! Where am I to find a carriage, for instance? I believe there's something black there at the corner. We'll see, we'll investigate. . . . Lord, have mercy on us!" our hero went on, bending his weak and tottering steps in the direction in which he saw something that looked like a cab.

"No, I know what I'll do; I'll go straight and fall on my knees, if I can, and humbly beg, saying, 'I put my fate in your hands, in the hands of my superiors'; saying, 'Your Excellency, be a protector and a benefactor'; and then I'll say this and that, and explain how it is and that it is an unlawful act; 'Do not destroy me, I look upon you as my father, do not abandon me . . . save my dignity, my honour, my name, my reputation . . . and save me from a miscreant, a vicious man. . . . He's another person, your Excellency, and I'm another person too; he's apart and I am myself by myself too; I am really myself by myself, your Excellency; really myself by myself,' that's what I shall say. 'I cannot be like him. Change him, dismiss him, give orders for him to be changed and a godless, licentious impersonation to be suppressed . . . that it may not be an example to others, your Excellency. I look upon you as a father'; those in authority over us, our benefactors and protectors, are bound, of course, to encourage such impulses. . . . There's something chivalrous about it: I shall say, 'I look upon you, my benefactor and superior, as a father, and trust my fate to you, and I will not say anything against it; I put myself in your hands, and retire from the affair myself' . . . that's what I would say."

"Well, my man, are you a cabman?"

"Yes . . ."

"I want a cab for the evening. . . ."

"And does your honour want to go far?"

"For the evening, for the evening; wherever I have to go, my man, wherever I have to go."

"Does your honour want to drive out of town?"

"Yes, my friend, out of town, perhaps. I don't quite know myself yet, I can't tell you for certain, my man. Maybe, you see, it will all be settled for the best. We all know, my friend . . ."

"Yes, sir, of course we all know. Please God it may."

"Yes, my friend, yes; thank you, my dear fellow, come, what's your fare, my good man? . . ."

"Do you want to set off at once?"

"Yes, at once, that is, no, you must wait at a certain place. . . . A little while, not long, you'll have to wait. . . ."

"Well, if you hire me for the whole time, I couldn't ask less than six roubles for weather like this. . . ."

"Oh, very well, my friend; and I thank you, my dear fellow. So, come, you can take me now, my good man."

"Get in; allow me, I'll put it straight a bit—now will your honour get in? Where shall I drive?"

"To the Ismailovsky Bridge, friend."

The driver plumped down on the box, with difficulty roused his pair of lean nags from the trough of hay, and was setting off for the Ismailovsky Bridge. But suddenly Mr. Golyadkin pulled the cord, stopped the cab, and besought him in an imploring voice not to drive to the Ismailovsky Bridge, but to turn back to another street. The driver turned into another street, and ten minutes later Mr. Golyadkin's newly hired equipage was standing before the house in which his Excellency had a flat. Mr. Golyadkin got out of the carriage, begged the driver to be sure to wait and with a sinking heart ran upstairs to the third storey and pulled the bell; the door was opened and our hero found himself in the entry of his Excellency's flat.

"Is his Excellency graciously pleased to be at home?" said Mr. Golyadkin, addressing the man who opened the door.

"What do you want?" asked the servant, scrutinizing Mr. Golyadkin from head to foot.

"I, my friend . . . I am Golyadkin, the titular councillor, Golyadkin. . . . To say . . . something or other . . . to explain . . ."

"You must wait; you cannot . . ."

"My friend, I cannot wait; my business is important, it's business that admits of no delay. . . ."

"But from whom have you come? Have you brought papers? . . ."

"No, my friend, I am on my own account. Announce me, my friend, say something or other, explain. I'll reward you, my good man. . . ."

"I cannot. His Excellency is not at home, he has visitors. Come at ten o'clock in the morning. . . ."

"Take in my name, my good man, I can't wait—it is impossible. . . . You'll have to answer for it, my good man."

"Why, go and announce him! What's the matter with you; want to save your shoe leather?" said another lackey, who was lolling on the bench and had not uttered a word till then.

"Shoe leather! I was told not to show any one up, you know; their time is the morning."

"Announce him, have you lost your tongue?"

"I'll announce him all right—I've not lost my tongue. It's not my orders; I've told you, it's not my orders. Walk inside."

Mr. Golyadkin went into the outermost room; there was a clock on the table. He glanced at it: it was half-past eight. His heart ached within him. Already he wanted to turn back, but at that very moment the footman standing at the door of the next room had already boomed out Mr. Golyadkin's name.

"Oh, what lungs," thought our hero in indescribable misery. "Why, you ought to have said: 'He has come most humbly and meekly to make an explanation . . . something . . . be graciously pleased to see him' . . . Now the whole business is ruined; all my hopes are scattered to the winds. But . . . however . . . never mind. . . ."

There was no time to think, moreover. The lackey, returning, said, "Please walk in," and led Mr. Golyadkin into the study.

When our hero went in, he felt as though he were blinded, for he could see nothing at all. . . . But three or four figures seemed flitting before his eyes: "Oh, yes, they are the visitors," flashed through Mr. Golyadkin's mind. At last our hero could distinguish clearly the star on the black coat of his Excellency, then by degrees advanced to seeing the black coat and at last gained the power of complete vision. . . .

"What is it?" said a familiar voice above Mr. Golyadkin.

"The titular councillor, Golyadkin, your Excellency."

"Well?"

"I have come to make an explanation. . . ."

"How? . . . What?"

"Why, yes. This is how it is. I've come for an explanation, your Excellency. . . ."

"But you . . . but who are you? . . ."

"M—m—m—mist—er Golyadkin, your Excellency, a titular councillor."

"Well, what is it you want?"

"Why, this is how it is, I look upon you as a father; I retire . . . defend me from my enemy! . . ."

"What's this? . . ."

"We all know . . ."

"What do we all know?"

Mr. Golyadkin was silent: his chin began twitching a little.

"Well?"

"I thought it was chivalrous, your Excellency. . . . 'There's something chivalrous in it,' I said, 'and I look upon my superior as a father' . . . this is what I thought; protect me, I tear-earfully . . . b-beg and that such imp-impulses ought . . . to . . . be encouraged. . . ."

His Excellency turned away, our hero for some minutes could distinguish nothing. There was a weight on his chest. His breathing was laboured; he did not know where he was standing. . . . He felt ashamed and sad. God knows what followed. . . . Recovering himself, our hero noticed that his Excellency was talking with his guests, and seemed to be briskly and emphatically discussing something with them. One of the visitors Mr. Golyadkin recognized at once. This was Andrey Filippovitch; he knew no one else; yet there was another person that seemed familiar—a tall, thick-set figure, middle-aged, possessed of very thick eyebrows and whiskers and a significant sharp expression. On his chest was an order and in his mouth a cigar. This gentleman was smoking and nodding significantly without taking the cigar out of his mouth, glancing from time to time at Mr. Golyadkin. Mr. Golyadkin felt awkward; he turned away his eyes and immediately saw another very strange visitor. Through a door which our hero had taken for a looking-glass, just as he had done once before—*he* made his appearance—we know who: a very intimate friend and acquaintance of Mr. Golyadkin's. Mr. Golyadkin junior had actually been till then in a little room close by, hurriedly writing something; now, apparently, he was needed—and he came in with papers under his arm, went up to his Excellency, and while waiting for exclusive attention to be paid him succeeded very adroitly in putting his spoke into the talk and consultation, taking his place a little behind Andrey Filippovitch's back and partly screening him from the gentleman smoking the cigar. Apparently Mr. Golyadkin junior took an extreme interest in the conversation, to which he was listening now in a gentlemanly way, nodding his head, fidgeting with his feet, smiling, continually looking at his Excellency—as it were, beseeching him with his eyes to let him put his word in.

"The scoundrel," thought Mr. Golyadkin, and involuntarily he took a step forward. At this moment his Excellency turned round, and came rather hesitatingly towards Mr. Golyadkin.

"Well, that's all right, that's all right; well, run along, now. I'll look into your case, and give orders for you to be taken . . ."

At this point his Excellency glanced at the gentleman with the thick whiskers. The latter nodded in assent.

Mr. Golyadkin felt and distinctly understood that they were taking him for something different and not looking at him in the proper light at all.

"In one way or another I must explain myself," he thought; "I must say, 'This is how it is, your Excellency.'"

At this point in his perplexity he dropped his eyes to the floor and to his great astonishment he saw a good-sized patch of something white on his Excellency's boots.

"Can there be a hole in them?" thought Mr. Golyadkin. Mr. Golyadkin was, however, soon convinced that his Excellency's boots were not split, but were only shining brilliantly—a phenomenon fully explained by the fact that they were patent leather and highly polished.

"It is what they call *blick*," thought our hero; "the term is used particularly in artists' studios; in other places such a reflected light is called a rib of light."

At this point Mr. Golyadkin raised his eyes and saw that the time had come to speak, for things might easily end badly. . . .

Our hero took a step forward.

"I say this is how it is, your Excellency," he said, "and there's no accepting impostors nowadays."

His Excellency made no answer, but rang the bell violently. Our hero took another step forward.

"He is a vile, vicious man, your Excellency," said our hero, beside himself and faint with terror, though he still pointed boldly and resolutely at his unworthy twin, who was fidgeting about near his Excellency. "I say this is how it is, and I am alluding to a well-known person."

There was a general sensation at Mr. Golyadkin's words. Andrey Fillippovitch and the gentleman with the cigar nodded their heads; his Excellency impatiently tugged at the bell to summon the servants. At this point Mr. Golyadkin junior came forward in his turn.

"Your Excellency," he said, "I humbly beg permission to speak." There was something very resolute in Mr. Golyadkin junior's voice; everything showed that he felt himself completely in the right.

"Allow me to ask you," he began again, anticipating his Excellency's reply in his eagerness, and this time addressing Mr. Golyadkin; "allow me to ask you, in whose presence you are making this explanation? Before whom are you standing, in whose room are you? . . ."

Mr. Golyadkin junior was in a state of extraordinary excitement, flushed and glowing with wrath and indignation; there were positively tears in his eyes.

A lackey, appearing in the doorway, roared at the top of his voice the name of some new arrivals, the Bassavryukovs.

"A good aristocratic name, hailing from Little Russia," thought Mr. Golyadkin, and at that moment he felt some one lay a very friendly hand on his back, then a second hand was laid on his back. Mr. Golyadkin's infamous twin was tripping about in front leading the way; and our hero saw clearly that he was being led to the big doors of the room.

"Just as it was at Olsufy Ivanovitch's," he thought, and he found himself in the hall. Looking round, he saw beside him two of his Excellency's lackeys and his twin.

"The greatcoat, the greatcoat, the greatcoat, the greatcoat, my friend! The greatcoat of my best friend!" whispered the depraved man, snatching the coat from one of the servants, and by way of a nasty and ungentlemanly joke flinging it straight at Mr. Golyadkin's head. Extricating himself from under his coat, Mr. Golyadkin distinctly heard the two lackeys snigger. But without listening to anything, or paying attention to it, he went out of the hall and found himself on the lighted stairs. Mr. Golyadkin junior following him.

"Good-bye, your Excellency!" he shouted after Mr. Golyadkin senior.

"Scoundrel!" our hero exclaimed, beside himself.

"Well, scoundrel, then . . ."

"Depraved man! . . ."

"Well, depraved man, then . . ." answered Mr. Golyadkin's unworthy enemy, and with his characteristic baseness he looked down from the top of the stairs straight into Mr. Golyadkin's face as though begging him to go on. Our hero spat with indignation and ran out of the front door; he was so shattered, so crushed, that he had no recollection of how he got into the cab or who helped him in. Coming to himself, he found that he was being driven to Fontanka. "To the Ismailovsky Bridge, then," thought Mr. Golyadkin. At this point, Mr. Golyadkin tried to think of something else, but could not; there was something so terrible that he could not explain it. . . . "Well, never mind," our hero concluded, and he drove to the Ismailovsky Bridge.

CHAPTER 13

... It seemed as though the weather meant to change for the better. The snow, which had till then been coming down in regular clouds, began growing less and less and at last almost ceased. The sky became visible and here and there tiny stars sparkled in it. It was only wet, muddy, damp and stifling, especially for Mr. Golyadkin, who could hardly breathe as it was. His greatcoat, soaked and heavy with wet, sent a sort of unpleasant warm dampness all through him and weighed down his exhausted legs. A feverish shiver sent sharp, shooting pains all over him; he was in a painful cold sweat of exhaustion, so much so that Mr. Golyadkin even forgot to repeat at every suitable occasion with his characteristic firmness and resolution his favourite phrase that "it all, maybe, most likely, indeed, might turn out for the best." "But all this does not matter for the time," our hero repeated, still staunch and not down-hearted, wiping from his face the cold drops that streamed in all directions from the brim of his round hat, which was so soaked that it could hold no more water. Adding that all this was nothing so far, our hero tried to sit on a rather thick clump of wood, which was lying near a heap of logs in Olsufy Ivanovitch's yard. Of course, it was no good thinking of Spanish serenades or silken ladders, but it was quite necessary to think of a modest corner, snug and private, if not altogether warm. He felt greatly tempted, we may mention in passing, by that corner in the back entry of Olsufy Ivanovitch's flat in which he had once, almost at the beginning of this true story, stood for more than two hours between a cupboard and an old screen among all sorts of domestic odds and ends and useless litter. The fact is that Mr. Golyadkin had been standing waiting for two whole hours on this occasion in Olsufy Ivanovitch's yard. But in regard to that modest and snug little corner there were certain drawbacks which had not existed before. The first drawback was the fact that it was probably now a marked place and that certain precautionary measures had been taken in regard to it since the scandal at Olsufy Ivanovitch's last ball. Secondly, he had to wait for a signal from Klara Olsufyevna, for there was bound to be some such signal, it was always a feature in such cases and, "it didn't begin with us and it won't end with us."

At this point Mr. Golyadkin very appropriately remembered a novel he had read long ago in which the heroine, in precisely similar circumstances, signalled to Alfred by tying a pink ribbon to her window. But now, at night, in the climate of Petersburg, famous for its dampness and unreliability, a pink ribbon was hardly appropriate and, in fact, was utterly out of the question.

"No, it's not a matter of silk ladders," thought our hero, "and I had better stay here quietly and comfortably. . . . I had better stand here."

And he selected a place in the yard exactly opposite the window, near a stack of firewood. Of course, many persons, grooms and coachmen, were continually crossing the yard, and there was, besides, the rumbling of wheels and the snorting of horses and so on; yet it was a convenient place, whether he was observed or not; but now, anyway, there was the advantage of being to some extent in shadow, and no one could see Mr. Golyadkin while he himself could see everything.

The windows were brightly lit up, there was some sort of ceremonious party at Olsufy Ivanovitch's. But he could hear no music as yet.

"So it's not a ball, but a party of some other sort," thought our hero, somewhat aghast. "Is it today?" floated the doubt through him. "Have I made a mistake in the date? Perhaps; anything is possible. . . . Yes, to be sure, anything is possible. . . . Perhaps she wrote a letter to me yesterday, and it didn't reach me, and perhaps it did not reach me because Petrushka put his spoke in, the rascal! Or it was tomorrow in the letter, that is, that I . . . should do everything tomorrow, that is—wait with a carriage. . . ."

At this point our hero turned cold all over and felt in his pocket for the letter, to make sure. But to his surprise the letter was not in his pocket.

"How's this?" muttered Mr. Golyadkin, more dead than alive. "Where did I leave it? Then I must have lost it. That is the last straw!" he moaned at last. "Oh, if it falls into evil hands! Perhaps it has already. Good Lord! What may it not lead to! It may lead to something such that . . . Ach, my miserable fate!" At this point Mr. Golyadkin began trembling like a leaf at the thought that perhaps his vicious twin had thrown the greatcoat at him with the object of stealing the letter of which he had somehow got an inkling from Mr. Golyadkin's enemies.

"What's more, he's stealing it," thought our hero, "as evidence . . . but why evidence! . . ."

After the first shock of horror, the blood rushed to Mr. Golyadkin's head. Moaning and gnashing his teeth, he clutched his burning head, sank back on his block of wood and relapsed into brooding. . . . But he could form no coherent thoughts. Figures kept flitting through his brain, incidents came back to his memory, now vaguely, now distinctly, the tunes of some foolish songs kept ringing in his ears. . . . He was in great distress, unnatural distress!

"My God, my God!" our hero thought, recovering himself a little, and suppressing a muffled sob, "give me fortitude in the immensity of my afflictions! That I am done for, utterly destroyed—of that there can be no doubt, and that's all in the natural order of things, since it cannot be otherwise. To begin with, I've lost my berth, I've certainly lost it, I must have lost it. . . . Well, supposing things are set right somehow. Supposing I have money enough to begin with: I must have another lodging, furniture of some sort. . . . In the first place, I shan't have Petrushka. I can get on without the rascal . . . somehow, with help from the people of the house; well, that will be all right! I can go in and out when I like, and Petrushka won't grumble at my coming in late—yes, that is so; that's why it's a good thing to have the people in the house. . . . Well, supposing that's all right; but all that's nothing to do with it, all that's nothing to do with it."

At this point the thought of the real position again dawned upon Mr. Golyadkin's memory. He looked round.

"Oh, Lord, have mercy on me, have mercy on me! What am I talking about?" he thought, growing utterly desperate and clutching his burning head in his hands. . . .

"Won't you soon be going, sir?" a voice pronounced above Mr. Golyadkin. Our hero started; before him stood his cabman, who was also drenched through and shivering; growing impatient, and having nothing to do, he had thought fit to take a look at Mr. Golyadkin behind the woodstack.

"I am all right, my friend. . . . I am coming soon, soon, very soon; you wait. . . ."

The cabman walked away, grumbling to himself. "What is he grumbling about?" Mr. Golyadkin wondered through his tears. "Why, I have hired him for the evening, why, I'm . . . within my rights now . . . that's so! I've hired him for the evening, and that's the end of it. If one stands still, it's just the same. That's for me to decide. I am free to drive on or not to drive on. And my staying here by the wood-stack has nothing to do with the case . . . and don't dare to say any-thing; think, the gentleman wants to stand behind the woodstack, and so he's standing behind it . . . and he is not disgracing any one's honour! That's the fact of the matter.

"I tell you what it is, madame, if you care to know. Nowadays, madame, nobody lives in a hut, or anything of that sort. No, indeed. And in our industrial age there's no getting on without morality, a fact of which you are a fatal example, madame. . . . You say we must get a job as a register clerk and live in a hut on the sea-shore. In the first place, madame, there are no register clerks on the sea-shore, and in the second place we can't get a job as a register clerk. For supposing, for example, I send in a petition, present myself— saying a register clerk's place or something of the sort . . . and defend me from my enemy . . . they'll tell you, madame, they'll say, to be sure . . . we've lots of register clerks, and here you are not at Ma-dame Falbalas', where you learnt the rules of good behaviour of which you are such a fatal example. Good behaviour, madame, means staying at home, honouring your father and not thinking about suitors prematurely. Suitors will come in good time, madame, that's so! Of course, you are bound to have some accomplishments, such as playing the piano sometimes, speaking French, history, geography, scripture and arithmetic, that's the truth of it! And that's all you need. Cooking, too, cooking certainly forms part of the education of a well-behaved girl! But as it is, in the first place, my fine lady, they won't let you go, they'll raise a hue and cry after you, and then they'll lock you up in a nunnery. How will it be then, madame? What will you have me do then? Would you have me, madame, follow the example of some stupid novels, and melt into tears on a neighbouring hillock, gazing at the cold walls of your prison house, and finally die, following the example of some wretched German poets and novelists. Is that it, madame? But, to begin with, allow me to tell you, as a friend, that things are not done like that, and in the second place I would have given you and your parents, too, a good thrashing for letting you read French books; for French books teach you no good. There's a poison in them . . . a pernicious poison, madame! Or do you imagine, allow me to ask you, or do you imagine that we shall elope with impunity, or something of that sort . . . that we shall have a hut on the shore of the sea and so on; and that we shall begin billing and cooing and talking about our feelings, and that so we shall spend our lives in happiness and content; and then there would be little ones—so then we shall . . . shall go to our father, the civil councillor, Olsufy Ivanovitch, and say, 'we've got a little one, and so, on this propitious occasion remove your curse, and bless the couple.' No, madame, I tell you again, that's not the way to do things, and for the first thing there'll be no billing and cooing, and please don't reckon on it. Nowadays, madame, the husband is the master and a good, well-brought-up wife should try and please him in every way. And endearments, madame, are not in favour, nowadays, in our industrial age; the day of Jean Jacques Rousseau is over. The husband comes home, for instance, hungry from the office, and asks, 'Isn't there something to eat, my love, a drop of vodka to drink, a bit of salt fish to eat?' So then, madame, you must have the vodka and the herring ready. Your husband will eat it with relish, and he won't so much as look at you, he'll only say 'Run into the kitchen, kitten,' he'll say, 'and look after the dinner,' and at most, once a week he'll kiss you, even then rather indifferently. . . . That's how it will be with us, my young lady! Yes, even then, indifferently. . . . That's how it will be, if one considers it, if it has come to one's looking at the thing in that way. . . . And how do I come in? Why have you mixed me up in your caprices? 'The noble man who is suffering for your sake and will be dear to your heart for ever,' and so on. But in the first place, madame, I am not suited to you, you know yourself, I'm not a great hand at compliments, I'm not fond of uttering perfumed trifles for the ladies. I'm not fond of lady-killers, and I must own, I've never been a beauty to look at. You won't find any swagger or false shame in me, and I tell you so now in all sincerity. This is the fact of the matter: we can boast of nothing but a straightforward, open character and common sense; we have nothing to do with intrigues. I am not one to intrigue, I say so and I'm proud of it—that's the fact of the matter! . . . I wear no mask among straightforward people, and to tell you the whole truth . . ."

Suddenly Mr. Golyadkin started. The red and perfectly sopping beard of the cabman appeared round the woodstack again. . . .

"I am coming directly, my friend. I'm coming at once, you know," Mr. Golyadkin responded in a trembling and failing voice.

The cabman scratched his head, then stroked his beard, and moved a step forward . . . stood still and looked suspiciously at Mr. Golyadkin.

"I am coming directly, my friend; you see, my friend . . . I . . . just a little, you see, only a second! . . . more . . . here, you see, my friend. . . ."

"Aren't you coming at all?" the cabman asked at last, definitely coming up to Mr. Golyadkin.

"No, my friend, I'm coming directly. I am waiting, you see, my friend. . . ."

"So I see. . . ."

"You see, my friend, I . . . What part of the country do you come from, my friend?"

"We are under a master . . ."

"And have you a good master? . . ."

"All right. . . ."

"Yes, my friend; you stay here, my friend, you see. . . . Have you been in Petersburg long, my friend?"

"It's a year since I came. . . ."

"And are you getting on all right, my friend?"

"Middling."

"To be sure, my friend, to be sure. You must thank Providence, my friend. You must look out for straightforward people. Straightforward people are none too common nowadays, my friend; he would give you washing, food, and drink, my good fellow, a good man would. But sometimes you see tears shed for the sake of gold, my friend . . . you see a lamentable example; that's the fact of the matter, my friend. . . ."

The cabman seemed to feel sorry for Mr. Golyadkin. "Well, your honour, I'll wait. Will your honour be waiting long?"

"No, my friend, no; I . . . you know . . . I won't wait any longer, my good man. . . . What do you think, my friend? I rely upon you. I won't stay any longer."

"Aren't you going at all?"

"No, my friend, no; I'll reward you, my friend . . . that's the fact of the matter. How much ought I to give you, my dear fellow?"

"What you hired me for, please, sir. I've been waiting here a long time; don't be hard on a man, sir."

"Well, here, my good man, here."

At this point Mr. Golyadkin gave six whole roubles to the cabman, and made up his mind in earnest to waste no more time, that is, to clear off straight away, especially as the cabman was dismissed and everything was over, and so it was useless to wait longer. He rushed out of the yard, went out of the gate, turned to the left and without looking round took to his heels, breathless and rejoicing. "Perhaps it will all be for the best," he thought, "and perhaps in this way I've run away from trouble." Mr. Golyadkin suddenly became all at once light-hearted. "Oh, if only it could turn out for the best!" thought our hero, though he put little faith in his own words. "I know what I'll do . . ." he thought. "No, I know, I'd better try the other tact. . . . Or wouldn't it be better to do this? . . ." In this way, hesitating and seeking for the solution of his doubts, our hero ran to the Semyonovsky Bridge; but while running to the Semyonovsky Bridge he very rationally and conclusively decided to return.

"It will be better so," he thought. "I had better try the other tact, that is . . . I will just go—I'll look on simply as an outsider, and that will be the end of it; I am simply an onlooker, an outsider—and nothing more, whatever happens—it's not my fault, that's the fact of the matter! That's how it shall be now."

Deciding to return, our hero actually did return, the more readily because with this happy thought he conceived of himself now as quite an outsider.

"It's the best thing; one's not responsible for anything, and one will see all that's necessary . . . that's the fact of the matter!"

It was a safe plan and that settled it. Reassured, he crept back under the peaceful shelter of his soothing and protecting woodstack, and began gazing intently at the window. This time he was not destined to gaze and wait for long. Suddenly a strange commotion became apparent at all the windows. Figures appeared, curtains were drawn back, whole groups of people were crowding to the windows at Olsufy Ivanovitch's flat. All were peeping out looking for something in the yard. From the security of his woodstack, our hero, too, began with curiosity watching the general commotion, and with interest craned forward to right and to left so far as he could within the shadow of the woodstack. Suddenly he started, held his breath and almost sat down with horror. It seemed to him —in short, he realized, that they were looking for nothing and for nobody but him, Mr. Golyadkin! Every one was looking in his direction. It was impossible to escape; they saw him. . . . In a flutter, Mr. Golyadkin huddled as closely as he could to the woodstack, and only then noticed that the treacherous shadow had betrayed him, that it did not cover him completely. Our hero would have been delighted at that moment to creep into a mouse hole in the woodstack, and there meekly to remain, if only it had been possible. But it was absolutely impossible. In his agony he began at last staring openly and boldly at the windows, it was the best thing to do. . . . And suddenly he glowed with shame. He had been fully discovered, every one was staring at him at once, they were all waving their hands, all were nodding their heads at him, all were calling to him; then several windows creaked as they opened, several voices shouted something to him at once. . . .

"I wonder why they don't whip these naughty girls as children," our hero muttered to himself, losing his head completely. Suddenly there ran down the steps *he* (we know who), without his hat or greatcoat, breathless, rubbing his hands, wriggling, capering, perfidiously displaying intense joy at seeing Mr. Golyadkin.

"Yakov Petrovitch," whispered this individual, so notorious for his worthlessness, "Yakov Petrovitch, are you here? You'll catch cold. It's chilly here, Yakov Petrovitch. Come indoors."

"Yakov Petrovitch! No, I'm all right, Yakov Petrovitch," our hero muttered in a submissive voice.

"No, this won't do, Yakov Petrovitch, I beg you, I humbly beg you to wait with us. 'Make him welcome and bring him in,' they say, 'Yakov Petrovitch.'"

"No, Yakov Petrovitch, you see, I'd better . . . I had better go home, Yakov Petrovitch . . ." said our hero, burning at a slow fire and freezing at the same time with shame and terror.

"No—no—no—no!" whispered the loathsome person. "No—no —no, on no account! Come along," he said resolutely, and he dragged Mr. Golyadkin senior to the steps. Mr. Golyadkin senior did not at all want to go, but as every one was looking at them, it would have been stupid to struggle and resist; so our hero went— though, indeed, one cannot say that he went, because he did not know in the least what was being done with him. Though, after all, it made no difference!

Before our hero had time to recover himself and come to his senses, he found himself in the drawing-room. He was pale, dishevelled, harassed; with lustreless eyes he scanned the crowd—horror! The drawing room, all the rooms, were full to overflowing. There were masses of people, a whole galaxy of ladies; and all were crowding round Mr. Golyadkin, all were pressing towards Mr. Golyadkin, all were squeezing Mr. Golyadkin and he perceived clearly that they were all forcing him in one direction.

"Not towards the door," was the thought that floated through Mr. Golyadkin's mind.

They were, in fact, forcing him not towards the door but Olsufy Ivanovitch's easy chair. On one side of the arm chair stood Klara Olsufyevna, pale, languid, melancholy, but gorgeously dressed. Mr. Golyadkin was particularly struck by a little white flower which rested on her superb hair. On the other side of the arm chair stood Vladimir Semyonovitch, clad in black, with his new order in his buttonhole. Mr. Golyadkin was led in, as we have described above, straight up to Olsufy Ivanovitch—on one side of him, Mr. Golyadkin junior, who had assumed an air of great decorum and propriety, to the immense relief of our hero, while on the other side was Andrey Filippovitch, with a very solemn expression on his face.

"What can it mean?" Mr. Golyadkin wondered.

When he saw that he was being led to Olsufy Ivanovitch, an idea struck him like a flash of lightning. The thought of the intercepted letter darted through his brain. In great agony our hero stood before Olsufy Ivanovitch's chair.

"What will he say now?" he wondered to himself. "Of course, it will be all aboveboard now, that is, straightforward and, one may say, honourable; I shall say this is how it is, and so on."

But what our hero apparently feared did not happen. Olsufy Ivanovitch received Mr. Golyadkin very warmly, and though he did not hold out his hand to him, yet as he gazed at our hero, he shook his grey and venerable head—shook it with an air of solemn melancholy and yet of good will. So, at least, it seemed to Mr. Golyadkin. He even fancied that a tear glittered in Olsufy Ivanovitch's lustreless eyes; he raised his eyes and saw that there seemed to be tears, too, on the eyelashes of Klara Olsufyevna, who was standing by—that there seemed to be something of the same sort even in the eyes of Vladimir Semyonovitch—that the unruffled and composed dignity of Andrey Filippovitch had the same significance as the general tearful sympathy—that even the young man who was so much like a civil councillor, seizing the opportunity, was sobbing bitterly. . . . Though perhaps this was only all Mr. Golyadkin's fancy, because he was so much moved himself, and distinctly felt the hot tears running down his cold cheeks. . . .

Feeling reconciled with mankind and his destiny, and filled with love at the moment, not only for Olsufy Ivanovitch, not only for the whole party collected there, but even for his noxious twin (who seemed now to be by no means noxious, and not even to be his twin at all, but a person very agreeable in himself and in no way connected with him), our hero, in a voice broken with sobs, tried to express his feelings to Olsufy Ivanovitch, but was too much overcome by all that he had gone through, and could not utter a word; he could only, with an expressive gesture, point meekly to his heart. . . .

At last, probably to spare the feelings of the old man, Andrey Filippovitch led Mr. Golyadkin a little away, though he seemed to leave him free to do as he liked. Smiling, muttering something to himself, somewhat bewildered, yet almost completely reconciled with fate and his fellow creatures, our hero began to make his way through the crowd of guests. Every one made way for him, every one looked at him with strange curiosity and with mysterious, unaccountable sympathy. Our hero went into another room; he met with the same attention everywhere; he was vaguely conscious of the whole crowd closely following him, noting every step he took, talking in undertones among themselves of something very interesting, shaking their heads, arguing and discussing in whispers. Mr. Golyadkin wanted very much to know what they were discussing in whispers. Looking round, he saw near him Mr. Golyadkin junior. Feeling an overwhelming impulse to seize his hand and draw him aside, Mr. Golyadkin begged the other Yakov Petrovitch most particularly to co-operate with him in all his future undertakings, and not to abandon him at a critical moment. Mr. Golyadkin junior nodded his head gravely and warmly pressed the hand of Mr. Golyadkin senior. Our hero's heart was quivering with the intensity of his emotion. He was gasping for breath, however; he felt so oppressed—so oppressed; he felt that all those eyes fastened upon him were oppressing and dominating him. . . . Mr. Golyadkin caught a glimpse of the councillor who wore a wig. The latter was looking at him with a stern, searching eye, not in the least softened by the general sympathy. . . .

Our hero made up his mind to go straight up to him in order to smile at him and have an immediate explanation, but this somehow did not come off. For one instant Mr. Golyadkin became almost unconscious, almost lost all memory, all feeling.

When he came to himself again, he noticed that he was the centre of a large ring formed by the rest of the party round him. Suddenly, Mr. Golyadkin's name was called from the other room; the shout was at once taken up by the whole crowd. All was noise and excitement, all rushed to the door of the first room, almost carrying our hero along with them. In the crush the hard-hearted councillor in the wig was side by side with Mr. Golyadkin, and, taking our hero by the hand, he made him sit down beside him opposite Olsufy Ivanovitch, at some distance from the latter, however. Every one in the room sat down; the guests were arranged in rows round Mr. Golyadkin and Olsufy Ivanovitch. Everything was hushed; every one preserved a solemn silence; every one was watching Olsufy Ivanovitch, evidently expecting something out of the ordinary. Mr. Golyadkin noticed that beside Olsufy Ivanovitch's chair and directly facing the councillor sat Mr. Golyadkin junior, with Andrey Filippovitch. The silence was prolonged; they were evidently expecting something.

"Just as it is in a family when some one is setting off on a far journey. We've only to stand up and pray now," thought our hero.

Suddenly there was a general stir which interrupted Mr. Golyadkin's reflections. Something they had long been waiting for happened.

"He is coming, he is coming!" passed from one to another in the crowd.

"Who is it that is coming?" floated through Mr. Golyadkin's mind, and he shuddered at a strange sensation. "High time too!" said the councillor, looking intently at Andrey Filippovitch. Andrey Filippovitch, for his part, glanced at Olsufy Ivanovitch. Olsufy Ivanovitch gravely and solemnly nodded his head.

"Let us stand up," said the councillor, and he made Mr. Golyadkin get up. All rose to their feet. Then the councillor took Mr. Golyadkin senior by the hand, and Andrey Filippovitch took Mr. Golyadkin junior, and in this way these two precisely similar persons were conducted through the expectant crowd surrounding them. Our hero looked about him in perplexity; but he was at once checked and his attention was called to Mr. Golyadkin junior, who was holding out his hand to him.

"They want to reconcile us," thought our hero, and with emotion he held out his hand to Mr. Golyadkin junior; and then—then bent his head forward towards him. The other Mr. Golyadkin did the same. . . .

At this point it seemed to Mr. Golyadkin senior that his perfidious friend was smiling, that he gave a sly, hurried wink to the crowd of onlookers, and that there was something sinister in the face of the worthless Mr. Golyadkin junior, that he even made a grimace at the moment of his Judas kiss. . . .

There was a ringing in Mr. Golyadkin's ears, and a darkness before his eyes; it seemed to him that an infinite multitude, an unending series of precisely similar Golyadkins were noisily bursting in at every door of the room; but it was too late . . . the resounding, treacherous kiss was over, and . . .

Then quite an unexpected event occurred. . . . The door opened noisily, and in the doorway stood a man, the very sight of whom sent a chill to Mr. Golyadkin's heart. He stood rooted to the spot. A cry of horror died away in his choking throat. Yet Mr. Golyadkin knew it all beforehand, and had had a presentiment of something of the sort for a long time. The new arrival went up to Mr. Golyadkin gravely and solemnly. Mr. Golyadkin knew this personage very well. He had seen him before, had seen him very often, had seen him that day. . . . This personage was a tall, thick-set man in a black dress-coat with a good-sized cross on his breast, and was possessed of thick, very black whiskers; nothing was lacking but the cigar in the mouth to complete the picture. Yet this person's eyes, as we have mentioned already, sent a chill to the heart of Mr. Golyadkin. With a grave and solemn air this terrible man approached the pitiable hero of our story. . . . Our hero held out his hand to him; the stranger took his hand and drew him along with him. . . . With a crushed and desperate air our hero looked about him.

"It's . . . it's Krestyan Ivanovitch Rutenspitz, doctor of medicine and surgery; your old acquaintance, Yakov Petrovitch!" a detestable voice whispered in Mr. Golyadkin's ear. He looked round: it was Mr. Golyadkin's twin, so revolting in the despicable meanness of his soul. A malicious, indecent joy shone in his countenance; he was rubbing his hands with rapture, he was turning his head from side to side in ecstasy, he was fawning round every one in delight and seemed ready to dance with glee. At last he pranced forward, took a candle from one of the servants and walked in front, showing the way to Mr. Golyadkin and Krestyan Ivanovitch. Mr. Golyadkin heard the whole party in the drawing-room rush out after him, crowding and squeezing one another, and all beginning to repeat after Mr. Golyadkin himself, "It is all right, don't be afraid, Yakov Petrovitch; this is your old friend and acquaintance, you know, Krestyan Ivanovitch Rutenspitz. . . ."

At last they came out on the brightly lighted stairs; there was a crowd of people on the stairs too. The front door was thrown open noisily, and Mr. Golyadkin found himself on the steps together with Krestyan Ivanovitch. At the entrance stood a carriage with four horses that were snorting with impatience. The malignant Mr. Golyadkin junior in three bounds flew down the stairs and opened the

carriage door himself. Krestyan Ivanovitch, with an impressive gesture, asked Mr. Golyadkin to get in. There was no need of the
impressive gesture, however; there were plenty of people to help
him in. . . . Faint with horror, Mr. Golyadkin looked back. The
whole of the brightly lighted staircase was crowded with people;
inquisitive eyes were looking at him from all sides; Olsufy Ivanovitch himself was sitting in his easy chair on the top landing, and
watching all that took place with deep interest. Every one was
waiting. A murmur of impatience passed through the crowd when
Mr. Golyadkin looked back.

"I hope I have done nothing . . . nothing reprehensible . . . or
that can call for severity . . . and general attention in regard to my
official relations," our hero brought out in desperation. A clamour
of talk rose all round him, all were shaking their heads, tears started
from Mr. Golyadkin's eyes.

"In that case I'm ready. . . . I have full confidence . . . and I
entrust my fate to Krestyan Ivanovitch. . . ."

No sooner had Mr. Golyadkin declared that he entrusted his
fate to Krestyan Ivanovitch than a dreadful, deafening shout of joy
came from all surrounding him and was repeated in a sinister echo
through the whole of the waiting crowd. Then Krestyan Ivanovitch
on one side and Andrey Filippovitch on the other helped Mr. Golyadkin into the carriage; his double, in his usual nasty way, was
helping to get him in from behind. The unhappy Mr. Golyadkin
senior took his last look on all and everything, and, shivering like a
kitten that has been drenched with cold water—if the comparison
may be permitted—got into the carriage. Krestyan Ivanovitch followed him in immediately. The carriage door slammed. There was
a swish of the whip on the horses' backs . . . the horses started off.
. . . The crowd dashed after Mr. Golyadkin. The shrill, furious shouts
of his enemies pursued him by way of good wishes for his journey.
For some time several persons were still running by the carriage
that bore away Mr. Golyadkin; but by degrees they were left behind, till at last they had all disappeared. Mr. Golyadkin's unworthy
twin kept up longer than any one. With his hands in the trouser
pockets of his green uniform he ran on with a satisfied air, skipping
first to one and then to the other side of the carriage, sometimes
catching hold of the window frame and hanging on by it, poking his

head in at the window, and throwing farewell kisses to Mr. Golyad-kin. But he began to get tired, he was less and less often to be seen, and at last vanished altogether. There was a dull ache in Mr. Gol-yadkin's heart; a hot rush of blood set Mr. Golyadkin's head throb-bing; he felt stifled, he longed to unbutton himself—to bare his breast, to cover it with snow and pour cold water on it. He sank at last into forgetfulness. . . .

When he came to himself, he saw that the horses were taking him along an unfamiliar road. There were dark patches of copse on each side of it; it was desolate and deserted. Suddenly he almost swooned; two fiery eyes were staring at him in the darkness, and those two eyes were glittering with malignant, hellish glee. "That's not Krestyan Ivanovitch! Who is it? Or is it he? It is. It is Krestyan Ivanovitch, but not the old Krestyan Ivanovitch, it's another Krestyan Ivanovitch! It's a terrible Krestyan Ivanovitch! . . ."

"Krestyan Ivanovitch, I . . . I believe . . . I'm all right, Krestyan Ivanovitch," our hero was beginning timidly in a trembling voice, hoping by his meekness and submission to soften the terrible Kres-tyan Ivanovitch a little.

"You get free quarters, wood, with light, and service, which you deserve not," Krestyan Ivanovitch's answer rang out, stern and terrible as a judge's sentence.

Our hero shrieked and clutched his head in his hands. Alas! For a long while he had been haunted by a presentiment of this.

Bartleby, the Scrivener

A Story of Wall-Street

HERMAN MELVILLE

I am a rather elderly man. The nature of my avocations for the last thirty years has brought me into more than ordinary contact with what would seem an interesting and somewhat singular set of men, of whom as yet nothing that I know of has ever been written: —I mean the law-copyists or scriveners. I have known very many of them, professionally and privately, and if I pleased, could relate divers histories, at which good-natured gentlemen might smile, and sentimental souls might weep. But I waive the biographies of all other scriveners for a few passages in the life of Bartleby, who was a scrivener the strangest I ever saw or heard of. While of other law-copyists I might write the complete life, of Bartleby nothing of that sort can be done. I believe that no materials exist for a full and satisfactory biography of this man. It is an irreparable loss to literature. Bartleby was one of those beings of whom nothing is ascertainable, except from the original sources, and in his case those are very small. What my own astonished eyes saw of Bartleby, *that* is all I know of him, except, indeed, one vague report which will appear in the sequel.

Ere introducing the scrivener, as he first appeared to me, it is fit I make some mention of myself, my *employées,* my business, my chambers, and general surroundings; because some such description is indispensable to an adequate understanding of the chief character about to be presented.

Imprimis: I am a man who, from his youth upwards, has been filled with a profound conviction that the easiest way of life is the best. Hence, though I belong to a profession proverbially energetic and nervous, even to turbulence, at times, yet nothing of that sort have I ever suffered to invade my peace. I am one of those unambitious lawyers who never addresses a jury, or in any way draws down public applause; but in the cool tranquillity of a snug retreat, do a snug business among rich men's bonds and mortgages and title-deeds. All who know me, consider me an eminently *safe* man. The late John Jacob Astor, a personage little given to poetic enthusiasm, had no hesitation in pronouncing my first grand point to be prudence; my next, method. I do not speak it in vanity, but simply record the fact, that I was not unemployed in my profession by the late John Jacob Astor; a name which, I admit, I love to repeat, for it hath a rounded and orbicular sound to it, and rings like unto bullion. I will freely add, that I was not insensible to the late John Jacob Astor's good opinion.

Some time prior to the period at which this little history begins, my avocations had been largely increased. The good old office, now extinct in the State of New York, of a Master in Chancery, had been conferred upon me. It was not a very arduous office, but very pleasantly remunerative. I seldom lose my temper; much more seldom indulge in dangerous indignation at wrongs and outrages; but I must be permitted to be rash here and declare that I consider the sudden and violent abrogation of the office of Master in Chancery, by the new Constitution, as a—premature act; inasmuch as I had counted upon a life-lease of the profits, whereas I only received those of a few short years. But this is by the way.

My chambers were up stairs at No.—Wall-street. At one end they looked upon the white wall of the interior of a spacious sky-light shaft, penetrating the building from top to bottom. This view might have been considered rather tame than otherwise, deficient in what landscape painters call "life." But if so, the view from the other end of my chambers offered, at least, a contrast, if nothing more. In that direction my windows commanded an unobstructed view of a lofty brick wall, black by age and everlasting shade; which wall required no spy-glass to bring out its lurking beauties, but, for the benefit of all near-sighted spectators, was pushed up to within ten feet of my window panes. Owing to the great height of the surrounding buildings, and my chambers being on the second floor, the interval between this wall and mine not a little resembled a huge square cistern.

At the period just preceding the advent of Bartleby, I had two persons as copyists in my employment, and a promising lad as an office-boy. First, Turkey; second Nippers; third, Ginger Nut. These may seem names the like of which are not usually found in the Directory. In truth they were nicknames, mutually conferred upon each other by my three clerks, and were deemed expressive of their respective persons or characters. Turkey was a short, pursy Englishman of about my own age, that is, somewhere not far from sixty. In the morning, one might say, his face was of a fine florid hue, but after twelve o'clock, meridian—his dinner hour—it blazed like a grate full of Christmas coals; and continued blazing—but, as it were, with a gradual wane—till 6 o'clock P. M. or thereabouts, after which I saw no more of the proprietor of the face, which gaining its meridian with the sun, seemed to set with it, to rise, culminate, and decline the following day, with the like regularity and undiminished glory. There are many singular coincidences I have known in the course of my life, not the least among which was the fact, that exactly when Turkey displayed his fullest beams from his red and radiant countenance, just then, too, at that critical moment, began the daily period when I considered his business capacities as seriously disturbed for the remainder of the twenty-four hours. Not that he was absolutely idle, or averse to business then; far from it. The difficulty was, he was apt to be altogether too energetic. There was a strange, inflamed, flurried, flighty recklessness of activity about him. He would be incautious in dipping his pen into his inkstand. All his blots upon my documents were dropped there after twelve o'clock, meridian. Indeed, not only would he be reckless and sadly given to making blots in the afternoon, but some days he went further, and was rather noisy. At such times, too, his face flamed with augmented blazonry, as if cannel coal had been heaped on anthracite. He made an unpleasant racket with his chair; spilled his sandbox; in mending his pens, impatiently split them all to pieces, and threw them on the floor in a sudden passion; stood up and leaned over his table, boxing his papers about in a most indecorous manner, very sad to behold in an elderly man like him. Nevertheless, as he was in many ways a most valuable person to me, and all the time before twelve o'clock, meridian, was the quickest, steadiest creature too, accomplishing a great deal of work in a style not easy to be matched—for these reasons, I was willing to overlook his eccentricities, though indeed, occasionally, I remonstrated with him. I did this very gently, however, because, though the civilest, nay, the blandest and most reverential of men in the morning, yet in the afternoon he was disposed, upon provocation, to be slightly rash with his tongue, in fact, insolent. Now, valuing his morning services as I did, and resolved not to lose them; yet, at the same time made uncomfortable by his inflamed ways after twelve o'clock; and being a man of peace, unwilling by my admonitions to call forth unseemly retorts from him; I took upon me, one Saturday noon (he was always worse on Saturdays), to hint to him, very kindly, that perhaps now that he was growing old, it might be well to abridge his labors; in short, he need not come to my chambers after twelve o'clock, but, dinner over, had best go home to his lodgings and rest himself till tea-time. But no; he insisted upon his afternoon devotions. His countenance became intolerably fervid, as he oratorically assured me—gesticulating with a long ruler at the other end of the room— that if his services in the morning were useful, how indispensable, then, in the afternoon?

"With submission, sir," said Turkey on this occasion, "I consider myself your right-hand man. In the morning I but marshal and deploy my columns; but in the afternoon I put myself at their head, and gallantly charge the foe, thus!"—and he made a violent thrust with the ruler.

"But the blots, Turkey," intimated I.

"True,—but, with submission, sir, behold these hairs! I am getting old. Surely, sir, a blot or two of a warm afternoon is not to be severely urged against gray hairs. Old age—even if it blot the page —is honorable. With submission, sir, we *both* are getting old."

This appeal to my fellow-feeling was hardly to be resisted. At all events, I saw that go he would not. So I made up my mind to let him stay, resolving, nevertheless, to see to it that during the afternoon he had to do with my less important papers.

Nippers, the second on my list, was a whiskered, sallow, and, upon the whole, rather piratical-looking young man of about five and twenty. I always deemed him the victim of two evil powers— ambition and indigestion. The ambition was evinced by a certain impatience of the duties of a mere copyist, an unwarrantable usurpation of strictly professional affairs, such as the original drawing up of legal documents. The indigestion seemed betokened in an occasional nervous testiness and grinning irritability, causing the teeth to audibly grind together over mistakes committed in copying; unnecessary maledictions, hissed, rather than spoken, in the heat of business; and especially by a continual discontent with the height of the table where he worked. Though of a very ingenious mechanical turn, Nippers could never get this table to suit him. He put chips under it, blocks of various sorts, bits of pasteboard, and at last went so far as to attempt an exquisite adjustment by final pieces of folded blotting-paper. But no invention would answer. If, for the sake of easing his back, he brought the table lid at a sharp angle well up towards his chin, and wrote there like a man using the steep roof of a Dutch house for his desk:—then he declared that it stopped the circulation in his arms. If now he lowered the table to his waistbands, and stooped over it in writing, then there was a sore aching in his back. In short, the truth of the matter was, Nippers knew not what he wanted. Or, if he wanted any thing, it was to be rid of a scrivener's table altogether. Among the manifestations of his diseased ambition was a fondness he had for receiving visits from certain ambiguous-looking fellows in seedy coats, whom he called his clients. Indeed I was aware that not only was he, at times, considerable of a ward-politician, but he occasionally did a little business at the Justices' courts, and was not unknown on the steps of the Tombs. I have good reason to believe, however, that one individual who called upon him at my chambers, and who, with a grand air, he insisted was his client, was no other than a dun, and the alleged title-deed, a bill. But with all his failings, and the annoyances he caused me, Nippers, like his compatroit Turkey, was a very useful man to me; wrote a neat, swift hand; and, when he chose, was not deficient in a gentlemanly sort of deportment. Added to this, he always dressed in a gentlemanly sort of way; and so, incidentally, reflected credit upon my chambers. Whereas with respect to Turkey, I had much ado to keep him from being a reproach to me. His clothes were apt to look oily and smell of eating-houses. He wore his pantaloons very loose and baggy in summer. His coats were execrable; his hat not to be handled. But while the hat was a thing of indifference to me, inasmuch as his natural civility and deference, as a dependent Englishman, always led him to doff it the moment he entered the room, yet his coat was another matter. Concerning his coats, I reasoned with him; but with no effect. The truth was, I suppose, that a man with so small an income, could not afford to sport such a lustrous face and a lustrous coat at one and the same time. As Nippers once observed. Turkey's money went chiefly for red ink. One winter day I presented Turkey with a highly-respectable looking coat of my own, a padded gray coat, of a most comfortable warmth, and which buttoned straight up from the knee to the neck. I thought Turkey would appreciate the favor, and abate his rashness and obstreperousness of afternoons. But no. I verily believe that buttoning himself up in so downy and blanket-like a coat had a pernicious effect upon him; upon the same principle that too much oats are bad for horses. In fact, precisely as a rash, restive horse is said to feel his oats, so Turkey felt his coat. It made him insolent. He was a man whom prosperity harmed.

Though concerning the self-indulgent habits of Turkey I had my own private surmises, yet touching Nippers I was well persuaded that whatever might be his faults in other respects, he was, at least, a temperate young man. But indeed, nature herself seemed to have been his vintner, and at his birth charged him so thoroughly with an irritable, brandy-like disposition, that all subsequent potations were needless. When I consider how, amid the stillness of my chambers, Nippers would sometimes impatiently rise from his seat, and stooping over his table, spread his arms wide apart, seize the whole desk, and move it, and jerk it, with a grim, grinding motion on the floor, as if the table were a perverse voluntary agent, intent on thwarting and vexing him, I plainly perceive that for Nippers, brandy and water were altogether superfluous.

It was fortunate for me that, owing to its peculiar cause—indigestion—the irritability and consequent nervousness of Nippers were mainly observable in the morning, while in the afternoon he was comparatively mild. So that Turkey's paroxysms only coming on about twelve o'clock, I never had to do with their eccentricities at one time. Their fits relieved each other like guards. When Nippers' was on, Turkey's was off; and *vice versa*. This was a good natural arrangement under the circumstances.

Ginger Nut, the third on my list, was a lad some twelve years old. His father was a carman, ambitious of seeing his son on the bench instead of a cart, before he died. So he sent him to my office as student at law, errand boy, and cleaner and sweeper, at the rate of one dollar a week. He had a little desk to himself, but he did not use it much. Upon inspection, the drawer exhibited a great array of the shells of various sorts of nuts. Indeed, to this quick-witted youth the whole noble science of the law was contained in a nut-shell. Not the least among the employments of Ginger Nut, as well as one which he discharged with the most alacrity, was his duty as cake and apple purveyor for Turkey and Nippers. Copying law papers being proverbially a dry, husky sort of business, my two scriveners were fain to moisten their mouths very often with Spitzenbergs to be had at the numerous stalls nigh the Custom House and Post Office. Also, they sent Ginger Nut very frequently for that peculiar cake—small, flat, round, and very spicy—after which he had been named by them. Of a cold morning when business was but dull, Turkey would gobble up scores of these cakes, as if they were mere wafers—indeed they sell them at the rate of six or eight for a penny—the scrape of his pen blending with the crunching of the crisp particles in his mouth. Of all the fiery afternoon blunders and flurried rashnesses of Turkey, was his once moistening a ginger-cake between his lips, and clapping it on to a mortgage for a seal. I came within an ace of dismissing him then. But he mollified me by making an oriental bow, and saying—"With submission, sir, it was generous of me to find you in stationery on my own account."

Now my original business—that of a conveyancer and title hunter, and drawer-up of recondite documents of all sorts—was considerably increased by receiving the master's office. There was now great work for scriveners. Not only must I push the clerks already with me, but I must have additional help. In answer to my advertisement, a motionless young man one morning stood upon my office threshold, the door being open, for it was summer. I can see that figure now—pallidly neat, pitiably respectable, incurably forlorn! It was Bartleby.

After a few words touching his qualifications, I engaged him, glad to have among my corps of copyists a man of so singularly sedate an aspect, which I thought might operate beneficially upon the flighty temper of Turkey, and the fiery one of Nippers.

I should have stated before that ground glass folding-doors divided my premises into two parts, one of which was occupied by my scriveners, the other by myself. According to my humor I threw open these doors, or closed them. I resolved to assign Bartleby a corner by the folding-doors, but on my side of them, so as to have this quiet man within easy call, in case any trifling thing was to be done. I placed his desk close up to a small side-window in that part of the room, a window which originally had afforded a lateral view of certain grimy back-yards and bricks, but which, owing to subsequent erections, commanded at present no view at all, though it gave some light. Within three feet of the panes was a wall, and the light came down from far above, between two lofty buildings, as from a very small opening in a dome. Still further to a satisfactory arrangement, I procured a high green folding screen, which might entirely isolate Bartleby from my sight, though not remove him from my voice. And thus, in a manner, privacy and society were conjoined.

At first Bartleby did an extraordinary quantity of writing. As if long famishing for something to copy, he seemed to gorge himself on my documents. There was no pause for digestion. He ran a day and night line, copying by sun-light and by candle-light. I should have been quite delighted with his application, had he been cheerfully industrious. But he wrote on silently, palely, mechanically.

It is, of course, an indispensable part of a scrivener's business to verify the accuracy of his copy, word by word. Where there are two or more scriveners in an office, they assist each other in this examination, one reading from the copy, the other holding the original. It is a very dull, wearisome, and lethargic affair. I can readily imagine that to some sanguine temperaments it would be altogether intolerable. For example, I cannot credit that the mettlesome poet Byron would have contentedly sat down with Bartleby to examine a law document of, say five hundred pages, closely written in a crimpy hand.

Now and then, in the haste of business, it had been my habit to assist in comparing some brief document myself, calling Turkey or Nippers for this purpose. One object I had in placing Bartleby so handy to me behind the screen, was to avail myself of his services on such trivial occasions. It was on the third day, I think, of his being with me, and before any necessity had arisen for having his own writing examined, that, being much hurried to complete a small affair I had in hand, I abruptly called to Bartleby. In my haste and natural expectancy of instant compliance, I sat with my head bent over the original on my desk, and my right hand sideways, and somewhat nervously extended with the copy, so that immediately upon emerging from his retreat, Bartleby might snatch it and proceed to business without the least delay.

In this very attitude did I sit when I called to him, rapidly stating what it was I wanted him to do—namely, to examine a small paper with me. Imagine my surprise, nay, my consternation, when without moving from his privacy, Bartleby in a singularly mild, firm voice, replied, "I would prefer not to."

I sat awhile in perfect silence, rallying my stunned faculties. Immediately it occurred to me that my ears had deceived me, or Bartleby had entirely misunderstood my meaning. I repeated my request in the clearest tone I could assume. But in quite as clear a one came the previous reply, "I would prefer not to."

"Prefer not to," echoed I, rising in high excitement, and crossing the room with a stride. "What do you mean? Are you moonstruck? I want you to help me compare this sheet here—take it," and I thrust it towards him.

"I would prefer not to," said he.

I looked at him steadfastly. His face was leanly composed; his gray eye dimly calm. Not a wrinkle of agitation rippled him. Had there been the least uneasiness, anger, impatience or impertinence in his manner; in other words, had there been any thing ordinarily human about him, doubtless I should have violently dismissed him from the premises. But as it was, I should have as soon thought of turning my pale plaster-of-paris bust of Cicero out of doors. I stood gazing at him awhile, as he went on with his own writing, and then reseated myself at my desk. This is very strange, thought I. What had one best do? But my business hurried me. I concluded to forget the matter for the present, reserving it for my future leisure. So calling Nippers from the other room, the paper was speedily examined.

A few days after this, Bartleby concluded four lengthy documents, being quadruplicates of a week's testimony taken before me in my High Court of Chancery. It became necessary to examine them. It was an important suit, and great accuracy was imperative. Having all things arranged I called Turkey, Nippers and Ginger Nut from the next room, meaning to place the four copies in the hands of my four clerks, while I should read from the original. Accordingly Turkey, Nippers and Ginger Nut had taken their seats in a row, each with his document in hand, when I called to Bartleby to join this interesting group.

"Bartleby! quick, I am waiting."

I heard a slow scrape of his chair legs on the uncarpeted floor, and soon he appeared standing at the entrance of his hermitage.

"What is wanted?" said he mildly.

"The copies, the copies," said I hurriedly. "We are going to examine them. There"—and I held towards him the fourth quadruplicate.

"I would prefer not to," he said, and gently disappeared behind the screen.

For a few moments I was turned into a pillar of salt, standing at the head of my seated column of clerks. Recovering myself, I advanced towards the screen, and demanded the reason for such extraordinary conduct.

"*Why* do you refuse?"

"I would prefer not to."

With any other man I should have flown outright into a dreadful passion, scorned all further words, and thrust him ignominiously from my presence. But there was something about Bartleby that not only strangely disarmed me, but in a wonderful manner touched and disconcerted me. I began to reason with him.

"These are your own copies we are about to examine. It is labor saving to you, because one examination will answer for your four papers. It is common usage. Every copyist is bound to help examine his copy. Is it not so? Will you not speak? Answer!"

"I prefer not to," he replied in a flute-like tone. It seemed to me that while I had been addressing him, he carefully revolved every statement that I made; fully comprehended the meaning; could not gainsay the irresistible conclusion; but, at the same time, some paramount consideration prevailed with him to reply as he did.

"You are decided, then, not to comply with my request—a request made according to common usage and common sense?"

He briefly gave me to understand that on that point my judgment was sound. Yes: his decision was irreversible.

It is not seldom the case that when a man is browbeaten in some unprecedented and violently unreasonable way, he begins to stagger in his own plainest faith. He begins, as it were, vaguely to surmise that, wonderful as it may be, all the justice and all the reason is on the other side. Accordingly, if any disinterested persons are present, he turns to them for some reinforcement for his own faltering mind.

"Turkey," said I, "what do you think of this? Am I not right?"

"With submission, sir," said Turkey, with his blandest tone, "I think that you are."

"Nippers," said I, "what do *you* think of it?"

"I think I should kick him out of the office."

(The reader of nice perceptions will here perceive that, it being morning, Turkey's answer is couched in polite and tranquil terms, but Nippers replies in ill-tempered ones. Or, to repeat a previous sentence, Nippers's ugly mood was on duty, and Turkey's off.)

"Ginger Nut," said I, willing to enlist the smallest suffrage in my behalf, "what do *you* think of it?"

"I think, sir, he's a little *luny*," replied Ginger Nut, with a grin.

"You hear what they say," said I, turning towards the screen, "come forth and do your duty."

But he vouchsafed no reply. I pondered a moment in sore perplexity. But once more business hurried me. I determined again to postpone the consideration of this dilemma to my future leisure. With a little trouble we made out to examine the papers without Bartleby, though at every page or two, Turkey deferentially dropped his opinion that this proceeding was quite out of the common; while Nippers, twitching in his chair with a dyspeptic nervousness, ground out between his set teeth occasional hissing maledictions against the stubborn oaf behind the screen. And for his (Nippers's) part, this was the first and the last time he would do another man's business without pay.

Meanwhile Bartleby sat in his hermitage, oblivious to every thing but his own peculiar business there.

Some days passed, the scrivener being employed upon another lengthy work. His late remarkable conduct led me to regard his ways narrowly. I observed that he never went to dinner; indeed that he never went any where. As yet I had never of my personal knowledge known him to be outside of my office. He was a perpetual sentry in the corner. At about eleven o'clock though, in the morning, I noticed that Ginger Nut would advance toward the opening in Bartleby's screen, as if silently beckoned thither by a gesture invisible to me where I sat. The boy would then leave the office jingling a few pence, and reappear with a handful of ginger-nuts which he delivered in the hermitage, receiving two of the cakes for his trouble.

He lives, then, on ginger-nuts, thought I; never eats a dinner, properly speaking; he must be a vegetarian then; but no; he never eats even vegetables, he eats nothing but ginger-nuts. My mind then ran on in reveries concerning the probable effects upon the human constitution of living entirely on ginger-nuts. Ginger-nuts are so called because they contain ginger as one of their peculiar constituents, and the final flavoring one. Now what was ginger? A hot, spicy thing. Was Bartleby hot and spicy? Not at all. Ginger, then, had no effect upon Bartleby. Probably he preferred it should have none.

Nothing so aggravates an earnest person as a passive resistance. If the individual so resisted be of a not inhumane temper, and the resisting one perfectly harmless in his passivity; then, in the better moods of the former, he will endeavor charitably to construe to his imagination what proves impossible to be solved by his judgment. Even so, for the most part, I regarded Bartleby and his ways. Poor fellow! thought I, he means no mischief; it is plain he intends no insolence; his aspect sufficiently evinces that his eccentricities are involuntary. He is useful to me. I can get along with him. If I turn him away, the chances are he will fall in with some less indulgent employer, and then he will be rudely treated, and perhaps driven forth miserably to starve. Yes. Here I can cheaply purchase a delicious self-approval. To befriend Bartleby; to humor him in his strange wilfulness, will cost me little or nothing, while I lay up in my soul what will eventually prove a sweet morsel for my conscience. But this mood was not invariable with me. The passiveness of Bartleby sometimes irritated me. I felt strangely goaded on to encounter him in new opposition, to elicit some angry spark from him answerable to my own. But indeed I might as well have essayed to strike fire with my knuckles against a bit of Windsor soap. But one afternoon the evil impulse in me mastered me, and the following little scene ensued:

"Bartleby," said I, "when those papers are all copied, I will compare them with you."

"I would prefer not to."

"How? Surely you do not mean to persist in that mulish vagary?"

No answer.

I threw open the folding-doors near by, and turning upon Turkey and Nippers, exclaimed in an excited manner—

"He says, a second time, he won't examine his papers. What do you think of it, Turkey?"

It was afternoon, be it remembered. Turkey sat glowing like a brass boiler, his bald head steaming, his hands reeling among his blotted papers.

"Think of it?" roared Turkey; "I think I'll just step behind his screen, and black his eyes for him!"

So saying, Turkey rose to his feet and threw his arms into a pugilistic position. He was hurrying away to make good his promise, when I detained him, alarmed at the effect of incautiously rousing Turkey's combativeness after dinner.

"Sit down, Turkey," said I, "and hear what Nippers has to say. What do you think of it, Nippers? Would I not be justified in immediately dismissing Bartleby?"

"Excuse me, that is for you to decide, sir. I think his conduct quite unusual, and indeed unjust, as regards Turkey and myself. But it may only be a passing whim."

"Ah," exclaimed I, "you have strangely changed your mind then —you speak very gently of him now."

"All beer," cried Turkey; "gentleness is effects of beer—Nippers and I dined together to-day. You see how gentle *I* am, sir. Shall I go and black his eyes?"

"You refer to Bartleby, I suppose. No, not to-day, Turkey," I replied; "pray, put up your fists."

I closed the doors, and again advanced towards Bartleby. I felt additional incentives tempting me to my fate. I burned to be rebelled against again. I remembered that Bartleby never left the office.

"Bartleby," said I, "Ginger Nut is away; just step round to the Post Office, won't you? (it was but a three minutes walk,) and see if there is any thing for me."

"I would prefer not to."

"You *will* not?"

"I *prefer* not."

I staggered to my desk, and sat there in a deep study. My blind inveteracy returned. Was there any other thing in which I could procure myself to be ignominiously repulsed by this lean, penniless wight?—my hired clerk? What added thing is there, perfectly reasonable, that he will be sure to refuse to do?

"Bartleby!"

No answer.

"Bartleby," in a louder tone.

No answer.

"Bartleby," I roared.

Like a very ghost, agreeably to the laws of magical invocation, at the third summons, he appeared at the entrance of his hermitage.

"Go to the next room, and tell Nippers to come to me."

"I prefer not to," he respectfully and slowly said, and mildly disappeared.

"Very good, Bartleby," said I, in a quiet sort of serenely severe self-possessed tone, intimating the unalterable purpose of some terrible retribution very close at hand. At the moment I half intended something of the kind. But upon the whole, as it was drawing towards my dinner-hour, I thought it best to put on my hat and walk home for the day, suffering much from perplexity and distress of mind.

Shall I acknowledge it? The conclusion of this whole business was, that it soon became a fixed fact of my chambers, that a pale young scrivener, by the name of Bartleby, had a desk there; that he copied for me at the usual rate of four cents a folio (one hundred words); but he was permanently exempt from examining the work done by him, that duty being transferred to Turkey and Nippers, one of compliment doubtless to their superior acuteness; moreover, said Bartleby was never on any account to be dispatched on the most trivial errand of any sort; and that even if entreated to take upon him such a matter, it was generally understood that he would prefer not to—in other words, that he would refuse point-blank.

As days passed on, I became considerably reconciled to Bartleby. His steadiness, his freedom from all dissipation, his incessant industry (except when he chose to throw himself into a standing revery behind his screen), his great stillness, his unalterableness of demeanor under all circumstances, made him a valuable acquisition. One prime thing was this,—*he was always there;*—first in the morning, continually through the day, and the last at night. I had a singular confidence in his honesty. I felt my most precious papers perfectly safe in his hands. Sometimes to be sure I could not, for the very soul of me, avoid falling into sudden spasmodic passions with him. For it was exceeding difficult to bear in mind all the time those strange peculiarities, privileges, and unheard of exemptions, forming the tacit stipulations on Bartleby's part under which he remained in my office. Now and then, in the eagerness of dispatching pressing business, I would inadvertently summon Bartleby, in a short, rapid tone, to put his finger, say, on the incipient tie of a bit of red tape with which I was about compressing some papers. Of course, from behind the screen the usual answer, "I prefer not to," was sure to come; and then, how could a human creature with the common infirmities of our nature, refrain from bitterly exclaiming upon such perverseness—such unreasonableness. However, every added repulse of this sort which I received only tended to lessen the probability of my repeating the inadvertence.

Here it must be said, that according to the custom of most legal gentlemen occupying chambers in densely populated law buildings, there were several keys to my door. One was kept by a woman residing in the attic, which person weekly scrubbed and daily swept and dusted my apartments. Another was kept by Turkey for convenience sake. The third I sometimes carried in my own pocket. The fourth I knew not who had.

Now, one Sunday morning I happened to go to Trinity Church, to hear a celebrated preacher, and finding myself rather early on the ground, I thought I would walk round to my chambers for a while. Luckily I had my key with me; but upon applying it to the lock, I found it resisted by something inserted from the inside. Quite surprised, I called out; when to my consternation a key was turned from within; and thrusting his lean visage at me, and holding the door ajar, the apparition of Bartleby appeared, in his shirt sleeves, and otherwise in a strangely tattered dishabille, saying quietly that he was sorry, but he was deeply engaged just then, and—preferred not admitting me at present. In a brief word or two, he moreover added, that perhaps I had better walk round the block two or three times, and by that time he would probably have concluded his affairs.

Now, the utterly unsurmised appearance of Bartleby, tenanting my law-chambers of a Sunday morning, with his cadaverously gentlemanly *nonchalance*, yet withal firm and self-possessed, had such a strange effect upon me, that incontinently I slunk away from my own door, and did as desired. But not without sundry twinges of impotent rebellion against the mild effrontery of this unaccountable scrivener. Indeed, it was his wonderful mildness chiefly, which not only disarmed me, but unmanned me, as it were. For I consider that one, for the time, is a sort of unmanned when he tranquilly permits his hired clerk to dictate to him, and order him away from his own premises. Furthermore, I was full of uneasiness as to what Bartleby could possibly be doing in my office in his shirt sleeves, and in an otherwise dismantled condition of a Sunday morning. Was any thing amiss going on? Nay, that was out of the question. It was not to be thought of for a moment that Bartleby was an immoral person. But what could he be doing there?—copying? Nay again, whatever might be his eccentricities, Bartleby was an eminently decorous person. He would be the last man to sit down to his desk in any state approaching to nudity. Besides, it was Sunday; and there was something about Bartleby that forbade the supposition that he would by any secular occupation violate the proprieties of the day.

Nevertheless, my mind was not pacified; and full of a restless curiosity, at last I returned to the door. Without hindrance I inserted my key, opened it, and entered. Bartleby was not to be seen. I looked round anxiously, peeped behind his screen; but it was very plain that he was gone. Upon more closely examining the place, I surmised that for an indefinite period Bartleby must have ate, dressed, and slept in my office, and that too without plate, mirror, or bed. The cushioned seat of a ricketty old sofa in one corner bore the faint impress of a lean, reclining form. Rolled away under his deck, I found a blanket; under the empty grate, a blacking box and brush; on a chair, a tin basin, with soap and a ragged towel; in a newspaper a few crumbs of ginger-nuts and a morsel of cheese. Yes, thought I, it is evident enough that Bartleby has been making his home here, keeping bachelor's hall all by himself. Immediately then the thought came sweeping across me, What miserable friendlessness and loneliness are here revealed! His poverty is great; but his solitude, how horrible! Think of it. Of a Sunday, Wall-street is deserted as Petra; and every night of every day it is an emptiness. This building too, which of week-days hums with industry and life, at nightfall echoes with sheer vacancy, and all through Sunday is forlorn. And here Bartleby makes his home; sole spectator of a solitude which he has seen all populous—a sort of innocent and transformed Marius brooding among the ruins of Carthage!

For the first time in my life a feeling of overpowering stinging melancholy seized me. Before, I had never experienced aught but a not-unpleasing sadness. The bond of a common humanity now drew me irresistibly to gloom. A fraternal melancholy! For both I and Bartleby were sons of Adam. I remembered the bright silks and sparkling faces I had seen that day, in gala trim, swan-like sailing down the Mississippi of Broadway; and I contrasted them with the pallid copyist, and thought to myself, Ah, happiness courts the light, so we deem the world is gay; but misery hides aloof, so we deem that misery there is none. These sad fancyings—chimeras, doubtless, of a sick and silly brain—led on to other and more special thoughts, concerning the eccentricities of Bartleby. Presentiments of strange discoveries hovered round me. The scrivener's pale form appeared to me laid out, among uncaring strangers, in its shivering winding sheet.

Suddenly I was attracted by Bartleby's closed desk, the key in open sight left in the lock.

I mean no mischief, seek the gratification of no heartless curiosity, thought I; besides, the desk is mine, and its contents too, so I will make bold to look within. Every thing was methodically arranged, the papers smoothly placed. The pigeon holes were deep, and removing the files of documents, I groped into their recesses. Presently I felt something there, and dragged it out. It was an old bandanna handkerchief, heavy and knotted. I opened it, and saw it was a savings' bank.

I now recalled all the quiet mysteries which I had noted in the man. I remembered that he never spoke but to answer; that though at intervals he had considerable time to himself, yet I had never seen him reading—no, not even a newspaper; that for long periods he would stand looking out, at his pale window behind the screen, upon the dead brick wall; I was quite sure he never visited any refectory or eating house; while his pale face clearly indicated that he never drank beer like Turkey, or tea and coffee even, like other men; that he never went any where in particular that I could learn; never went out for a walk, unless indeed that was the case at present; that he had declined telling who he was, or whence he came, or whether he had any relatives in the world; that though so thin and pale, he never complained of ill health. And more than all, I remembered a certain unconscious air of pallid—how shall I call it?—of pallid haughtiness, say, or rather an austere reserve about him, which had positively awed me into my tame compliance with his eccentricities, when I had feared to ask him to do the slightest incidental thing for me, even though I might know, from his long-continued motionlessness, that behind his screen he must be standing in one of these dead-wall reveries of his.

Revolving all these things, and coupling them with the recently discovered fact that he made my office his constant abiding place and home, and not forgetful of his morbid moodiness; revolving all these things, a prudential feeling began to steal over me. My first emotions had been those of pure melancholy and sincerest pity; but just in proportion as the forlornness of Bartleby grew and grew to my imagination, did that same melancholy merge into fear, that pity into repulsion. So true it is, and so terrible too, that up to

a certain point the thought or sight of misery enlists our best affections; but, in certain special cases, beyond that point it does not.
They err who would assert that invariably this is owing to the inherent selfishness of the human heart. It rather proceeds from a certain hopelessness of remedying excessive and organic ill. To a sensitive being, pity is not seldom pain. And when at last it is perceived
that such pity cannot lead to effectual succor, common sense bids
the soul be rid of it. What I saw that morning persuaded me that
the scrivener was the victim of innate and incurable disorder. I
might give alms to his body; but his body did not pain him; it was
his soul that suffered, and his soul I could not reach.

I did not accomplish the purpose of going to Trinity Church
that morning. Somehow, the things I had seen disqualified me for
the time from church-going. I walked homeward, thinking what I
would do with Bartleby. Finally, I resolved upon this;—I would put
certain calm questions to him the next morning, touching his history, &c., and if he declined to answer them openly and unreservedly
(and I supposed he would prefer not), then to give him a twenty
dollar bill over and above whatever I might owe him, and tell him
his services were no longer required; but that if in any other way I
could assist him, I would be happy to do so, especially if he desired
to return to his native place, wherever that might be, I would willingly help to defray the expenses. Moreover, if, after reaching home,
he found himself at any time in want of aid, a letter from him
would be sure of a reply.

The next morning came.

"Bartleby," said I, gently calling to him behind his screen.

No reply.

"Bartleby," said I, in a still gentler tone, "come here; I am not
going to ask you to do any thing you would prefer not to do—I
simply wish to speak to you."

Upon this he noiselessly slid into view.

"Will you tell me, Bartleby, where you were born?"

"I would prefer not to."

"Will you tell me *any thing* about yourself?"

"I would prefer not to."

"But what reasonable objection can you have to speak to me? I
feel friendly towards you."

He did not look at me while I spoke, but kept his glance fixed upon my bust of Cicero, which as I then sat, was directly behind me, some six inches above my head.

"What is your answer, Bartleby?" said I, after waiting a considerable time for a reply, during which his countenance remained immovable, only there was the faintest conceivable tremor of the white attenuated mouth.

"At present I prefer to give no answer," he said, and retired into his hermitage.

It was rather weak in me I confess, but his manner on this occasion nettled me. Not only did there seem to lurk in it a certain calm disdain, but his perverseness seemed ungrateful, considering the undeniable good usage and indulgence he had received from me.

Again I sat ruminating what I should do. Mortified as I was at his behavior, and resolved as I had been to dismiss him when I entered my office, nevertheless I strangely felt something superstitious knocking at my heart, and forbidding me to carry out my purpose, and denouncing me for a villain if I dared to breathe one bitter word against this forlornest of mankind. At last, familiarly drawing my chair behind his screen, I sat down and said: "Bartleby, never mind then about revealing your history; but let me entreat you, as a friend, to comply as far as may be with the usages of this office. Say now you will help to examine papers to-morrow or next day: in short, say now that in a day or two you will begin to be a little reasonable:—say so, Bartleby."

"At present I would prefer not to be a little reasonable," was his mildly cadaverous reply.

Just then the folding-doors opened, and Nippers approached. He seemed suffering from an unusually bad night's rest, induced by severer indigestion than common. He overheard those final words of Bartleby.

"*Prefer not*, eh?" gritted Nippers—"I'd *prefer* him, if I were you, sir," addressing me—"I'd *prefer* him; I'd give him preferences, the stubborn mule! What is it, sir, pray, that he *prefers* not to do now?"

Bartleby moved not a limb.

"Mr. Nippers," said I, "I'd prefer that you would withdraw for the present."

Somehow, of late I had got into the way of involuntarily using this word "prefer" upon all sorts of not exactly suitable occasions. And I trembled to think that my contact with the scrivener had already and seriously affected me in a mental way. And what further and deeper aberration might it not yet produce? This apprehension had not been without efficacy in determining me to summary means.

As Nippers, looking very sour and sulky, was departing, Turkey blandly and deferentially approached.

"With submission, sir," said he, "yesterday I was thinking about Bartleby here, and I think that if he would but prefer to take a quart of good ale every day, it would do much towards mending him, and enabling him to assist in examining his papers."

"So, you have got the word too," said I, slightly excited.

"With submission, what word, sir," asked Turkey, respectfully crowding himself into the contracted space behind the screen, and by so doing, making me jostle the scrivener. "What word, sir?"

"I would prefer to be left alone here," said Bartleby, as if offended at being mobbed in his privacy.

"*That's* the word, Turkey," said I—"*that's* it."

"Oh, *prefer?* oh yes—queer word. I never use it myself. But, sir, as I was saying, if he would but prefer—"

"Turkey," interrupted I, "you will please withdraw."

"Oh, certainly, sir, if you prefer that I should."

As he opened the folding-door to retire, Nippers at his desk caught a glimpse of me and asked whether I would prefer to have a certain paper copied on blue paper or white. He did not in the least roguishly accent the word prefer. It was plain that it involuntarily rolled from his tongue. I thought to myself, surely I must get rid of a demented man, who already has in some degree turned the tongues, if not the heads of myself and clerks. But I thought it prudent not to break the dismission at once.

The next day I noticed that Bartleby did nothing but stand at his window in his dead-wall revery. Upon asking him why he did not write, he said that he had decided upon doing no more writing.

"Why, how now? what next?" exclaimed I, "do no more writing?"

"No more."

"And what is the reason?"

"Do you not see the reason for yourself," he indifferently replied.

I looked steadfastly at him, and perceived that his eyes looked dull and glazed. Instantly it occurred to me that his unexampled diligence in copying by his dim window for the first few weeks of his stay with me might have temporarily impaired his vision.

I was touched. I said something in condolence with him. I hinted that of course he did wisely in abstaining from writing for a while; and urged him to embrace that opportunity of taking wholesome exercise in the open air. This, however, he did not do. A few days after this, my other clerks being absent, and being in a great hurry to dispatch certain letters by the mail, I thought that, having nothing else earthly to do, Bartleby would surely be less inflexible than usual, and carry these letters to the post-office. But he blankly declined. So, much to my inconvenience, I went myself.

Still added days went by. Whether Bartleby's eyes improved or not, I could not say. To all appearance, I thought they did. But when I asked him if they did, he vouchsafed no answer. At all events, he would do no copying. At last, in reply to my urgings, he informed me that he had permanently given up copying.

"What!" exclaimed I; "suppose your eyes should get entirely well—better than ever before—would you not copy then?"

"I have given up copying," he answered, and slid aside.

He remained as ever, a fixture in my chamber. Nay—if that were possible—he became still more of a fixture than before. What was to be done? He would do nothing in the office: why should he stay there? In plain fact, he had now become a millstone to me, not only useless as a necklace, but afflictive to bear. Yet I was sorry for him. I speak less than truth when I say that, on his own account, he occasioned me uneasiness. If he would but have named a single relative or friend, I would instantly have written, and urged their taking the poor fellow away to some convenient retreat. But he seemed alone, absolutely alone in the universe. A bit of wreck in the mid-Atlantic. At length, necessities connected with my business tyrannized over all other considerations. Decently as I could, I told Bartleby that in six days' time he must unconditionally leave the office. I warned him to take measures, in the interval, for procuring some other abode. I offered to assist him in this endeavor, if he himself would but take the first step towards a removal. "And when you finally quit me, Bartleby," added I, "I shall see that you go not away entirely unprovided. Six days from this hour, remember."

At the expiration of that period, I peeped behind the screen, and lo! Bartleby was there.

I buttoned up my coat, balanced myself; advanced slowly towards him, touched his shoulder, and said, "The time has come; you must quit this place; I am sorry for you; here is money; but you must go."

"I would prefer not," he replied, with his back still towards me.

"You *must*."

He remained silent.

Now I had an unbounded confidence in this man's common honesty. He had frequently restored to me sixpences and shillings carelessly dropped upon the floor, for I am apt to be very reckless in such shirt-button affairs. The proceeding then which followed will not be deemed extraordinary.

"Bartleby," said I, "I owe you twelve dollars on account; here are thirty-two; the odd twenty are yours.—Will you take it?" and I handed the bills towards him.

But he made no motion.

"I will leave them here then," putting them under a weight on the table. Then taking my hat and cane and going to the door I tranquilly turned and added—"After you have removed your things from these offices, Bartleby, you will of course lock the door—since every one is now gone for the day but you—and if you please, slip your key underneath the mat, so that I may have it in the morning. I shall not see you again; so good-bye to you. If hereafter in your new place of abode I can be of any service to you, do not fail to advise me by letter. Good-bye, Bartleby, and fare you well."

But he answered not a word; like the last column of some ruined temple, he remained standing mute and solitary in the middle of the otherwise deserted room.

As I walked home in a pensive mood, my vanity got the better of my pity. I could not but highly plume myself on my masterly management in getting rid of Bartleby. Masterly I call it, and such it must appear to any dispassionate thinker. The beauty of my procedure seemed to consist in its perfect quietness. There was no vulgar bullying, no bravado of any sort, no choleric hectoring, and striding to and fro across the apartment, jerking out vehement commands for Bartleby to bundle himself off with his beggarly traps. Nothing of the kind. Without loudly bidding Bartleby depart—as an inferior genius might have done—I *assumed* the ground that depart he must; and upon that assumption built all I had to say. The more I thought over my procedure, the more I was charmed with it. Nevertheless, next morning, upon awakening, I had my doubts,—I had somehow slept off the fumes of vanity. One of the coolest and wisest hours a man has, is just after he awakes in the morning. My procedure seemed as sagacious as ever,—but only in theory. How it would prove in practice—there was the rub. It was truly a beautiful thought to have assumed Bartleby's departure; but, after all, that assumption was simply my own, and none of Bartleby's. The great point was, not whether I had assumed that he would quit me, but whether he would prefer so to do. He was more a man of preferences than assumptions.

After breakfast, I walked down town, arguing the probabilities *pro* and *con*. One moment I thought it would prove a miserable failure, and Bartleby would be found all alive at my office as usual; the next moment it seemed certain that I should see his chair empty. And so I kept veering about. At the corner of Broadway and Canal-street, I saw quite an excited group of people standing in earnest conversation.

"I'll take odds he doesn't," said a voice as I passed.

"Doesn't go?—done!" said I, "put up your money."

I was instinctively putting my hand in my pocket to produce my own, when I remembered that this was an election day. The words I had overheard bore no reference to Bartleby, but to the success or non-success of some candidate for the mayoralty. In my intent frame of mind, I had, as it were, imagined that all Broadway shared in my excitement, and were debating the same question with me. I passed on, very thankful that the uproar of the street screened my momentary absent-mindedness.

As I had intended, I was earlier than usual at my office door. I stood listening for a moment. All was still. He must be gone. I tried the knob. The door was locked. Yes, my procedure had worked to a charm; he indeed must be vanished. Yet a certain melancholy mixed with this: I was almost sorry for my brilliant success. I was fumbling under the door mat for the key, which Bartleby was to have left there for me, when accidentally my knee knocked against a panel, producing a summoning sound, and in response a voice came to me from within—"Not yet; I am occupied."

It was Bartleby.

I was thunderstruck. For an instant I stood like the man who, pipe in mouth, was killed one cloudless afternoon long ago in Virginia, by summer lightning; at his own warm open window he was killed, and remained leaning out there upon the dreamy afternoon, till some one touched him, when he fell.

"Not gone!" I murmured at last. But again obeying that wondrous ascendancy which the inscrutable scrivener had over me, and from which ascendency, for all my chafing, I could not completely escape, I slowly went down stairs and out into the street, and while walking round the block, considered what I should next do in this unheard-of perplexity. Turn the man out by an actual thrusting I could not; to drive him away by calling him hard names would not do; calling in the police was an unpleasant idea; and yet, permit him to enjoy his cadaverous triumph over me,—this too I could not think of. What was to be done? or, if nothing could be done, was there any thing further that I could *assume* in the matter? Yes, as before I had prospectively assumed that Bartleby would depart, so now I might retrospectively assume that departed he was. In the legitimate carrying out of this assumption, I might enter my office in a great hurry, and pretending not to see Bartleby at all, walk straight against him as if he were air. Such a proceeding would in a singular degree have the appearance of a home-thrust. It was hardly possible that Bartleby could withstand such an application of the doctrine of assumptions. But upon second thoughts the success of the plan seemed rather dubious. I resolved to argue the matter over with him again.

"Bartleby," said I, entering the office, with a quietly severe expression, "I am seriously displeased. I am pained, Bartleby. I had thought better of you. I had imagined you of such a gentlemanly organization, that in any delicate dilemma a slight hint would suffice—in short, an assumption. But it appears I am deceived. Why," I added, unaffectedly starting, "you have not even touched that

money yet," pointing to it, just where I had left it the evening
previous.

He answered nothing.

"Will you, or will you not, quit me?" I now demanded in a
sudden passion, advancing close to him.

"I would prefer *not* to quit you," he replied, gently emphasizing
the *not*.

"What earthly right have you to stay here? Do you pay any
rent? Do you pay my taxes? Or is this property yours?"

He answered nothing.

"Are you ready to go on and write now? Are your eyes recovered? Could you copy a small paper for me this morning? or help
examine a few lines? or step round to the post-office? In a word, will
you do any thing at all, to give a coloring to your refusal to depart
the premises?"

He silently retired into his hermitage.

I was now in such a state of nervous resentment that I thought
it but prudent to check myself at present from further demonstra-
tions. Bartleby and I were alone. I remembered the tragedy of the
unfortunate Adams and the still more unfortunate Colt in the solitary office of the latter; and how poor Colt, being dreadfully incensed by Adams, and imprudently permitting himself to get wildly
excited, was at unawares hurried into his fatal act—an act which
certainly no man could possibly deplore more than the actor himself. Often it had occurred to me in my ponderings upon the subject,
that had that altercation taken place in the public street, or at a
private residence, it would not have terminated as it did. It was the
circumstance of being alone in a solitary office, up stairs, of a building entirely unhallowed by humanizing domestic associations—an
uncarpeted office, doubtless, of a dusty, haggard sort of appearance;
—this it must have been, which greatly helped to enhance the irritable desperation of the hapless Colt.

But when this old Adam of resentment rose in me and tempted
me concerning Bartleby, I grappled him and threw him. How? Why,
simply by recalling the divine injunction: "A new commandment
give I unto you, that ye love one another." Yes, this it was that
saved me. Aside from higher considerations, charity often operates
as a vastly wise and prudent principle—a great safeguard to its

possessor. Men have committed murder for jealousy's sake, and anger's sake, and hatred's sake, and selfishness' sake, and spiritual pride's sake; but no man that ever I heard of, ever committed a diabolical murder for sweet charity's sake. Mere self-interest, then, if no better motive can be enlisted, should, especially with high-tempered men, prompt all beings to charity and philanthropy. At any rate, upon the occasion in question, I strove to drown my exasperated feelings towards the scrivener by benevolently construing his conduct. Poor fellow, poor fellow! thought I, he don't mean any thing; and besides, he has seen hard times, and ought to be indulged.

I endeavored also immediately to occupy myself, and at the same time to comfort my despondency. I tried to fancy that in the course of the morning, at such time as might prove agreeable to him, Bartleby, of his own free accord, would emerge from his hermitage, and take up some decided line of march in the direction of the door. But no. Half-past twelve o'clock came; Turkey began to glow in the face, overturn his inkstand, and become generally obstreperous; Nippers abated down into quietude and courtesy; Ginger Nut munched his noon apple; and Bartleby remained standing at his window in one of his profoundest dead-wall reveries. Will it be credited? Ought I to acknowledge it? That afternoon I left the office without saying one further word to him.

Some days now passed, during which, at leisure intervals I looked a little into "Edwards on the Will," and "Priestley on Necessity." Under the circumstances, those books induced a salutary feeling. Gradually I slid into the persuasion that these troubles of mine touching the scrivener had been all predestinated from eternity, and Bartleby was billeted upon me for some mysterious purpose of an all-wise Providence, which it was not for a mere mortal like me to fathom. Yes, Bartleby, stay there behind your screen, thought I; I shall persecute you no more; you are harmless and noiseless as any of these old chairs; in short, I never feel so private as when I know you are here. At least I see it, I feel it; I penetrate to the predestinated purpose of my life. I am content. Others may have loftier parts to enact; but my mission in this world, Bartleby, is to furnish you with office-room for such period as you may see fit to remain.

I believe that this wise and blessed frame of mind would have continued with me had it not been for the unsolicited and uncharitable remarks obtruded upon me by my professional friends who visited the rooms. But thus it often is, that the constant friction of illiberal minds wears out at last the best resolves of the more generous. Though to be sure, when I reflected upon it, it was not strange that people entering my office should be struck by the peculiar aspect of the unaccountable Bartleby, and so be tempted to throw out some sinister observations concerning him. Sometimes an attorney having business with me, and calling at my office, and finding no one but the scrivener there, would undertake to obtain some sort of precise information from him touching my whereabouts; but without heeding his idle talk, Bartleby would remain standing immovable in the middle of the room. So after contemplating him in that position for a time, the attorney would depart, no wiser than he came.

Also, when a Reference was going on, and the room full of lawyers and witnesses and business was driving fast; some deeply occupied legal gentleman present, seeing Bartleby wholly unemployed, would request him to run round to his (the legal gentleman's) office and fetch some papers for him. Thereupon, Bartleby would tranquilly decline, and yet remain idle as before. Then the lawyer would give a great stare, and turn to me. And what could I say? At last I was made aware that all through the circle of my professional acquaintance, a whisper of wonder was running round, having reference to the strange creature I kept at my office. This worried me very much. And as the idea came upon me of his possibly turning out a long-lived man, and keep occupying my chambers, and denying my authority; and perplexing my visitors; and scandalizing my professional reputation; and casting a general gloom over the premises; keeping soul and body together to the last upon his savings (for doubtless he spent but half a dime a day), and in the end perhaps outlive me, and claim possession of my office by right of his perpetual occupancy: as all these dark anticipations crowded upon me more and more, and my friends continually intruded their relentless remarks upon the apparition in my room; a great change was wrought in me. I resolved to gather all my faculties together, and for ever rid me of this intolerable incubus.

Ere resolving any complicated project, however, adapted to this end, I first simply suggested to Bartleby the propriety of his permanent departure. In a calm and serious tone, I commended the idea to his careful and mature consideration. But having taken three days to meditate upon it, he apprised me that his original determination remained the same; in short, that he still preferred to abide with me.

What shall I do? I now said to myself, buttoning up my coat to the last button. What shall I do? what ought I to do? what does conscience say I *should* do with this man, or rather ghost. Rid myself of him, I must; go, he shall. But how? You will not thrust him, the poor, pale, passive mortal,—you will not thrust such a helpless creature out of your door? you will not dishonor yourself by such cruelty? No, I will not, I cannot do that. Rather would I let him live and die here, and then mason up his remains in the wall. What then will you do? For all your coaxing, he will not budge. Bribes he leaves under your own paperweight on your table; in short, it is quite plain that he prefers to cling to you.

Then something severe, something unusual must be done. What! surely you will not have have him collared by a constable, and commit his innocent pallor to the common jail? And upon what ground could you procure such a thing to be done?—a vagrant, is he? What! he a vagrant, a wanderer, who refuses to budge? It is because he will *not* be a vagrant, then, that you seek to count him *as* a vagrant. That is too absurd. No visible means of support: there I have him. Wrong again: for indubitably he *does* support himself, and that is the only unanswerable proof that any man can show of his possessing the means so to do. No more then. Since he will not quit me, I must quit him. I will change my offices; I will move elsewhere; and give him fair notice, that if I find him on my new premises I will then proceed against him as a common trespasser.

Acting accordingly, next day I thus addressed him: "I find these chambers too far from the City Hall; the air is unwholesome. In a word, I propose to remove my offices next week, and shall no longer require your services. I tell you this now, in order that you may seek another place."

He made no reply, and nothing more was said.

On the appointed day I engaged carts and men, proceeded to my chambers, and having but little furniture, every thing was removed in a few hours. Throughout, the scrivener remained standing behind the screen, which I directed to be removed the last thing.

It was withdrawn; and being folded up like a huge folio, left him the motionless occupant of a naked room. I stood in the entry watching him a moment, while something from within me upbraided me.

I re-entered, with my hand in my pocket—and—and my heart in my mouth.

"Good-bye, Bartleby; I am going—good-bye, and God some way bless you; and take that," slipping something in his hand. But it dropped upon the floor, and then,—strange to say—I tore myself from him whom I had so longed to be rid of.

Established in my new quarters, for a day or two I kept the door locked, and started at every footfall in the passages. When I returned to my rooms after any little absence, I would pause at the threshold for an instant, and attentively listen, ere applying my key. But these fears were needless. Bartleby never came nigh me.

I thought all was going well, when a perturbed looking stranger visited me, inquiring whether I was the person who had recently occupied rooms at No.—Wall-street.

Full of forebodings, I replied that I was.

"Then sir," said the stranger, who proved a lawyer, "you are responsible for the man you left there. He refuses to do any copying; he refuses to do any thing; he says he prefers not to; and he refuses to quit the premises."

"I am very sorry, sir," said I, with assumed tranquillity, but an inward tremor, "but, really, the man you allude to is nothing to me—he is no relation or apprentice of mine, that you should hold me responsible for him."

"In mercy's name, who is he?"

"I certainly cannot inform you. I know nothing about him. Formerly I employed him as a copyist; but he has done nothing for me now for some time past."

"I shall settle him then,—good morning, sir."

Several days passed, and I heard nothing more; and though I often felt a charitable prompting to call at the place and see poor Bartleby, yet a certain squeamishness of I know not what withheld me.

All is over with him, by this time, thought I at last, when through another week no further intelligence reached me. But coming to my room the day after, I found several persons waiting at my door in a high state of nervous excitement.

"That's the man—here he comes," cried the foremost one, whom I recognized as the lawyer who had previously called upon me alone.

"You must take him away, sir, at once," cried a portly person among them, advancing upon me, and whom I knew to be the landlord of No.—Wall-street. "These gentlemen, my tenants, cannot stand it any longer; Mr. B——" pointing to the lawyer, "has turned him out of his room, and he now persists in haunting the building generally, sitting upon the banisters of the stairs by day, and sleeping in the entry by night. Every body is concerned; clients are leaving the offices; some fears are entertained of a mob; something you must do, and that without delay."

Aghast at this torrent, I fell back before it, and would fain have locked myself in my new quarters. In vain I persisted that Bartleby was nothing to me—no more than to any one else. In vain:—I was the last person known to have any thing to do with him, and they held me to the terrible account. Fearful then of being exposed in the papers (as one person present obscurely threatened) I considered the matter, and at length said, that if the lawyer would give me a confidential interview with the scrivener, in his (the lawyer's) own room, I would that afternoon strive my best to rid them of the nuisance they complained of.

Going up stairs to my old haunt, there was Bartleby silently sitting upon the banister at the landing.

"What are you doing here, Bartleby?" said I.

"Sitting upon the banister," he mildly replied.

I motioned him into the lawyer's room, who then left us.

"Bartleby," said I, "are you aware that you are the cause of great tribulation to me, by persisting in occupying the entry after being dismissed from the office?"

No answer.

"Now one of two things must take place. Either you must do something, or something must be done to you. Now what sort of business would you like to engage in? Would you like to re-engage in copying for some one?"

"No; I would prefer not to make any change."

"Would you like a clerkship in a dry goods store?"

"There is too much confinement about that. No, I would not like a clerkship; but I am not particular."

"Too much confinement," I cried, "why you keep yourself confined all the time!"

"I would prefer not to take a clerkship," he rejoined, as if to settle that little item at once.

"How would a bartender's business suit you? There is no trying of the eyesight in that."

"I would not like it at all; though, as I said before, I am not particular."

His unwonted wordiness inspirited me. I returned to the charge.

"Well then, would you like to travel through the country collecting bills for the merchants? That would improve your health."

"No, I would prefer to be doing something else."

"How then would going as a companion to Europe, to entertain some young gentleman with your conversation,—how would that suit you?"

"Not at all. It does not strike me that there is any thing definite about that. I like to be stationary. But I am not particular."

"Stationary you shall be then," I cried, now losing all patience, and for the first time in all my exasperating connection with him fairly flying into a passion. "If you do not go away from these premises before night, I shall feel bound—indeed I *am* bound—to—to—to quit the premises myself!" I rather absurdly concluded, knowing not with what possible threat to try to frighten his immobility into compliance. Despairing of all further efforts, I was precipitately leaving him, when a final thought occurred to me—one which had not been wholly unindulged before.

"Bartleby," said I, in the kindest tone I could assume under such exciting circumstances, "will you go home with me now—not to my office, but my dwelling—and remain there till we can conclude upon some convenient arrangement for you at our leisure? Come, let us start now, right away."

"No: at present I would prefer not to make any change at all."

I answered nothing; but effectually dodging every one by the suddenness and rapidity of my flight, rushed from the building, ran up Wall-street towards Broadway, and jumping into the first omnibus was soon removed from pursuit. As soon as tranquillity returned I distinctly perceived that I had now done all that I possibly could, both in respect to the demands of the landlord and his tenants, and with regard to my own desire and sense of duty, to benefit Bartleby, and shield him from rude persecution. I now strove to be entirely care-free and quiescent; and my conscience justified me in the attempt; though indeed it was not so successful as I could have wished. So fearful was I of being again hunted out by the incensed landlord and his exasperated tenants, that, surrendering my business to Nippers, for a few days I drove about the upper part of the town and through the suburbs, in my rockaway; crossed over to Jersey City and Hoboken, and paid fugitive visits to Manhattanville and Astoria. In fact I almost lived in my rockaway for the time.

When again I entered my office, lo, a note from the landlord lay upon the desk. I opened it with trembling hands. It informed me that the writer had sent to the police, and had Bartleby removed to the Tombs as a vagrant. Moreover, since I knew more about him than any one else, he wished me to appear at that place, and make a suitable statement of the facts. These tidings had a conflicting effect upon me. At first I was indignant; but at last almost approved. The landlord's energetic, summary disposition, had led him to adopt a procedure which I do not think I would have decided upon myself; and yet as a last resort, under such peculiar circumstances, it seemed the only plan.

As I afterwards learned, the poor scrivener, when told that he must be conducted to the Tombs, offered not the slightest obstacle, but in his pale unmoving way, silently acquiesced.

Some of the compassionate and curious bystanders joined the party; and headed by one of the constables arm in arm with Bartleby, the silent procession filed its way through all the noise, and heat, and joy of the roaring thoroughfares at noon.

The same day I received the note I went to the Tombs, or to speak more properly, the Halls of Justice. Seeking the right officer, I stated the purpose of my call, and was informed that the individual I described was indeed within. I then assured the functionary that Bartleby was a perfectly honest man, and greatly to be compassionated, however unaccountably eccentric. I narrated all I knew, and closed by suggesting the idea of letting him remain in as indul-

gent confinement as possible till something less harsh might be done
—though indeed I hardly knew what. At all events, if nothing else
could be decided upon, the alms house must receive him. I then
begged to have an interview.

Being under no disgraceful charge, and quite serene and harmless in all his ways, they had permitted him freely to wander about
the prison, and especially in the inclosed grass-platted yards thereof.
And so I found him there, standing all alone in the quietest of the
yards, his face towards a high wall, while all around, from the narrow slits of the jail windows, I thought I saw peering out upon him
the eyes of murderers and thieves.

"Bartleby!"

"I know you," he said, without looking round,—"and I want
nothing to say to you."

"It was not I that brought you here, Bartleby," said I, keenly
pained at his implied suspicion. "And to you, this should not be so
vile a place. Nothing reproachful attaches to you by being here.
And see, it is not so sad a place as one might think. Look, there is
the sky, and here is the grass."

"I know where I am," he replied, but would say nothing more,
and so I left him.

As I entered the corridor again, a broad meat-like man, in an
apron, accosted me, and jerking his thumb over his shoulder said—
"Is that your friend?"

"Yes."

"Does he want to starve? If he does, let him live on the prison
fare, that's all."

"Who are you?" asked I, not knowing what to make of such an
unofficially speaking person in such a place.

"I am the grub-man. Such gentleman as have friends here hire
me to provide them with something good to eat."

"Is this so?" said I, turning to the turnkey.

He said it was.

"Well then," said I, slipping some silver into the grub-man's
hands (for so they called him), "I want you to give particular attention to my friend there; let him have the best dinner you can get.
And you must be as polite to him as possible."

"Introduce me, will you?" said the grub-man, looking at me with an expression which seemed to say he was all impatience for an opportunity to give a specimen of his breeding.

Thinking it would prove of benefit to the scrivener, I acquiesced; and asking the grub-man his name, went up with him to Bartleby.

"Bartleby, this is Mr. Cutlets; you will find him very useful to you."

"Your sarvant, sir, your sarvant," said the grub-man, making a low salutation behind his apron. "Hope you find it pleasant here, sir;—spacious grounds—cool apartments, sir—hope you'll stay with us some time—try to make it agreeable. May Mrs. Cutlets and I have the pleasure of your company to dinner, sir, in Mrs. Cutlets' private room?"

"I prefer not to dine to-day," said Bartleby, turning away. "It would disagree with me; I am unused to dinners." So saying he slowly moved to the other side of the inclosure, and took up a position fronting the dead-wall.

"How's this?" said the grub-man, addressing me with a stare of astonishment. "He's odd, aint he?"

"I think he is a little deranged," said I, sadly.

"Deranged? deranged is it? Well now, upon my word, I thought that friend of yourn was a gentleman forger; they are always pale and genteel-like, them forgers. I can't help pity 'em—can't help it, sir. Did you know Monroe Edwards?" he added touchingly, and paused. Then, laying his hand pityingly on my shoulder, sighed, "he died of consumption at Sing-Sing. So you weren't acquainted with Monroe?"

"No, I was never socially acquainted with any forgers. But I cannot stop longer. Look to my friend yonder. You will not lose by it. I will see you again."

Some few days after this, I again obtained admission to the Tombs, and went through the corridors in quest of Bartleby; but without finding him.

"I saw him coming from his cell not long ago," said a turnkey, "may be he's gone to loiter in the yards."

So I went in that direction.

"Are you looking for the silent man?" said another turnkey passing me. "Yonder he lies—sleeping in the yard there. 'Tis not twenty minutes since I saw him lie down."

The yard was entirely quiet. It was not accessible to the common prisoners. The surrounding walls, of amazing thickness, kept off all sounds behind them. The Egyptian character of the masonry weighted upon me with its gloom. But a soft imprisoned turf grew under foot. The heart of the eternal pyramids, it seemed, wherein, by some strange magic, through the clefts, grass seed, dropped by birds, had sprung.

Strangely huddled at the base of the wall, his knees drawn up, and lying on his side, his head touching the cold stones, I saw the wasted Bartleby. But nothing stirred. I paused; then went close up to him; stooped over, and saw that his dim eyes were open; otherwise he seemed profoundly sleeping. Something prompted me to touch him. I felt his hand, when a tingling shiver ran up my arm and down my spine to my feet.

The round face of the grub-man peered upon me now. "His dinner is ready. Won't he dine to-day either? Or does he live without dining?"

"Lives without dining," said I, and closed the eyes.

"Eh!—He's asleep, aint he?"

"With kings and counsellors," murmured I.

❊ ❊ ❊ ❊ ❊ ❊ ❊ ❊ ❊ ❊ ❊ ❊ ❊ ❊ ❊ ❊

There would seem little need for proceeding further in this history. Imagination will readily supply the meagre recital of poor Bartleby's interment. But ere parting with the reader, let me say, that if this little narrative has sufficiently interested him, to awaken curiosity as to who Bartleby was, and what manner of life he led prior to the present narrator's making his acquaintance, I can only reply, that in such curiosity I fully share, but am wholly unable to gratify it. Yet here I hardly know whether I should divulge one little item of rumor, which came to my ear a few months after the scrivener's decease. Upon what basis it rested, I could never ascertain; and hence, how true it is I cannot now tell. But inasmuch as this vague report has not been without a certain strange suggestive interest to me, however sad, it may prove the same with some others; and so I will briefly mention it. The report was this: that Bartleby had been a subordinate clerk in the Dead Letter Office at Washington, from which he had been suddenly removed by a change in the administration. When I think over this rumor, I cannot adequately express the emotions which seize me. Dead letters! does it not sound like dead men? Conceive a man by nature and misfortune prone to a pallid hopelessness, can any business seem more fitted to heighten it than that of continually handling these dead letters, and assorting them for the flames? For by the cart-load they are annually burned. Sometimes from out the folded paper the pale clerk takes a ring:—the finger it was meant for, perhaps, moulders in the grave; a bank-note sent in swiftest charity:—he whom it would relieve, nor eats nor hungers any more; pardon for those who died despairing; hope for those who died unhoping; good tidings for those who died stifled by unrelieved calamities. On errands of life, these letters speed to death.

Ah Bartleby! Ah humanity!

The Strange Case of
Dr. Jekyll and Mr. Hyde

ROBERT LOUIS STEVENSON

STORY OF THE DOOR

Mr. Utterson the lawyer was a man of a rugged countenance, that was never lighted by a smile; cold, scanty and embarrassed in discourse; backward in sentiment; lean, long, dusty, dreary and yet somehow lovable. At friendly meetings, and when the wine was to his taste, something eminently human beaconed from his eye; something indeed which never found its way into his talk, but which spoke not only in these silent symbols of the after-dinner face, but more often and loudly in the acts of his life. He was austere with himself; drank gin when he was alone, to mortify a taste for vintages; and though he enjoyed the theatre, had not crossed the doors of one for twenty years. But he had an approved tolerance for others; sometimes wondering, almost with envy, at the high pressure of spirits involved in their misdeeds; and in any extremity inclined to help rather than to reprove. "I incline to Cain's heresy," he used to say quaintly: "I let my brother go to the devil in his own way." In this character, it was frequently his fortune to be the last reputable acquaintance and the last good influence in the lives of down-going men. And to such as these, so long as they came about his chambers, he never marked a shade of change in his demeanour.

No doubt the feat was easy to Mr. Utterson; for he was undemonstrative at the best, and even his friendship seemed to be founded in a similar catholicity of good-nature. It is the mark of a modest man to accept his friendly circle ready-made from the hands of opportunity; and that was the lawyer's way. His friends were those of his own blood or those whom he had known the longest; his affections, like ivy, were the growth of time, they implied no aptness in the object. Hence, no doubt, the bond that united him to Mr. Richard Enfield, his distant kinsman, the well-known man about town. It was a nut to crack for many, what these two could see in each other, or what subject they could find in common. It was reported by those who encountered them in their Sunday walks, that they said nothing, looked singularly dull, and would hail with obvious relief the appearance of a friend. For all that, the two men put the greatest store by these excursions, counted them the chief jewel of each week, and not only set aside occasions of pleasure, but even resisted the calls of business, that they might enjoy them uninterrupted.

It chanced on one of these rambles that their way led them down a by-street in a busy quarter of London. The street was small and what is called quiet, but it drove a thriving trade on the weekdays. The inhabitants were all doing well, it seemed, and all emulously hoping to do better still, and laying out the surplus of their gains in coquetry; so that the shop fronts stood along that thoroughfare with an air of invitation, like rows of smiling saleswomen. Even on Sunday, when it veiled its more florid charms and lay comparatively empty of passage, the street shone out in contrast to its dingy neighbourhood, like a fire in a forest; and with its freshly painted shutters, well-polished brasses, and general cleanliness and gaiety of note, instantly caught and pleased the eye of the passenger.

Two doors from one corner, on the left hand going east, the line was broken by the entry of a court; and just at that point, a certain sinister block of building thrust forward its gable on the street. It was two storeys high; showed no window, nothing but a door on the lower storey and a blind forehead of discoloured wall on the upper; and bore in every feature, the marks of prolonged and sordid negligence. The door, which was equipped with neither bell nor knocker, was blistered and distained. Tramps slouched into the recess and struck matches on the panels; children kept shop upon the steps; the schoolboy had tried his knife on the mouldings;

and for close on a generation, no one had appeared to drive away these random visitors or to repair their ravages.

Mr. Enfield and the lawyer were on the other side of the by-street; but when they came abreast of the entry, the former lifted up his cane and pointed.

"Did you ever remark that door?" he asked; and when his companion had replied in the affirmative, "It is connected in my mind," added he, "with a very odd story."

"Indeed?" said Mr. Utterson, with a slight change of voice, "and what was that?"

"Well, it was this way," returned Mr. Enfield: "I was coming home from some place at the end of the world, about three o'clock of a black winter morning, and my way lay through a part of town where there was literally nothing to be seen but lamps. Street after street, and all the folks asleep—street after street, all lighted up as if for a procession and all as empty as a church—till at last I got into that state of mind when a man listens and listens and begins to long for the sight of a policeman. All at once, I saw two figures: one a little man who was stumping along eastward at a good walk, and the other a girl of maybe eight or ten who was running as hard as she was able down a cross street. Well, sir, the two ran into one another naturally enough at the corner; and then came the horrible part of the thing; for the man trampled calmly over the child's body and left her screaming on the ground. It sounds nothing to hear, but it was hellish to see. It wasn't like a man; it was like some damned Juggernaut. I gave a view halloa, took to my heels, collared my gentleman, and brought him back to where there was already quite a group about the screaming child. He was perfectly cool and made no resistance, but gave me one look, so ugly that it brought out the sweat on me like running. The people who had turned out were the girl's own family; and pretty soon, the doctor, for whom she had been sent, put in his appearance. Well, the child was not much the worse, more frightened, according to the Sawbones; and there you might have supposed would be an end to it. But there was one curious circumstance. I had taken a loathing to my gentleman at first sight. So had the child's family, which was only natural. But the doctor's case was what struck me. He was the usual cut

and dry apothecary, of no particular age and colour, with a strong
Edinburgh accent, and about as emotional as a bagpipe. Well, sir,
he was like the rest of us; every time he looked at my prisoner, I
saw that Sawbones turn sick and white with the desire to kill him.
I knew what was in his mind, just as he knew what was in mine;
and killing being out of the question, we did the next best. We
told the man we could and would make such a scandal out of this,
as should make his name stink from one end of London to the other.
If he had any friends or any credit, we undertook that he should
lose them. And all the time, as we were pitching it in red hot, we
were keeping the women off him as best we could, for they were
as wild as harpies. I never saw a circle of such hateful faces; and
there was the man in the middle, with a kind of black, sneering
coolness—frightened too, I could see that—but carrying it off, sir,
really like Satan. 'If you choose to make capital out of this accident,' said he, 'I am naturally helpless. No gentleman but wishes to
avoid a scene,' says he. 'Name your figure.' Well, we screwed him
up to a hundred pounds for the child's family; he would have clearly
liked to stick out; but there was something about the lot of us that
meant mischief, and at last he struck. The next thing was to get the
money; and where do you think he carried us but to that place with
the door?—whipped out a key, went in, and presently came back
with the matter of ten pounds in gold and a cheque for the balance
on Coutts's, drawn payable to bearer and signed with a name that
I can't mention, though it's one of the points of my story, but it
was a name at least very well known and often printed. The figure
was stiff; but the signature was good for more than that, if it was
only genuine. I took the liberty of pointing out to my gentleman
that the whole business looked apocryphal, and that a man does
not, in real life, walk into a cellar door at four in the morning and
come out of it with another man's cheque for close upon a hundred
pounds. But he was quite easy and sneering. 'Set your mind at rest,'
says he, 'I will stay with you till the banks open and cash the cheque
myself.' So we all set off, the doctor, and the child's father, and our
friend and myself, and passed the rest of the night in my chambers;
and next day, when we had breakfasted, went in a body to the bank.
I gave in the check myself, and said I had every reason to believe
it was a forgery. Not a bit of it. The cheque was genuine."

"Tut-tut," said Mr. Utterson.

"I see you feel as I do," said Mr. Enfield. "Yes, it's a bad story. For my man was a fellow that nobody could have to do with, a really damnable man; and the person that drew the cheque is the very pink of the proprieties, celebrated too, and (what makes it worse) one of your fellows who do what they call good. Blackmail, I suppose; an honest man paying through the nose for some of the capers of his youth. Black Mail House is what I call that place with the door, in consequence. Though even that, you know, is far from explaining all," he added, and with the words fell into a vein of musing.

From this he was recalled by Mr. Utterson asking rather suddenly: "And you don't know if the drawer of the cheque lives there?"

"A likely place, isn't it?" returned Mr. Enfield. "But I happen to have noticed his address; he lives in some square or other."

"And you never asked about the—place with the door?" said Mr. Utterson.

"No, sir: I had a delicacy," was the reply. "I feel very strongly about putting questions; it partakes too much of the style of the day of judgment. You start a question, and it's like starting a stone. You sit quietly on the top of a hill; and away the stone goes, starting others; and presently some bland old bird (the last you would have thought of) is knocked on the head in his own back garden and the family have to change their name. No, sir, I make it a rule of mine: the more it looks like Queer Street, the less I ask."

"A very good rule, too," said the lawyer.

"But I have studied the place for myself," continued Mr. Enfield. "It seems scarcely a house. There is no other door, and nobody goes in or out of that one but, once in a great while, the gentleman of my adventure. There are three windows looking on the court on the first floor; none below; the windows are always shut but they're clean. And then there is a chimney which is generally smoking; so somebody must live there. And yet it's not so sure; for the buildings are so packed together about that court, that it's hard to say where one ends and another begins."

The pair walked on again for a while in silence; and then "Enfield," said Mr. Utterson, "that's a good rule of yours."

"Yes, I think it is," returned Enfield.

"But for all that," continued the lawyer, "there's one point I want to ask: I want to ask the name of that man who walked over the child."

"Well," said Mr. Enfield, "I can't see what harm it would do. It was a man of the name of Hyde."

"H'm," said Mr. Utterson. "What sort of a man is he to see?"

"He is not easy to describe. There is something wrong with his appearance; something displeasing, something downright detestable. I never saw a man I so disliked, and yet I scarce know why. He must be deformed somewhere; he gives a strong feeling of deformity, although I couldn't specify the point. He's an extraordinary looking man, and yet I really can name nothing out of the way. No, sir; I can make no hand of it; I can't describe him. And it's not want of memory; for I declare I can see him this moment."

Mr. Utterson again walked some way in silence and obviously under a weight of consideration. "You are sure he used a key?" he inquired at last.

"My dear sir . . ." began Enfield, surprised out of himself.

"Yes, I know," said Utterson; "I know it must seem strange. The fact is, if I do not ask you the name of the other party, it is because I know it already. You see, Richard, your tale has gone home. If you have been inexact in any point, you had better correct it."

"I think you might have warned me," returned the other with a touch of sullenness. "But I have been pedantically exact, as you call it. The fellow had a key; and what's more, he has it still. I saw him use it, not a week ago."

Mr. Utterson sighed deeply but said never a word; and the young man presently resumed. "Here is another lesson to say nothing," said he. "I am ashamed of my long tongue. Let us make a bargain never to refer to this again."

"With all my heart," said the lawyer. "I shake hands on that, Richard."

SEARCH FOR MR. HYDE

That evening Mr. Utterson came home to his bachelor house in
sombre spirits and sat down to dinner without relish. It was his custom of a Sunday, when this meal was over, to sit close by the fire,
a volume of some dry divinity on his reading desk, until the clock
of the neighbouring church rang out the hour of twelve, when he
would go soberly and gratefully to bed. On this night, however, as
soon as the cloth was taken away, he took up a candle and went
into his business room. There he opened his safe, took from the most
private part of it a document endorsed on the envelope as Dr. Jekyll's
Will, and sat down with a clouded brow to study its contents. The
will was holograph, for Mr. Utterson, though he took charge of it
now that it was made, had refused to lend the least assistance in the
making of it; it provided not only that, in case of the decease of
Henry Jekyll, M.D., D.C.L., LL.D., F.R.S., etc., all his possessions
were to pass into the hands of his "friend and benefactor Edward
Hyde," but that in case of Dr. Jekyll's "disappearance or unexplained
absence for any period exceeding three calendar months," the said
Edward Hyde should step into the said Henry Jekyll's shoes without
further delay and free from any burthen or obligation, beyond the
payment of a few small sums to the members of the doctor's house-
hold. This document had long been the lawyer's eyesore. It offended
him both as a lawyer and as a lover of the sane and customary sides
of life, to whom the fanciful was the immodest. And hitherto it was
his ignorance of Mr. Hyde that had swelled his indignation; now,
by a sudden turn, it was his knowledge. It was already bad enough
when the name was but a name of which he could learn no more.
It was worse when it began to be clothed upon with detestable
attributes; and out of the shifting, insubstantial mists that had so
long baffled his eye, there leaped up the sudden, definite present-
ment of a fiend.

"I thought it was madness," he said, as he replaced the obnoxious paper in the safe, "and now I begin to fear it is disgrace."

With that he blew out his candle, put on a greatcoat, and set forth in the direction of Cavendish Square, that citadel of medicine, where his friend, the great Dr. Lanyon, had his house and received his crowding patients. "If anyone knows, it will be Lanyon," he had thought.

The solemn butler knew and welcomed him; he was subjected to no stage of delay, but ushered direct from the door to the dining-room where Dr. Lanyon sat alone over his wine. This was a hearty, healthy, dapper, red-faced gentleman, with a shock of hair prematurely white, and a boisterous and decided manner. At sight of Mr. Utterson, he sprang up from his chair and welcomed him with both hands. The geniality, as was the way of the man, was somewhat theatrical to the eye; but it reposed on genuine feeling. For these two were old friends, old mates both at school and college, both thorough respecters of themselves and of each other, and, what does not always follow, men who thoroughly enjoyed each other's company.

After a little rambling talk, the lawyer led up to the subject which so disagreeably preoccupied his mind.

"I suppose, Lanyon," said he, "you and I must be the two oldest friends that Henry Jekyll has?"

"I wish the friends were younger," chuckled Dr. Lanyon. "But I suppose we are. And what of that? I see little of him now."

"Indeed?" said Utterson. "I thought you had a bond of common interest."

"We had," was the reply. "But it is more than ten years since Henry Jekyll became too fanciful for me. He began to go wrong, wrong in mind; and though of course I continue to take an interest in him for old sake's sake, as they say, I see and I have seen devilish little of the man. Such unscientific balderdash," added the doctor, flushing suddenly purple, "would have estranged Damon and Pythias."

This little spirt of temper was somewhat of a relief to Mr. Utterson. "They have only differed on some points of science," he thought; and being a man of no scientific passions (except in the matter of conveyancing), he even added: "It is nothing worse than that!" He gave his friend a few seconds to recover his composure, and then approached the question he had come to put. "Did you ever come across a protégé of his—one Hyde?" he asked.

"Hyde?" repeated Lanyon. "No. Never heard of him. Since my time."

That was the amount of information that the lawyer carried back with him to the great, dark bed on which he tossed to and fro, until the small hours of the morning began to grow large. It was a night of little ease to his toiling mind, toiling in mere darkness and besieged by questions.

Six o'clock struck on the bells of the church that was so conveniently near to Mr. Utterson's dwelling, and still he was digging at the problem. Hitherto it had touched him on the intellectual side alone; but now his imagination also was engaged, or rather enslaved; and as he lay and tossed in the gross darkness of the night and the curtained room, Mr. Enfield's tale went by before his mind in a scroll of lighted pictures. He would be aware of the great field of lamps of a nocturnal city; then of the figure of a man walking swiftly; then of a child running from the doctor's; and then these met, and that human Juggernaut trod the child down and passed on regardless of her screams. Or else he would see a room in a rich house, where his friend lay asleep, dreaming and smiling at his dreams; and then the door of that room would be opened, the curtains of the bed plucked apart, the sleeper recalled, and lo! there would stand by his side a figure to whom power was given, and even at that dead hour, he must rise and do its bidding. The figure in these two phases haunted the lawyer all night; and if at any time he dozed over, it was but to see it glide more stealthily through sleeping houses, or move the more swiftly and still the more swiftly, even to dizziness, through wider labyrinths of lamplighted city, and at every street corner crush a child and leave her screaming. And still the figure had no face by which he might know it; even in his dreams, it had no face, or one that baffled him and melted before his eyes; and thus it was that there sprang up and grew apace in the lawyer's mind a singularly strong, almost an inordinate, curiosity to behold the features of the real Mr. Hyde. If he could but once set eyes on him, he thought the mystery would lighten and perhaps roll altogether away, as was the habit of mysterious things when well examined. He might see a reason for his friend's strange preference or bondage (call it which you please) and even for the startling clause of the will. At least it would be a face worth seeing: the face of a man who was without bowels of mercy: a face which had but to show itself to raise up, in the mind of the unimpressionable Enfield, a spirit of enduring hatred.

From that time forward, Mr. Utterson began to haunt the door in the by-street of shops. In the morning before office hours, at noon when business was plenty, and time scarce, at night under the face of the fogged city moon, by all lights and at all hours of solitude or concourse, the lawyer was to be found on his chosen post.

"If he be Mr. Hyde," he had thought, "I shall be Mr. Seek."

And at last his patience was rewarded. It was a fine dry night; frost in the air; the streets as clean as a ballroom floor; the lamps, unshaken by any wind, drawing a regular pattern of light and shadow. By ten o'clock, when the shops were closed, the by-street was very solitary and, in spite of the low growl of London from all round, very silent. Small sounds carried far; domestic sounds out of the houses were clearly audible on either side of the roadway; and the rumour of the approach of any passenger preceded him by a long time. Mr. Utterson had been some minutes at his post, when he was aware of an odd, light footstep drawing near. In the course of his nightly patrols, he had long grown accustomed to the quaint effect with which the footfalls of a single person, while he is still a great way off, suddenly spring out distinct from the vast hum and clatter of the city. Yet his attention had never before been so sharply and decisively arrested; and it was with a strong, superstitious prevision of success that he withdrew into the entry of the court.

The steps drew swiftly nearer, and swelled out suddenly louder as they turned the end of the street. The lawyer, looking forth from the entry, could soon see what manner of man he had to deal with. He was small and very plainly dressed, and the look of him, even at that distance, went somehow strongly against the watcher's inclination. But he made straight for the door, crossing the roadway to save time; and as he came, he drew a key from his pocket like one approaching home.

Mr. Utterson stepped out and touched him on the shoulder as he passed. "Mr. Hyde, I think?"

Mr. Hyde shrank back with a hissing intake of the breath. But his fear was only momentary; and though he did not look the lawyer in the face, he answered coolly enough: "That is my name. What do you want?"

"I see you are going in," returned the lawyer. "I am an old friend of Dr. Jekyll's—Mr. Utterson of Gaunt Street—you must have heard my name; and meeting you so conveniently, I thought you might admit me."

"You will not find Dr. Jekyll; he is from home," replied Mr. Hyde, blowing in the key. And then suddenly, but still without looking up, "How did you know me?" he asked.

"On your side," said Mr. Utterson, "will you do me a favour?"

"With pleasure," replied the other. "What shall it be?"

"Will you let me see your face?" asked the lawyer.

Mr. Hyde appeared to hesitate, and then, as if upon some sudden reflection, fronted about with an air of defiance; and the pair stared at each other pretty fixedly for a few seconds. "Now I shall know you again," said Mr. Utterson. "It may be useful."

"Yes," returned Mr. Hyde, "it is as well we have met; and *à propos,* you should have my address." And he gave a number of a street in Soho.

"Good God!" thought Mr. Utterson, "can he, too, have been thinking of the will?" But he kept his feelings to himself and only grunted in acknowledgment of the address.

"And now," said the other, "how did you know me?"

"By description," was the reply.

"Whose description?"

"We have common friends," said Mr. Utterson.

"Common friends?" echoed Mr. Hyde, a little hoarsely. "Who are they?"

"Jekyll, for instance," said the lawyer.

"He never told you," cried Mr. Hyde, with a flush of anger. "I did not think you would have lied."

"Come," said Mr. Utterson, "that is not fitting language."

The other snarled aloud into a savage laugh; and the next moment, with extraordinary quickness, he had unlocked the door and disappeared into the house.

The lawyer stood awhile when Mr. Hyde had left him, the picture of disquietude. Then he began slowly to mount the street, pausing every step or two and putting his hand to his brow like a man in mental perplexity. The problem he was thus debating as he walked, was one of a class that is rarely solved. Mr. Hyde was pale and dwarfish, he gave an impression of deformity without any name-able malformation, he had a displeasing smile, he had borne himself to the lawyer with a sort of murderous mixture of timidity and boldness, and he spoke with a husky, whispering and somewhat broken voice; all these were points against him, but not all of these together could explain the hitherto unknown disgust, loathing and fear with which Mr. Utterson regarded him. "There must be some-thing else," said the perplexed gentleman. "There is something more, if I could find a name for it. God bless me, the man seems hardly human! Something troglodytic, shall we say? or can it be the old story of Dr. Fell? or is it the mere radiance of a foul soul that thus transpires through, and transfigures, its clay continent? The last, I think; for, O my poor old Harry Jekyll, if ever I read Satan's signa-ture upon a face, it is on that of your new friend."

Round the corner from the by-street, there was a square of an-cient, handsome houses, now for the most part decayed from their high estate and let in flats and chambers to all sorts and conditions of men: map-engravers, architects, shady lawyers and the agents of obscure enterprises. One house, however, second from the corner, was still occupied entire; and at the door of this, which wore a great air of wealth and comfort, though it was now plunged in darkness except for the fanlight, Mr. Utterson stopped and knocked. A well-dressed, elderly servant opened the door.

"Is Dr. Jekyll at home, Poole?" asked the lawyer.

"I will see, Mr. Utterson," said Poole, admitting the visitor, as he spoke, into a large, low-roofed, comfortable hall, paved with flags, warmed (after the fashion of a country house) by a bright, open fire, and furnished with costly cabinets of oak. "Will you wait here by the fire, sir? or shall I give you a light in the dining-room?"

"Here, thank you," said the lawyer, and he drew near and leaned on the tall fender. This hall, in which he was now left alone, was a pet fancy of his friend the doctor's; and Utterson himself was wont to speak of it as the pleasantest room in London. But to-night there was a shudder in his blood; the face of Hyde sat heavy on his memory; he felt (what was rare with him) a nausea and distaste of life; and in the gloom of his spirits, he seemed to read a menace in the flickering of the firelight on the polished cabinets and the uneasy starting of the shadow on the roof. He was ashamed of his relief, when Poole presently returned to announce that Dr. Jekyll was gone out.

"I saw Mr. Hyde go in by the old dissecting-room door, Poole," he said. "Is that right, when Dr. Jekyll is from home?"

"Quite right, Mr. Utterson, sir," replied the servant. "Mr. Hyde has a key."

"Your master seems to repose a great deal of trust in that young man, Poole," resumed the other musingly.

"Yes, sir, he do indeed," said Poole. "We have all orders to obey him."

"I do not think I ever met Mr. Hyde?" asked Utterson.

"O, dear no, sir. He never *dines* here," replied the butler. "Indeed we see very little of him on this side of the house; he mostly comes and goes by the laboratory."

"Well, good-night, Poole."

"Good-night, Mr. Utterson."

And the lawyer set out homeward with a very heavy heart. "Poor Harry Jekyll," he thought, "my mind misgives me he is in deep waters! He was wild when he was young; a long while ago to be sure; but in the law of God, there is no statute of limitations. Ay, it must be that; the ghost of some old sin, the cancer of some concealed disgrace: punishment coming, *pede claudo,* years after memory has forgotten and self-love condoned the fault." And the lawyer, scared by the thought, brooded awhile on his own past, groping in all the corners of memory, least by chance some Jack-in-the-Box of an old iniquity should leap to light there. His past was fairly blameless; few men could read the rolls of their life with less apprehension; yet he was humbled to the dust by the many ill things he had done, and raised up again into a sober and fearful gratitude by the many that he had come so near to doing, yet avoided. And then by a return on his former subject, he conceived a spark of hope. "This Master Hyde, if he were studied," thought he, "must have secrets of his own; black secrets, by the look of him; secrets compared to which poor Jekyll's worst would be like sunshine. Things cannot continue as they are. It turns me cold to think of this creature stealing like a thief to Harry's bedside; poor Harry, what a wakening! And the danger of it; for if this Hyde suspects the existence of the will, he may grow impatient to inherit. Ay, I must put my shoulder to the wheel—if Jekyll will but let me," he added, "if Jekyll will only let me." For once more he saw before his mind's eye, as clear as a transparency, the strange clauses of the will.

DR. JEKYLL WAS QUITE AT EASE

A fortnight later, by excellent good fortune, the doctor gave one of his pleasant dinners to some five or six old cronies, all intelligent, reputable men and all judges of good wine; and Mr. Utterson so contrived that he remained behind after the others had departed. This was no new arrangement, but a thing that had befallen many scores of times. Where Utterson was liked, he was liked well. Hosts loved to detain the dry lawyer, when the light-hearted and the loose-tongued had already their foot on the threshold; they liked to sit awhile in his unobtrusive company, practising for solitude, sobering their minds in the man's rich silence after the expense and strain of gaiety. To this rule, Dr. Jekyll was no exception; and as he now sat on the opposite side of the fire—a large, well-made, smooth-faced man of fifty, with something of a slyish cast perhaps, but every mark of capacity and kindness—you could see by his looks that he cherished for Mr. Utterson a sincere and warm affection.

"I have been wanting to speak to you, Jekyll," began the latter. "You know that will of yours?"

A close observer might have gathered that the topic was distasteful; but the doctor carried it off gaily. "My poor Utterson," said he, "you are unfortunate in such a client. I never saw a man so distressed as you were by my will; unless it were that hide-bound pedant, Lanyon, at what he called my scientific heresies. O, I know he's a good fellow—you needn't frown—an excellent fellow, and I always mean to see more of him; but a hide-bound pedant for all that; an ignorant, blatant pedant. I was never more disappointed in any man than Lanyon."

"You know I never approved of it," pursued Utterson, ruthlessly disregarding the fresh topic.

"My will? Yes, certainly, I know that," said the doctor, a trifle sharply. "You have told me so."

"Well, I tell you so again," continued the lawyer. "I have been learning something of young Hyde."

The large handsome face of Dr. Jekyll grew pale to the very lips, and there came a blackness about his eyes. "I do not care to hear more," said he. "This is a matter I thought we had agreed to drop."

"What I heard was abominable," said Utterson.

"It can make no change. You do not understand my position," returned the doctor, with a certain incoherency of manner. "I am painfully situated, Utterson; my position is a very strange—a very strange one. It is one of those affairs that cannot be mended by talking."

"Jekyll," said Utterson, "you know me: I am a man to be trusted. Make a clean breast of this in confidence; and I make no doubt I can get you out of it."

"My good Utterson," said the doctor, "this is very good of you, this is downright good of you, and I cannot find words to thank you in. I believe you fully; I would trust you before any man alive, ay, before myself, if I could make the choice; but indeed it isn't what you fancy; it is not so bad as that; and just to put your good heart at rest, I will tell you one thing: the moment I choose, I can be rid of Mr. Hyde. I give you my hand upon that; and I thank you again and again; and I will just add one little word, Utterson, that I'm sure you'll take in good part: this is a private matter, and I beg of you to let it sleep."

Utterson reflected a little, looking in the fire.

"I have no doubt you are perfectly right," he said at last, getting to his feet.

"Well, but since we have touched upon this business, and for the last time I hope," continued the doctor, "there is one point I should like you to understand. I have really a very great interest in poor Hyde. I know you have seen him; he told me so; and I fear he was rude. But I do sincerely take a great, a very great interest in that young man; and if I am taken away, Utterson, I wish you to promise me that you will bear with him and get his rights for him. I think you would, if you knew all; and it would be a weight off my mind if you would promise."

"I can't pretend that I shall ever like him," said the lawyer.

"I don't ask that," pleaded Jekyll, laying his hand upon the other's arm; "I only ask for justice; I only ask you to help him for my sake, when I am no longer here."

Utterson heaved an irrepressible sigh. "Well," said he, "I promise."

THE CAREW MURDER CASE

Nearly a year later, in the month of October, 18—, London was startled by a crime of singular ferocity and rendered all the more notable by the high position of the victim. The details were few and startling. A maid servant living alone in a house not far from the river, had gone upstairs to bed about eleven. Although a fog rolled over the city in the small hours, the early part of the night was cloudless, and the lane, which the maid's window overlooked, was brilliantly lit by the full moon. It seems she was romantically given, for she sat down upon her box, which stood immediately under the window, and fell into a dream of musing. Never (she used to say, with streaming tears, when she narrated that experience), never had she felt more at peace with all men or thought more kindly of the world. And as she so sat she became aware of an aged and beautiful gentleman with white hair, drawing near along the lane; and advancing to meet him, another and very small gentleman, to whom at first she paid less attention. When they had come within speech (which was just under the maid's eyes) the older man bowed and accosted the other with a very pretty manner of politeness. It did not seem as if the subject of his address were of great importance; indeed, from his pointing, it sometimes appeared as if he were only inquiring his way; but the moon shone on his face as he spoke, and the girl was pleased to watch it, it seemed to breathe such an innocent and old-world kindness of disposition, yet with something high too, as of a well-founded self-content. Presently her eye wandered to the other, and she was surprised to recognise in him a certain Mr. Hyde, who had once visited her master and for whom she had conceived a dislike. He had in his hand a heavy cane, with which he was trifling; but he answered never a word, and seemed to listen with an ill-contained impatience. And then all of a sudden he broke out in a great flame of anger, stamping with his foot, brandishing the cane, and carrying on (as the maid described it) like a madman. The old gentleman took a step back, with the air of one very much surprised and a trifle hurt; and at that Mr. Hyde broke out of all bounds and clubbed him to the earth. And next moment, with ape-like fury, he was trampling his victim under foot and hailing down a storm of blows, under which the bones were audibly shattered and the body jumped upon the roadway. At the horror of these sights and sounds, the maid fainted.

It was two o'clock when she came to herself and called for the police. The murderer was gone long ago; but there lay his victim in the middle of the lane, incredibly mangled. The stick with which the deed had been done, although it was of some rare and very tough and heavy wood, had broken in the middle under the stress of this insensate cruelty; and one splintered half had rolled in the neighbouring gutter—the other, without doubt, had been carried away by the murderer. A purse and a gold watch were found upon the victim: but no cards or papers, except a sealed and stamped envelope, which he had been probably carrying to the post, and which bore the name and address of Mr. Utterson.

This was brought to the lawyer the next morning, before he was out of bed; and he had no sooner seen it, and been told the circumstances, than he shot out a solemn lip. "I shall say nothing till I have seen the body," said he; "this may be very serious. Have the kindness to wait while I dress." And with the same grave countenance he hurried through his breakfast and drove to the police station, whither the body had been carried. As soon as he came into the cell, he nodded.

"Yes," said he, "I recognise him. I am sorry to say that this is Sir Danvers Carew."

"Good God, sir," exclaimed the officer, "is it possible?" And the next moment his eye lighted up with professional ambition. "This will make a deal of noise," he said. "And perhaps you can help us to the man." And he briefly narrated what the maid had seen, and showed the broken stick.

Mr. Utterson had already quailed at the name of Hyde; but when the stick was laid before him, he could doubt no longer; broken and battered as it was, he recognised it for one that he had himself presented many years before to Henry Jekyll.

"Is this Mr. Hyde a person of small stature?" he inquired.

"Particularly small and particularly wicked-looking, is what the maid calls him," said the officer.

Mr. Utterson reflected; and then, raising his head, "If you will come with me in my cab," he said, "I think I can take you to his house."

It was by this time about nine in the morning, and the first fog of the season. A great chocolate-coloured pall lowered over heaven, but the wind was continually charging and routing these embattled vapours; so that as the cab crawled from street to street, Mr. Utterson beheld a marvellous number of degrees and hues of twilight; for here it would be dark like the back-end of evening; and there would be a glow of a rich, lurid brown, like the light of some strange conflagration; and here, for a moment, the fog would be quite broken up, and a haggard shaft of daylight would glance in between the swirling wreaths. The dismal quarter of Soho seen under these changing glimpses, with its muddy ways, and slatternly passengers, and its lamps, which had never been extinguished or had been kindled afresh to combat this mournful reïnvasion of darkness, seemed, in the lawyer's eyes, like a district of some city in a nightmare. The thoughts of his mind, besides, were of the gloomiest dye; and when he glanced at the companion of his drive, he was conscious of some touch of that terror of the law and the law's officers, which may at times assail the most honest.

As the cab drew up before the address indicated, the fog lifted a little and showed him a dingy street, a gin palace, a low French eating house, a shop for the retail of penny numbers and twopenny salads, many ragged children huddled in the doorways, and many women of many different nationalities passing out, key in hand, to have a morning glass; and the next moment the fog settled down again upon that part, as brown as umber, and cut him off from his blackguardly surroundings. This was the home of Henry Jekyll's favourite; of a man who was heir to quarter of a million sterling.

An ivory-faced and silvery-haired old woman opened the door. She had an evil face, smoothed by hypocrisy; but her manners were excellent. Yes, she said, this was Mr. Hyde's, but he was not at home; he had been in that night very late, but had gone away again in less than an hour; there was nothing strange in that; his habits were very irregular, and he was often absent; for instance, it was nearly two months since she had seen him till yesterday.

"Very well, then, we wish to see his rooms," said the lawyer; and when the woman began to declare it was impossible, "I had better tell you who this person is," he added. "This is Inspector Newcomen of Scotland Yard."

A flash of odious joy appeared upon the woman's face. "Ah!" said she, "he is in trouble! What has he done?"

Mr. Utterson and the inspector exchanged glances. "He don't seem a very popular character," observed the latter. "And now, my good woman, just let me and this gentleman have a look about us."

In the whole extent of the house, which but for the old woman remained otherwise empty, Mr. Hyde had only used a couple of rooms; but these were furnished with luxury and good taste. A closet was filled with wine; the plate was of silver, the napery elegant; a good picture hung upon the walls, a gift (as Utterson supposed) from Henry Jekyll, who was much of a connoisseur; and the carpets were of many plies and agreeable in colour. At this moment, however, the rooms bore every mark of having been recently and hurriedly ransacked; clothes lay about the floor, with their pockets inside out; lock-fast drawers stood open; and on the hearth there lay a pile of gray ashes, as though many papers had been burned. From these embers the inspector disinterred the butt end of a green cheque book, which had resisted the action of the fire; the other half of the stick was found behind the door; and as this clinched his suspicions, the officer declared himself delighted. A visit to the bank, where several thousand pounds were found to be lying to the murderer's credit, completed his gratification.

"You may depend upon it, sir," he told Mr. Utterson: "I have him in my hand. He must have lost his head, or he never would have left the stick or, above all, burned the cheque book. Why, money's life to the man. We have nothing to do but wait for him at the bank, and get out the handbills."

This last, however, was not so easy of accomplishment; for Mr. Hyde had numbered few familiars—even the master of the servant maid had only seen him twice; his family could nowhere be traced; he had never been photographed; and the few who could describe him differed widely, as common observers will. Only on one point, were they agreed; and that was the haunting sense of unexpressed deformity with which the fugitive impressed his beholders.

INCIDENT OF THE LETTER

It was late in the afternoon when Mr. Utterson found his way to Dr. Jekyll's door, where he was at once admitted by Poole, and carried down by the kitchen offices and across a yard which had once been a garden, to the building which was indifferently known as the laboratory or the dissecting rooms. The doctor had bought the house from the heirs of a celebrated surgeon; and his own tastes being rather chemical than anatomical, had changed the destination of the block at the bottom of the garden. It was the first time that the lawyer had been received in that part of his friend's quarters; and he eyed the dingy, windowless structure with curiosity, and gazed round with a distasteful sense of strangeness as he crossed the theatre, once crowded with eager students and now lying gaunt and silent, the tables laden with chemical apparatus, the floor strewn with crates and littered with packing straw, and the light falling dimly through the foggy cupola. At the further end, a flight of stairs mounted to a door covered with red baize; and through this, Mr. Utterson was at last received into the doctor's cabinet. It was a large room, fitted round with glass presses, furnished, among other things, with a cheval-glass and a business table, and looking out upon the court by three dusty windows barred with iron. A fire burned in the grate; a lamp was set lighted on the chimney shelf, for even in the houses the fog began to lie thickly; and there, close up to the warmth, sat Dr. Jekyll, looking deadly sick. He did not rise to meet his visitor, but held out a cold hand and bade him welcome in a changed voice.

"And now," said Mr. Utterson, as soon as Poole had left them, "you have heard the news?"

The doctor shuddered. "They were crying it in the square," he said. "I heard them in my dining-room."

"One word," said the lawyer. "Carew was my client, but so are you, and I want to know what I am doing. You have not been mad enough to hide this fellow?"

"Utterson, I swear to God," cried the doctor, "I swear to God I will never set eyes on him again. I bind my honour to you that I am done with him in this world. It is all at an end. And indeed he does not want my help; you do not know him as I do; he is safe, he is quite safe; mark my words, he will never more be heard of."

The lawyer listened gloomily; he did not like his friend's feverish manner. "You seem pretty sure of him," said he; "and for your sake, I hope you may be right. If it came to a trial, your name might appear."

"I am quite sure of him," replied Jekyll; "I have grounds for certainty that I cannot share with anyone. But there is one thing on which you may advise me. I have—I have received a letter; and I am at a loss whether I should show it to the police. I should like to leave it in your hands, Utterson; you would judge wisely, I am sure; I have so great a trust in you."

"You fear, I suppose, that it might lead to his detection?" asked the lawyer.

"No," said the other. "I cannot say that I care what becomes of Hyde; I am quite done with him. I was thinking of my own character, which this hateful business has rather exposed."

Utterson ruminated awhile; he was surprised at his friend's selfishness, and yet relieved by it. "Well," said he, at last, "let me see the letter."

The letter was written in an odd, upright hand and signed "Edward Hyde": and it signified, briefly enough, that the writer's benefactor, Dr. Jekyll, whom he had long so unworthily repaid for a thousand generosities, need labour under no alarm for his safety, as he had means of escape on which he placed a sure dependence. The lawyer liked this letter well enough; it put a better colour on the intimacy than he had looked for; and he blamed himself for some of his past suspicions.

"Have you the envelope?" he asked.

"I burned it," replied Jekyll, "before I thought what I was about. But it bore no postmark. The note was handed in."

"Shall I keep this and sleep upon it?" asked Utterson.

"I wish you to judge for me entirely," was the reply. "I have lost confidence in myself."

"Well, I shall consider," returned the lawyer. "And now one word more: it was Hyde who dictated the terms in your will about that disappearance?"

The doctor seemed seized with a qualm of faintness; he shut his mouth tight and nodded.

"I knew it," said Utterson. "He meant to murder you. You have had a fine escape."

"I have had what is far more to the purpose," returned the doctor solemnly: "I have had a lesson—O God, Utterson, what a lesson I have had!" And he covered his face for a moment with his hands.

On his way out, the lawyer stopped and had a word or two with Poole. "By the bye," said he, "there was a letter handed in to-day: what was the messenger like?" But Poole was positive nothing had come except by post; "and only circulars by that," he added.

This news sent off the visitor with his fears renewed. Plainly the letter had come by the laboratory door; possibly, indeed, it had been written in the cabinet; and if that were so, it must be differently judged, and handled with the more caution. The newsboys, as he went, were crying themselves hoarse along the footways: "Special edition. Shocking murder of an M. P." That was the funeral oration of one friend and client; and he could not help a certain apprehension lest the good name of another should be sucked down in the eddy of the scandal. It was, at least, a ticklish decision that he had to make; and self-reliant as he was by habit, he began to cherish a longing for advice. It was not to be had directly; but perhaps, he thought, it might be fished for.

Presently after, he sat on one side of his own hearth, with Mr. Guest, his head clerk, upon the other, and midway between, at a nicely calculated distance from the fire, a bottle of a particular old wine that had long dwelt unsunned in the foundations of his house. The fog still slept on the wing above the drowned city, where the lamps glimmered like carbuncles; and through the muffle and smother of these fallen clouds, the procession of the town's life was still rolling in through the great arteries with a sound as of a mighty wind. But the room was gay with firelight. In the bottle the acids were long ago resolved; the imperial dye had softened with time, as the colour grows richer in stained windows; and the glow of hot autumn afternoons on hillside vineyards was ready to be set free and to disperse the fogs of London. Insensibly the lawyer melted. There was no man from whom he kept fewer secrets than Mr. Guest; and he was not always sure that he kept as many as he meant. Guest had often been on business to the doctor's; he knew Poole; he could scarce have failed to hear of Mr. Hyde's familiarity about the house; he might draw conclusions: was it not as well, then, that he should see a letter which put that mystery to rights? and above all since Guest, being a great student and critic of handwriting, would consider the step natural and obliging? The clerk, besides, was a man of counsel; he would scarce read so strange a document without dropping a remark; and by that remark Mr. Utterson might shape his future course.

"This is a sad business about Sir Danvers," he said.

"Yes, sir, indeed. It has elicited a great deal of public feeling," returned Guest. "The man, of course, was mad."

"I should like to hear your views on that," replied Utterson. "I have a document here in his handwriting; it is between ourselves, for I scarce know what to do about it; it is an ugly business at the best. But there it is; quite in your way: a murderer's autograph."

Guest's eyes brightened, and he sat down at once and studied it with passion. "No, sir," he said: "not mad; but it is an odd hand."

"And by all accounts a very odd writer," added the lawyer.

Just then the servant entered with a note.

"Is that from Dr. Jekyll, sir?" inquired the clerk. "I thought I knew the writing. Anything private, Mr. Utterson?"

"Only an invitation to dinner. Why? Do you want to see it?"

"One moment. I thank you, sir;" and the clerk laid the two sheets of paper alongside and sedulously compared their contents. "Thank you, sir," he said at last, returning both; "it's a very interesting autograph."

There was a pause, during which Mr. Utterson struggled with himself. "Why did you compare them, Guest?" he inquired suddenly.

"Well, sir," returned the clerk, "there's a rather singular resemblance; the two hands are in many points identical: only differently sloped."

"Rather quaint," said Utterson.

"It is, as you say, rather quaint," returned Guest.

"I wouldn't speak of this note, you know," said the master.

"No, sir," said the clerk. "I understand."

But no sooner was Mr. Utterson alone that night than he locked the note into his safe, where it reposed from that time forward. "What!" he thought. "Henry Jekyll forge for a murderer!" And his blood ran cold in his veins.

REMARKABLE INCIDENT OF DR. LANYON

Time ran on; thousands of pounds were offered in reward, for the death of Sir Danvers was resented as a public injury; but Mr. Hyde had disappeared out of the ken of the police as though he had never existed. Much of his past was unearthed, indeed, and all disreputable: tales came out of the man's cruelty, at once so callous and violent; of his vile life, of his strange associates, of the hatred that seemed to have surrounded his career; but of his present whereabouts, not a whisper. From the time he had left the house in Soho on the morning of the murder, he was simply blotted out; and gradually, as time drew on, Mr. Utterson began to recover from the hotness of his alarm, and to grow more at quiet with himself. The death of Sir Danvers was, to his way of thinking, more than paid for by the disappearance of Mr. Hyde. Now that that evil influence had been withdrawn, a new life began for Dr. Jekyll. He came out of his seclusion, renewed relations with his friends, became once more their familiar guest and entertainer; and whilst he had always been known for charities, he was now no less distinguished for religion. He was busy, he was much in the open air, he did good; his face seemed to open and brighten, as if with an inward consciousness of service; and for more than two months, the doctor was at peace.

On the 8th of January Utterson had dined at the doctor's with a small party; Lanyon had been there; and the face of the host had looked from one to the other as in the old days when the trio were inseparable friends. On the 12th, and again on the 14th, the door was shut against the lawyer. "The doctor was confined to the house," Poole said, "and saw no one." On the 15th, he tried again, and was again refused; and having now been used for the last two months to see his friend almost daily, he found this return of solitude to weigh upon his spirits. The fifth night he had in Guest to dine with him; and the sixth he betook himself to Dr. Lanyon's.

There at least he was not denied admittance; but when he came in, he was shocked at the change which had taken place in the doctor's appearance. He had his death warrant written legibly upon his face. The rosy man had grown pale; his flesh had fallen away; he was visibly balder and older; and yet it was not so much these tokens of a swift physical decay that arrested the lawyer's notice, as a look in the eye and quality of manner that seemed to testify to some deep-seated terror of the mind. It was unlikely that the doctor should fear death; and yet that was what Utterson was tempted to suspect. "Yes," he thought; "he is a doctor, he must know his own state and that his days are counted; and the knowledge is more than he can bear." And yet when Utterson remarked on his ill-looks, it was with an air of great firmness that Lanyon declared himself a doomed man.

"I have had a shock," he said, "and I shall never recover. It is a question of weeks. Well, life has been pleasant; I liked it; yes, sir, I used to like it. I sometimes think if we knew all, we should be more glad to get away."

"Jekyll is ill, too," observed Utterson. "Have you seen him?"

But Lanyon's face changed, and he held up a trembling hand. "I wish to see or hear no more of Dr. Jekyll," he said in a loud, unsteady voice. "I am quite done with that person; and I beg that you will spare me any allusion to one whom I regard as dead."

"Tut-tut," said Mr. Utterson; and then after a considerable pause, "Can't I do anything?" he inquired. "We are three very old friends, Lanyon; we shall not live to make others."

"Nothing can be done," returned Lanyon; "ask himself."

"He will not see me," said the lawyer.

"I am not surprised at that," was the reply. "Some day, Utterson, after I am dead, you may perhaps come to learn the right and wrong of this. I cannot tell you. And in the meantime, if you can sit and talk with me of other things, for God's sake, stay and do so; but if you cannot keep clear of this accursed topic, then, in God's name, go, for I cannot bear it."

As soon as he got home, Utterson sat down and wrote to Jekyll, complaining of his exclusion from the house, and asking the cause of this unhappy break with Lanyon; and the next day brought him a long answer, often very pathetically worded, and sometimes darkly mysterious in drift. The quarrel with Lanyon was incurable. "I do not blame our old friend," Jekyll wrote, "but I share his view that we must never meet. I mean from henceforth to lead a life of extreme seclusion; you must not be surprised, nor must you doubt my friendship, if my door is often shut even to you. You must suffer me to go my own dark way. I have brought on myself a punishment and a danger that I cannot name. If I am the chief of sinners, I am the chief of sufferers also. I could not think that this earth contained a place for sufferings and terrors so unmanning; and you can do but one thing, Utterson, to lighten this destiny, and that is to respect my silence." Utterson was amazed; the dark influence of Hyde had been withdrawn, the doctor had returned to his old tasks and amities; a week ago, the prospect had smiled with every promise of a cheerful and an honoured age; and now in a moment, friendship, and peace of mind, and the whole tenor of his life were wrecked. So great and unprepared a change pointed to madness; but in view of Lanyon's manner and words, there must lie for it some deeper ground.

A week afterwards Dr. Lanyon took to his bed, and in something less than a fortnight he was dead. The night after the funeral, at which he had been sadly affected, Utterson locked the door of his business room, and sitting there by the light of a melancholy candle, drew out and set before him an envelope addressed by the hand and sealed with the seal of his dead friend. "PRIVATE: for the hands of G. J. Utterson ALONE, and in case of his predecease *to be destroyed unread,*" so it was emphatically superscribed; and the lawyer dreaded to behold the contents. "I have buried one friend today," he thought: "what if this should cost me another?" And then he condemned the fear as a disloyalty, and broke the seal. Within there was another enclosure, likewise sealed, and marked upon the cover as "not to be opened till the death or disappearance of Dr. Henry Jekyll." Utterson could not trust his eyes. Yes, it was disappearance; here again, as in the mad will which he had long ago restored to its author, here again were the idea of a disappearance and the name of Henry Jekyll bracketed. But in the will, that idea had sprung from the sinister suggestion of the man Hyde; it was set there with a purpose all too plain and horrible. Written by the hand of Lanyon, what should it mean? A great curiosity came on the trustee, to disregard the prohibition and dive at once to the bottom of these mysteries; but professional honour and faith to his dead friend were stringent obligations; and the packet slept in the inmost corner of his private safe.

It is one thing to mortify curiosity, another to conquer it; and it may be doubted if, from that day forth, Utterson desired the society of his surviving friend with the same eagerness. He thought of him kindly; but his thoughts were disquieted and fearful. He went to call indeed; but he was perhaps relieved to be denied admittance; perhaps, in his heart, he preferred to speak with Poole upon the doorstep and surrounded by the air and sounds of the open city, rather than to be admitted into that house of voluntary bondage, and to sit and speak with its inscrutable recluse. Poole had, indeed, no very pleasant news to communicate. The doctor, it appeared, now more than ever confined himself to the cabinet over the laboratory, where he would sometimes even sleep; he was out of spirits, he had grown very silent, he did not read; it seemed as if he had something on his mind. Utterson became so used to the unvarying character of these reports, that he fell off little by little in the frequency of his visits.

INCIDENT AT THE WINDOW

It chanced on Sunday, when Mr. Utterson was on his usual walk with Mr. Enfield, that their way lay once again through the by-street; and that when they came in front of the door, both stopped to gaze on it.

"Well," said Enfield, "that story's at an end at least. We shall never see more of Mr. Hyde."

"I hope not," said Utterson. "Did I ever tell you that I once saw him, and shared your feeling of repulsion?"

"It was impossible to do the one without the other," returned Enfield. "And by the way, what an ass you must have thought me, not to know that this was a back way to Dr. Jekyll's! It was partly your own fault that I found it out, even when I did."

"So you found it out, did you?" said Utterson. "But if that be so, we may step into the court and take a look at the windows. To tell you the truth, I am uneasy about poor Jekyll; and even outside, I feel as if the presence of a friend might do him good."

The court was very cool and a little damp, and full of premature twilight, although the sky, high up overhead, was still bright with sunset. The middle one of the three windows was half way open; and sitting close beside it, taking the air with an infinite sadness of mien, like some disconsolate prisoner, Utterson saw Dr. Jekyll.

"What! Jekyll!" he cried. "I trust you are better."

"I am very low, Utterson," replied the doctor, drearily, "very low. It will not last long, thank God."

"You stay too much indoors," said the lawyer. "You should be out, whipping up the circulation like Mr. Enfield and me. (This is my cousin—Mr. Enfield—Dr. Jekyll.) Come now; get your hat and take a quick turn with us."

"You are very good," sighed the other. "I should like to very much; but no, no, no, it is quite impossible; I dare not. But indeed, Utterson, I am very glad to see you; this is really a great pleasure; I would ask you and Mr. Enfield up, but the place is really not fit."

"Why then," said the lawyer, good-naturedly, "the best thing we can do is to stay down here and speak with you from where we are."

"That is just what I was about to venture to propose," returned the doctor with a smile. But the words were hardly uttered, before the smile was struck out of his face and succeeded by an expression of such abject terror and despair, as froze the very blood of the two gentlemen below. They saw it but for a glimpse, for the window was instantly thrust down; but that glimpse had been sufficient, and they turned and left the court without a word. In silence, too, they traversed the by-street; and it was not until they had come into a neighbouring thoroughfare, where even upon a Sunday there were still some stirrings of life, that Mr. Utterson at last turned and looked at his companion. They were both pale; and there was an answering horror in their eyes.

"God forgive us, God forgive us," said Mr. Utterson.

But Mr. Enfield only nodded his head very seriously, and walked on once more in silence.

THE LAST NIGHT

Mr. Utterson was sitting by his fireside one evening after dinner, when he was surprised to receive a visit from Poole.

"Bless me, Poole, what brings you here?" he cried; and then taking a second look at him, "What ails you?" he added; "is the doctor ill?"

"Mr. Utterson," said the man, "there is something wrong."

"Take a seat, and here is a glass of wine for you," said the lawyer. "Now, take your time, and tell me plainly what you want."

"You know the doctor's ways, sir," replied Poole, "and how he shuts himself up. Well, he's shut up again in the cabinet; and I don't like it, sir—I wish I may die if I like it. Mr. Utterson, sir, I'm afraid."

"Now, my good man," said the lawyer, "be explicit. What are you afraid of?"

"I've been afraid for about a week," returned Poole, doggedly disregarding the question, "and I can bear it no more."

The man's appearance amply bore out his words; his manner was altered for the worse; and except for the moment when he had first announced his terror, he had not once looked the lawyer in the face. Even now, he sat with the glass of wine untasted on his knee, and his eyes directed to a corner of the floor. "I can bear it no more," he repeated.

"Come," said the lawyer, "I see you have some good reason, Poole; I see there is something seriously amiss. Try to tell me what it is."

"I think there's been foul play," said Poole, hoarsely.

"Foul play!" cried the lawyer, a good deal frightened and rather inclined to be irritated in consequence. "What foul play? What does the man mean?"

"I daren't say, sir," was the answer; "but will you come along with me and see for yourself?"

Mr. Utterson's only answer was to rise and get his hat and great coat; but he observed with wonder the greatness of the relief that appeared upon the butler's face, and perhaps with no less, that the wine was still untasted when he set it down to follow.

It was a wild, cold, seasonable night of March, with a pale moon, lying on her back as though the wind had tilted her, and a flying wrack of the most diaphanous and lawny texture. The wind made talking difficult, and flecked the blood into the face. It seemed to have swept the streets unusually bare of passengers, besides; for Mr. Utterson thought he had never seen that part of London so deserted. He could have wished it otherwise; never in his life had he been conscious of so sharp a wish to see and touch his fellow-creatures; for struggle as he might, there was born in upon his mind a crushing anticipation of calamity. The square, when they got there, was all full of wind and dust, and the thin trees in the garden were lashing themselves along the railing. Poole, who had kept all the way a pace or two ahead, now pulled up in the middle of the pavement, and in spite of the biting weather, took off his hat and mopped his brow with a red pocket-handkerchief. But for all the hurry of his coming, these were not the dews of exertion that he wiped away, but the moisture of some strangling anguish; for his face was white and his voice, when he spoke, harsh and broken.

"Well, sir," he said, "here we are, and God grant there be nothing wrong."

"Amen, Poole," said the lawyer.

Thereupon the servant knocked in a very guarded manner; the door was opened on the chain; and a voice asked from within, "Is that you, Poole?"

"It's all right," said Poole. "Open the door."

The hall, when they entered it, was brightly lighted up; the fire was built high; and about the hearth the whole of the servants, men and women, stood huddled together like a flock of sheep. At the sight of Mr. Utterson, the housemaid broke into hysterical whimpering; and the cook, crying out "Bless God! it's Mr. Utterson," ran forward as if to take him in her arms.

"What, what? Are you all here?" said the lawyer peevishly. "Very irregular, very unseemly; your master would be far from pleased."

"They're all afraid," said Poole.

Blank silence followed, no one protesting; only the maid lifted up her voice and now wept loudly.

"Hold your tongue!" Poole said to her, with a ferocity of accent that testified to his own jangled nerves; and indeed, when the girl had so suddenly raised the note of her lamentation, they had all started and turned towards the inner door with faces of dreadful expectation. "And now," continued the butler, addressing the knife-boy, "reach me a candle, and we'll get this through hands at once." And then he begged Mr. Utterson to follow him, and led the way to the back garden.

"Now, sir," said he, "you come as gently as you can. I want you to hear, and I don't want you to be heard. And see here, sir, if by any chance he was to ask you in, don't go."

Mr. Utterson's nerves, at this unlooked-for termination, gave a jerk that nearly threw him from his balance; but he recollected his courage and followed the butler into the laboratory building and through the surgical theatre, with its lumber of crates and bottles, to the foot of the stair. Here Poole motioned him to stand on one side and listen; while he himself, setting down the candle and making a great and obvious call on his resolution, mounted the steps and knocked with a somewhat uncertain hand on the red baize of the cabinet door.

"Mr. Utterson, sir, asking to see you," he called; and even as he did so, once more violently signed to the lawyer to give ear.

A voice answered from within: "Tell him I cannot see anyone," it said complainingly.

"Thank you, sir," said Poole, with a note of something like triumph in his voice; and taking up his candle, he led Mr. Utterson back across the yard and into the great kitchen, where the fire was out and the beetles were leaping on the floor.

"Sir," he said, looking Mr. Utterson in the eyes, "was that my master's voice?"

"It seems much changed," replied the lawyer, very pale, but giving look for look.

"Changed? Well, yes, I think so," said the butler. "Have I been twenty years in this man's house, to be deceived about his voice? No, sir; master's made away with; he was made away with, eight days ago, when we heard him cry out upon the name of God; and *who's* in there instead of him, and *why* it stays there, is a thing that cries to Heaven, Mr. Utterson!"

"This is a very strange tale, Poole; this is rather a wild tale, my man," said Mr. Utterson, biting his finger. "Suppose it were as you suppose, supposing Dr. Jekyll to have been—well, murdered, what could induce the murderer to stay? That won't hold water; it doesn't commend itself to reason."

"Well, Mr. Utterson, you are a hard man to satisfy, but I'll do it yet," said Poole. "All this last week (you must know) him, or it, or whatever it is that lives in that cabinet, has been crying night and day for some sort of medicine and cannot get it to his mind. It was sometimes his way—the master's, that is—to write his orders on a sheet of paper and throw it on the stair. We've had nothing else this week back; nothing but papers, and a closed door, and the very meals left there to be smuggled in when nobody was looking.

Well, sir, every day, ay, and twice and thrice in the same day, there have been orders and complaints, and I have been sent flying to all the wholesale chemists in town. Every time I brought the stuff back, there would be another paper telling me to return it, because it was not pure, and another order to a different firm. This drug is wanted bitter bad, sir, whatever for."

"Have you any of these papers?" asked Mr. Utterson.

Poole felt in his pocket and handed out a crumpled note, which the lawyer, bending nearer to the candle, carefully examined. Its contents ran thus: "Dr. Jekyll presents his compliments to Messrs. Maw. He assures them that their last sample is impure and quite useless for his present purpose. In the year 18—, Dr. J. purchased a somewhat large quantity from Messrs. M. He now begs them to search with the most sedulous care, and should any of the same quality be left, to forward it to him at once. Expense is no consideration. The importance of this to Dr. J. can hardly be exaggerated." So far the letter had run composedly enough, but here with a sudden splutter of the pen, the writer's emotion had broken loose. "For God's sake," he had added, "find me some of the old."

"This is a strange note," said Mr. Utterson; and then sharply, "How do you come to have it open?"

"The man at Maw's was main angry, sir, and he threw it back to me like so much dirt," returned Poole.

"This is unquestionably the doctor's hand, do you know?" resumed the lawyer.

"I thought it looked like it," said the servant rather sulkily; and then, with another voice, "But what matters hand of write?" he said. "I've seen him!"

"Seen him?" repeated Mr. Utterson. "Well?"

"That's it!" said Poole. "It was this way. I came suddenly into the theatre from the garden. It seems he had slipped out to look for this drug or whatever it is; for the cabinet door was open, and there he was at the far end of the room digging among the crates. He looked up when I came in, gave a kind of cry, and whipped upstairs into the cabinet. It was but for one minute that I saw him, but the hair stood upon my head like quills. Sir, if that was my master, why had he a mask upon his face? If it was my master, why did he cry out like a rat, and run from me? I have served him long enough. And then . . ." The man paused and passed his hand over his face.

"These are all very strange circumstances," said Mr. Utterson, "but I think I begin to see daylight. Your master, Poole, is plainly seized with one of those maladies that both torture and deform the sufferer; hence, for aught I know, the alteration of his voice; hence the mask and the avoidance of his friends; hence his eagerness to find this drug, by means of which the poor soul retains some hope of ultimate recovery—God grant that he be not deceived! There is my explanation; it is sad enough, Poole, ay, and appalling to consider; but it is plain and natural, hangs well together, and delivers us from all exorbitant alarms."

"Sir," said the butler, turning to a sort of mottled pallor, "that thing was not my master, and there's the truth. My master"—here he looked round him and began to whisper—"is a tall, fine build of a man, and this was more of a dwarf." Utterson attempted to protest. "O, sir," cried Poole, "do you think I do not know my master after twenty years? Do you think I do not know where his head comes to in the cabinet door, where I saw him every morning of my life? No, sir, that thing in the mask was never Dr. Jekyll— God knows what it was, but it was never Dr. Jekyll; and it is the belief of my heart that there was murder done."

"Poole," replied the lawyer, "if you say that, it will become my duty to make certain. Much as I desire to spare your master's feelings, much as I am puzzled by this note which seems to prove him to be still alive, I shall consider it my duty to break in that door."

"Ah, Mr. Utterson, that's talking!" cried the butler.

"And now comes the second question," resumed Utterson: "Who is going to do it?"

"Why, you and me," was the undaunted reply.

"That's very well said," returned the lawyer; "and whatever comes of it, I shall make it my business to see you are no loser."

"There is an axe in the theatre," continued Poole; "and you might take the kitchen poker for yourself."

The lawyer took that rude but weighty instrument into his hand, and balanced it. "Do you know, Poole," he said, looking up, "that you and I are about to place ourselves in a position of some peril?"

"You may say so, sir, indeed," returned the butler.

"It is well, then, that we should be frank," said the other. "We both think more than we have said; let us make a clean breast. This masked figure that you saw, did you recognise it?"

"Well, sir, it went so quick, and the creature was so doubled up, that I could hardly swear to that," was the answer. "But if you mean, was it Mr. Hyde?—why, yes, I think it was! You see, it was much of the same bigness; and it had the same quick, light way with it; and then who else could have got in by the laboratory door? You have not forgot, sir, that at the time of the murder he had still the key with him? But that's not all. I don't know, Mr. Utterson, if ever you met this Mr. Hyde?"

"Yes," said the lawyer, "I once spoke with him."

"Then you must know as well as the rest of us that there was something queer about that gentleman—something that gave a man a turn—I don't know rightly how to say it, sir, beyond this: that you felt it in your marrow kind of cold and thin."

"I own I felt something of what you describe," said Mr. Utterson.

"Quite so, sir," returned Poole. "Well, when that masked thing like a monkey jumped from among the chemicals and whipped into the cabinet, it went down my spine like ice. O, I know it's not evidence, Mr. Utterson; I'm book-learned enough for that; but a man has his feelings, and I give you my bible-word it was Mr. Hyde!"

"Ay, ay," said the lawyer. "My fears incline to the same point. Evil, I fear, founded—evil was sure to come—of that connection. Ay, truly, I believe you; I believe poor Harry is killed; and I believe his murderer (for what purpose, God alone can tell) is still lurking in his victim's room. Well, let our name be vengeance. Call Bradshaw."

The footman came at the summons, very white and nervous.

"Pull yourself together, Bradshaw," said the lawyer. "This suspense, I know, is telling upon all of you; but it is now our intention to make an end of it. Poole, here, and I are going to force our way into the cabinet. If all is well, my shoulders are broad enough to bear the blame. Meanwhile, lest anything should really be amiss, or any malefactor seek to escape by the back, you and the boy must go round the corner with a pair of good sticks and take your post at the laboratory door. We give you ten minutes, to get to your stations."

As Bradshaw left, the lawyer looked at his watch. "And now, Poole, let us get to ours," he said; and taking the poker under his arm, led the way into the yard. The scud had banked over the moon, and it was now quite dark. The wind, which only broke in puffs and draughts into that deep well of building, tossed the light of the candle to and fro about their steps, until they came into the shelter of the theatre, where they sat down silently to wait. London hummed solemnly all around; but nearer at hand, the stillness was only broken by the sounds of a footfall moving to and fro along the cabinet floor.

"So it will walk all day, sir," whispered Poole; "ay, and the better part of the night. Only when a new sample comes from the chemist, there's a bit of a break. Ah, it's an ill conscience that's such an enemy to rest! Ah, sir, there's blood foully shed in every step of it! But hark again, a little closer—put your heart in your ears, Mr. Utterson, and tell me, is that the doctor's foot?"

The steps fell lightly and oddly, with a certain swing, for all they went so slowly; it was different indeed from the heavy creaking tread of Henry Jekyll. Utterson sighed. "Is there never anything else?" he asked.

Poole nodded. "Once," he said. "Once I heard it weeping!"

"Weeping? how that?" said the lawyer, conscious of a sudden chill of horror.

"Weeping like a woman or a lost soul," said the butler. "I came away with that upon my heart, that I could have wept too."

But now the ten minutes drew to an end. Poole disinterred the axe from under a stack of packing straw; the candle was set upon the nearest table to light them to the attack; and they drew near with bated breath to where that patient foot was still going up and down, up and down, in the quiet of the night.

"Jekyll," cried Utterson, with a loud voice, "I demand to see you." He paused a moment, but there came no reply. "I give you fair warning, our suspicions are aroused, and I must and shall see you," he resumed; "if not by fair means, then by foul—if not of your consent, then by brute force!"

"Utterson," said the voice, "for God's sake, have mercy!"

"Ah, that's not Jekyll's voice—it's Hyde's!" cried Utterson. "Down with the door, Poole!"

Poole swung the axe over his shoulder; the blow shook the building, and the red baize door leaped against the lock and hinges. A dismal screech, as of mere animal terror, rang from the cabinet. Up went the axe again, and again the panels crashed and the frame bounded; four times the blow fell; but the wood was tough and the fittings were of excellent workmanship; and it was not until the fifth, that the lock burst in sunder and the wreck of the door fell inwards on the carpet.

The besiegers, appalled by their own riot and the stillness that had succeeded, stood back a little and peered in. There lay the cabinet before their eyes in the quiet lamplight, a good fire glowing and chattering on the hearth, the kettle singing its thin strain, a drawer or two open, papers neatly set forth on the business table, and nearer the fire, the things laid out for tea: the quietest room, you would have said, and, but for the glazed presses full of chemicals, the most commonplace that night in London.

Right in the midst there lay the body of a man sorely contorted and still twitching. They drew near on tip-toe, turned it on its back and beheld the face of Edward Hyde. He was dressed in clothes far too large for him, clothes of the doctor's bigness; the cords of his face still moved with a semblance of life, but life was quite gone: and by the crushed phial in the hand and the strong smell of kernels that hung upon the air, Utterson knew that he was looking on the body of a self-destroyer.

"We have come too late," he said sternly, "whether to save or punish. Hyde is gone to his account; and it only remains for us to find the body of your master."

The far greater proportion of the building was occupied by the theatre, which filled almost the whole ground story and was lighted from above, and by the cabinet, which formed an upper story at one end and looked upon the court. A corridor joined the theatre to the door on the by-street; and with this the cabinet communicated separately by a second flight of stairs. There were besides a few dark closets and a spacious cellar. All these they now thoroughly examined. Each closet needed but a glance, for all were empty, and all, by the dust that fell from their doors, had stood long unopened. The cellar, indeed, was filled with crazy lumber, mostly dating from the times of the surgeon who was Jekyll's predecessor; but even as they opened the door they were advertised of the uselessness of further search, by the fall of a perfect mat of cobweb which had for years sealed up the entrance. Nowhere was there any trace of Henry Jekyll, dead or alive.

Poole stamped on the flags of the corridor. "He must be buried here," he said, hearkening to the sound.

"Or he may have fled," said Utterson, and he turned to examine the door in the by-street. It was locked; and lying near by on the flags, they found the key, already stained with rust.

"This does not look like use," observed the lawyer.

"Use!" echoed Poole. "Do you not see, sir, it is broken? much as if a man had stamped on it."

"Ay," continued Utterson, "and the fractures, too, are rusty." The two men looked at each other with a scare. "This is beyond me, Poole," said the lawyer. "Let us go back to the cabinet."

They mounted the stair in silence, and still with an occasional awestruck glance at the dead body, proceeded more thoroughly to examine the contents of the cabinet. At one table, there were traces of chemical work, various measured heaps of some white salt being laid on glass saucers, as though for an experiment in which the unhappy man had been prevented.

"That is the same drug that I was always bringing him," said Poole; and even as he spoke, the kettle with a startling noise boiled over.

This brought them to the fireside, where the easychair was drawn cosily up, and the tea things stood ready to the sitter's elbow, the very sugar in the cup. There were several books on a shelf; one lay beside the tea things open, and Utterson was amazed to find it a copy of a pious work, for which Jekyll had several times expressed a great esteem, annotated, in his own hand, with startling blasphemies.

Next, in the course of their review of the chamber, the searchers came to the cheval-glass, into whose depths they looked with an involuntary horror. But it was so turned as to show them nothing but the rosy glow playing on the roof, the fire sparkling in a hundred repetitions along the glazed front of the presses, and their own pale and fearful countenances stooping to look in.

"This glass has seen some strange things, sir," whispered Poole.

"And surely none stranger than itself," echoed the lawyer in the same tones. "For what did Jekyll"—he caught himself up at the word with a start, and then conquering the weakness—"what could Jekyll want with it?" he said.

"You may say that!" said Poole.

Next they turned to the business table. On the desk, among the neat array of papers, a large envelope was uppermost, and bore, in the doctor's hand, the name of Mr. Utterson. The lawyer unsealed it, and several enclosures fell to the floor. The first was a will, drawn in the same eccentric terms as the one which he had returned six months before, to serve as a testament in case of death and as a deed of gift in case of disappearance; but in place of the name of Edward Hyde, the lawyer, with indescribable amazement, read the name of Gabriel John Utterson. He looked at Poole, and then back at the paper, and last of all at the dead malefactor stretched upon the carpet.

"My head goes round," he said. "He has been all these days in possession; he had no cause to like me; he must have raged to see himself displaced; and he has not destroyed this document."

He caught up the next paper; it was a brief note in the doctor's hand and dated at the top. "O Poole!" the lawyer cried, "he was alive and here this day. He cannot have been disposed of in so short a space; he must be still alive, he must have fled! And then, why fled? and how? and in that case, can we venture to declare this suicide? O, we must be careful. I foresee that we may yet involve your master in some dire catastrophe."

"Why don't you read it, sir?" asked Poole.

"Because I fear," replied the lawyer solemnly. "God grant I have no cause for it!" And with that he brought the paper to his eyes and read as follows:

My Dear Utterson,—

When this shall fall into your hands, I shall have disappeared, under what circumstances I have not the penetration to foresee, but my instinct and all the circumstances of my nameless situation tell me that the end is sure and must be early. Go then, and first read the narrative which Lanyon warned me he was to place in your hands; and if you care to hear more, turn to the confession of

Your unworthy and unhappy friend,
Henry Jekyll.

"There was a third enclosure?" asked Utterson.

"Here, sir," said Poole, and gave into his hands a considerable packet sealed in several places.

The lawyer put it in his pocket. "I would say nothing of this paper. If your master has fled or is dead, we may at least save his credit. It is now ten; I must go home and read these documents in quiet; but I shall be back before midnight, when we shall send for the police."

They went out, locking the door of the theatre behind them; and Utterson, once more leaving the servants gathered about the fire in the hall, trudged back to his office to read the two narratives in which this mystery was now to be explained.

DR. LANYON'S NARRATIVE

On the ninth of January, now four days ago, I received by the evening delivery a registered envelope, addressed in the hand of my colleague and old school companion, Henry Jekyll. I was a good deal surprised by this; for we were by no means in the habit of correspondence; I had seen the man, dined with him, indeed, the night before; and I could imagine nothing in our intercourse that should justify formality of registration. The contents increased my wonder; for this is how the letter ran:

10th December, 18—

DEAR LANYON,—

You are one of my oldest friends; and although we may have differed at times on scientific questions, I cannot remember, at least on my side, any break in our affection. There was never a day when, if you had said to me, 'Jekyll, my life, my honour, my reason, depend upon you,' I would not have sacrificed my left hand to help you. Lanyon, my life, my honour, my reason, are all at your mercy; if you fail me to-night I am lost. You might suppose, after this preface, that I am going to ask you for something dishonourable to grant. Judge for yourself.

I want you to postpone all other engagements for to-night—

ay, even if you were summoned to the bedside of an emperor; to take a cab, unless your carriage should be actually at the door; and with this letter in your hand for consultation, to drive straight to my house. Poole, my butler, has his orders; you will find him waiting your arrival with a locksmith. The door of my cabinet is then to be forced: and you are to go in alone; to open the glazed press (letter E) on the left hand, breaking the lock if it be shut; and to draw out, *with all its contents as they stand*, the fourth drawer from the top or (which is the same thing) the third from the bottom. In my extreme distress of mind, I have a morbid fear of misdirecting you; but even if I am in error, you may know the right drawer by its contents: some powders, a phial and a paper book. This drawer I beg of you to carry back with you to Cavendish Square exactly as it stands.

That is the first part of the service: now for the second. You should be back, if you set out at once on the receipt of this, long before midnight; but I will leave you that amount of margin, not only in the fear of one of those obstacles that can neither be prevented nor foreseen, but because an hour when your servants are in bed is to be preferred for what will then remain to do. At midnight, then, I have to ask you to be alone in your consulting room, to admit with your own hand into the house a man who will present himself in my name, and to place in his hands the drawer that you will have brought with you from my cabinet. Then you will have played your part and earned my gratitude completely. Five minutes afterwards, if you insist upon an explanation, you will have understood that these arrangements are of capital importance; and that by the neglect of one of them, fantastic as they must appear, you might have charged your conscience with my death or the shipwreck of my reason.

Confident as I am that you will not trifle with this appeal, my heart sinks and my hand trembles at the bare thought of such a possibility. Think of me at this hour, in a strange place, labouring under a blackness of distress that no fancy can exaggerate, and yet well aware that, if you will but punctually serve me, my troubles will roll away like a story that is told. Serve me, my dear Lanyon, and save

Your friend,

H. J.

P.S.—I had already sealed this up when a fresh terror struck upon my soul. It is possible that the post-office may fail me, and this letter not come into your hands until to-morrow morning. In that case, dear Lanyon, do my errand when it shall be most convenient for you in the course of the day; and once more expect my messenger at midnight. It may then already be too late; and if that night passes without event, you will know that you have seen the last of Henry Jekyll.

Upon the reading of this letter, I made sure my colleague was insane; but till that was proved beyond the possibility of doubt, I felt bound to do as he requested. The less I understood of this farrago, the less I was in a position to judge of its importance; and an appeal so worded could not be set aside without a grave responsibility. I rose accordingly from table, got into a hansom, and drove straight to Jekyll's house. The butler was awaiting my arrival; he had received by the same post as mine a registered letter of instruction, and had sent at once for a locksmith and a carpenter. The tradesmen came while we were yet speaking; and we moved in a body to old Dr. Denman's surgical theatre, from which (as you are doubtless aware) Jekyll's private cabinet is most conveniently entered. The door was very strong, the lock excellent; the carpenter avowed he would have great trouble and have to do much damage, if force were to be used; and the locksmith was near despair. But this last was a handy fellow, and after two hours' work, the door stood open. The press marked E was unlocked; and I took out the drawer, had it filled up with straw and tied in a sheet, and returned with it to Cavendish Square.

Here I proceeded to examine its contents. The powders were neatly enough made up, but not with the nicety of the dispensing chemist; so that it was plain they were of Jekyll's private manufacture: and when I opened one of the wrappers I found what seemed to me a simple crystalline salt of a white colour. The phial, to which I next turned my attention, might have been about half full of a blood-red liquor, which was highly pungent to the sense of smell and seemed to me to contain phosphorus and some volatile ether. At the other ingredients I could make no guess. The book was an ordinary version book and contained little but a series of dates.

These covered a period of many years, but I observed that the entries ceased nearly a year ago and quite abruptly. Here and there a brief remark was appended to a date, usually no more than a single word: "double" occurring perhaps six times in a total of several hundred entries; and once very early in the list and followed by several marks of exclamation, "total failure!!!" All this, though it whetted my curiosity, told me little that was definite. Here were a phial of some tincture, a paper of some salt, and the record of a series of experiments that had led (like too many of Jekyll's investigations) to no end of practical usefulness. How could the presence of these articles in my house affect either the honour, the sanity, or the life of my flighty colleague? If his messenger could go to one place, why could he not go to another? And even granting some impediment, why was this gentleman to be received by me in secret? The more I reflected the more convinced I grew that I was dealing with a case of cerebral disease; and though I dismissed my servants to bed, I loaded an old revolver, that I might be found in some posture of self-defence.

Twelve o'clock had scarce rung out over London, ere the knocker sounded very gently on the door. I went myself at the summons, and found a small man crouching against the pillars of the portico.

"Are you come from Dr. Jekyll?" I asked.

He told me "yes" by a constrained gesture; and when I had bidden him enter, he did not obey me without a searching backward glance into the darkness of the square. There was a policeman not far off, advancing with his bull's eye open; and at the sight, I thought my visitor started and made greater haste.

These particulars struck me, I confess, disagreeably; and as I followed him into the bright light of the consulting room, I kept my hand ready on my weapon. Here, at last, I had a chance of clearly seeing him. I had never set eyes on him before, so much was certain. He was small, as I have said; I was struck besides with the shocking expression of his face, with his remarkable combination of great muscular activity and great apparent debility of constitution, and—last but not least—with the odd, subjective disturbance caused by his neighbourhood. This bore some resemblance to incipient rigour, and was accompanied by a marked sinking of the pulse. At the time, I set it down to some idiosyncratic, personal distaste, and merely wondered at the acuteness of the symptoms; but I have since had reason to believe the cause to lie much deeper in the nature of man, and to turn on some nobler hinge than the principle of hatred.

This person (who had thus, from the first moment of his entrance, struck in me what I can only describe as a disgustful curiosity) was dressed in a fashion that would have made an ordinary person laughable; his clothes, that is to say, although they were of rich and sober fabric, were enormously too large for him in every measurement—the trousers hanging on his legs and rolled up to keep them from the ground, the waist of the coat below his haunches, and the collar sprawling wide upon his shoulders. Strange to relate, this ludicrous accoutrement was far from moving me to laughter. Rather, as there was something abnormal and misbegotten in the very essence of the creature that now faced me—something seizing, surprising and revolting—this fresh disparity seemed but to fit in with and to reinforce it; so that to my interest in the man's nature and character, there was added a curiosity as to his origin, his life, his fortune and status in the world.

These observations, though they have taken so great a space to be set down in, were yet the work of a few seconds. My visitor was, indeed, on fire with sombre excitement.

"Have you got it?" he cried. "Have you got it?" And so lively was his impatience that he even laid his hand upon my arm and sought to shake me.

I put him back, conscious at his touch of a certain icy pang along my blood. "Come, sir," said I. "You forget that I have not yet the pleasure of your acquaintance. Be seated, if you please." And I showed him an example, and sat down myself in my customary seat and with as fair an imitation of my ordinary manner to a patient, as the lateness of the hour, the nature of my preoccupations, and the horror I had of my visitor, would suffer me to muster.

"I beg your pardon, Dr. Lanyon," he replied civilly enough. "What you say is very well founded; and my impatience has shown its heels to my politeness. I come here at the instance of your colleague, Dr. Henry Jekyll, on a piece of business of some moment; and I understood . . ." He paused and put his hand to his throat, and I could see, in spite of his collected manner, that he was wrestling against the approaches of the hysteria—"I understood, a drawer . . ."

But here I took pity on my visitor's suspense, and some perhaps on my own growing curiosity.

"There it is, sir," said I, pointing to the drawer, where it lay on the floor behind a table and still covered with the sheet.

He sprang to it, and then paused, and laid his hand upon his heart: I could hear his teeth grate with the convulsive action of his jaws; and his face was so ghastly to see that I grew alarmed both for his life and reason.

"Compose yourself," said I.

He turned a dreadful smile to me, and as if with the decision of despair, plucked away the sheet. At sight of the contents, he uttered one loud sob of such immense relief that I sat petrified. And the next moment, in a voice that was already fairly well under control, "Have you a graduated glass?" he asked.

I rose from my place with something of an effort and gave him what he asked.

He thanked me with a smiling nod, measured out a few minims of the red tincture and added one of the powders. The mixture, which was at first of a reddish hue, began, in proportion as the crystals melted, to brighten in colour, to effervesce audibly, and to throw off small fumes of vapour. Suddenly and at the same moment, the ebullition ceased and the compound changed to a dark purple, which faded again more slowly to a watery green. My visitor, who had watched these metamorphoses with a keen eye, smiled, set down the glass upon the table, and then turned and looked upon me with an air of scrutiny.

"And now," said he, "to settle what remains. Will you be wise? will you be guided? will you suffer me to take this glass in my hand and to go forth from your house without further parley? or has the greed of curiosity too much command of you? Think before you answer, for it shall be done as you decide. As you decide, you shall be left as you were before, and neither richer nor wiser, unless the sense of service rendered to a man in mortal distress may be counted as a kind of riches of the soul. Or, if you shall so prefer to choose, a new province of knowledge and new avenues to fame and power shall be laid open to you, here, in this room, upon the instant; and your sight shall be blasted by a prodigy to stagger the unbelief of Satan."

"Sir," said I, affecting a coolness that I was far from truly possessing, "you speak enigmas, and you will perhaps not wonder that I hear you with no very strong impression of belief. But I have gone too far in the way of inexplicable services to pause before I see the end."

"It is well," replied my visitor. "Lanyon, you remember your vows: what follows is under the seal of our profession. And now, you who have so long been bound to the most narrow and material views, you who have denied the virtue of transcendental medicine, you who have derided your superiors—behold!"

He put the glass to his lips and drank at one gulp. A cry followed; he reeled, staggered, clutched at the table and held on, staring with injected eyes, gasping with open mouth; and as I looked there came, I thought, a change—he seemed to swell—his face became suddenly black and the features seemed to melt and alter—and the next moment, I had sprung to my feet and leaped back against the wall, my arm raised to shield me from that prodigy, my mind submerged in terror.

"O God!" I screamed, and "O God!" again and again; for there before my eyes—pale and shaken, and half fainting, and groping before him with his hands, like a man restored from death—there stood Henry Jekyll!

What he told me in the next hour, I cannot bring my mind to set on paper. I saw what I saw, I heard what I heard, and my soul sickened at it; and yet now when that sight has faded from my eyes, I ask myself if I believe it, and I cannot answer. My life is shaken to its roots; sleep has left me; the deadliest terror sits by me at all hours of the day and night; I feel that my days are numbered, and that I must die; and yet I shall die incredulous. As for the moral turpitude that man unveiled to me, even with tears of penitence, I cannot, even in memory, dwell on it without a start of horror. I will say but one thing, Utterson, and that (if you can bring your mind to credit it) will be more than enough. The creature who crept into my house that night was, on Jekyll's own confession, known by the name of Hyde and hunted for in every corner of the land as the murderer of Carew.

HENRY JEKYLL'S FULL STATEMENT
OF THE CASE

I was born in the year 18— to a large fortune, endowed besides with excellent parts, inclined by nature to industry, fond of the respect of the wise and good among my fellow men, and thus, as might have been supposed, with every guarantee of an honourable and distinguished future. And indeed the worst of my faults was a certain impatient gaiety of disposition, such as has made the happiness of many, but such as I found it hard to reconcile with my imperious desire to carry my head high, and wear a more than commonly grave countenance before the public. Hence it came about that I concealed my pleasures; and that when I reached years of reflection, and began to look round me and take stock of my progress and position in the world, I stood already committed to a profound duplicity of life. Many a man would have even blazoned such irregularities as I was guilty of; but from the high views that I had set before me, I regarded and hid them with an almost morbid sense of shame. It was thus rather the exacting nature of my aspirations than any particular degradation in my faults, that made me what I was, and, with even a deeper trench than in the majority of men, severed in me those provinces of good and ill which divide and compound man's dual nature. In this case, I was driven to reflect deeply and inveterately on that hard law of life, which lies at the root of religion and is one of the most plentiful springs of distress. Though so profound a double-dealer, I was in no sense a hypocrite; both sides of me were in dead earnest; I was no more myself when I laid aside restraint and plunged in shame, than when I laboured, in the eye of day, at the furtherance of knowledge or the relief of sorrow and suffering. And it chanced that the direction of my scientific studies, which led wholly towards the mystic and the transcendental, reäcted and shed a strong light on this consciousness of the perennial war among my members. With every day, and from both sides of my intelligence, the moral and the intellectual, I thus drew steadily nearer to that truth, by whose partial discovery I have been doomed to such a dreadful shipwreck: that man is not truly one, but truly two. I say two, because the state of my own knowledge does not pass beyond that point. Others will follow, others will outstrip me on the same lines; and I hazard the guess that man will be ultimately known for a mere polity of multifarious, incongruous and independent denizens. I, for my part, from the nature of my life, advanced infallibly in one direction and in one direction only. It was on the moral side, and in my own person, that I learned to recognise the thorough and primitive duality of man; I saw that, of the two natures that contended in the field of my consciousness, even if I could rightly be said to be either, it was only because I was radically both; and from an early date, even before the course of my scientific discoveries had begun to suggest the most naked possibility of such a miracle, I had learned to dwell with pleasure, as a beloved day-dream, on the thought of the separation of these elements. If each, I told myself, could but be housed in separate identities, life would be relieved of all that was unbearable; the unjust might go his way, delivered from the aspirations and remorse of his more upright twin; and the just could walk steadfastly and securely on his upward path, doing the good things in which he found his pleasure, and no longer exposed to disgrace and penitence by the hands of this extraneous evil. It was the curse of mankind that these incongruous faggots were thus bound together—that in the agonised womb of consciousness, these polar twins should be continuously struggling. How, then, were they dissociated?

I was so far in my reflections when, as I have said, a side light began to shine upon the subject from the laboratory table. I began to perceive more deeply than it has ever yet been stated, the trembling immateriality, the mist-like transience, of this seemingly so solid body in which we walk attired. Certain agents I found to have the power to shake and to pluck back that fleshly vestment, even as a wind might toss the curtains of a pavilion. For two good reasons, I will not enter deeply into this scientific branch of my confession.

First, because I have been made to learn that the doom and burthen of our life is bound forever on man's shoulders, and when the attempt is made to cast it off, it but returns upon us with more unfamiliar and more awful pressure. Second, because, as my narrative will make, alas! too evident, my discoveries were incomplete. Enough, then, that I not only recognised my natural body for the mere aura and effulgence of certain of the powers that made up my spirit, but managed to compound a drug by which these powers should be dethroned from their supremacy, and a second form and countenance substituted, none the less natural to me because they were the expression, and bore the stamp, of lower elements in my soul.

I hesitated long before I put this theory to the test of practice. I knew well that I risked death; for any drug that so potently controlled and shook the very fortress of identity, might by the least scruple of an overdose or at the least inopportunity in the moment of exhibition, utterly blot out that immaterial tabernacle which I looked to it to change. But the temptation of a discovery so singular and profound, at last overcame the suggestions of alarm. I had long since prepared my tincture; I purchased at once, from a firm of wholesale chemists, a large quantity of a particular salt which I knew, from my experiments, to be the last ingredient required; and late one accursed night, I compounded the elements, watched them boil and smoke together in the glass, and when the ebullition had subsided, with a strong glow of courage, drank off the potion.

The most racking pangs succeeded: a grinding in the bones, deadly nausea, and a horror of the spirit that cannot be exceeded at the hour of birth or death. Then these agonies began swiftly to subside, and I came to myself as if out of a great sickness. There was something strange in my sensations, something indescribably new and, from its very novelty, incredibly sweet. I felt younger, lighter, happier in body; within I was conscious of a heady recklessness, a current of disordered sensual images running like a mill race in my fancy, a solution of the bonds of obligation, an unknown but not an innocent freedom of the soul. I knew myself, at the first breath of this new life, to be more wicked, tenfold more wicked, sold a slave to my original evil; and the thought, in that moment, braced and delighted me like wine. I stretched out my hands, exulting in the freshness of these sensations; and in the act, I was suddenly aware that I had lost in stature.

There was no mirror, at that date, in my room; that which stands beside me as I write, was brought there later on and for the very purpose of these transformations. The night, however, was far gone into the morning—the morning, black as it was, was nearly ripe for the conception of the day—the inmates of my house were locked in the most rigorous hours of slumber; and I determined, flushed as I was with hope and triumph, to venture in my new shape as far as to my bedroom. I crossed the yard, wherein the constellations looked down upon me, I could have thought, with wonder, the first creature of that sort that their unsleeping vigilance had yet disclosed to them; I stole through the corridors, a stranger in my own house; and coming to my room, I saw for the first time the appearance of Edward Hyde.

I must here speak by theory alone, saying not that which I know, but that which I suppose to be most probable. The evil side of my nature, to which I had now transferred the stamping efficacy, was less robust and less developed than the good which I had just deposed. Again, in the course of my life, which had been, after all, nine-tenths a life of effort, virtue and control, it had been much less exercised and much less exhausted. And hence, as I think, it came about that Edward Hyde was so much smaller, slighter and younger than Henry Jekyll. Even as good shone upon the countenance of the one, evil was written broadly and plainly on the face of the other. Evil besides (which I must still believe to be the lethal side of man) had left on that body an imprint of deformity and decay. And yet when I looked upon that ugly idol in the glass, I was conscious of no repugnance, rather of a leap of welcome. This, too, was myself. It seemed natural and human. In my eyes it bore a livelier image of the spirit, it seemed more express and single, than the imperfect and divided countenance I had been hitherto accustomed to call mine. And in so far I was doubtless right. I have observed that when I wore the semblance of Edward Hyde, none could come near to me at first without a visible misgiving of the flesh. This, as I take it, was because all human beings, as we meet them, are commingled out of good and evil: and Edward Hyde, alone in the ranks of man-kind, was pure evil.

I lingered but a moment at the mirror: the second and conclu-sive experiment had yet to be attempted; it yet remained to be seen if I had lost my identity beyond redemption and must flee before daylight from a house that was no longer mine; and hurrying back to my cabinet, I once more prepared and drank the cup, once more suffered the pangs of dissolution, and came to myself once more with the character, the stature and the face of Henry Jekyll.

That night I had come to the fatal cross roads. Had I approached my discovery in a more noble spirit, had I risked the experiment while under the empire of generous or pious aspirations, all must have been otherwise, and from these agonies of death and birth, I had come forth an angel instead of a fiend. The drug had no discrimi-nating action; it was neither diabolical nor divine; it but shook the doors of the prison-house of my disposition; and like the captives of Philippi, that which stood within ran forth. At that time my virtue slumbered; my evil, kept awake by ambition, was alert and swift to seize the occasion; and the thing that was projected was Edward Hyde. Hence, although I had now two characters as well as two appearances, one was wholly evil, and the other was still the old Henry Jekyll, that incongruous compound of whose reformation and improvement I had already learned to despair. The movement was thus wholly towards the worse.

Even at that time, I had not yet conquered my aversion to the dryness of a life of study. I would still be merrily disposed at times; and as my pleasures were (to say the least) undignified, and I was not only well known and highly considered, but growing towards the elderly man, this incoherency of my life was daily growing more unwelcome. It was on this side that my new power tempted me un-til I fell in slavery. I had but to drink the cup, to doff at once the body of the noted professor, and to assume, like a thick cloak, that of Edward Hyde. I smiled at the notion; it seemed to me at the time to be humorous; and I made my preparations with the most studious care. I took and furnished that house in Soho, to which Hyde was tracked by the police; and engaged as housekeeper a creature whom I well knew to be silent and unscrupulous. On the other side, I announced to my servants that a Mr. Hyde (whom I described) was to have full liberty and power about my house in the square; and to parry mishaps, I even called and made myself a familiar object, in my second character. I next drew up that will to which you so much objected; so that if anything befell me in the person of Dr. Jekyll, I could enter on that of Edward Hyde without pecuniary loss. And thus fortified, as I supposed, on every side, I began to profit by the strange immunities of my position.

Men have before hired bravos to transact their crimes, while their own person and reputation sat under shelter. I was the first that ever did so for his pleasures. I was the first that could thus plod in the public eye with a load of genial respectability, and in a moment, like a schoolboy, strip off these lendings and spring headlong into the sea of liberty. But for me, in my impenetrable mantle, the safety was complete. Think of it—I did not even exist! Let me but escape into my laboratory door, give me but a second or two to mix and swallow the draught that I had always standing ready; and whatever he had done, Edward Hyde would pass away like the stain of breath upon a mirror; and there in his stead, quietly at home, trimming the midnight lamp in his study, a man who could afford to laugh at suspicion, would be Henry Jekyll.

The pleasures which I made haste to seek in my disguise were, as I have said, undignified; I would scarce use a harder term. But in the hands of Edward Hyde, they soon began to turn towards the monstrous. When I would come back from these excursions, I was often plunged into a kind of wonder at my vicarious depravity. This familiar that I called out of my own soul, and sent forth alone to do his good pleasure, was a being inherently malign and villainous; his every act and thought centered on self; drinking pleasure with bestial avidity from any degree of torture to another; relentless like a man of stone. Henry Jekyll stood at times aghast before the acts of Edward Hyde; but the situation was apart from ordinary laws, and insidiously relaxed the grasp of conscience. It was Hyde, after all, and Hyde alone, that was guilty. Jekyll was no worse; he woke again to his good qualities seemingly unimpaired; he would even make haste, where it was possible, to undo the evil done by Hyde. And thus his conscience slumbered.

Into the details of the infamy at which I thus connived (for even now I can scarce grant that I committed it) I have no design of entering; I mean but to point out the warnings and the successive steps with which my chastisement approached. I met with one accident which, as it brought on no consequence, I shall no more than mention. An act of cruelty to a child aroused against me the anger of a passer-by, whom I recognised the other day in the person of your kinsman; the doctor and the child's family joined him; there were moments when I feared for my life; and at last, in order to pacify their too just resentment, Edward Hyde had to bring them to the door, and pay them in a cheque drawn in the name of Henry Jekyll. But this danger was easily eliminated from the future, by opening an account at another bank in the name of Edward Hyde himself; and when, by sloping my own hand backward, I had supplied my double with a signature, I thought I sat beyond the reach of fate.

Some two months before the murder of Sir Danvers, I had been out for one of my adventures, had returned at a late hour, and woke the next day in bed with somewhat odd sensations. It was in vain I looked about me; in vain I saw the decent furniture and tall proportions of my room in the square; in vain that I recognised the pattern of the bed curtains and the design of the mahogany frame; something still kept insisting that I was not where I was, that I had not wakened where I seemed to be, but in the little room in Soho where I was accustomed to sleep in the body of Edward Hyde. I smiled to myself, and, in my psychological way began lazily to inquire into the elements of this illusion, occasionally, even as I did so, dropping back into a comfortable morning doze. I was still so engaged when, in one of my more wakeful moments, my eyes fell upon my hand. Now the hand of Henry Jekyll (as you have often remarked) was professional in shape and size: it was large, firm, white and comely. But the hand which I now saw, clearly enough, in the yellow light of a mid-London morning, lying half shut on the bed clothes, was lean, corded, knuckly, of a dusky pallor and thickly shaded with a swart growth of hair. It was the hand of Edward Hyde.

I must have stared upon it for near half a minute, sunk as I was in the mere stupidity of wonder, before terror woke up in my breast as sudden and startling as the crash of cymbals; and bounding from my bed, I rushed to the mirror. At the sight that met my eyes, my blood was changed into something exquisitely thin and icy. Yes, I had gone to bed Henry Jekyll, I had awakened Edward Hyde. How was this to be explained? I asked myself; and then, with another bound of terror—how was it to be remedied? It was well on in the morning; the servants were up; all my drugs were in the cabinet—a long journey down two pair of stairs, through the back passage, across the open court and through the anatomical theatre, from where I was then standing horror-struck. It might indeed be possible to cover my face; but of what use was that, when I was unable to conceal the alteration in my stature? And then with an overpowering sweetness of relief, it came back upon my mind that the servants were already used to the coming and going of my second self. I had soon dressed, as well as I was able, in clothes of my own size: had soon passed through the house, where Bradshaw stared and drew back at seeing Mr. Hyde at such an hour and in such a strange array; and ten minutes later, Dr. Jekyll had returned to his own shape and was sitting down, with a darkened brow, to make a feint of breakfasting.

Small indeed was my appetite. This inexplicable incident, this reversal of my previous experience, seemed, like the Babylonian finger on the wall, to be spelling out the letters of my judgment; and I began to reflect more seriously than ever before on the issues and possibilities of my double existence. That part of me which I had the power of projecting had lately been much exercised and nourished; it had seemed to me of late as though the body of Edward Hyde had grown in stature, as though (when I wore that form) I were conscious of a more generous tide of blood; and I began to spy a danger that, if this were much prolonged, the balance of my nature might be permanently overthrown, the power of voluntary change be forfeited, and the character of Edward Hyde become irrevocably mine. The power of the drug had not been always equally displayed. Once, very early in my career, it had totally failed me; since then I had been obliged on more than one occasion to double, and once, with infinite risk of death, to treble the amount; and these rare uncertainties had cast hitherto the sole shadow on my contentment. Now, however, and in the light of that morning's accident, I was led to remark that whereas, in the beginning, the difficulty had been to throw off the body of Jekyll, it had of late gradually but decidedly transferred itself to the other side. All things therefore seemed to point to this: that I was slowly losing hold of my original and better self, and becoming slowly incorporated with my second and worse.

Between these two, I now felt I had to choose. My two natures had memory in common, but all other faculties were most unequally shared between them. Jekyll (who was composite) now with the most sensitive apprehensions, now with a greedy gusto, projected and shared in the pleasures and adventures of Hyde; but Hyde was indifferent to Jekyll, or but remembered him as the mountain bandit remembers the cavern in which he conceals himself from pursuit. Jekyll had more than a father's interest; Hyde had more than a son's indifference. To cast in my lot with Jekyll, was to die to those appetites which I had long secretly indulged and had of late begun to pamper. To cast it in with Hyde, was to die to a thousand interests and aspirations, and to become, at a blow and forever, despised and friendless. The bargain might appear unequal; but there was still another consideration in the scales; for while Jekyll would suffer smartingly in the fires of abstinence, Hyde would be not even conscious of all that he had lost. Strange as my circumstances were, the terms of this debate are as old and commonplace as man; much the same inducements and alarms cast the die for any tempted and trembling sinner; and it fell out with me, as it falls with so vast a majority of my fellows, that I chose the better part and was found wanting in the strength to keep to it.

Yes, I preferred the elderly and discontented doctor, surrounded by friends and cherishing honest hopes; and bade a resolute farewell to the liberty, the comparative youth, the light step, leaping impulses and secret pleasures, that I had enjoyed in the disguise of Hyde. I made this choice perhaps with some unconscious reservation, for I neither gave up the house in Soho, nor destroyed the clothes of Edward Hyde, which still lay ready in my cabinet. For two months, however, I was true to my determination; for two months I led a life of such severity as I had never before attained to, and enjoyed the compensations of an approving conscience. But time began at last to obliterate the freshness of my alarm; the praises of conscience began to grow into a thing of course; I began to be tortured with throes and longings, as of Hyde struggling after freedom; and at last, in an hour of moral weakness, I once again compounded and swallowed the transforming draught.

I do not suppose that, when a drunkard reasons with himself upon his vice, he is once out of five hundred times affected by the dangers that he runs through his brutish, physical insensibility; neither had I, long as I had considered my position, made enough allowance for the complete moral insensibility and insensate readiness to evil, which were the leading characters of Edward Hyde. Yet it was by these that I was punished. My devil had been long caged, he came out roaring. I was conscious, even when I took the draught, of a more unbridled, a more furious propensity to ill. It must have been this, I suppose, that stirred in my soul that tempest of impatience with which I listened to the civilities of my unhappy victim; I declare, at least, before God, no man morally sane could have been guilty of that crime upon so pitiful a provocation; and that I struck in no more reasonable spirit than that in which a sick child may break a plaything. But I had voluntarily stripped myself of all those balancing instincts by which even the worst of us continues to walk with some degree of steadiness among temptations; and in my case, to be tempted, however slightly, was to fall.

Instantly the spirit of hell awoke in me and raged. With a transport of glee, I mauled the unresisting body, tasting delight from every blow; and it was not till weariness had begun to succeed, that I was suddenly, in the top fit of my delirium, struck through the heart by a cold thrill of terror. A mist dispersed; I saw my life to be forfeit; and fled from the scene of these excesses, at once glorifying and trembling, my lust of evil gratified and stimulated, my love of live screwed to the topmost peg. I ran to the house in Soho, and (to make assurance doubly sure) destroyed my papers; thence I set out through the lamplit streets, in the same divided ecstasy of mind, gloating on my crime, light-headedly devising others in the future, and yet still hastening and still hearkening in my wake for the steps of the avenger. Hyde had a song upon his lips as he compounded the draught, and as he drank it, pledged the dead man. The pangs of transformation had not done tearing him, before Henry Jekyll, with streaming tears of gratitude and remorse, had fallen upon his knees and lifted his clasped hands to God. The veil of self-indulgence was rent from head to foot. I saw my life as a whole: I followed it up from the days of childhood, when I had walked with my father's hand, and through the self-denying toils of my professional life, to arrive again and again, with the same sense of unreality, at the damned horrors of the evening. I could have screamed aloud; I sought with tears and prayers to smother down the crowd of hideous images and sounds with which my memory swarmed against me; and still, between the petitions, the ugly face of my iniquity stared into my soul. As the acuteness of this remorse began to die away, it was succeeded by a sense of joy. The problem of my conduct was solved. Hyde was thenceforth impossible; whether I would or not, I was now confined to the better part of my existence; and O, how I rejoiced to think it! with what willing humility, I embraced anew the restrictions of natural life! with what sincere renunciation, I locked the door by which I had so often gone and come, and ground the key under my heel!

The next day, came the news that the murder had been overlooked, that the guilt of Hyde was patent to the world, and that the victim was a man high in public estimation. It was not only a crime, it had been a tragic folly. I think I was glad to know it; I think I was glad to have my better impulses thus buttressed and guarded by the terrors of the scaffold. Jekyll was now my city of refuge; let but Hyde peep out an instant, and the hands of all men would be raised to take and slay him.

I resolved in my future conduct to redeem the past; and I can say with honesty that my resolve was fruitful of some good. You know yourself how earnestly in the last months of last year, I laboured to relieve suffering; you know that much was done for others, and that the days passed quietly, almost happily for myself. Nor can I truly say that I wearied of this beneficent and innocent life; I think instead that I daily enjoyed it more completely; but I was still cursed with my duality of purpose; and as the first edge of my penitence wore off, the lower side of me, so long indulged, so recently chained down, began to growl for license. Not that I dreamed of resuscitating Hyde; the bare idea of that would startle me to frenzy: no, it was in my own person, that I was once more tempted to trifle with my conscience; and it was as an ordinary secret sinner, that I at last fell before the assualts of temptation.

There comes an end to all things; the most capacious measure is filled at last; and this brief condescension to my evil finally destroyed the balance of my soul. And yet I was not alarmed; the fall seemed natural, like a return to the old days before I had made my discovery. It was a fine, clear, January day, wet under foot where the frost had melted, but cloudless overhead; and the Regent's Park was full of winter chirrupings and sweet with spring odours. I sat in the sun on a bench; the animal within me licking the chops of memory; the spiritual side a little drowsed, promising subsequent penitence, but not yet moved to begin. After all, I reflected, I was like my neighbours; and then I smiled, comparing myself with other men, comparing my active goodwill with the lazy cruelty of their neglect. And at the very moment of that vain-glorious thought, a qualm came over me, a horrid nausea and the most deadly shuddering. These passed away, and left me faint; and then as in its turn the faintness subsided, I began to be aware of a change in the temper of my thoughts, a greater boldness, a contempt of danger, a solution of the bonds of obligation. I looked down; my clothes hung formlessly on my shrunken limbs; the hand that lay on my knee was corded and hairy. I was once more Edward Hyde. A moment before I had been safe of all men's respect, wealthy, beloved—the cloth laying for me in the dining-room at home; and now I was the common quarry of mankind, hunted, houseless, a known murderer, thrall to the gallows.

My reason wavered, but it did not fail me utterly. I have more than once observed that, in my second character, my faculties seemed sharpened to a point and my spirits more tensely elastic; thus it came about that, where Jekyll perhaps might have succumbed, Hyde rose to the importance of the moment. My drugs were in one of the presses of my cabinet; how was I to reach them? That was the problem that (crushing my temples in my hands) I set myself to solve. The laboratory door I had closed. If I sought to enter by the house, my own servants would consign me to the gallows. I saw I must employ another hand, and thought of Lanyon. How was he to be reached? how persuaded? Supposing that I escaped capture in the streets, how was I to make my way into his presence? and how should I, an unknown and displeasing visitor, prevail on the famous physician to rifle the study of his colleague, Dr. Jekyll? Then I remembered that of my original character, one part remained to me:

I could write my own hand; and once I had conceived that kindling spark, the way that I must follow became lighted up from end to end.

Thereupon, I arranged my clothes as best I could, and summoning a passing hansom, drove to an hotel in Portland Street, the name of which I chanced to remember. At my appearance (which was indeed comical enough, however tragic a fate these garments covered) the driver could not conceal his mirth. I gnashed my teeth upon him with a gust of devilish fury; and the smile withered from his face—happily for him—yet more happily for myself, for in another instant I had certainly dragged him from his perch. At the inn, as I entered, I looked about me with so black a countenance as made the attendants tremble; not a look did they exchange in my presence; but obsequiously took my orders, led me to a private room, and brought me wherewithal to write. Hyde in danger of his life was a creature new to me; shaken with inordinate anger, strung to the pitch of murder, lusting to inflict pain. Yet the creature was astute; mastered his fury with a great effort of the will; composed his two important letters, one to Lanyon and one to Poole; and that he might receive actual evidence of their being posted, sent them out with directions that they should be registered.

Thenceforward, he sat all day over the fire in the private room, gnawing his nails; there he dined, sitting alone with his fears, the waiter visibly quailing before his eye; and thence, when the night was fully come, he set forth in the corner of a closed cab, and was driven to and fro about the streets of the city. He, I say—I cannot say, I. That child of Hell had nothing human; nothing lived in him but fear and hatred. And when at last, thinking the driver had begun to grow suspicious, he discharged the cab and ventured on foot, attired in his misfitting clothes, an object marked out for observation, into the midst of the nocturnal passengers, these two base passions raged within him like a tempest. He walked fast, hunted by his fears, chattering to himself, skulking through the less frequented thoroughfares, counting the minutes that still divided him from midnight. Once a woman spoke to him, offering, I think, a box of lights. He smote her in the face, and she fled.

When I came to myself at Lanyon's, the horror of my old friend perhaps affected me somewhat: I do not know; it was at least but a drop in the sea to the abhorrence with which I looked back upon these hours. A change had come over me. It was no longer the fear of the gallows, it was the horror of being Hyde that racked me. I received Lanyon's condemnation partly in a dream; it was partly in a dream that I came home to my own house and got into bed. I slept after the prostration of the day, with a stringent and profound slumber which not even the nightmares that wrung me could avail to break. I awoke in the morning shaken, weakened, but refreshed. I still hated and feared the thought of the brute that slept within me, and I had not of course forgotten the appalling dangers of the day before; but I was once more at home, in my own house and close to my drugs; and gratitude for my escape shone so strong in my soul that it almost rivalled the brightness of hope.

I was stepping leisurely across the court after breakfast, drinking the chill of the air with pleasure, when I was seized again with those indescribable sensations that heralded the change; and I had but the time to gain the shelter of my cabinet, before I was once again raging and freezing with the passions of Hyde. It took on this occasion a double dose to recall me to myself; and alas! six hours after, as I sat looking sadly in the fire, the pangs returned, and the drug had to be readministered. In short, from that day forth it seemed only by a great effort as of gymnastics, and only under the immediate stimulation of the drug, that I was able to wear the countenance of Jekyll. At all hours of the day and night, I would be taken with the premonitory shudder; above all, if I slept, or even dozed for a moment in my chair, it was always as Hyde that I awakened. Under the strain of this continually impending doom and by the sleeplessness to which I now condemned myself, ay, even beyond what I had thought possible to man, I became, in my own person, a creature eaten up and emptied by fever, languidly weak both in body and mind, and solely occupied by one thought: the horror of my other self. But when I slept, or when the virtue of the medicine wore off, I would leap almost without transition (for the pangs of transformation grew daily less marked) into the possession of a fancy brimming with images of terror, a soul boiling with causeless hatreds, and a body that seemed not strong enough to contain the raging energies of life. The powers of Hyde seemed to have grown with the sickliness of Jekyll. And certainly the hate that now divided them was equal on each side. With Jekyll, it was a thing of vital instinct. He had now seen the full deformity of that creature that shared with him some of the phenomena of consciousness, and was co-heir with him to death: and beyond these links of community, which in themselves made the most poignant part of his distress, he thought of Hyde, for all his energy of life, as of something not only hellish but inorganic. This was the shocking thing; that the slime of the pit seemed to utter cries and voices; that the amorphous dust gesticulated and sinned; that what was dead, and had no shape, should usurp the offices of life. And this again, that that insurgent horror was knit to him closer than a wife, closer than an eye; lay caged in his flesh, where he heard it mutter and felt it struggle to be born; and at every hour of weakness, and in the confidence of slumber, prevailed against him, and deposed him out of life. The hatred of Hyde for Jekyll was of a different order. His terror of the gallows drove him continually to commit temporary suicide, and return to his subordinate station of a part instead of a person; but he loathed the necessity, he loathed the despondency into which Jekyll was now fallen, and he resented the dislike with which he was himself regarded. Hence the apelike tricks that he would play me, scrawling in my own hand blasphemies on the pages of my books, burning the letters and destorying the portrait of my father; and indeed, had it not been for his fear of death, he would long ago have ruined himself in order to involve me in the ruin. But his love of life is wonderful; I go further: I, who sicken and freeze at the mere thought of him, when I recall the abjection and passion of this attachment, and when I know how he fears my power to cut him off by suicide, I find it in my heart to pity him.

It is useless, and the time awfully fails me, to prolong this description; no one has ever suffered such torments, let that suffice; and yet even to these, habit brought—no, not alleviation—but a certain callousness of soul, a certain acquiescence of despair; and my punishment might have gone on for years, but for the last calamity which has now fallen, and which has finally severed me from my own face and nature. My provision of the salt, which had never been renewed since the date of the first experiment, began to run low. I sent out for a fresh supply, and mixed the draught; the ebullition followed, and the first change of colour, not the second; I drank it and it was without efficiency. You will learn from Poole how I have had London ransacked; it was in vain; and I am now persuaded that my first supply was impure, and that it was that unknown impurity which lent efficacy to the draught.

About a week has passed, and I am now finishing this statement under the influence of the last of the old powders. This, then, is the last time, short of a miracle, that Henry Jekyll can think his own thoughts or see his own face (now how sadly altered!) in the glass. Nor must I delay too long to bring my writing to an end; for if my narrative has hitherto escaped destruction, it has been by a combination of great prudence and great good luck. Should the throes of change take me in the act of writing it, Hyde will tear it in pieces; but if some time shall have elapsed after I have laid it by, his wonderful selfishness and circumscription to the moment will probably save it once again from the action of his apelike spite. And indeed the doom that is closing on us both, has already changed and crushed him. Half an hour from now, when I shall again and forever reindue that hated personality, I know how I shall sit shuddering and weeping in my chair, or continue, with the most strained and fearstruck ecstasy of listening, to pace up and down this room (my last earthly refuge) and give ear to every sound of menace. Will Hyde die upon the scaffold? or will he find courage to release himself at the last moment? God knows; I am careless; this is my true hour of death, and what is to follow concerns another than myself. Here then, as I lay down the pen and proceed to seal up my confession, I bring the life of that unhappy Henry Jekyll to an end.

The Shadow Within:
The Conscious and
Unconscious Use of the Double

CLAIRE ROSENFIELD

The "symposium" of Plato has amused us with the comic image that each of us has a Double to whom we were once physically attached. Mistaken identity, the birth and later separation of twins, a god assuming the bodily form of an absent husband—indeed, all the absurd and irrational portrayals of Doubles inherent in the comedies of civilized literature from the "Amphitryon" of Plautus to "The Comedy of Errors" by Shakespeare—have provoked our unthinking laughter. To the sophisticated audiences of the Classical World, the Middle Ages, and the Renaissance, Doubles were either facsimiles, bodily duplicates manipulated to divert us, or allegorized opposites to instruct us. Perhaps not until after the development of the novel, have we been made aware of what primitives have always intuitively known: that duality inspires both terror and awe whether that duality be manifested in a twin birth, or in a man and his shadow, or in one's reflection in water or in a mirror, or in the creation of an artifact resembling the exterior self. Not until Freud revealed the importance of the irrational in man have we been willing to admit the possiblity that each of us has within us a second or a shadow self dwelling beside the eminently civilized, eminently rational self, a Double who may at any time assert its anti-social tendencies.

Reprinted from *Daedalus*, Spring, 1967, by permission of the author and *Daedalus*.

By analyzing superstitions, folk beliefs, and modern literature, Otto Rank has attempted to show the evolution of the Double: that "What we really have in common with our remote ancestors is a *spiritual*, not a primitive self."[1] Frightened by the possible destruction of his ego and the loss of his individuality in death, primitive man created a body-soul which he located in his shadow or his reflection, and which he deemed immortal. His very real dreams provided him with the proof that a soul must exist independent of the body, for in his dreams he saw the souls of the absent, of others who had died, of enemies whom he had killed. Motivated by what Freud has called his "primary narcissism," he could not grant life to others and not to himself.[2] Though his body would die and disintegrate—as had the bodies of the dead he had seen—his soul would survive as his shadow or Double.

How man came to see the soul in his shadow may be explained by the assumption that he first saw his own image in it, inseparable from himself and yet not only changing in its form but also disappearing at night. It seems to me that this observation of the human shadow disappearing with the fertilizing sun to reappear with its return made it a perfect symbol for the idea of an immortal soul. . . . It is then, in my opinion, not so much the resemblance of the shadow to the self as its appearance and disappearance, its regular return to life, as it were, which made the shadow a symbol of the returning soul still surviving in our spiritual belief in immortality. In the original duality of the soul concept, I am inclined to see the root of man's two endeavors to preserve his self and to maintain the belief in its immortality: religion and psychology. From the belief in a soul of the dead in one form or another sprang all religion; from the belief in the soul of the living, psychology eventually developed.[3]

Possessing this belief in an immortal soul, man was able gradually to develop a personality which seemed to have an essential totality.

[1] Otto Rank, "The Double as Immortal Self," *Beyond Psychology*. New York: Dover Publications, 1958, 63. See also "Der Doppelgänger," *Imago*, III (1914).

[2] Otto Rank, "Religion and Belief in the Soul," *Psychology and The Soul*, trans. by William D. Turner. New York: A. S. Barnes and Company, Inc., 1961, 14.

[3] Rank, "The Double as Immortal Self," *Beyond Psychology*, 74.

But, Rank points out, modern literature presents the Double as a symbol not of eternal life but of death,[4] a representation which anticipates the division of the personality into two opposing forces, and a subsequent loss of a sense of identity and continuity in time.

Because the Romantic Movement made the inner life of man—spontaneity of feeling, imagination, spiritual exploration—fashionable if not respectable, nineteenth century audiences generally accepted works which revealed the two opposing selves within the human personality. But they accepted these only on terms which would not destroy communal or personal complacency, either in folk songs and stories which portrayed a primitive self in which they believed they no longer shared, or in fairy tales written down for children, or in fantasies or mystery stories which titillated the senses without disrupting equanimity. In the romance, a *genre* where by definition the imagination was allowed free play, the hero might lose his shadow as in "The Wonderful History of Peter Schlemihl," or sell his reflection to the devil as in Hoffmann's "Story of a Lost Reflection." When, however, the reader approached a work in which the disintegration of the personality was plausibly presented, he ignored it as completely as he ignored Melville's *Pierre.* Or else he dismissed it as the work of a monster, as De Vogüé, who introduced Russian literature to France, dismissed Dostoevsky.[5] Dickens' terrifying *Edwin Drood* offered no threat to the mind which had created a defense mechanism almost as satisfactory as the dream work, and called the book a mystery story. And Emily Brontë, perhaps unwittingly, made her amoral, passionate fictional world palatable by sifting it through the consciousness of two extraordinarily conventional and imperceptive narrators.

That the motif of the Double should manifest itself so abundantly in the nineteenth century can be explained both culturally and psychologically. The French Revolution betrayed an irrationality in direct proportion to earlier oppression. With the "Rights of Man" came a new emphasis upon the individual. Not only did the Romantic Movement sanction introspection; it also reintroduced into society the collective inheritance of the folk. As I have already noted,

[4] *Ibid.,* 66.
[5] André Gide, *Dostoevsky,* intro. by Albert J. Guerard. Norfolk, Conn.: New Directions, 1961, 168.

the Double or *Doppelgänger* was made initially respectable in romance, fairy tale, and mystery story where repressed fantasies asserted themselves with particular vengeance in extravagant plots. But the novel requires that the opposing selves submit to the canons of plausibility. Therefore, the novelist who consciously or unconsciously exploits psychological Doubles may either juxtapose or duplicate two characters; the one representing the socially acceptable or conventional personality, the other externalizing the free, uninhibited, often criminal self. Conrad's *The Secret Sharer*, Mann's *Doctor Faustus*, Dostoevsky's *The Double* all reveal this pattern. Or he may present two characters who complement each other both physically and psychologically and who together are projections of the crippled or struggling personality of a third character with whom the author is primarily concerned, as in Dostoevsky's *Crime and Punishment* or Melville's *Pierre*. These complementary Doubles may appear in the narrative as simple opposites; what is important is not their contrary natures and descriptions, but the way in which they reveal the loss of identity of the main character. When the passionate, uninhibited self is a woman, she more often than not is dark and the sister or half-sister of the protagonist, thus introducing the suggestion of incest, the most horrific of crimes in Christian culture. Again, the presence of biological Doubles or Twins in a novel of psychic disintegration can suggest authorial awareness of the problem of inner duality and the subsequent terrors involved.

The first novelist to use duality consciously in order to reveal the mental struggles of his characters was Goethe. Because he was contemplating a Faust play before writing *Wilhelm Meister's Apprenticeship*, the Double motif in the former may illuminate authorial intention in the latter. What Mephistopheles mirrors in the drama is the demonic forces within the titanic Faust himself. This dynamic tension between good and evil does not appear overtly in the novel, where the young Wilhelm seeks harmony through active humanism. Part of his search for personal fulfillment involves the search for a wife. The various women he encounters seem to him but fragmentary parts of himself; many of them—actresses—appear to him first dressed as boys, playing a male role. Even the mysterious Mignon, who refuses to dress like a girl and who reveals a diabolic disorder which he has never experienced, momentarily excites his orderly soul: "He longed to incorporate this forsaken being within his own heart, to take her in his arms, and with a father's love to awaken in her the joy of existence."[6] Finally, he realizes totality in his union with Natalie, the "beautiful soul" with whom he reconciles all contraries. The modern disintegration of the self, on the other hand, is seen in the story of Mignon's parents, Sperata and Augustin, the brother and sister who unknowingly commit incest. Mignon, whose frantic artistry and behavior exist within the realm of madness, duplicates in her gradual decline the previous degradation of her parents. Because Goethe achieved a balance between the classic and romantic aspects of his own life and nature, he could construct both a positive representation of harmony and a negative picture of personality decay; few other novelists, however, were able to do the same.

When the reader confronts a novelist like Emily Brontë, all presuppositions about conscious creation disappear. So intimate was she with the projections of her own unconscious life that she may have been only intuitively aware that Cathy and Heathcliff are themselves exact Doubles differing in sex alone, and that each possesses a complementary self in his choice of a mate. Both are dark; both are accustomed to roam freely over the moors; both are proud and headstrong; both carry into maturity an energy and violence which normally is pushed into the buried self by conventional society. Both realize their similar natures. Cathy, when deciding to marry Edgar Linton, explains why she cannot forsake Heathcliff:

My love for Heathcliff resembles the eternal rocks beneath—a source of little visible delight, but necessary. . . . I *am* Heathcliff—he's always, always in my mind—not as a pleasure, any more than I am always a pleasure to myself—but as my own being—so, don't talk of our separation again—it is impracticable; and. . . .

When dying she claims "'That is not *my* Heathcliff. I shall love mine yet; and take him with me—he's in my soul.'" To Heathcliff, Cathy is not merely a second self but also his immortal soul. It is a

---

[6] No quotations from individual novels will be footnoted.

soul which he had destroyed, yet one which he hopes will return to haunt him.

> The murdered *do* haunt their murderers. I believe—I know that ghosts *have* wandered on earth. Be with me always—take any form—drive me mad! only *do* not leave me in this abyss where I cannot find you! Oh God! it is unutterable! I *cannot* live without my life! I *cannot* live without my soul!

Cathy marries the blond and pallid Edgar, hoping to reconcile the refined, conventional, civilized society of the Lintons and the unconscious, passionate, natural world of childhood; she, in other words, "adopt[s] a double character without exactly intending to deceive any one." Heathcliff marries the blond and pallid Isabella not that the two worlds may coexist but rather that the world of the Lintons may be destroyed by his strength. Cathy wills her death when she discovers that she cannot reconcile these divided selves; and yet, alone, she and Heathcliff are incomplete selves. Heathcliff wills his death when he discovers that the biological entity, the child, does combine within itself those qualities which could not join within the psychological Doubles, that young Cathy does possess sweetness to tame her mother's wildness, that Hareton cannot be entirely brutalized. Cathy and Heathcliff can exist only in the world of childhood or death where capacity for freedom is infinite, where the claims of others do not impinge upon the self. The amoral landscape of *Wuthering Heights*, moreover, could only be made *respectable* by being filtered through the sensibilities of two narrators in whom Victorian mores have been so internalized that the outlaw self is completely misunderstood because completely submerged.

That Melville in *Pierre* was aware of the essential oppositions which he establishes between Lucy and Isabel, between the blond, socially sanctioned, spiritual creature and the dark, desirable, sexually forbidden half-sister Isabel, is undeniable. What he probably did not realize is the fact that these apparently conventional opposites are Doubles in the psychological sense: together they externalize the total personality Pierre must experience as an artist; separately, the disintegration he chose as a man. Professor Henry Murray is right in claiming that only Isabel, for whom Pierre thinks he possesses fraternal compassion but to whom he is really sexually attracted, can rescue him from the narrow maternal paradise which confines him. She alone can provide him with the tragic awareness necessary to manhood.[7] Her mysterious force suggests both madness, a longing for death, and the world of the unconscious with which society has never allowed Pierre to be troubled. In abandoning the acceptable Lucy for the desirable Isabel, he deserts the God of his Puritan fathers and his community. Once his choice is made, however, he is unable to bear the consequences of his incest, of his discovery of the abyss, of the revelation that his new God is his society's devil. When the light, rational world once more collides with his irrational one, when his now avowed "good angel" appears in the form of Lucy, Pierre has already begun to shun Isabel and her potentially tragic self as he had earlier shunned Lucy. Ironically, Lucy wishes to live as a sister with the couple whom she believes are husband and wife; but she cannot be made to live with the anarchy of incest. Finally, Pierre must die, a poor artist for the same reason he is an incomplete man: he is unable to balance the creative and destructive forces within himself.

In 1845, Charles Dickens parodied a "romance" in "Count Ludwig," a comic tale in which the Double theme is disguised by the narrative distortions. Here are no visible threats to the ego. At the end of his career in 1870 he began but never finished *The Mystery of Edwin Drood*, in which the disguised Double is less fantastic, more realistic. Choirmaster Jack Jasper is torn between his genuine devotion to his nephew and his love of that nephew's betrothed, between the respectable boredom of his occupation and his unconscious striving. His antisocial impulses reveal themselves in his predilection for opium, in his habitual appearances in the night world, and in his rambles through the privacy of the graveyard. Since the novel was never finished, we can only conjecture that Jasper's eventual disintegration culminates in the murder (or, at least, the abduction) of that nephew, a "good self." Though on a narrative level Jasper is Edwin's guardian; on a symbolic level, Edwin is the guardian angel whom Jasper dispatches. Henceforth, the forbidden dominates Jasper's behavior: he is described as possessing

[7] Henry A. Murray, "Introduction," *Pierre*, by Herman Melville. New York: Hendricks House, 1949, liii.

"destructive power"; he seems "an older devil." Dickens' conscious intention becomes obvious when we see that the novel contains two sets of biological Doubles: the "lovers" Edwin and Rosa who by agreement become like brother and sister, and the strange twins Neville and Helena Landless who are direct opposites. While the former are English and fair, the latter are exceedingly dark, foreign, "land less"; there is "something untamed about them both." When Neville is accused of Edwin's murder, one feels that his situation and physical characteristics alone rather than any intrinsic passion for the demonic mark him as an unconscious, criminal force and that Dickens is yielding to the romantic stereotype. Although these conventionalized Doubles add to the intricacies of the Dickensian plot, the dramatic tensions which exist within the divided soul of Jack Jasper, at once struggling for some balance and sinking deeper and deeper into the underground of the irrational, are the real energizing force of the novel.

Dostoevsky, whatever his own fears might have been, was sufficiently sensible of the tyranny of his unconscious to respond to the motif of the divided self. Throughout his career he consciously wrought variations on this theme. In 1874 in *A Raw Youth* Versilov actually describes his visual hallucination, his apparent perception which possesses no object. Although the narrator, Versilov's illegitimate son Arkady, finally gives the negative clinical diagnosis of madness to his father's disordered state, he himself accepts only the less damning idea of a split between the real man and his ego ideal.

What is a second self, exactly? The second self, according to a medical book written by an expert that I purposely read afterward, is nothing else than the first stage of serious mental derangement, which may lead to something very bad. And in the scene at my Mother's, Versilov himself had with strange frankness described the "duality" of his will and feelings. But I repeat again, . . . that scene at Mother's and that broken ikon were undoubtedly partly due to the influence of a real "second self."

In *The Double*, Golyadkin, before the appearance of a Mr. Golyadkin Junior, evidences most of the symptoms of a developing split personality. He acts, as it were, because of a perverse inner

compulsion which he cannot control. The appearance of Mr. Golyadkin Junior, who is "a double in every respect," reinforces all the
protagonist's insecurities, for the new Mr. Golyadkin is not an "insect" or a "rag"; though physically similar, he possesses all those
qualities for advancement—self-possession, wit, the power of decision
—which the original Mr. Golyadkin lacks. Persecuted by this Double,
Golyadkin Senior grows more indecisive and declines finally into
madness. While he is being carried to an asylum by the doctor he
had earlier consulted, he imagines that he is confronted in the darkness by this doctor's infernal presence whose eyes glitter in "hellish
glee."

In Conrad's *The Secret Sharer* and *Heart of Darkness,* a bodily
Double is present whose outlaw freedom is evidence for the narrator and the reader that even the most rational man possesses a
dual nature, that no man is above the threat of the irrational. As
Albert J. Guerard has pointed out, both Marlow and the young
captain must "come to know themselves . . . , must recognize their
own potential criminality and test their own resources, *must travel
through Kurtz and Leggatt,* before they will be capable of manhood. . . ."[8] In both short novels the actual journeys which the
two narrators take "exploit the ancient myth or archetypal experience of the 'night journey,' of the provisional descent into the primitive and unconscious sources of being."[9] The final choice each makes
symbolizes the choice between internal division or personal coherence.
The young captain hides the murderer Leggatt with whom he
identifies himself even though this new allegiance may mean his
isolation from a crew and a command which he does not know,
may foster irresponsibility to his fellow men. Surely the repeated
use of such phrases as "the secret sharer of my cabin," "my secret
double" indicates Conrad's intentional pursuit of the *Doppelgänger*
motif. Marlow's journey into the Congo for Kurtz is also a journey
into the recesses of the mind; the actual jungle and its darkness
mirror the intricacies of the internal landscape. When Marlow
pursues a crawling Kurtz driven to the last extremity of madness,
he describes him as "that Shadow," "the nightmare of my choice,"

[8] Albert J. Guerard, "Introduction," *Heart of Darkness* and *The Secret Sharer,*
by Joseph Conrad. New York: The American Library, 1961, 9.
[9] *Loc. Cit.*

"the shade." Both the captain and Marlow emerge from their visions of criminal freedom. In so far as the hero does return from the underworld of his being and is able to use his new knowledge for the benefit of his fellow men—as do the captain and Marlow—the Double novel reveals not a disintegration of the personality but a reintegration, a recognition of the necessary balance between order and freedom.[10]

When Henry James attempts a variation on the Double theme in *The Jolly Corner,* he consciously employs the alter-ego to suggest possible future events which might have occurred had Spencer Brydon remained in America. Brydon pursues and, finally, is pursued by his projection of his "real," "waiting life." Because this "life" appears as a prediction of what he might have been, it suggests the primitive belief that the sight of one's self may be an anticipation of death. Indeed, Spencer's second self appears twice in Alice Staverton's dreams—the primitive's evidence of the immortal soul. But Spencer's vision is a vision of an evil self pursuing him:

> It came upon him nearer now, quite as one of those expanding fantastic images projected by the magic lantern of childhood: for the stranger, whoever he might be, evil, odious, blatant, vulgar, had advanced as for aggression, and he knew himself give ground.
> . . . His head went round; he was going; he had gone.

His loss of consciousness is a symbolic death; his revival of "rich consciousness" is in his own eyes a rebirth: "He had come back, yes—come back from further away than any man but himself had ever traveled." And he says to Alice Staverton: " 'You brought me literally to life.' " He, too, has achieved knowledge on his "night journey," but he denies the major implication of his descent into the irrational; that is, that the possibility of such a horrible life still exists within him. " 'But this brute, with his awful face—this brute's a black stranger. He's none of me, even as I *might* have been.' "

[10] See Otto Rank, *The Myth of the Birth of the Hero* for an account of the various stages of the hero's quest as well as its psychological origins. For the theory relating the meaning of the archetypal night journey to the integration of the personality see C. G. Jung, *The Archetypes and the Collective Unconscious,* trans. by R. F. C. Hull, New York: Pantheon Books Inc., 1959.

Double novels become Devil novels in a social context which places a negative value upon what is free and uninhibited. Freud states that psychologically, the Devil is simply the projection into the external world of man's buried instinctual life.[11] But Hebraic-Christian mythology, not Freud, assigned the perjorative word "evil" to that projection. Primitive religions made no distinction between gods and devils; the gods were both worshipped and feared. According to Rank, the original Double, when it was insurance against the destruction of the self, was a guardian angel; later it "appears as precisely the opposite, a reminder of the individual's mortality, indeed the announcer of death itself."[12] The Church, which used the belief in immortality as a means of distributing rewards and punishments, created the Devil as we know him today and the destructive concept of the Double. Poe's "William Wilson" is one of the few examples in which the whispering Double appears as a "guardian angel" seeking to annul the evil of the narrator.

In *The Private Memoirs and Confessions of a Justified Sinner*, one of the clearest examples of the Devil Novel, James Hogg has skillfully juxtaposed primitive superstition, diabolism, religious fanaticism, and psychic disintegration in a perilous equilibrium which threatens constantly to dissolve. The bodily Doubles are two brothers: George Colwan, the legitimate heir of the gay laird of Dalcastle who has a fanatic wife; and Robert Wringhim, the son of that wife and her spiritual guide. Usually, the Double-Devil Novel makes the "free" self the evil self. To promote Hogg's religious satire, however, the evil brother is not the gay, spontaneous, fun-loving George, who has instinctive moral goodness, but the son of Wringhim who is obsessed with his belief in absolute predestination, that salvation depends upon the grace of God alone. Moreover, he believes that he is one of God's elect and, in the name of that election but actually because of a classic split personality, he commits the most criminal acts, including the murder of his own brother. The novel's formal structure reproduces the double motif: the first part purports to be an objective account of "traditionary facts," using

[11]Sigmund Freud, "Neurosis of Demoniacal Possession," *Collected Papers*, authorized trans. under supervision of Joan Riviere. New York: Basic Books, Inc., IV, 450–451.
[12]Rank, "The Double as Immortal Self," *Beyond Psychology*, 76.

the third person point of view of an editor who is not James Hogg; the second part is the private memoirs of Robert Wringhim.

In the second part, the extent of Robert's madness is finally ascertained. In these confessions we see that all Robert's evil acts are sanctioned by his "friend" who he does not realize is the Devil until it is too late. Now demonology bows to pathology. Is his friend simply a projection of his mental aberration and a manifestation of his disorder? Not only is he completely driven by his belief in his own divine justification, but he reveals several psychotic symptoms. He hates women; he suffers from some nervous disease which he attributes to witchcraft.

Immediately after this I was seized with a strange distemper, which neither my friends nor physicians could comprehend, and it confined me to my chamber for many days; but I knew, myself, that I was bewitched, and suspected my father's reputed concubine of the deed. I told my fears to my reverend protector, who hesitated concerning them, but I knew by his words and looks that he was conscious I was right. I generally conceived myself to be two people. When I lay in bed, I deemed there were two of us in it; when I sat up I always beheld another person, and always in the same position from the place where I sat or stood, which was about three paces off me towards my left side. It mattered not how many or how few were present: this my second self was sure to be present in his place, and this occasioned a confusion in all my words and ideas that utterly astounded my friends, who all declared that, instead of being deranged in my intellect, they had never heard my conversation manifest so much energy or sublimity of conception; but, for all that, over the singular delusion that I was two persons my reasoning faculties had no power. The most perverse part of it was that I rarely conceived *myself* to be any of the two persons. I thought for the most part that my companion was one of them, and my brother the other; and I found that, to be obliged to speak and answer in the character of another man, was a most awkward business in the long run.

In the end Robert accepts the idea of the demonic because, believing in an external moral order, he cannot accept any other explanation. "To be in a state of consciousness and unconsciousness, at the same time, in the same body and same spirit, was impossible." Only in very few instances, however, are the events unexplainable in psychological terms.

In the twentieth century the author's intentional use of the *Doppelgänger* is rarely in doubt. The rapid rise of Freudian psychology as a discipline and the gradual decline of the influence of religion as an absolute external sanction have determined the Devil's role in the Double novel. When inner duality is externalized as a Devil, that Devil is clearly a hallucination. After all, the *diabolus ex machina* is too naïve for modern taste; not so the *diabolus ex capite*. Or else realistic characters, by assuming traditional demonic attributes, symbolize the illicit freedom of unconscious processes.

In Mann's *Doctor Faustus* Adrian Leverkühn's bargain with the Devil for twenty-four years of intensely creative life is clearly internal. Moreover, we might prosaically impute that "Devil" to visions consequent on the syphilis to which he exposes himself in order to heighten his genius. But the inhabitants of Adrian's world are themselves plausible manifestations of personal and social diabolism. The subversive teachings of Schleppfuss recall the fallacious logic of Satanic dialectic, which assigns its own qualities to the Divine; the word "freedom" becomes a theological obscenity in his mouth. His name means "dragfoot"—the Devil is usually lame in oral and written accounts; he is red-haired, sports a pointed beard, has pointed teeth, wears a black cloak. There are other characters with demonic attributes: Saul Fitelberg, who wishes Mephistophelean-like, to bear Adrian "on my mantle through the air and show you the kingdoms of the earth and the glory of them"; or Doctor Zimbalist, the red-headed, criminal physician; or Hetaera Esmeralda, the prostitute from whom Adrian contracts the syphilis which is to nourish his creativity and to destroy his sanity; or the pimp who introduces him to Esmeralda, who reminds him of Schleppfuss and who wears an infernal red cap—all these signify the "soulless instinct" of this Germanic universe. Adrian's dialogues with the Devil are imaginary; however, on the final page, the pedantic narrator, Serenus Zeitblom, Ph.D., sees a stranger at Adrian's grave "a veiled unknown, who disappeared as the final clods fell on the coffin." This ambiguity is, indeed, a mark of the modern novel when it deals with the dark powers of Western religion.

Moreover, the narrative structure enforces the interpretation that the demonic and the irrational are one. Serenus constantly juxtaposes thematically and technically Adrian's insanity and his country's descent into Naziism, the personal and the national anarchy, the demonic within and the demonic without.

Germany, the hectic on her cheek, was reeling then at the height of her dissolute triumphs, about to gain the whole world by virtue of the one pact she was minded to keep, which she had signed with her blood. Today, clung round by demons, a hand over one eye, with the other staring into horrors, down she flings from despair to despair. When will she reach the bottom of the abyss? When, out of uttermost hopelessness—a miracle beyond the power of belief—will the light of hope dawn? A lonely man folds his hands and speaks: "God be merciful to thy poor soul, my friend, my Fatherland!"

Adrian Leverkühn evokes our sympathy because of the magnitude of his suffering, because he is unable to love, and because he is presented through the tolerant eyes of a character we like. Though this narrator is pedantic and bourgeois, though he is a foil for Adrian's dynamic demonism, though he is Adrian's alter-ego and complementary Double, Serenus is humane, is finally perceptive, and lives to denounce Naziism. But what are we to make of the constant parallel between Adrian and Germany herself descending into "naked instinct"? A good novel must transcend time and place; but are we—and is the author, himself a German—sufficiently distant from the atrocities of Nazi Germany to accept sympathetically the theme of mental disintegration when it is juxtaposed to the conflict within the German nation. Time may dispel some of the weight of moral judgment for the reader; fortunately it cannot dispel the ambiguity between sympathy and judgment within Mann during the process of creation.

In Flannery O'Connor's *The Violent Bear It Away* some of the same pattern is apparent. The divided self of a boy manifests its loss of identity in a hallucination of the Devil, called the "stranger." But throughout the book realistic characters appear whom the author describes in traditional demonic terms. Authorial and reader sympathy is reserved for a Southern fundamentalist preacher who is clearly insane and for his disciple and grand nephew Tarwater, who is gradually becoming insane. Tarwater's conflict between his uncle's divinely inflicted teaching and the world of temptation is dramatized in the fanciful dialogue between himself and the imaginary "stranger" when the former is trying to bury his dead uncle according to instructions. That the stranger is Tarwater's second self is apparent; the Negro Buford does *not* see him. But the teacher Rayber, who represents a sterile and corrupting rationalism, and the real stranger, the "old-looking young man" in the black suit and lavender shirt who sexually assaults Tarwater after getting him drunk, are both on the Devil's side. While walking with Rayber, while riding with the stranger, Tarwater sees in a store window and in the car window respectively, his Double, his own inner soul which must be saved at all costs.

But *The Violent Bear It Away*, above all, shows the growing complexity in aesthetic and moral ambiguity in the *Doppelgänger* novel. Even when religion is its subject matter, that religion no longer provides a frame of reference by which values may be measured. The modern novelist, although conscious of using the Double motif technically, does not place a moral judgment upon the irrational; or, at least, he reveals a tension between his sympathy for amoral freedom and his judgment of the fictional creatures he has given life. Flannery O'Connor's characters for whom we as readers —and for whom the author herself[13]—care immensely are the two religious fanatics, uncle and nephew. Described as a prophet of old, the uncle is deranged in his obsessive concerns and his inability to live in the real world. Tarwater does in the end become a prophet "in the dark city, where the children of God lay sleeping." Yet the child evangelist whom he sees at the meeting is a freak in whom he recognizes a possible self but at whom he says he wants to spit. He does baptize the idiot child Bishop according to his uncle's demand, but he drowns that child in the process, according to the command of his second self, "the stranger." He does not bury his uncle, nor does he burn the preacher's body, as he at first intended. Symbolically, the man in the lavender shirt steals the hat which

[13]John Hawkes, "Flannery O'Connor's Devil," *The Sewanne Review*, LXX, (Summer 1962), 3.

his uncle had left him and which represents his sense of identity. Yet that identity is already seriously impaired by divine precepts. He sets the woods on fire in order to escape the manifestations of his madness—the "violet shadow," the "grinning presence." But as he rushes away to save the city and so win his eternal salvation, he is preceded by a "jagged shadow," the threat to his soul. Again, the disintegration of the self is, in effect, a denial of salvation. The reader may be torn between sympathy and judgment but Flannery O'Connor is on the Devil's side without knowing it.

John Knowles has demonstrated in A *Separate Peace* that even novels dealing with preparatory schools can benefit from the *Doppelgänger* technique. Nor does the complex relationship between moral judgment and sympathy in these modern novels diminish because the characters are young or ostensibly free from intense suffering. An imperceptive narrator, Gene, becomes aware of the principle of anarchy when he meets his bodily Double Phineas at school. Finny breaks the rules, lives in a child's world of daring and invention, says what he thinks, possesses a primitive energy which at once attracts and repels. But, although this relationship causes Gene to commit an irrational act in which he cripples Finny, he refuses to admit that he himself is capable of such disorder. When his friend Leper, whose instability finally leads to madness and to truth, states: "'You always were a savage underneath,'" he rushes away in anger. Indeed, he destroys Phineas by destroying his will to live—still neglecting his responsibility for his deed. Phineas is presented as "the good bad boy" in the sentimental American tradition. What redeems him and convinces his teachers that he is a model boy is his love of his school and the fact that he has the "right" instincts. No Satanic hate deforms him. But what are we to think of Gene, who is not evil in any objective sense, merely incredibly imperceptive and callous. When he says,

> I never killed anybody and I never developed an intense level of hatred for the enemy. Because my war ended before I ever put on a uniform; I was on active duty all my time at school; I killed my enemy there.

who are we as readers to regard as the enemy? Phineas, his second self, whose being finally fills Gene, is a free self but not a criminal self. If Phineas is the "enemy," then Gene's final statement is his moment of revelation, his recognition that the instinctual and free is not to be crippled or killed but made to coexist, to balance in a new unity.

All of them, all except Phineas, constructed at infinite cost to themselves these Maginot Lines against this enemy they thought they saw across the frontier, this enemy who never attacked that way—if he ever attacked at all; if he was indeed the enemy.

Ironically, Gene thinks he has killed the enemy, has destroyed that irrational externalized by Finny. And even in this moment of truth, he subconsciously still denies that "they" are the same as "he."

William Faulkner's *Sartoris* and *Go Down Moses* both explore the idea of the psychic unity of twins and, therefore, reveal Faulkner's fascination with bodily Doubles. Young Bayard Sartoris consciously yields to his self-destructive tendencies after the death of his twin John in the First World War. This is the modern ironic reversal of the primitive social tradition in which the founding of cultures demanded the positive sacrifice of one twin.[14] John's death in the war is a parody of that ritual sacrifice, and is symptomatic both of Bayard's internal disorder and of the decay of the South and of modern mechanized society.

In *Absalom, Absalom!* Faulkner's awareness of the *Doppelgänger* as a motif for exploiting personal and social disintegration and loss of identity combine with his emphasis upon formal ingenuity. Here the complexity of the psychological Double affects the story of Thomas Sutpen, whose dominant nature seems to change according to which observer reveals his "truth" more than fifty years later to Quentin Compson. Amid constant chronological violation in the narrative, three observers tell the same story to Quentin; each provides a different picture of the same man in a fictional technique which approximates the incremental repetition of the ballad. To Miss Rosa, Sutpen's essential quality is his demonism; to Quentin's grandfather it is his innocence. Sutpen's refusal to allow Charles Bon, his illegitimate son, to marry Judith, his daughter, is attributed first to fear of bigamy; then, to fear of incest; then, to fear of misceg-

---

[14] Rank, "The Double as Immortal Self," *Beyond Psychology*, 92.

enation. Sutpen's own dual nature is externalized in shifting relationships among his children; for the child is man's attempt to duplicate
himself and, hence, insure his immortality. Judith and her brother
Henry are described as a composite. Charles fascinates both in turn
because "of that relationship between them—that single personality
with two bodies both of which had been seduced almost simultaneously by a man whom at the time Judith had never seen. . . ." But
Henry's allegiance to Bon is also a repressed incestuous desire for the
sister with whom he would like to unite sexually as well as psychi-
cally, and with whom Bon would, indeed, be committing incest.

> . . . So it must have been Henry who seduced Judith, not Bon:
> seduced her along with himself from that distance between Oxford
> and Sutpen's Hundred, between herself and the man whom she
> had not even seen yet, as though by means of that telepathy
> with which as children they seemed at times to anticipate one
> another's actions as two birds leave a limb at the same instant;
> that rapport not like the conventional delusion of that between
> twins but rather such as might exist between two people who,
> regardless of sex or age or heritage of race or tongue, had been
> marooned at birth on a desert island: the island here Sutpen's
> Hundred. . . .

Ultimately Faulkner's insistence upon Bon's almost womanly
"elegance," his conversion into the "woman, the loved, the bride,"
while it does affect our sympathy for him adversely, functions to
exploit the fascination which ungoverned yearnings have for Henry.
In killing Bon, Henry buries back in his childhood all the antisocial
tendencies which Bon's effeminate presence inspires. Again, Quentin,
who himself commits incest in desire though not in fact; and Shreve,
his Harvard roommate, with whom he is brooding over Sutpen's
story—South and North—project themselves into the past and into
the figures of Henry and Charles: "Charles-Shreve and Quentin-
Henry." Shreve becomes so obsessed by Bon that he attempts to
guess the latter's thoughts while he waits for Sutpen's paternal
acknowledgment, while he consents to the final ride which he knows
will end in fratricide. The fateful ride before Charles's death is for
both Quentin and Shreve a descent into the self, the "night journey"
without which there is neither understanding nor wholeness.

Not only does Charles Bon synthesize the feminine and the masculine but also the light and dark, good and evil, within his being; he reunites his father's demonism and his father's innocence. In not admitting his paternity, Sutpen continues to believe he can establish his design upon wholly rational and conscious foundations, that his obsession can fasten upon the ideal alone without the balance which the irrational furnishes. In not admitting his paternity, he ironically thwarts his own role as the father of a dynasty and of a culture. Finally in not admitting his paternity, Sutpen denies not only Charles's identity, but his own as well.

In its dramatization of a constant threat to our identity and our internal selves, the modern *Doppelgänger* novel reveals an ambiguity in authorial and reader sympathy and judgment, a failure to assign negative value to the socially undesirable. Paradoxically, an author's growing sympathy for anarchy and illicit freedom has led him to a new emphasis upon technique—as if this yearning for the abyss requires the restraint of intricate form. Denied an absolute external order, aware of enormous internal oppositions, he seems forced to create that order in an extreme concern for structure and style.

All the characteristics of the modern Double novel converge in *Pale Fire* by Vladimir Nabokov. A pedantic academician, Charles Kinbote, edits the manuscript of a neighbor and poet who is accidentally shot and killed. John Shade's name alone assigns him his major role in his relationship to Kinbote: he is a second or shadow self. Like Adrian Leverkühn and Serenus Zeitblom in *Doctor Faustus*, Shade and Kinbote are foils, the two sides of a single personality. Formally, the book is divided into two parts—the Foreword, Notes, and Index of the scholar; and the Four Cantos (minus one line) of the poet's contemplative, almost Wordsworthian spiritual autobiography in verse. The scholar constantly imposes his presence upon the poet in order to tell him the account of the exiled king of Zembla. He hopes to inspire Shade to write the national epic of this land. The Notes, which alternate between the everyday details of Wordsmith College in New Wye, where Kinbote teaches and Shade is poet in residence, and the political unrest in Zembla, finally reveal that Kinbote is the exiled king, Charles the Beloved. Kinbote insists that the bullet of the assassin which killed Shade was meant for him, since his enemies at home have penetrated his disguise.

But narrative events imply that Kinbote himself is mad, that the kingdom of Zembla is an imaginary realm to which he wishes Shade to give artistic life; and Gradus, the Assassin, is but an escapee from a mental institution who shoots Shade by chance. With Shade's death Kinbote loses at once his *raison d'être* and any hope of eventual recovery. This *Doppelgänger* novel, then—and Nabokov is sufficiently thoughtful to use the word "doubleganger" once in the text —explores both the disintegrating personality and the problem of identity. Not only can we not trust Kinbote, but Shade proves to be a drunkard. One deleted line of Shade's poem quotes Alexander Pope: " '. . . The sot a hero, lunatic a king.' " Given the madness of one and the weakness and name of the other, we cannot determine which man represents the disintegration within. Even the real artist is in doubt, for Kinbote's artistic achievement in giving life to his fictional world of pedantic Notes far exceeds that of Shade in his competent but pedestrian poem.

Nor does Nabokov spare his readers a new use of the stylistic and technical devices of the traditional Double novel. The imaginary king's escape from Zembla is facilitated, he claims, by numerous subjects who adopt his disguise of a red cap and red sweater—a parody of demonic dress. His incessant concern with Shade's life often appears as mere voyeurism; he is constantly peering into Shade's window and speculating upon the poet's sexual prowess. (Perhaps this may establish a new motif—the Double as Voyeur.) Mirrors and windows, water used to reflect, "crystal lakes"—all these are multiplied infinitely so that the reader cannot mistake Nabokov's intention.[15]

The reader may question if any real tension exists between our sympathy and our judgment as readers. Any threat to the unconscious which we may feel the personality of Kinbote exercises over us is dispelled by the ingenuity of the technique. The novel arouses both our very real admiration and our equally real laughter, but only occasionally our sympathy. Perhaps the threat *is* there, but what dissipates it and deceives us is that we do laugh.

In the twentieth century *Doppelgänger* novel there can no longer be any question of whether the author realizes that he is exploiting

[15]For an extended analysis of the Doubles in *Pale Fire*, see Mary McCarthy, "A Bolt from the Blue." *The New Republic* (June 4, 1962).

the conflict between the conscious and the unconscious life, the constant menace of personal disintegration which apparently threatens us all and the loss of identity consequent both upon mental disorder and the necessity that the character mask his internal life by creating roles to play. The dream of reconciliation between conflicting selves is but a dream after all. What the novelist does to compensate for his and his reader's loss of the primitive's secure belief based on a religious world-view is to find order in artistry and form, an order which is imposed from without rather than inherent in his material. Moreover, to save his individuality, he relies not upon the primitive's belief in an immortal self; rather, he creates that immortality in a work which is a mirror of his soul-mind, a "mutual daydream."[16] The author's vision of life is his public confession that he is both criminal and prosecutor, and that we, as second selves, unconsciously share his guilt.

---

[16] Hans Sachs, "The Community of Daydreams," *The Creative Unconscious*, ed. by A. A. Roback. Cambridge, Mass.: Sci-Art Publishers, 1951, 31.